Magic Happens!

Romancing the Lakes of Minnesota
~Autumn~

Rhonda Brutt
Jude Wiesner
Jill Revak
Kristy Johnson
Ingrid Anderson Sampo
Peg Pierson
Ann Nardone
Rachael Passan
Christopher Edmund
Diane Wiggert
Rose Marie Meuwissen
Kathleen Nordstrom
Angeline Fortin
KT Alexander

Published by

nordic
PUBLISHING

Nordic Publishing, LLC.
P. O. Box 923, Prior Lake, MN. 55372
www.NordicPublishing.biz

ISBN: 1501059556
ISBN-13: 978-1501059551

ACKNOWLEDGEMENTS

We would like to offer a special thanks to published authors for Beta Reads and the Minnesota Lakes Anthology Committee. Also for the services provided in publishing this anthology, we would like to thank our cover artist Christopher Edmund, our editor, Ursula Avery and Paula Miller for formatting this book.

ROMANCING THE LAKES OF MINNESOTA ~AUTUMN~

1. **A Splash with Fate** by ***Rhonda Brutt***

   Lake Harriet

   When their paths crossed, Kaitlyn and Samuel had no idea how an act of charity, along with a few homeless animals, would change their lives.

2. **Always a Wedding Planner** by ***Jude Wiesner***

   Lake Minnetonka

   Until Tessa can recognize that the one man totally wrong for her could be mister right, she will remain always a wedding planner, never a bride.

3. **Camp Crooked Lake** by ***Jill Revak***

   Crooked Lake

   After seventeen years, city-girl Molly Rhodes revisits her childhood camp and reconnects with her first crush.

4. **Cara's Swim** by ***Kristy Johnson***

   Lake Sylvia

   On the quiet shores of Lake Sylvia, amongst the golden colors of fall, Cara Waters expected to spend her days overseeing renovations of camp Chi-Ro and working on her novel. Instead she inadvertently exposed an old mystery, and found the love of her life.

5. **Cup a' Java** by ***Ingrid Anderson Sampo***

   Big Moose Lake

   A parcel of the citizens of Foulwell, a motley group, come together at the Cup 'a Java for caffeine, a chat and some playful razzing. Tall tales of an alleged romance figure prominently in the conversation.

6. **Fish Flirt Too** by ***Peg Pierson***

   North Long Lake

   To save her beloved lakeside Inn from the clutches of her greedy stepdaughter, Savanah needs a miracle. Not a merman…

7. **For the Love of Bertha** by ***Ann Nardone***

   Trout Lake

   An old legend leads a lost soul to find answers … and maybe love.

8. **Ghost Light** by ***Rachael Passan***

   Eagle Lake

   The spark between a paranormal investigator and a theater owner is given a helping "hand" from three card-playing seniors in a being-renovated Minnesota movie house.

9. **Knight of the Witching Hour** by ***Christopher Edmund***

   Devil Track Lake

   Caden Lee Wester was a drifter. A lone wolf seeking solitude on a peaceful night at the lake until a young woman, in desperate need of help, plucked him from reality, tossing him head first into a fantastical adventure filled with magic, monsters, and witches

10. **Magic at Moose Lake** by ***Diane Wiggert***

    Moose Lake

    While Shelby Maguire escapes to her friend's cabin to find peace, quiet and to seek the answers to her man troubles. Tanner Burke heads to the same cabin to seek the illusive whitetail. But will an unexpected week together lead them to find something else?

11. **Railroad Ties** by ***Rose Marie Meuwissen***

    Lake Superior

    Little did Kayla know, by following her late husband's love of trains to the shores of Lake Superior, she would end up on the right track to fall in love again.

12. **The Inheritance** by ***Kathleen Nordstrom***

    Big Stone Lake

All in one day, Katie lost her inheritance, was unable to carry out her dead grandmother's burial wishes and found love in a horse stable.

13. **The Leap** by ***Angeline Fortin***

Lake Minnetonka

A passionate confession at a lakeside celebration sends a single mother reeling and wondering if she should take a leap of her own.

14. **Third Time's a Charm** by ***KT Alexander***

Lake Minnetonka

A witch, with a forbidden old flame, and the power of Samhain.

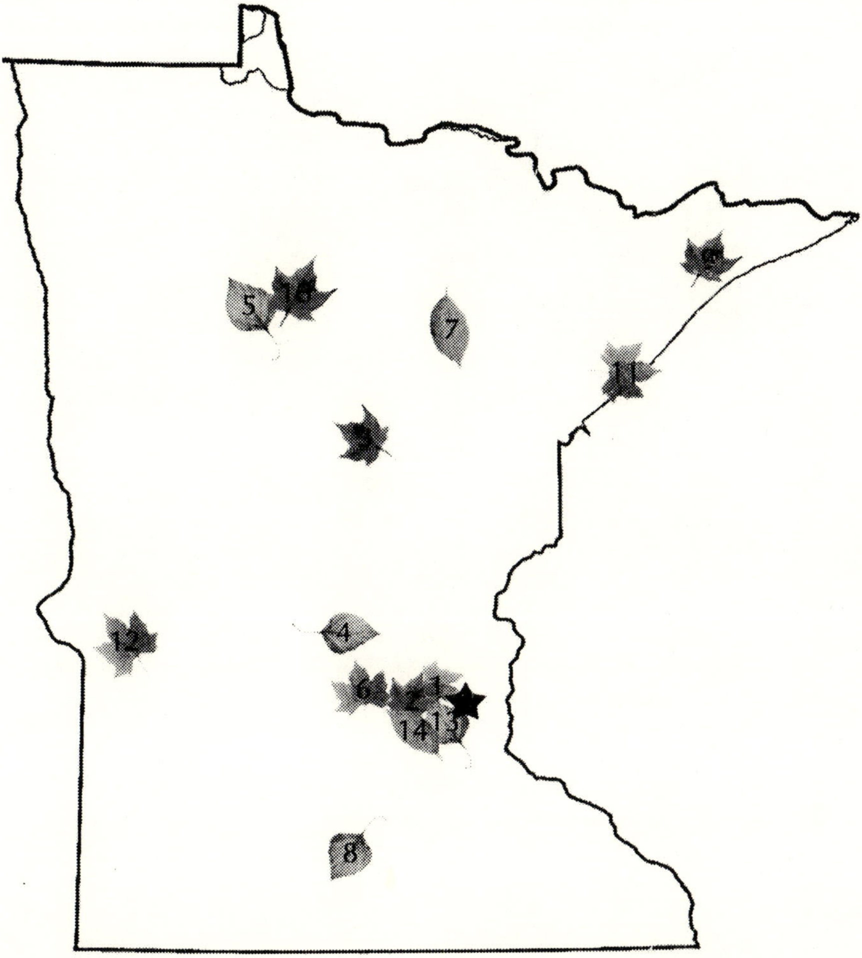

1 Lake Harriet, Minneapolis
2 Lake Minnetonka, Wayzata
3 Crooked Lake, Deerwood
4 Lake Sylvia, Annandale
5 Big Moose Lake, Bemidji
6 North Long Lake, No. Long Lake
7 Trout Lake, Coleraine
8 Eagle Lake, Mankato
9 Devil Track Lake, Grand Marais
10 Moose Lake, Bemidji
11 Lake Superior, Two Harbors
12 Big Stone Lake, Ortonville
13 Lake Minnetonka, Wayzata
14 Lake Minnetonka, Excelsior

A SPLASH WITH FATE

Rhonda Brutt

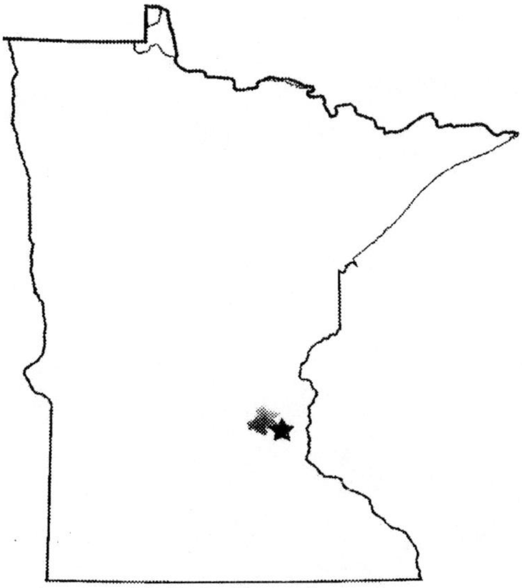

Lake Harriet, Minneapolis

The pavilion platform overlooking Lake Harriet, in Minneapolis, bustled with activity. Several hundred people, along with an interesting array of pets, had gathered to participate in the annual *Walk for the Animals*. This charity event was held every October, and the money that was raised helped to defray the costs of running the local animal shelter.

Kaitlyn Jergaine sat on the large cement platform, dangling her legs over the edge of the wall that kept the lake from spilling over into the band shell area and park. Several feet below her, tiny ripples of water lapped rhythmically against the lake's retaining wall as the cool morning breeze blew new fallen leaves around her. By her side sat her grandmother's dog, Regis, who had participated in this event ever since its inception. Kaitlyn's grandmother, a long time champion of animal rights, was at home, recovering from surgery. Kaitlyn had agreed to take the little Yorkshire terrier and go in her place.

"Just look at those sailboats out there Regis." Kaitlyn nodded towards the boats that glided silently on the water. "If we could ride around the lake in one of those, I bet I wouldn't have to carry you that last mile, huh old fellow?" The Yorkie just cocked his head and lifted his nose to the breeze.

Kaitlyn gave his head a pat. "I suppose you like it better right here on land, surrounded by all these—"

"Hey! Get back here! Somebody stop that dog!" Commotion erupted directly behind her. Kaitlyn jerked her head around just in time to realize that the largest dog she'd ever seen was barreling towards her with amazing speed.

"Move!" the voice yelled again, but the warning came too late. Without enough time to react, the large dog plowed directly into Kaitlyn, sending her and the little Yorkie into the shallow waters of the lake below.

Kaitlyn was only submerged for a second before quickly standing up. Water dripped from her long blonde hair and she leaned forward to spit lake water from her mouth. Taking a few breaths to regain herself, she frantically looked around for her dog. "Regis! Where are you? My dog!

Where's my dog?"

A crowd quickly formed along the lake wall, looking down at her.

"He's over there!" A woman pointed along the shoreline. Several yards away Kaitlyn could see the head of the little Yorkie sticking out of the water as he dog-paddled to safety.

People began questioning her as they tried to help.

"Are you alright?"

"Quick! Get out of that water before you freeze to death!"

"Is anything broken?"

Curious on-lookers offered her their hands as they lifted her out of the water and back onto the platform. A towel suddenly appeared and soon she was trying to dry herself off.

"Here's your dog." A boy handed her a soaking wet Regis, who was still wearing his collar and leash.

She cradled the shivering animal close. "It's alright fella," she cooed as she stroked his wet fur.

The man who had lost control of the large dog approached. "I can't believe this just happened! I'm sorry! Truly, I am *so* sorry! Here, take my jacket!" He quickly removed his jacket and offered it to her.

Taking it from his outstretched hand, she suddenly felt embarrassed by all of the staring eyes.

"I've got blankets in the van. If you come with me I'll—"

"Go with you?" She sputtered as the cold started to penetrate her body. "I'm not going anywhere with you, or that horse!" Kaitlyn pointed to the enormous dog at the end of the leash the man was once again holding. "You are supposed to be in control of your animal at all times! What kind of a pet owner are you anyway?" Kaitlyn's anger was beginning to overtake her initial embarrassment at falling into the lake in front of so many people. She only hoped this wouldn't end up on the web in a video.

"I'm not his owner, really I'm not! I'm here as a volunteer for the shelter. This dog was found earlier this week and no one has claimed him. They'd hoped someone here might recognize him and help us find his home. Otherwise he might be at the shelter a long time. They say it's really hard to get people to adopt Great Danes."

"Gee, I can't imagine why…" Kaitlyn rolled her eyes before unzipping the pocket of her soaking wet hoodie. She pulled her car keys out.

"I'm leaving. Let's go, Regis. I guess you won't be walking with the animals this year huh?" She wrapped the jacket around him.

"I really *am* sorry! I had no idea this Dane would act like that. I don't know what else I can say." The man's shoulders slumped in resignation.

"Whatever. It was an accident." Kaitlyn wasn't one to hold a grudge. "I smell like the lake and I'm freezing. Good luck finding his owner; you're going to need it."

Kate watched as the enormous dog gave the man's hand an affectionate lick.

"You are not forgiven! Got it? Let's go." She heard him mumble as he turned to lead the canine back to the animal shelter's van.

* * *

"So you actually fell in the lake?" Kaitlyn's grandmother looked amused as Kaitlyn relayed the events of the morning over lunch.

Kaitlyn slowly returned the smile. "I guess it was kind of funny."

"Well, at least neither of you got hurt, and a bath never hurt Regis, that's for sure." Kaitlyn's grandmother could always find something positive with just about any circumstance.

"What did the doctor say about your ankle this morning, Grandma?" Kaitlin took another bite of her sandwich.

"This will be my last week of therapy. I should be able to return to most of my normal activities after that. Unfortunately, I'll still need some help this week."

"If we've told you once, we've told you a thousand times, it's no problem helping you. And truth be told, I've done very little for you. I told mom it was my turn, so I purposely didn't accept any teaching jobs for the week. Like it or not, I'm your guest for seven whole days. Whatever you need, all you have to do is ask."

"It's such a shame you didn't get a full-time position. Have you heard back yet from your interview?"

"Not yet. I have to give it time, I'm only 24. Most teachers start out working as substitutes their first year. Until something permanent comes along, it gives me flexibility. So what can I do for you?"

"Well, there is one thing. I forgot to cancel one of my volunteer jobs, and now I'm afraid it's too late." She wrung her hands before continuing. "I'm sure they are expecting me to come back this week but if you could go in my place, that would be just lovely."

"Whatever you need" Kaitlyn gave her grandmother's hand a reassuring pat.

"Good. I need you to fill in for my shift at the animal shelter this Monday."

For a brief moment, Kaitlyn was too shocked to speak. While she loved animals, she didn't quite share her grandmother's enthusiasm for committing her time to them. But how could she refuse?

"Of course I'll go Grandma."

"Wonderful! I'm sure you'll have fun, dear!"

Fun? Kaitlyn could only let out a sigh. Taking care of her grandmother was going to be no easy task. No wonder her mother was exhausted. It was going to be a long week.

* * *

"Well, Samuel, there's no surgery scheduled this week. I'm afraid there won't be much to learn," the woman behind the counter of the animal shelter apologized.

"Good, I need a break anyway. This internship has proven to be as grueling as veterinary school was. I'll gladly do something that doesn't require much skill." The man shrugged nonchalantly.

"Nevertheless, I sent the other two guys back to help clear kennels, no point in having a vet do that. What I need for you to do is to take our van and pick up a load of donated cat food from this warehouse." The receptionist handed the keys and the map to him. "It's a bit of a drive. It'll be late in the afternoon by the time you return. The van is parked out back. Why don't you go get it and pull up to the front? Our director, Dennis, will send someone out to go with you."

"Just as long as I don't have to take that Great Dane with me again, I'll be fine." Samuel took the keys from her.

"I promise the dog won't be going with you. In fact, we won't send you near a lake either," she chuckled.

"So you heard about that." His face reddened at the memory of the embarrassing episode at the lake. Even soaking wet, he could tell the woman he had encountered was good looking. Not only that, she was obviously an animal lover like himself, or she probably wouldn't have been there. Why did he always look like such a fool in front of attractive women? Even in college, his track record with the ladies was less than stellar.

"No matter what they taught you in vet school, that is *not* the way to meet women, Dr. Pearson," the receptionist teased, interrupting his thoughts.

"I'll remember that." Samuel muttered as he turned to go.

"Wait. I want to tell you something." She lowered her voice and looked cautiously around before continuing. "Some of these helpers are here this week because they've been ordered to do volunteer work or community service as part of a plea bargain, or a sentence handed out by a judge, you know, that kind of thing."

Samuel grinned. "Well, no, thankfully I don't know."

"At any rate, none of these volunteers are dangerous or anything. The things they get sent here for is your basic misdemeanor stuff. We've never had a single problem with any of them, in fact, we're usually pleasantly surprised. Still…a nice fellow with your career just starting out, well you don't want to be handing out too much personal information. It's always best to error on the side of caution."

"It's cool. I can take care of myself," he assured her.

"Of course you can. Well, Dennis is in the back giving the rest of today's volunteers their assignments. He'll send someone right out. My kid is home sick, so I'm leaving for the day. Call him if there's a problem."

Samuel stepped out into the brisk air to retrieve the van. *Community service huh?* He smiled. *This should be an interesting day.*

* * *

Kaitlyn stood at the back of the room on Monday morning as one by one; varying tasks were assigned to the volunteers who had reported to work at the shelter.

"Let's see, you're filling in for one of our regular volunteers today right?" Dennis pointed to her.

Kaitlyn nodded. "Yes, I'm here for my grandmother."

"I'm going to have you ride along to pick up a pallet of cat food for us, if that's alright with you?"

"That'll be fine." Kaitlyn breathed a sigh of relief. Cleaning out kennels definitely wasn't what she wanted to do. Riding in a vehicle to run an errand was more to her liking any day of the week.

"Before you go though, there's something I want to warn you about." His voice was suddenly hushed. "One week each month, we participate in a program where judges send us people who need to perform some community service hours as part of their sentencing. Of course, we get a lot of regular volunteers, ones who aren't required to be here, such as your grandmother."

Kaitlyn's eyes widened a bit. This was something her grandmother had never told her. But that wasn't surprising, her grandmother accepted everyone, no matter what.

"I don't know who our receptionist got to drive the van, but it's only fair to warn you that this individual could be in a bit of trouble. With that being said, you don't want to give out too many details about yourself. Keep it generic if you know what I mean."

"Is it safe?" Kaitlyn asked slowly.

"Perfectly safe. We've never had any issues." He waved his hand dismissively. "These are petty things, such as non-payment of child support, stuff like that. These people aren't in jail, they just need to do some sort of restitution. Of course, if you'd rather not—"

"No! It's fine. I'll go." Kaitlyn picked up her bag and headed out the door.

As the van pulled up, Kaitlyn barely noticed the driver's face behind the sunglasses. But when she opened the door to get in, she froze in place. It was the same man whose Great Dane had sent her to parting the waters of Lake Harriet.

"Oh hey! How about that? It's you!" Samuel removed his glasses and smiled. He had been right about her the other day. She was extremely pretty.

"I didn't expect to see you again." Kaitlyn climbed into the passenger seat and closed the door.

Samuel put the glasses in his pocket and pulled the car out onto the road. "Sorry again about that little mishap at the lake," he apologized.

"Yeah, well it's over now, so…" Kaitlyn wanted to change the subject. "So, do you volunteer for the shelter often?"

"Nah, I'm just here for this week. It's all they require of us."

So he was sent here from the courts! Kaitlyn wasn't sure if she should be afraid or not. There was something about his demeanor that instantly made her feel relaxed. Perhaps it was his dark blonde hair and sparkling blue eyes that had put her at ease. She hadn't noticed his good looks during their initial encounter at the lake. He sure didn't look like the criminals on TV shows. He looked more like a super hero, with the exception that he had of course been responsible for her trip to the bottom of the lake.

"We should probably introduce ourselves. I'm uh… Sam."

He hesitated. Maybe He didn't want to tell me his real name. Maybe he thinks I'll look up his record. "And I'm..." Kaitlyn paused. *Don't give him your full name. Good looks can be deceiving. You don't know what he's done yet.* "Kate," she finished.

"Well, Kate, it's nice to officially meet you." He held out his hand in introduction.

"Please keep both hands on the wheel. If you can lose control of a dog, I can't imagine what you'd do to a moving vehicle," Kaitlyn chastised.

"I'm a perfectly safe driver. Well, I am most of the time." He drummed his fingers lightly on the steering wheel.

"What do you mean, most of the time?" Kaitlyn looked at him sideways.

"Well, I do have a problem with parking. It's just that no matter where I go in the Twin Cities, I'm destined to not find an available space. It seems to be my curse in life." Samuel grinned.

Parking tickets! That's it. He's had too many unpaid parking tickets. That's not so bad. But what if it's really something else? "Well, I never have a problem with parking, so we're good," she told him. Suddenly Kate wanted to know more. After all, she was spending the day with him.

"So besides trying to drown unsuspecting people at charity events, what else do you like to do?"

"Well, let's see." He tipped his head as if in thought. "My life has been a real blur the last year or so. I haven't been able to do much."

A blur? Was he a drug addict? Kaitlyn sat up straighter.

"Oh wait!" He piped up as though a sudden thought occurred to him.

"Some friends of mine opened a wine bar in Minneapolis this past year. I've discovered…much to my surprise…that I love trying new wines. That's something I definitely like to do!" He grinned.

Great. Was he an alcoholic? Could he have a problem with the bottle? Kaitlyn shifted in her seat. The possibilities here were a little disturbing, and yet there was something so normal about him. Even when they were at the lake, he didn't have the aura of someone who was in trouble.

"You look like you're deep in thought." Samuel looked over at her.

Kaitlyn shook her head as if to clear it. "It's nothing." She forced a weak smile.

"I hope you don't mind me saying this but…I must confess…you are much prettier when you're not in wet baggy clothes." Samuel sounded sincere.

"Yeah, well the *drowned rat* look doesn't do much for anyone." She blushed.

"I did intend it to be a compliment, Kate." He reached over and touched her hand. As he did, a shiver went through her body. *Do not fall for this guy. So what if he's drop-dead gorgeous? It will only bring you trouble.* Suddenly, the song lyrics from an old TV show reverberated through her head.

"*Bad boys, bad boys, Whatcha gonna do?*"

* * *

Samuel could hardly believe his luck. What were the odds he would get to spend the day with such an attractive woman? In his life, that number was zero. Even better was the fact that although he'd screwed up their initial first encounter at the lake, she was super easy to talk to. Getting through veterinary college had been hard work. There had been little room for a social life. No time like the present to start, though. Of course, there was just one minor thing to consider. Kate's record. As the morning ticked away, it became difficult for him to imagine she could possibly possess a rap sheet. She was friendly and easy to talk with. Getting closer to their destination, he finally couldn't stand it anymore. He just had to find out what her deal was. Perhaps he could help her.

I wonder if I should just ask her. Would that be rude? Probably. After all, I wouldn't want to embarrass her. I already did that at the lake. Maybe a little bit of investigation work would uncover something. Samuel decided he had nothing to lose.

"So do you volunteer at the shelter regularly?" He hoped he sounded casual.

"No. Today was the first day I've ever been there. But my …" Kaitlyn abruptly looked down. Samuel wondered why she had stopped talking. What was it she was about to say? Her parole officer? What was she hiding? He hoped a different approach might work.

"I told you what I like to do. Now it's your turn, Kate," he encouraged.

"Well, uhh…I guess one thing I like to do is to go shopping," she admitted sheepishly.

Shopping? Had she been caught shop-lifting? He wondered how many hours she would have to volunteer to make restitution for that.

"Another thing I like to do, and some people might think this is weird, but…well, I like to people watch. If you go into downtown Minneapolis, on weekend evenings, you see so many interesting people. Do you ever do that?" She tipped her head and stared intently at him as she asked.

"Do what?"

"Walk down Hennepin Avenue, late at night. It's so energetic and exotic!" She smiled.

Are you kidding? Downtown? On Hennepin Avenue? At night? Exotic? Who uses that word except for a…? No way! Could she have been picked up for prostitution? Is that her vice? "Uh…no. I can't say that I have. I mean, do you think that's safe?" He stammered.

"Sure. I don't go alone." Kaitlyn shrugged.

Words seemed to elude him for the moment. *What did she mean?* He tried picturing her dressed as though she was working the streets, but he just couldn't see it. Maybe he didn't want to see it. There seemed to be an innocent quality to her, but he was no idiot. He knew people could be misleading.

"Oh, here we are. The building is up ahead." Samuel nodded toward the large pet food warehouse. He was glad they had arrived. He definitely needed a diversion. It would be just like him to fall for someone he shouldn't. Now he would have something else to focus on instead of the striking blonde sitting next to him. There were just too many things a person could get in trouble for doing and it seemed as though his brain was warping into overdrive. Yet as they got out of the van, he couldn't help but wonder and hope. Hope that whatever reason she had for volunteering, wasn't half as bad as he could imagine.

* * *

As Kaitlyn and Samuel were about to leave the warehouse with their newly loaded van, a rather disheveled, elderly woman walked in. In her hands was a large cardboard box and it appeared as though she was struggling with the weight of it.

"Here, you look like you could use some help." Samuel rushed to her side to relieve her of the box. Suddenly the box began to wiggle and soft little sounds came from within.

"What's in here?" Samuel carefully set the box down and Kaitlyn reached to open the lid.

"Kittens!" Kaitlyn exclaimed as she peered down at the contents. "Look how adorable they are!"

Samuel quickly counted seven kittens. "How old are they?"

"Nine weeks old and they're fully weaned from their mamma. I am a responsible cat owner, I am. I don't care what anyone says!" The old woman wrung her hands. "I can't keep them. The neighbors will call the police again if I get any more cats. I promised that animal control man I wouldn't be collecting no more cats. Four cats is my limit, it's all the city says I can have now. If I don't do as they say, they'll take them all away from me."

The man from the warehouse shook his head. "Lady, you can't leave them here. We only sell supplies, not pets. We aren't licensed to sell animals. You have to take them somewhere else to surrender them."

Kaitlyn stroked the soft fur of the kittens as they rubbed and mewed gently by her hands. They were so young, so innocent. What would become of these tiny creatures? She looked up at Samuel with pleading eyes and mouthed one word. "Please."

"Kate, can I talk to you?" Sam nodded toward the door. "Alone?" He added quietly.

After stepping outside, Kaitlyn turned to face him. "Sam, I know what you're thinking, but what will become of those poor little things? We have to help that lady. I mean look at her! Did you see her jacket? She obviously can't afford to keep them."

"Yeah, did you notice that she smells as well? She definitely has that *crazy cat lady* look about her." Samuel sighed as he looked at Kaitlyn's imploring face. He was a sucker and he knew it. How could he possibly refuse?

"I'll help find homes for them. I promise." Kaitlyn grabbed both of his hands with hers. It may have been his imagination but Samuel thought he felt a rush of warmth generating from her hands. He didn't want her to let them go.

"Okay," He nodded in agreement. Kaitlyn dropped his hands and flung her arms around him in a huge hug instead.

Sam laughed. "Whoa there, don't knock me over! But Kate…" He pulled back to look at her. A somber expression crept across his face.

"What?"

"There's one thing she's got to do before we agree to take them." Samuel turned for the door and walked back inside with Kaitlyn on his heels.

"Where's the mother cat?" Samuel asked the woman.

"Out in my car. I thought they'd travel better with her around. But I wasn't planning on getting rid of her. She's one of the four cats they'll let me keep without a permit, and my interfering neighbors are keeping a close eye on me, they are." She crossed her arms in front of her stubbornly.

"I'll take these kittens from you, but only if you give me that mother cat as well. She needs to be spayed, and quite frankly, even four cats is an awful lot for one person to take care of," he insisted with authority.

"I love all my cats, no matter what anyone says." The woman looked down at the floor.

Samuel spoke sternly to her. "If you really loved them, you would give them to someone who could take care of them. Properly."

The woman was silent for a few moments before raising her head. "Will you be able to find a home for her?"

"I'll do my best," Samuel assured her.

"Well, I guess, if you promise…" She backed up towards the door. "I won't be saying goodbye to them. It's just too hard," The old woman sniffed as she backed up towards the door.

"I'll go with you to get the mother cat," Kaitlyn gently offered as she followed the woman out.

The man from the warehouse smiled knowingly at Samuel as he nodded towards Kaitlyn. "A good looking gal like her will break you down every time. She'll eventually turn your heart to putty."

"I think she's already begun." Samuel sighed as he picked up the box of kittens and headed out to join Kaitlyn.

* * *

With a box of active, mewing kittens who were continually trying to escape from their confinement, and a terrified mother cat who kept hissing, the ride home seemed to take much longer than the ride there. Both Kaitlyn and Samuel were able to put their suspicions of the other from their minds as they talked about what they would do with the kittens once they'd returned to the shelter.

"Do you think we should call Dennis to warn him that we picked up some cats to go with the cat food?" Kaitlyn asked.

"What's the point? If they can't take them, I guess we'll implement plan B." Samuel ran his hand through his hair.

"What's plan B?"

"I don't have a clue. I'm still working on that," he confessed.

"My apartment doesn't allow pets," Kaitlyn fussed.

"Maybe you should have thought of that before we took them."

"I guess I am a little impulsive," Kate admitted. "But what were we supposed to do?"

"Kate, I'm just messing with you. I'm sure things will be fine."

"You sound like my grandmother."

"Do I now? Old before my time, I suppose?" He grinned.

"No, just compassionate. My grandmother is a staunch believer in fate. You know, everything happens for a reason."

"She might be on to something." He had a faraway look in his eyes. Was it fate that had brought them together? Samuel sure hoped so.

As they neared the shelter, Samuel realized his time with Kaitlyn was almost up. He wasn't sure how he was going to say goodbye to her. He wondered if he should ask for her phone number. He didn't even know if she had a boyfriend. Then of course, there was the nagging question of what possible crime had landed her in this position as a volunteer in the first place. Perhaps he should have just asked her. At least then he'd know what he was dealing with. Still, would it matter? She seemed so easy going and happy. He felt relaxed around her and it sure didn't hurt that she was extremely attractive.

"So, maybe we could meet back at the shelter in a few days, you know, to see how the kittens are doing." Kaitlyn interrupted his thoughts.

Samuel broke into a smile. "That would be great!"

* * *

Kaitlyn breathed a sigh of relief that he hadn't said no. This would mean she would get to see him at least one more time. Until then, she hoped she could do a little investigating to see if she could find out more about him. Was he as genuinely nice as he appeared to be? Kaitlyn certainly hoped so.

Upon arriving at the animal shelter, Samuel and Kaitlyn carefully carried the box together into the building.

Dennis, the director, got up from the desk. "What have we got here?" He lifted the lid and peered inside. "You were supposed to pick up cat food, not cats," he added good-naturedly.

Samuel began, "No worries, we got the cat food. It's just that—"

"The kittens are my fault. I was the one who…" Kaitlyn wasn't sure what to say.

Samuel came to her rescue. "It was both of us. We both accept responsibility for—"

"Kaitlyn! Is that you?" A familiar voice chimed in.

Kaitlyn turned to find her grandmother standing with a cane behind her.

"Grandma, what are you doing? How did you get here?" Kaitlyn hoped her grandmother hadn't driven herself there.

"I had my neighbor bring me. Dennis said he'd take me home later." Her grandmother looked over at Dennis, who nodded in agreement.

"I came because I wanted to be the first one to give you the good news!" Her grandmother held up Kaitlyn's cell phone. "You left this at my house this morning. You kept getting calls from the school. So I finally decided to answer it. I hope you don't mind."

"I actually hadn't noticed it was gone." Kailyn look puzzled. "I guess I was having such a nice day."

"Well, your day is about to get even nicer. They want to hire you! Permanently. To teach third grade!" Her grandmother's eyes danced with excitement. "You got that job you interviewed for! I told them you would call them first thing tomorrow morning."

Kaitlyn stood there speechless. Then she noticed Samuel's puzzled expression.

"You're a teacher?" He asked incredulously.

Before Kaitlyn could respond, her grandmother piped up, "Of course she is! And you must be Dr. Pearson. We're always so grateful when one of our local vets volunteers for us."

"You're a doctor?" Kaitlyn's mouth hung partly open as she absorbed this new bit of information.

Dennis looked back and forth between both of them. "Do you mean to tell me that you two just spent almost an entire day together, and you didn't even *talk* to each other?"

"Well yes, we talked. Sort of." Samuel confessed.

"We talked a lot actually, just not about that I guess." Kaitlyn added.

"Oh Kaitlyn! Your mother taught you better than that! Where are your manners?" Her grandmother sounded flabbergasted.

Ignoring her grandmother, Kaitlyn looked at Samuel. "So you're volunteering here then for *what* reason?"

"I just got my veterinary license this year. The clinic I'm working for requires all new interns to volunteer at these types of facilities. It gives us experience." Samuel's eyes never left hers. "And you? Why are you here?"

"I'm filling in for my grandmother. She volunteers here every Monday, but she broke her ankle, so she wanted me to cover today's shift for her," Kaitlyn answered.

"You young people are weird," Dennis added shaking his head. "Now, back to the problem at hand. What are we going to do with all these felines?"

Kaitlyn blinked. For a moment, she had forgotten all about the kittens. From the shocked look on Samuel's face, it appeared he had temporarily forgotten them as well.

"If you can keep the mother cat here, I'll get her spayed next week sometime. I'd like to make sure she's healthy before I operate. As for the kittens," Samuel looked down into the box. "I could take them to my practice and see if we could give them away to our clients. It would help alleviate the crowding here," he offered.

"Sounds fine by me." Dennis looked relieved.

"Do you need us to unload the cat food out of the van first?" Samuel asked.

Dennis shook his head. "No. You two have done enough. We'll get it unloaded."

"I'll help you get the kittens to your car," Kaitlyn quickly offered as Samuel prepared to leave.

"Thanks. That would be great." They both knelt down and picked up the box.

"Grandma, I'll be right back for you," Kaitlyn called out as they were leaving.

"No you won't. Dennis will help me tonight. Go and have some fun. Celebrate that new job! Just don't leave your phone lying around anymore," her grandmother chastised.

Samuel and Kaitlyn both carried the box between them to Samuel's car.

"So Kate is your nickname then, Kaitlyn?"

She nodded. "That's what my friend's call me. And Sam is your nickname, Samuel?" She echoed.

Now it was Samuel's turn to nod. "That's what my friends call me. So I guess that means we're both friends then as well."

Kaitlyn smiled as they carefully slid the box into the backseat of his car. After shutting the door, Kaitlyn decided to take a chance. "If I ask you something Sam, will you answer me truthfully?"

"Yes." Samuel held up his hand as if taking an oath.

"Did you think the reason I was here today was because I was fulfilling some kind of community service obligation, like some of their volunteers do?"

"You caught me." He shook his head slightly. "And did you think the same thing about me, Kate?"

"Guilty as charged," she grinned.

Samuel threw his head back and laughed.

"So what heinous crime did you think I must have committed to be here today with you?" He wanted to know.

"Well, at first I thought maybe you had unpaid parking tickets…"

"Too boring!" He chuckled.

"Then you mentioned living in a blur for the past year, so I thought that perhaps you were an addict of some sort."

"That's a fair assumption."

"But then you said you liked wine—"

"So I became an alcoholic?" His gorgeous eyes sparkled with amusement.

"Uh, basically, yes." Kaitlyn answered sheepishly.

"Those were good guesses. Wrong of course, but your observations are accurate." A thoughtful look crossed his face.

"And what about me?" Kaitlyn crossed her arms in front of her. "What had you supposed I was guilty of?"

"No. We are NOT going there!" Samuel raised both hands in surrender even as a playful smile spread across his lips.

"I told you what I thought, now return the favor. You said you would," she reminded him.

"Okay. But before you hit me, just know that my parents forked over a lot of money to an orthodontist for this smile!"

"Then I guess you'll have to duck fast!" she teased back. "So go on then, Sam. Tell me what crimes I had supposedly committed."

"Oh you know, just ordinary girly types of things…like shoplifting…and prostitution—"

"WHAT?" Kaitlyn stomped her foot and scowled. But a second later, she burst out laughing. Samuel's playful expression was just too cute to even try to be mad at.

"Kate, I think you and I missed our callings in life. People with our imaginations should be living in Los Angeles, writing soap opera scripts!"

"Or romance novels," Kaitlyn added.

"Now that would be taking it a bit too far." He laughed.

Suddenly, a noise from inside the vehicle caught their attention. The kittens had escaped from their box and were exploring the interior of his car.

"How am I going to drive with them climbing all over the place?" He moaned.

"I could ride along and keep them in the box for you," Kaitlyn offered.

"Well, I suppose so, but under one condition."

"And what condition would that be?"

"That you'll go out to dinner with me later tonight."

Kaitlyn stepped closer to him.

"Well, I do still have your jacket to return to you from Saturday's lakeside fiasco."

"Forget the jacket, you can keep it. So what do you say? How about dinner?" He leaned down until he was inches from her face. Kate's heart thumped wildly in her chest.

"Will you promise to be honest with me from now on?" She whispered.

Samuel nodded. "Only if you'll promise the same to me."

"Then yes, Dr. Pearson. I'll go to dinner with you."

Right after they kissed, Kaitlyn saw her grandmother standing in the window. A look of approval was evident by the warm smile on her face. Kaitlyn gave her a wave and her grandmother acknowledged it with a nod. Perhaps her grandmother was onto something when she said she believed everything happened for a reason. Maybe there really weren't any accidents. Breaking an ankle, falling in a lake, even volunteering, could that all have been pre-determined?

Kate gave a contented sigh as she turned to get in the car. From that first splash at Lake Harriet, well…perhaps they were both just meant to be together. Maybe that's what her grandmother had always meant. The proof was right in front of her. It was called Fate.

ABOUT THE AUTHOR

Rhonda Brutt moved to Minnesota over twenty years ago after growing up in Florida. A lifelong reader, she finds herself still pouring over young adult novels as well as science fiction and romance. When she's not reading or writing she enjoys visiting coffee shops, swimming, traveling, rock music, attending concerts, going to the theater, and trying to come up with creative excuses to get out of cooking.

Rhonda attended Florida State University but withdrew and moved Minnesota. It was several years before she returned to finish her schooling. She graduated from Normandale Community College, Phi Theta Kappa, with high academic honors.

Rhonda is proof that it is never too late to finish your education or achieve your goals; a message that she stresses to the young people she now mentors in her community, as well as to her own three children. Her first Young Adult novel, *Voyance*, was published in 2011 and the sequel, *Redeemed* was published in 2013. She lives with her husband in the Minneapolis metropolitan area. She also has a short story published in the *Romancing the Lakes of Minnesota Summer* anthology, published in 2013.

Visit Rhonda's website ar http://RhondaBrutt.com or LIKE her Facebook page at Rhonda Brutt Author.

ALWAYS A WEDDING PLANNER

Jude Wiesner

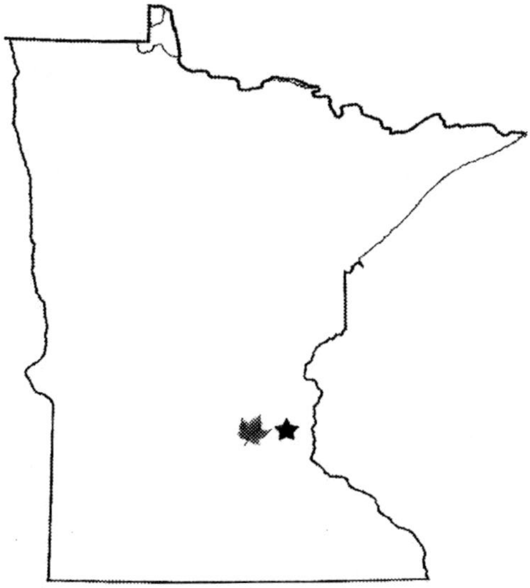

Lake Minnetonka, Wayzata

Tessa thrust her hand out, palm forward like an over-zealous school crossing guard. "Don't say a word."

He stood there, black tuxedo jacket slung over his shoulder, dangling from one finger as though time had little consequence.

"You won't need that." She snatched the coat from his hand and tossed it over a chair.

A smile tugged at the corner of his mouth and Tessa couldn't help but notice how gorgeous he was with his dark hair curling over the edge of his collar. She wasn't dead, just harried. But looks or not, he had screwed up her perfectly timed schedule.

"I think–," he began.

"You're not here to think or talk. Your job is to listen and then follow my instructions to the letter." Already on tiptoes in her three-inch heels, she barely reached his shoulders. "Sloppy." She yanked him forward by the loose ends of the tie that dangled around his neck. She deftly tied the bow and patted it in place firm enough to momentarily cut off his air.

Tessa indicated the table next to her. "We have less than an hour." She turned to glare at him. "Because you're late. Each table in the tent, all thirty-five of them have to be dressed." The idiot stood there and grinned at her.

"Now pay attention. Sprinkle a light smattering of silver stars over the middle of the table." She demonstrated as she talked. "Place a round mirror in the center, a vase of flowers in the center of the mirror, and five votive candles around the vase." She raised her hand, fingers spread like a turkey's tail and counted out. "Not four, not six, five. Do you think you can manage that?"

"Yes ma'am." His voice rolled over her, soft and sexy.

She thrust a large box straight into his midsection and Brady caught it by reflex. "Pre-nuptial photographs are due to start in one hour and she may want to use the tent so you better hop to it."

* * *

Brady appreciated every swing of her slender hips as Tessa strode through the terrace doors and into the hotel. A mass of thick auburn hair was twisted in a knot at the back of her neck. He wanted to tug it loose and see if it reached that pretty little backside.

Grinning, Brady hoisted the box in his arms and proceeded to follow her instructions. He couldn't think of anything better to do for an hour anyway. The wedding party table had already been decorated and the guest tables were set up in an ever-widening half circle that covered two-thirds of the transparent vinyl tent. The other third held a small area for the orchestra and wood flooring for dancing later in the evening. The entire facade was strung with fairy lights and balls of white mums suspended from wide satin ribbons. By sunset it would look like a castle in the sky. He figured it must have set old man Matthews back a nice chunk of change.

The job wasn't rocket science and Brady prided himself on his deft execution. When finished he exited the tent, entered the hotel and took the open staircase to the third floor. He opened the door to suite 306 and walked into a wall of testosterone.

* * *

Tessa walked between the tent tables, pleased to see the crisp russet linen table cloths covered by a smaller white cloth. The center arrangements looked stunning and the bride's choice of apricot roses, fern, and preserved oak leaves in russet and mauve were magnificent.

"Ten minutes and the ballroom is all yours." Gwen's voice came over Tessa's earpiece.

"See you in ten then."

Tessa could always count on her partner Gwen to do a stellar job with the flowers. Each table had been properly dressed and Tessa was relieved the guy had fulfilled his task. The question being, where had he gone off to now?

She checked her watch against her schedule and set off toward the hotel at a rapid clip. Swinging the double doors of the ballroom wide she smiled at the sight. Gwen's crew was filling the impromptu riser with a bank of the same flowers.

"What do think?" Gwen adjusted one container about three degrees.

"They're magnificent."

Lavish large brass tubs were set amongst thick tall white candles. The back of each aisle chair bore a cluster of flowers tied with russet ribbons.

"I never doubted you for a minute." Tessa turned in a circle as she surveyed the room.

Massive windows overlooked Lake Minnetonka and the expansive hotel grounds, always groomed to the point where a blade of grass didn't dare to rise above the others, made a magnificent backdrop. Tessa watched the tail end of the wedding party wind their way toward the fountain at the lake's edge. The light laughter of women and booming voices of men along with some shoulder punching were all typical. She watched as Mazie grouped the still casually dressed party not in the usual straight line, but in a cluster with the groom scooping the bride up into his arms. At this distance without her glasses, Tessa couldn't make out any of the faces, but knew they enjoyed themselves. She wished she had time to stick around while Mazie ran the group through the rest of their paces as she worked for the perfect shot.

"Mazie always gets the best of the deal." Gwen threw an arm over Tessa's shoulders.

"We each have our talents and complement each other. Besides you get to be there when Mazie snaps shots of the men dressing."

"Well, there is that slight compensation.," Tessa laughed.

"All I ever get is over aggressive mothers and fathers that have had too much to drink."

"And you love it." Gwen stacked large boxes of flowers in her arms.

Tessa smiled. "I wouldn't have it any other way."

As university roommates, Gwen and Mazie had been her best friends and shared their dreams of running their own businesses where they could control their own destiny. Tessa, having grown up in the posh society of Minnetonka, had a plethora of contacts and nursed them shamelessly. She was a wedding planner with access to all the right venues and knew the families who would provide her with enough business to rocket her to the forefront.

After a couple years and countless glasses of wine, Tessa had convinced her roommates to join her venture and offer the complete package for any wedding at any price point. The only person missing was the fourth roommate Grace who moved to New York after graduation to hone her culinary skills cooking for a fine restaurant. Tessa still hoped they could lure her home to complete the one missing piece of the puzzle.

Her dream materialized when Tessa was a young girl playing Cinderella. There were no wicked step sisters to muck up her story. It began when the prince whisked Cinderella away to the elaborate palace wedding. Tessa's dog Grunt pulled the wagon coach decorated in flowers and crape paper. Much to Grunt's credit he wore a plumed hat with dignity and tolerance. Dolls and various stuffed animals completed the retinue. The groom was most often represented by a large stuffed bear or, on special occasions, her little cousin Tim if she could bribe him with enough ice cream. Mostly Tessa liked the organization part of the event and took enough pictures to fill countless photo albums. Today she still organized events but had Mazie to take the photographs and create one of a kind albums.

Leaving Mazie to record the exceptional moments of both joy and tears, Tessa made a dash for the kitchen. If she could just lure Grace back, she wouldn't have to rely on anyone else. And that included wait staff. Where had the guy gone off to anyway? Never trust a good-looking man. They invariably turned into egotistical little boys who needed to be fawned over. Not that she didn't appreciate a handsome face, but her business took all her time and she frankly didn't have the energy to pamper any of them the way they expected. She'd rather put her time into pampering brides and running interference for them with Godzilla mothers.

Speaking of mothers, the mother of the bride swept right into the kitchen chaos. Tessa raced around a counter and cut her off before she could accost the chef who only tolerated Tessa as an annoying necessity.

"Mrs. Matthews, just look at you. Your dress is divine and you wouldn't want to get anything on it. Goodness, there's any number of splatters just flying around the kitchen. "

"I only wanted to sample those little quiches. I'm worried they might be too pedestrian."

At the growl from the chef, Tessa turned Mrs. Matthews around and ushered her out of the kitchen. "I can assure you Mrs. Matthews, nothing about the food will be pedestrian. The truffle oil used in the sauce makes them spectacular."

Just then, Tessa's ear-piece buzzed. She pressed the button to hear Mazie.

"The wedding party is heading back into the hotel and I'm escorting them up the back way to ensure they stay out of sight of guests who have begun to roam about the grounds."

"Gotcha." Tessa clicked off.

"You're needed upstairs. The photographer wants to catch your last sight of your little girl before she becomes a wife."

Mrs. Matthews began to tear up and Tessa deftly pulled a tissue from her suit jacket pocket. "No tears. This is a jubilant occasion and you wouldn't want to ruin your makeup." Tessa patted her back, while she steered her in the right direction.

With a sigh of relief, Tessa checked off the next item on her list. She wanted to ensure the violinist and pianist would begin to play fifteen minutes before the guests were escorted down the ballroom aisle and seated appropriately, all three hundred fifty of them.

The volume of conversation in the lobby had risen to a mild roar as guests milled about and greeted each other. The men were all in tuxedos and the women in seasonal appropriate dresses, jewels, and elaborate hats. It looked as though many would have their view considerably obstructed. She consulted her list and checked off the six ushers as more guests came inside and queued up at the doorway. Even though the day was sunny and seventy-five glorious degrees, the sun would set early and there would be a distinct autumn chill in the air.

Once again, her ear-piece buzzed.

"I've delivered the men's boutonnieres and I'm on the way to deliver the flowers to the ladies. Mazie will want to get pictures."

"You will probably run into her. She should still be with the bride."

Tessa took a moment to catch her breath. Once the wedding began, she would have to oversee a number things and this might be the only opportunity she had to fortify herself. She navigated the twists and turns of the hallways and exited the back door to the pool area. The clear blue of the salt-water pool lapped against the tiled edges. A light breeze caused ripples and leaves floated on the surface of the water and skittered along the expansive stone patio. Tessa turned her face up into the sun to absorb the last warmth of the fall season. She breathed in the smell of newly mown grass and dried leaves. With reluctance, she turned back toward the hotel. She would rather strip off her hose and dangle her already aching feet in the water. But duty as well as a lucrative wedding contract required her undivided attention.

* * *

He saw her the moment she came through the door. The pale yellow silk suit with the short slim skirt revealed a mile of leg, the perfect compliment to her hair the color of autumn leaves. Brady stopped at the bottom step until she noticed him. Her head jerked up and her eyes flashed.

"Where have you been?" She marched up to him as he took the final step down.

"Hi again."

"Don't hi me." Tessa reached up and plucked the boutonniere from his lapel and tossed it on a small table against the wall. "Just what do you think you're doing? You have no business upstairs with the wedding party and these flowers aren't for you."

"I don't suppose you want an explanation."

"No. You can march yourself outside and help park cars." She gave him a scowl that made him grin. "Oh, and eighty-six the jacket. I definitely don't want you confused with a guest." Tessa turned to stalk down the hall.

Brady stood and watched her go. She made a very pleasing package and he had every intention of finding out just how tightly wrapped she was. He inserted the flower back in his lapel before walking away.

* * *

When Tessa turned the corner, she almost ran over Mazie. "You look hot and bothered."

"It's a hormone attack. I just finished photographing the guys in various stages of undress." Mazie ran a hand through her short spiky dark hair as she shifted her camera case higher on her shoulder. "What's revving your engine?"

"It's one of the crew. I don't know who hired him but I intend to find out and blacklist him. He doesn't seem to know his place and is never around when I need him."

"Never mind him. Wait until you get a good look at the wedding party. That'll perk you up. Until now, we've only met with the bride and groom. The frosting on the cake is the rest of these men. I swear I could print a calendar and sell a million of them. I'm seriously thinking of making one shot into a poster and papering my bedroom wall with it." She fanned her flushed cheeks with her hand. "Be still my heart."

Tessa laughed. "I'm afraid I won't have the time until the reception is in full swing. I'll take your word for it." She tucked her arm in Mazie's as they walked toward the ballroom.

The last guests were being seated as the bride and her father came down the curved hotel staircase. Tessa caught her breath. The slender bride wore a lace covered, long strapless gown with a whisper thin veil that trailed behind her on the stairs. She was gorgeous. Just as she looked up into the eyes of her father, handsome and dignified in his tuxedo, Mazie caught the shot. Tears glittered in both their eyes and Tessa felt a little ping in her heart. She designed weddings for countless others, never her own.

Four bridesmaids lined up outside the door. Their dresses were a mixture of styles that ranged in color from copper satin to burnt orange crepe. They blended into a tableau of blazing autumn. Mazie squeezed past them to station herself down the aisle to photograph the procession. One by one, as the music played, they entered the ballroom to make their way down the aisle, only to be met by a groomsman who escorted them up the two steps where the minister stood to officiate the occasion.

When the music reached a crescendo and changed to the wedding march the bride stood on her toes to kiss her father's cheek. Step by step they glided down the aisle as the guests rose and turned to greet them. The wedding had begun.

Tessa had one-half hour to make sure the wait staff was ready to serve. Why wasn't she surprised to see her mystery man wasn't front and center in the kitchen? Trays of small canapés were lined up along the counters and servers stood at the ready to mingle through the crowd as soon as the ceremony was finished. The canapés along with the champagne would be served outside around the tent as the last vestiges of daylight lingered.

"I'm bushed." Gwen pulled a stool from under the counter where she slouched and lowered her head. "Every flower is blooming and I've wilted. Call me when it's time to dismantle."

Tessa stroked her hand over Gwen's springy dark curls and gave them a motherly pat. "Poor baby. But you won't get any more sympathy than that out of me. At least you get to rest for a few hours."

"Indeed I do and have every intention of taking advantage. Our staging room should be empty by now and I plan on a good long nap. Wake me when the festivities are finished."

"Mazie said the men are above the standard. You might want to sneak a look."

"After the thousands of flowers we've arranged, there isn't a man on earth who could interest me tonight." Gwen stood, stretched and then hugged Tessa. "Be a good girl and wake me before the witching hour, will you?"

"Count on it. Mazie can show you the pictures in the morning and you can see how much muscle you missed."

"You ever notice we excel at producing spectacular weddings week after week and not one of us has the time to even date. What's wrong with this picture?"

"We will. One day your prince will come."

Gwen gave an unladylike snort and reached for the plate of food set before her. She waved to Tessa over her shoulder.

Tessa gave her hair a once over before she checked on the tent. The sun low in the sky gleamed on Lake Minnetonka and cast the fairy lights in a pink glow. By the time the happy couple came outside it would look like a galaxy of stars against the first evening light. It would be a perfect night with the tent to ward off the autumn chill. Unlike the summer, there was no need to worry about those pesky mosquitos because the first frost had come a week earlier and rendered them unconscious.

Tessa crossed to the main doors. She pulled them wide, kicked the foot pads in place to lock them open just as the bride and groom came through the ballroom doors. They stopped and turned to each other with looks of wonder on their faces. As the groom crushed the bride in his arms and kissed her with total abandon, Mazie breezed out the door to catch the kiss with her camera. Mazie was always in the right spot.

"I'm off the clock for about forty-five minutes. Shots of people with their mouths open either yammering or stuffing them with food is never flattering." As the guests began to file into the tent and pick up their name cards to reveal their table assignment, Mazie plopped into a chair outside the tent and kicked off her shoes.

"Here, you can take care of this for me." A guest thrust an elaborately wrapped box into Mazie hands. "You're so sweet. Thank you sooo much."

"And you are sooo welcome." Mazie's smile was stiff.

"Tut, tut," Tessa responded.

"Sorry, but some people just tick me off with their sense of entitlement. I'm not some flunky to do their bidding."

"Yes, I know. We have flunkies to do that sort of thing." Tessa took the gift and tucked it under her arm.

"Don't mind me. I think I enjoy the weddings done on a shoestring more. These rich folks always look at me as though I'm invisible."

"Isn't that the idea? You take the photographs without anyone realizing you're there."

"Yeah, yeah. I need a vacation."

"We all do. I've kept the first week in November wide open so don't book any appointments. I've commandeered my folk's condo in Hilton Head for the week. We'll have nothing but sun and sand for a solid seven days."

"With that in mind I just might make it through the night." Mazie crossed her legs at the ankles, folded her arms across her chest, and closed her eyes. "Nudge me when dinner is over."

Tessa laughed and headed off with the gift.

* * *

Brady held a glass of champagne in hand, half listened to what the woman next to him was saying, and kept an eye out for a flash of yellow silk. He didn't know her name, but he intended to know more than that about her before the night's end. It was obvious she ran the show and was doing a very fine job of it, if he were any judge.

* * *

"Mazie, you're on in two." Tessa over saw the clearing of dishes, made sure the trolley holding small stacked boxes had been placed for the packaging of wedding cake to be taken home by the guests. There was some oddball tradition about sleeping with the cake under your pillow and you're wishes would be granted. Tessa figured all she'd get was a mass of guck on her pillowcase.

She slipped her glasses on to scan the crowd for the bride and groom who were going from table to table to talk with guests and that's when she saw him. He had some nerve, she'd give him that. There he stood, bolder than life, with a glass of champagne in his hand talking with one of the bridesmaids. He wouldn't orchestrate a pick-up on her watch.

"Go head off the lovebirds," she told Mazie as she approached. "While they cut the cake I'm going to cut this guy off at the knees."

Tessa streaked across the floor, a false smile stretched across her face as she passed the tables. She came up behind the head table and grabbed Brady's arm.

"Hi," he said. "I've been looking for you."

"Excuse us a moment, won't you?" She clutched his sleeve and steered him away from the woman he was hitting on. When she hauled him off to the side, she turned her back on the guests. "You're fired," she said through gritted teeth and removed the glass from his hand.

"Great. Now I can finally enjoy the rest of the evening."

"No, you get out of here right now or I'll have you thrown out and charged with trespassing." When Brady just smiled at her, she clamped her hands together to keep from smacking him. "You think I'm kidding buster, well try me." She gave him her best scowl before she turned her back and walked away. She needed to get herself under control before she barked at a guest.

* * *

Brady watched her go. It was probably time he stopped playing with her. It was quite probable that irritating the woman over the edge wouldn't ingratiate him for any future relationship. But just like his years as an incorrigible little kid, he wanted to see how far he could push the situation. Not wise perhaps, but definitely entertaining. He stepped back into the shadows and watched as she turned around to check on him. When she put her glasses on he took another step back out of sight. Apparently satisfied she had chastised him into submission, she removed her glasses and stuffed them back into her tidy jacket pocket and walked out through the open tent flaps. Brady turned to get a fresh glass of champagne.

The father of the bride stood and tapped his glass with his fork. Conversation dwindled and everyone gave him their attention as he began the last of the evening's speeches.

"I would like to thank you all for sharing this wonderful evening with us. It isn't every day a father gives his daughter away. But I'm pleased to say Charlotte, Katie's mother, and I couldn't be more pleased than to welcome Paul and the Westin family into our own." He raised his glass. "To Katie and Paul. Salute."

"Salute." Everyone responded in unison.

Brady raised his glass with the others. After a string of toasts, Brady got up on the platform. "I'd like to thank Mr. and Mrs. Maxwell for the extravagant evening, and being such gracious hosts. It has been a pleasure to be part of this wedding. To Katie and Paul."

The small band began to play and the bride and groom took to the floor.

* * *

Tessa couldn't believe her ears. He not only had the audacity to stay after she threatened him with repercussions but the gall to actually draw attention to himself by giving a toast. As she was about to turn and call security, Brady caught her by the arm. She began to sputter as he swept her out onto the dance floor.

"You…you," she stammered as he pulled her into his arms.

Brady pressed her head against his shoulder. "Hush, you wouldn't want to make a scene."

She yanked her head back. "I don't know what kind of game you're playing but this is going to end here and now." Tessa tried to pull free but he only held her tighter.

"Haven't you ever seen the movie Wedding Crashers?"

She pulled her hand free to poke him in the chest. "Look, slick, no one crashes my weddings."

Brady laughed. "There's a first time for everything." He snatched her hand back and twirled her stiff little body in a circle. "By the way, my name's Brady. What's yours?"

"My name is of no concern to you. Now let me go."

It only caused him to snuggle her closer against him. "I should probably end this little charade right now."

"No. You should have ended it a long time ago." She stopped moving and Brady almost fell over her.

"I meant I'd like to explain."

Before Tessa could fire off a response, the bride and groom approached them and she struggled to regain her poise. Good God, it was all going to come crashing down right here on the dance floor where she had no business being in the first place. She would take full responsibility when they voiced their displeasure.

"Tessa." Katie put her arms around her and hugged her. "I can't thank you enough. It is everything I dreamed it would be and more. It's all so wondrous." Katie's eyes filled with tears.

Paul leaned close to kiss Tessa's cheek and clap Brady on the back. "I didn't realize you had met our extraordinary wedding planner."

"We… that is I…" Tessa stammered, her face flushed with mortification.

"Not formally," Brady said.

"Brady, I'd like you to meet Tessa Chase. I was a little leery of all this planning business in the beginning, but Tessa made the whole thing painless." Paul smiled. "Tessa, this is my big brother, Brady."

"Brother? He's your brother?"

"The only one I have."

"And definitely the best man." Brady winked at her.

She turned to him with a formal nod. "It's nice to meet you." Her face was pale and poker straight. She turned back to Katie and Paul. "Mazie will have your wedding albums complete by the time you get back from your honeymoon. Now, if you'll excuse me I have to deal with the kitchen staff. The last of the cake is being boxed as we speak. And again, congratulations." Tessa turned on her heels and walked out of the tent.

* * *

Brady intercepted her before she was half way across the lawn. "Tessa, please wait."

She didn't stop, didn't say a word, just yanked the hotel door open to let it swing shut in his face.

"At least let me apologize." Brady caught up and took her arm.

Tessa inhaled a deep breath and stopped. "Look, you're a guest and what's more, a member of the bridal party. And because of that I make it my policy to see you get whatever you want."

"I want you."

"Well that's where I draw the line. You made a fool out of me. So, apology accepted." She glared at him. "Now let me go."

Brady removed his hand. "First of all it wasn't my fault. You mistook me for a waiter or something and I thought it was funny. I had some time to kick around so I fixed up your pretty tables."

"You could have said something."

"As you recall, I tried."

She wiped a hand over her brow. "When I caught you coming down the stairs I should have known. You should have told me the truth then."

"You were so wound up and so darn cute I just didn't think."

Cute, she thought. Just what she'd always aspired to. She hadn't wanted to be cute since she was six. "Fine, let's leave it at that and chalk it up to a very embarrassing misunderstanding. Now, I really do have things to do."

He took her hand and started to tug her back out the door.

"Don't do this. Don't make this anymore humiliating than it already is."

"I think you owe me one more dance for making me fix tables and park cars."

"Oh my God, you didn't really go out and park cars did you?"

With the small orchestra playing a slow song Brady took her in his arms. "No, I drew the line at cars."

Tessa banged her head against his shoulder. "I took your champagne away and threatened you with security."

"I've never been threatened by such a beautiful woman."

She looked up into his eyes. And they were magnificent. A deep brown surrounded by thick lashes women would pay big money to have. She sighed as Brady drew her close.

Just then Mazie called out from the tent door. "Hey Tessa, the bride is about to throw the bouquet."

"C'mon," Tessa said. "I need to do crowd control."

Brady followed and they stood at the back of the anxious group of single women.

"You're not married, are you?" He asked.

"No. You?"

"Always the best man, never the groom."

"Me too. Always a wedding planner."

Just then the bride threw her bouquet with a strong arm. Brady lurched to the side and the bouquet landed in Tessa's hands.

"Maybe we can change all that," Brady said and kissed the shock off her lips.

ABOUT THE AUTHOR

Jude Wiesner has studied creative writing for several years under an award-winning author and mentor. She is the author of a memoir in the 2013 Midwest Book Award winning St. Paul Almanac and will be published again the in the upcoming 2015 edition.

She writes travel articles, literary fiction, and romance. Jude is active in four writing organizations.

CAMP CROOKED LAKE

Jill Revak

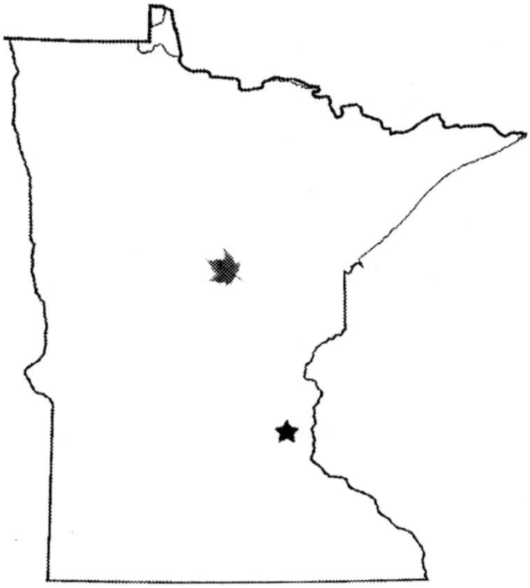

Crooked Lake, Deerwood

"I can't believe I agreed to this," I said as I shut down my computer.

"Molly, it's a camp, not prison," Elsie said.

Elsie secretly signed me up for my childhood camp reunion, ambushing me at work. I hadn't been back there in seventeen years, and really had no desire to. But when your best friend/coworker packs your bag, covers for your meetings, and flashes the most sincere pouty face, how was I to say no?

"What's the difference?" I scowled as we waited.

Elsie grabbed my shoulders. "It's either this or you're dressing up for Halloween this weekend."

"No way."

"Think of this as an adventure." Elsie grabbed a hair tie from her wrist and wrapped her auburn hair up in a messy bun. "And who knows, there might be some single guys there. It's time for you to do something crazy."

I snorted. "These are people I haven't seen since I was twelve."

"And now they're twenty-nine, like you."

"I don't really want to reconnect with the past."

Elsie sighed. "It's been six months since you and Colin broke up, and you've been sitting around pouting. You need to trust again."

"Can't I just live vicariously through you and your crazy escapades?"

Elsie pushed me toward the elevator. She was mighty strong for someone who was a 110 pounds soaking wet. "You might be surprised and actually have fun."

I rolled my eyes, like any mature twenty-nine-year-old would do. "I doubt it." The elevator dinged and opened. "A weekend in the wilderness. You owe me," I said as I rolled my suitcase into the elevator and faced her.

She smiled. "Maybe I'll be saying that to you when you get back."

I pressed G for the ground level and the doors started to close. "I doubt it!" I yelled as the elevator descended down and down.

* * *

The temperature was warmer than normal for late October. I had the window cracked as I drove, enjoying the smell of nature and the crisp air. There was definitely something about getting out of the city that was refreshing. As an adult it was a novelty. Work and the craziness of life usually took precedence over vacations, especially those in the wilderness. The days of skipping rocks and nature hikes were now taken over by spreadsheets and conference meetings.

As I reached the entrance to the camp, I slowed down to take in the view. It was amazing. Everything looked the exact same as it did when I was a kid, albeit a little smaller. The wooden archway that canopied over the entrance read CROOKED LAKE CAMP in bright yellow paint, just like it had been painted seventeen years earlier.

After parking my car, I walked up the sidewalk to the Welcoming Lodge, taking in the beautiful foliage that towered over the entire camp. Sky-high oak and cottonwood trees bearing red, orange and yellow leaves were breathtaking. Camp Crooked Lake was completely covered by forests, where the lake wasn't, making it a very remote location. I remembered being spooked at night as a kid when we would play flashlight tag in the back woods, convinced Michael Myers was coming for us.

Before I could reach the door, an older women came bustling out, nearly bumping into me. She was holding a giant box in her hands and was having a conversation with an older gentleman. I didn't have to ask who she was as she came toward me. Marge, the owner of the camp, looked the exact same as she did when I was kid, with the addition of a few wrinkles and grey wisps of hair.

"Hello," I said to them. "Hello, Marge?" I called after her again.

"It's Miss Marge around here," she said as she walked up to me. She wiped her hand on her shirt and extended it to me. "You must be the lawyer from Parsons and Eckleburd?"

I looked down at my clothes, regretting my decision not to change before heading on the road. I guess a business suit and heels wasn't quite the camping attire she was used to. "No, no. I'm Molly Rhodes. I used to spend the summers here."

Miss Marge gave me a once over. Her eyebrows drew together in confusion and in a second they lifted in surprise. "Molly. Molly Rhodes. Yes! Same blonde hair and cute dimples." She gave me a hug. "Thank God for that! I thought I'd have to fake a pleasant conversation and I wasn't up for that today." She grabbed my arm and pulled me up the walkway. "What the heck are you in those shoes for, Molly Melon?"

I couldn't believe she'd called me that. I hadn't heard that name in ages. Molly Melon was my camp name. We were all nicknamed after a fruit or vegetable. Miss Marge said everyone deserved a nickname, but I hated mine. I developed early in the chest department, so my nickname also became a sexual innuendo for twelve-year-old boys. It goes without further explanation that there were hand gestures involved whenever my name was spoken.

"I left work right before I came here." I followed Miss Marge as she sprinted at lightning speed toward the check-in desk inside. "My friend Elsie talked me into coming." I wasn't sure why I'd told her that. Maybe the fresh air had a guileless effect on the brain. "I never thought I'd be back here."

Miss Marge smiled as she pulled a folder out from behind the counter. "We're glad to have you. We've had great reunions over the years. And I know there's one person particularly interested in see—"

My phone dinged, showing a text message. "Sorry, that might be work." I swiped my phone to find a text from Elsie.

U arrive? Any hot lumberjacks? ☺

I typed quickly, aware that Miss Marge was staring at me.

Very funny. Just arrived. Feels weird.

In seconds Elsie's response came.

U need a better attitude, girly!

I smiled and typed.

Whatever. Call u when . . .

Before I could finish my text, Miss Marge had confiscated my phone. I didn't know what to do or say as she shook her head at me.

"Sorry, Molly Melon, no phones here. We'll keep this locked up for safety until the weekend's over."

I shook my head. What was she saying? "You're kidding, right?"

Miss Marge shook her head. "I'm as serious as a heart attack. We didn't have phones back in the day, so we don't allow them now." She wrote something down on a piece of paper. "Cellphones only give you brain cancer and take you away from the joys of nature. You'll thank me by the end of your visit."

I felt like I was just slapped in the face. I loved my cellphone; it was like an extra limb. How could one cope with an unexpected amputation? I wasn't prepared for this. "I have some work stuff I need to do this weekend. I'll just hold on to my phone and only use it for business purposes, okay?

Miss Marge shook her head and laughed. "Oh, silly girl. There's no business working this weekend, unless you count the work you'll be doing around here." She handed me a map of the property with a cabin number written on it, just like back in the day. "Here you go, honey. Do you still remember your way around here?"

I took the map while my head still reeled with all the information she'd dumped on me. No cellphones? Working around the camp? This was now the epitome of hell. "Um . . . I think so."

She shooed me with her hand. "Hurry along, dear. The sun is falling and the bell will be ringing for dinner soon." She walked toward the front door. "Be sure to dress warm tonight! Camp songs by the bonfire happen directly after dinner!"

Camp songs?

Crap.

I'm gonna kill Elsie.

* * *

It took about twenty minutes to find Cabin 10 after fetching my suitcase from my car, thankful I had my watch on since my phone was gone. I thought it odd that I didn't see anyone as I nearly twisted both ankles along the gravel path. High heels are not camping shoes, clearly.

I opened the door to the cabin and noticed other luggage along with personal belongings scattered about. I started to worry I was in someone else's cabin until I looked closer at the map and it had Cabin 10 Bunk 5 written on it. Yikes. I was sharing a cabin with four other people. I hadn't shared a room with anyone else since college.

After I changed and unpacked my things, I beelined it to the restroom to freshen up. But when I reached the door, it was stuck. I tried the knob, pushing with all of my might, but the darn thing wouldn't move. It now had been approximately four hours since I'd used the restroom, and any longer, I'd break out in a child-like pee pee dance.

Glancing to the left and right, not seeing anyone, I sneaked around the side of the building to use the men's restroom. And as I briskly ran into a stall, I realized the last time I'd broken this rule was here at camp. It felt really strange to be back, yet somewhat familiar at the same time.

After washing my hands, I was just about to grab a paper towel from the holder when I heard a noise coming from the back. I paused for a moment, then ran to the side wall to hide. I didn't know why I didn't just run out, but I regretted my decision when a man came around the corner, fresh out of the shower, with just a towel on.

I put my hands over my mouth, not knowing what to do. Just in case the man exposed himself, I decided to speak up and save us both from humiliation. "I'm sorry, sir. The door to the ladies' room was stuck and I . . ."

The man faced me, and I was surprised to see how young he looked. My mouth gaped open as I took in his tanned, tightly toned muscles that glistened with tiny drops of water. He ran his hand through his dark, wet hair and it stuck up in an adorable sexy way in the front.

Eat your heart out, Elsie.

"I guess I'll have to fix that," he said as he adjusted his towel. He didn't seem fazed by my intrusion.

I suddenly felt the need to take a shower myself. "Great . . . okay . . . 'bye." I headed for the door, making a conscious decision not to gawk at him on my way out.

"Hey, wait up! Um . . . what's your name?"

When I turned around, the man had one arm extended to greet me and the other on his hip. Man, he was sexy. I swallowed hard and took a few reluctant steps toward him, placing my hand against his. His skin was silky soft and warm. "Molly. Molly Rhodes."

"Hello, Molly. Welcome to camp."

The man looked familiar as he flashed a friendly smile at me. I just stood there, mesmerized by him, until I realized we were standing in an awkward silence. "Right. Thanks. Um, 'bye." I ran out of the bathroom so fast I actually walked in the wrong direction. Once I got a hold of myself, I headed back to my cabin. When I reached the door, I heard lots of laughter going on inside. One high-pitched laugh in particular struck a chord with me. My arch enemy from camp days. Jessica Mason.

"Oh. My. Goodness!" I heard a women say as I entered the cabin.

"Look, ladies! It's Molly Melon! We never thought we'd see you here!"

I waved at all the ladies who were staring at me. They definitely looked familiar, but it had been seventeen years since I'd seen any of them, so I couldn't be positive on names. "Hello. Nice to see you all." I wiped the sweat that was building across my forehead.

"Oh, don't let the girls scare you, Molly." The slightly curvaceous women put her arm around my shoulders. "I'm Rebecca 'Romaine,' do you remember me?

My mouth dropped. The Rebecca Romaine I'd remembered was tall and lanky. But when I looked closer, I could still see that same girl, just with adult curves. I thought she looked better with some weight on; her body looked healthy.

"No relation to the actress," she teased as she sat on her bunk. "Though, I'd have never let that Stamos guy go if that was the case."

"Remember me?" A woman with curly red hair walked closer to me. "You look incredible, Molly!"

I looked at her for a moment.

"Stacy Strawberry?"

She smiled and gave me a hug, and just like that is was like being back together all those years ago.

"Where was everyone? When I got here no one was in sight."

"Mandatory nature scavenger hunt," Stacy said. "Just be glad you missed it. I think I may have poison ivy in a very private place."

The room erupted in laughter.

"Okay, enough about Strawberry's private parts," I heard a girl say behind Rebecca. "You couldn't forget me, now could you?" The women was sitting on her bunk, drinking something out of a large coffee mug.

I knew by the long, straight dark hair and dark eyes that it was Tiffany Spencer. "Tiffany Turnip," I said. She gave me a face. "Yes, I know, you always hated that name. At least it's better than Molly Melon, right?"

I heard a high pitched laugh and out from the corner appeared Jessica Mason. She looked just as stunning as she did as a kid, just in a grown-up, models-for-Victoria's-Secret way. She fluffed her blonde curls as she strutted toward me. "Well, you've grown into those melons, we see." Jessica laughed again, high-pitched and all. "Whatever brought you back to camp?"

As Jessica narrowed her eyes at me, all my childhood insecurities rushed back. "Um … I …"

She put her hand on her chest. "Oh, my, gosh. It's not for Travis, is it?" Then she let out another high-pitched laugh, but this time it was clearly filled with sarcasm.

Before I could wrap my brain around what she was saying, the bell for dinner rang with loud anticipation. I grabbed my purse and made a quick B-line for the door. My brain was still reeling from Jessica's question. Travis? As in Travis Wellington, my first crush and the first boy I ever kissed? The same boy that told everyone at camp that we made out, then moved on to Jessica Mason. There was no way I came to see him!

"So, tell us all about your life," Tiffany said a while later as we all sat down at one of the dining tables in the main lodge.

It was crazy how many people came for the reunion. I looked around the packed cafeteria, seeing if I recognized anyone else. I kind of wanted to stall on the whole "life questions" section of reconnecting with these girls. I looked down at the food, which seemed to not have changed since I was a kid. There was some kind of hotdish, a Jell-O dessert, and a bun with butter. I suddenly missed takeout from Murray's and my usual glass of red wine.

"Don't feel on the spot," Stacy said from across the table. "I'm just so happy you're here!"

Before I could get into the details about my life, the man from the bathroom walked into the dining lodge. Gone was the towel and he now was dressed in jeans and an old vintage T-shirt. I quickly hide behind Tiffany before he could see me.

"What are you doing?" Her breath smelled like liquor; clearly the coffee mug she was drinking earlier didn't have coffee in it.

"I'm trying to hide. Hold still." Tiffany was moving to get a better look at me. "Do you see that guy that just walked in?" I whispered. She looked and nodded. "I walked in on him half-naked, in the bathroom earlier."

Tiffany belted out of loud laugh and waved her hands at the man. "Yoo-hoo! Over here!"

"What are you doing?!" I snapped at her. "Don't call him over here!"

Tiffany shook her head and smiled. I was about to get up and leave when the man's eyes caught mine. He smiled and started walking toward us. Damned drunken Tiffany Turnip! I stared at my plate, mushing the pile of hotdish around with my fork.

"Travis!" I heard Jessica squeal. "Come sit next to me!"

Jessica wrapped her arms around the man. Travis? I gulped. Suddenly I felt all hot and sweaty. Travis pulled Jessica's arms off his shoulders, placing his hands on top of hers. She smiled seductively at him, and suddenly it all came clear. Travis Wellington. Crap. Hot guy in the bathroom was my childhood love. I mean, crush. Not love. Definitely not love.

"Good evening, ladies," Travis said as removed his hands from Jessica's perfect little shoulder's. "How was the scavenger hunt? I'm sorry I missed it."

I noticed the effect he still had on all the ladies. Nothing had changed since we were twelve. Travis had the talent to silence a room and gain everyone's attention. I ignored him and started to eat the hotdish, which luckily looked worse than it tasted.

"Hello, Molly." I raised my head, gulping down the noodles. Travis's brown eyes were staring at me and his lips turned upward in a smirk. "It's lovely to see you again."

Before I could say anything, he walked away from the table, to the food line. I was grateful I didn't have to have an awkward conversation with him. Besides, clearly there was something going on between him and Jessica. It was best if we didn't talk.

"Isn't he good looking?" Stacy said when she noticed me watching him. "I mean, as a kid he was cute, but now—"

"Totally doable," Tiffany finished for her. "That's if I was single. I have a boyfriend." She turned her attention to me. "I'm also divorced. Don't ask."

"Well, I wasn't going to say that," Stacy said shyly. "I'm married. Four kids." She grabbed a picture out of her purse and handed it to me. There were four little kids, all huddled together on a bed of grass.

"They're adorable," I said, and handed her back the picture.

"You know what's adorable," Tiffany said. "Travis's chest." She turned to me. "Did you see more of him in the bathroom? Maybe some manly parts you wanna tell us about?"

"What are we talking about ladies?" Rebecca was late to the conversation. "I heard 'manly parts'?"

"I bet it's really bi—"

"Okay," I said quickly, cutting Tiffany off on her speculation. "We're all eating here."

"What are we talking about?" Rebecca inquired insistently.

"Travis." Tiffany nudged me with her elbow. "Molly Melon here saw his privates."

The other ladies gasped while I rolled my eyes. "I did not see his privates. Okay? He had a towel on."

"Excuse me," I heard a snarly voice say from the other end of the table. "Did I just hear you ladies right?"

Rebecca put her hand up to quiet Jessica. "Whoa, whoa, whoa. How did you get to see Travis with only a towel on?"

"In the boys' . . . men's room," Tiffany quickly answered for me.

"*Thank* you, Tiffany," I said sarcastically. And as the girls all stared at me with overly excited eyes, Jessica made her way down to our end of the table. "There's a perfect explanation for why I was in there."

"And?" All four of them said in unison.

"The women's door was stuck," I said matter-of-factly.

Tiffany made an indignant face. "That's it?"

She was still the same old Tiffany: wild and crazy.

"Yes. That's it."

"So you didn't see anything," Jessica said.

"Nope. Sorry, ladies." Everyone apart from Jessica looked mildly disappointed. I grabbed my plate and stood up to throw it away. "Well, you all have a nice night."

Stacy's brows closed together. "You're not going to the bonfire?"

"No, I think I'll watch some TV and call it an early night." Everyone around the table laughed. "What's so funny?"

"The cabins aren't furnished with TVs, Molly. In fact, the only TV is in Miss Marge's office," Rebecca said. "And that's off-limits."

No TVs? You'd think after seventeen years that'd get with the times a little. What the heck was I going to do without my phone, and now no TV?

"Anyway, the bonfire is mandatory," Tiffany said as she stood up. "And if you don't go, you'll get bathroom duty." She laughed. "And we all know you're not successful in the bathroom department."

I rolled my eyes. Ha. Ha. What were we twelve again? It kind of felt like it. Okay, I guess I had to concede to some of the camping shenanigans. But

I was an adult now. Miss Marge could make me attend the bonfire, but she couldn't make me sing "Kumbaya."

* * *

Okay, so I sang "Kumbaya." Miss Marge insisted we all sing. I was hesitant at first, but when she came over and placed her arm around my shoulder, what choice did I have? It surprised me how much fun the bonfire actually ended up being. There were some pretty good singers in the bunch, and a couple not-so-good ones, too, which made it more fun.

"Nice night, isn't it?" Travis handed me a mug as he took a seat next to me.

I scooted down on the log as Travis's leg brushed mine. "Yes, it is." The warm mug felt good against my cold hands. I sniffed the contents. "What is this?"

"Apple cider. It's spiked, so take it easy."

"Thank you." I took a sip. Hmmm. It was delicious. "Isn't that against the rules?"

He shrugged. "I'm a rule breaker kind of guy." He placed his mug on the ground and stood up to put another log on the fire. "Kind of like you."

I met his gaze, all radiant with the glow of the fire behind him. Why did he have to be so damn hot? "Yes, well, the restroom was my last broken rule here. I'm on good behavior from now on."

His smile reached up to his dark brown eyes and I felt like I was going to burn a hole right through the log. "That's too bad."

"I had no idea who you were in the restroom," I said. "I feel like an idiot now."

"Why? I wouldn't expect you to recognize me." He reached for his mug and took a sip as he sat down again. "I mean, I hope I've changed a little since then."

I laughed. "Um, yes, you have." Feeling a little uncomfortable, I said, "But your eyes are the same. You always had friendly eyes."

"Ahhh, you like my eyes?" Travis said smoothly.

Oh, boy. What did I say that for? "No, I said your eyes are friendly."

"So you don't like my eyes?"

Seriously?

"You know what?" I said. I could beat him at his own game. "I take that back. You haven't changed at all."

Travis laughed and put a hand on his chest like he'd just been hit. "I remembered you."

"You did? But you asked for my name?"

"I'm not sure why I did that." He locked eyes with mine. "I could never forget your face."

I was stunned. What could I say to that? Before I could articulate a response he said, "Remember that time we booby trapped the dining hall with those buckets of water, and every time someone came out they got soaked?"

Where did that come from? It had been a long time since I'd thought about our crazy camp antics. But that was what really bonded us when I think about it. Travis would come up with some crazy idea and beg me to help him, which usually entailed some harmless prank. I was Travis's buddy, his partner in crime. I wasn't someone he had a crush on.

"We did some crazy things. We were pretty good *buddies*."

Travis's expression was hard to read. "Buddies. Right. Those were the days. It's too bad Miss Marge might have to sell the place. I have a cabin not too far from here, so I've been helping her with repair stuff for quite some time. I'm gonna miss coming out here."

"She has to sell the place?" I was suddenly overcome by sadness, which totally surprised me. I loved this place as a kid. I felt guilty for not coming back over the years to help out.

"It's disappointing. She's been meeting with some hot-shot lawyer from some land development company. I guess they want to build luxury cabins. She has the best views on Crooked Lake."

"But this isn't a concrete deal, right?" I couldn't believe Camp Crooked Lake would be bulldozed to the ground. The thought of it had left me feeling nauseous.

"I've been wracking my brain, trying to come up with a way for her to keep it. We're looking at all options."

With this news and the effect of the alcohol, I decided I'd better call it a night. Besides, Jessica had been glaring at me from across the fire, tentatively watching my conversation with Travis. I had so many mixed emotions swirling inside me, I didn't know what to do with myself. "I'm going to head back to my cabin. Thanks for the cider." I handed him back the mug.

"You sure you want to leave? I think Benny Anderson is telling ghost stories over there." He nodded across the fire to Benny Banana. Benny still looked like the same twelve-year-old boy from back in the day: stocky, short. The only difference now was the prominent beard on his face. "And I have much better ideas up my sleeve than the water buckets."

I sighed. "I think I'm a little too old for ghost stories and pranks," I said as I started to walk away.

"Chicken!" Travis called after me.

But I wasn't going to be reeled in by his childish mockery. Not anymore. Travis wanted a buddy again, a partner in crime. But that girl who'd succumbed to peer pressure all because of a secret crush had moved on.

So I shook my head and waved goodnight.

* * *

"But . . . I don't do costumes," I said as Stacy pushed me toward the Activity Center. It was dusk and the Halloween party was going to start in another hour.

"It's mandatory, Molly." She pushed me a little more.

I was exhausted from a day of nature hiking, kayaking relays, and kitchen duty. The last thing I wanted to do was dress up in a stupid costume. "Can't we just pretend we're going? Where does she get these costumes from anyway?"

"Her sister owns a Halloween store in Brainerd."

"Oh my goodness!" I yelped as I nearly walked into a giant fake spider web that was strewn around the entire room. Tables were dressed with orange and black table coverings, and ghosts, witches and monsters were pinned up on every wall. I guess Miss Marge loved the festivities that Halloween brought with it. "Wow, she really gets into this."

"Shoot," Stacy said as we walked into the back storage room. There were some leftover costumes hanging on a rack. "I forgot, I told Tiffany I'd do her hair in pin curls for tonight."

"Go ahead," I told her, combing through the undesirable selection of costumes. "Shouldn't take me long here."

"You sure?" Stacy seemed hesitant.

"Yes," I said, shooing her out. I smiled. "I'll surprise you."

While Stacy left to play hairstylist, I picked out the only costume I could find that didn't show ninety percent of my skin. Elsie came to mind when I grabbed the Spider girl costume, pulling at the unforgivable spandex. Thank goodness my phone was confiscated.

On my way out of the closet, I heard a noise close by. The Activity Center was still empty, and with the darkness of the place and it being Halloween, it had me spooked. I was just about to walk out of the door when someone jumped out, wearing a creepy mask. "Ahhhhh!" I screamed. Then, reflexively, I punched the creepy face square in the nose.

"Oooouch!" the person cried as they kneeled on the ground.

I was shocked when the person pulled off their mask. "Travis? Oh, shit!" I kneeled on the ground in front of him. "Are you okay?"

"Ahhh, I think so. Is my nose bleeding?" He laughed. "You pack a mean punch for being so little."

"I'm so sorry. It was instinctual." I leaned in closer to his face to make sure he wasn't bleeding. When I went to touch his nose, he grabbed my hand. Immediately it was like a jolt of energy surged through my body. I thought I could actually hear my heart beating in my chest.

"You were always easy to scare." He smirked mischievously. "Happy Halloween."

I pulled my hand away and hit him on the shoulder. "You deserve that one! Scaring a poor girl in the middle of the wilderness! You're lucky I didn't hit you somewhere else!" I stood up and grabbed my costume off the grass.

Travis got up as well, albeit he winced a few times. "What'd you find for a costume?"

I unfolded the ridiculous dress to show him. "Spider girl. It was slim pickings in there."

Travis just stared at me for a moment, which had me suddenly feeling insecure. I hated the way he could make me feel like I was twelve again, all smitten and tongue-tied.

"Well, I better get back to the cabin," I said.

He put his hands up. "Just wait here for a moment."

A cool breeze blew across me as the clouds covered the moon. I started to get chilled as I waited for him, not exactly sure what he was up to. I could smell the smoke from a nearby bonfire, probably the main one near my cabin, and then a moment later, Travis came out holding something.

"Here, this should fit you." He handed me what looked like a princess dress and a tiara.

"A princess?"

"A royal Duchess."

"Ah, that's better. Thank you." I took the dress from him.

"You'd look great in either one," he said. "But I think this one fits your personality better." He moved closer to me. "Hey, I'm sorry for scaring you."

I took a step back. "Sorry I broke your nose."

He smiled, rubbing the tip of his nose. "It's not broken. Just a little bruised."

With my heart beating at a runner's pace, I waved and walked away toward my cabin. And as I was getting ready, I couldn't stop thinking of Travis, which had me unnerved. Travis was a good-looking, perfect-body kind of specimen. He wasn't a settle down, one women kind of man. I kept trying to tell myself this as I curled my hair and applied my makeup for the night. If I was smart, I had to stay away from him. He may have gotten rid of his braces, matured some with age, and grew substantial inches, but one thing still hadn't changed. Travis Wellington was still a heartbreaker.

* * *

"You look so pretty," Stacy said as I arrived at the Halloween party. She was dressed in a mermaid costume, complete with tail.

"Thanks," I said. "I feel a bit silly in it. Costumes aren't my thing."

"Look at you!" Tiffany came up and gave me a hug. She was dressed in a sexy cat costume. "Did you and Travis plan that?"

"What?" I asked, confused. I looked around the room until I found Travis by the punch bowl, talking to some guy with a pirate costume on. It was hard to see in the dark, but he looked like he was wearing a costume that resembled mine, except of course it was for a man.

"Look at you!" Rebecca said as she joined the conversation. "You carry royalty well!"

I forced a smile at Rebecca, then made my way across the room to where Travis was. He smiled and waved at me when he saw me coming.

"Wow, Molly. You look amazing."

My cheeks flushed. "Thank you." The pirate walked away and I took a deep breath. "Do you notice anything familiar about my costume?"

Travis cocked his head to the side. "Um, it's the one I found for you earlier."

I raised my eyebrows at him. "That's it?"

Travis's lips curled in that adorable way. "Okay. Are you mad?" He looked down at his costume. "I couldn't very well wear this costume without a Duchess, now could I?"

"People are going to talk, you know."

Travis shrugged. "So let them talk."

"Shouldn't you have given this costume to Jessica?" The minute I said it I felt like an idiot. It just sort of came out.

"Jessica? Are you kidding me?"

I shook my head. Right. Did he think I was stupid? The man had a total crush on Jessica when we were kids and it clearly hadn't changed. But before I could say anything Stacy ran up to me.

"C'mon, Molly! Miss Marge is on the dance floor. We have to whoop it up with her!" She grabbed my hand and dragged me into the crowded circle, where Miss Marge and a group of girls, including my cabin mates, were singing and dancing to "YMCA."

An hour later my feet felt like they were going to bleed from dancing nonstop, so I took a seat at one of the tables. As I removed my shoes and rubbed my poor feet, an 80s slow song came on.

"May I have this dance?" I heard a voice say.

I looked up to see Travis standing there. He bowed and extended his hand like a royal would do. I swallowed hard, trying to quickly come up with some excuse. "I . . . I . . . um," I stammered.

"C'mon on." Travis grabbed my hand. "Dance with me."

I reluctantly followed his lead out on the dance floor, placing my hands on his shoulders. The disco ball turned above us, casting circles of light around us.

"Are you having fun?"

I studied his big brown eyes. "Yes, are you?"

"I usually need some liquid courage before I get on the dance floor."

"I'm not much of a dancer myself."

"What do you say we get outta here? Do something really fun?"

"Nah ah. I'm too old for pranks."

"You keep saying that, but I'm having a hard time believing you."

"Well, it's the truth."

"I wasn't talking about a prank anyway. I'm talking about something fun."

I rolled my eyes. "Fun?"

Travis laughed. "Don't roll your eyes at me. Besides, you owe me."

I guffawed. "I owe you?"

"Yes. You nearly broke my nose tonight."

"That was an accident." I pushed his shoulder playfully. "And you scared the living daylights out of me."

Instead of responding, Travis grabbed my hand and pulled me across the room. Before I could even protest we were already outside.

"What are we doing?" I stage-whispered. "We can't leave!"

Travis had this adorable, mischievous look on his face. "Says who?"

I just stood there, not knowing what to do.

"Okay," Travis said, "you can go back and do the conga with Miss Marge." He jingled some keys in the air. "Or you could sneak into her office with me and check your texts before we sneak off the property." He extended his hand.

I narrowed my eyes at him. He knew exactly what he was doing. I gave one last glance at the Activity Lodge before I placed my hand in his, and we were off running.

* * *

After checking my phone and finding out it was dead, the trek through the woods only took twenty minutes to get to the Lonesome Pine Bar. I enjoyed the log cabin feel of the place, which was crammed with tables and a long bar with some TVs hanging on the wall. We navigated through the crowd of people dressed for the holiday and found a small two-top in the back. I felt silly as the crowd of local strangers bowed and curtseyed to us as if we were truly royalty.

"What do you think?" Travis said over the loud conversations around us. "Worth sneaking out for?"

"It's great. How'd you find this place?"

"I've been here before with some friends. Never went through the woods before, though."

"Here you go," a server said as she dropped off two shots at our table. "Compliments of the ladies over there." She gestured toward a group of older ladies dressed as witches. They wiggled their fingers at Travis.

Travis lifted his shot to thank them. "You ready for this?"

I smelled the contents. "Tequila? I don't know."

Travis shrugged. "I know, it's not my kind of drink, but how about we do it on three." He lifted his glass. "To Camp Crooked Lake."

Although hesitant, I lifted my glass and said, "To Camp Crooked Lake."

"Ahhhh." After filling each other in on the last seventeen years, Travis slammed his fourth shot glass down. "These people need to quit sending us tequila."

"I know," I giggled, feeling very tipsy. "It's so hard to be royalty."

Travis laughed, then turned serious as he pushed the shot glass to the edge of the table. "I have a question for you."

I laughed, shoving popcorn into my mouth. "Okaaay."

"Why did you think something was going on with me and Jessica?"

I narrowed my eyes. "C'mon, Travis. She's had her claws in you since the moment I arrived. I mean, I don't know her situation, but she seemed to be staking her claim."

Travis looked bemused. "What do you mean?"

I rolled my eyes. "I mean, not much has changed since we were kids."

Travis grabbed my hand from across the table. "Don't roll your eyes at me, Molls." He smiled. "What are you talking about? Nothing has ever been going on between me and Jessica, nor will there ever be."

I took a sip of my drink of choice—a glass of red—and set it down. "Well, I'm over it now, but when you kissed me and blabbed about it to the entire camp, then moved on to Jessica, you broke my heart." It was amazing what liquid courage could do for you.

"Is that what you think?"

I waved it off. "Doesn't matter now. It was ages ago. We were just kids."

"That's why you left camp? Why you didn't answer any of my letters?" His brows furrowed. "Geez, Molly. You have it all wrong. I never told anyone that we kissed. And I never had any interest in Jessica."

I took a rather large sip of my wine. "And we were just friends."

Before Travis could reply an older man dressed as a priest came over to our table. "Well, looky here," he slurred. "We have royalty in the house." He reached out his hand to Travis. "Father Willy Jeffers." Then he leaned into me. "I'm not *really* a priest, you know."

I smiled at Travis, who was holding the man steady as he swayed forward.

"Bless me Father, for I have sinned," Travis said to the man. "It's been seventeen years since my last confession."

I just stared at Travis, whose face was stone-cold serious. What was he doing?

"Go on my child," the drunken man said as he leaned into our table. I put my hands up in case he fell on me.

"I've had impure thoughts about a girl, Father," Travis said.

"Oooh, lad, do tell." The man leaned in to look Travis square in the eyes.

"You see," Travis went on. "I've had a crush on this girl for many years now, but I was always too chicken to do anything about it." The old man rolled his finger around for Travis to continue. "And now she's back into my life and I don't know what to do."

"Wells," the drunken 'priest' said, "if it's meant to be, yous be togetheeer."

Travis locked eyes with mine. "That's easier said than done. You see, she thinks I broke her heart, but I never would have done that. And all this time I thought it was my heart that had been broken. . . ."

I looked down at the table, then at the drunken priest who was almost asleep as he stood there. Then an older women came over and apologized and led him back to his table near the center of the room. When I looked back at Travis, he was staring intently at me. "Travis, I . . ."

"I'm crazy about you, Molly. Always have been. All those times I had us doing crazy stuff as kids was just an excuse to be close to you." His face turned beet-red. "I've even stalked you on Facebook but was too chicken to send a friend request."

I narrowed my eyes. "Stalking on Facebook, huh? I don't know, Travis. That might be crossing a line." I smiled at him.

Travis stood up from the table and playfully pulled me off my stool. He ran his hand along my cheek and sighed heavily. "What am I going to do with you, Molly Melon?"

I looked up into his beautiful dark eyes, wanting to get lost in them. That's when we heard the loud clinks start up across the bar. It was just a few at first, then the entire room started in. We were surrounded by the repetitive chants of, "Kiss! Kiss! Kiss!"

Travis pulled me close to him, really close, then pressed his lips against mine. I heard the bellowing of cheers for just a moment, before I let myself get lost, and they completely drifted away.

* * *

"I had an amazing time last night." Travis said. He pressed his lips against mine.

We were squeezed together on the small twin bed, in an empty cabin that wasn't being used. I never anticipated going on a wild adventure with Travis, making out in front of an entire bar, and waking up in his arms. But there it was.

"We broke a lot of rules." I kissed him again, enjoying his hand caressing my bare back.

"And nearly broke this teeny twin bed," he joked.

I laughed and nuzzled into his neck. And then we were kissing again until we heard someone burst through the door.

"What the hell?!" Jessica said. "You've got to be kidding me?!"

"Wow, way to go, Molls." Tiffany nodded approvingly.

"What are you doing in here?!" Travis yelled.

"I've been looking everywhere for you, Travis!" Jessica yelled back. "I need to talk to you—now!"

Travis jumped out of bed, quickly got dressed around the corner, and then ran after Jessica. I suddenly felt like I was twelve again. Only this time Travis and I didn't just kiss. I looked up to see Tiffany with a mischievous smile across her face.

"So?" she said, twirling her long hair around her fingers. "What about those manly parts?"

I covered my head with the sheet, ignoring her childish behavior. After she wouldn't shut up, I did the walk of shame back to my cabin, in full Duchess gown. She kept trying to pry dirty details of my night with Travis, but I wasn't in the mood. After everything we'd been through the night before, one little plea from Jessica and he was back under her spell.

Before I got to the cabin, I saw a group of people standing in a circle. When I got closer, I noticed it was Travis and Miss Marge in a heated discussion with some man. Miss Marge seemed to be crying. Jessica was beside Travis, and when she saw me she shot me a look of disgust.

A larger crowd formed as I made my way past them, needing to get to the ladies' room. Before I could get too far, I heard Travis call my name. I ignored him, pressing on.

"Molly, wait up!" Travis was right behind me now. "Molly, stop!"

I turned around. "What?"

"You're mad at me."

"Very intuitive."

"Because I ran out on you," he said. "And followed Jessica." He ran his hands through his hair. "I swear, Molly, this has nothing to do with her."

I shrugged, unconvinced. I hated being insecure, but she had that effect on me just as much as Travis could make my heart go pitter patter. "Okay."

"I'm serious, Molly. I'm crazy about you."

I just stood there, feeling like an idiot, as fellow campers started to show up, now forming a circle around us. Wearing our costumes from the night before and having a makeup smeared face didn't help in the humiliation department.

"The man we were talking to is the lawyer working with the company wanting to bulldoze the camp. Jessica's a lawyer. She's been helping me figure out a way to keep this place."

I shook my head. Jessica a lawyer? "Why didn't you tell me?"

"I didn't want you to think it was anything more." Travis grabbed my hand and led me to where Miss Marge was standing with the lawyer and Jessica. "I want everyone to listen," he said as we approached them.

I pulled on his arm. "Travis, what are you doing?"

"Let me do this," he said to me.

I just stood there, not knowing what to do or say at his point.

"I've been coming here since I was seven," Travis said to the lawyer as he continued to hold my hand. "And through the years I've met some amazing people here. This weekend I've reconnected with this girl," he held up my hand, "and no matter what happens, you'll never take that away from me." He turned to me, while our fellow campers looked on with curiosity. "I might lose this camp, but that wouldn't compare to the pain of losing you again, Molly."

I looked around the crowd, seeing Tiffany, Rebecca and Stacy with smiles on their faces. "Well, Travis, you're just going to have to deal with it," I started, hearing audible gasps fill the air. "Because whether you like it or not, you're stuck with me."

Travis pulled me close to him, placed his hand across my cheek, and kissed me more passionately than I had ever been kissed in my entire life. One thing came to mind as my lips moved expertly against his. Eat your heart out, Jessica Mason.

* * *

"Wait a minute," Elsie said as the waitress brought us our drinks. "You did what?"

It was the following Monday and I was on my lunch break. "You heard me right."

Elsie looked stunned. "You bought Camp Crooked Lake? Are you serious?"

I laughed. "Well, not the entire thing, of course. But with Miss Marge and Travis, Camp Crooked Lake is not going anywhere."

Elsie's eyes were as wide as I'd ever seen them. "This is crazy!"

"You told me to do something crazy, so I did."

She laughed. "Well, I guess so. This Travis guy must be special."

Before I could answer her, I noticed a tall, handsome man walk into the restaurant, wearing a striped dress shirt and dark jeans. Elsie turned around in her seat to see what had caught my attention. Her jaw dropped when she saw Travis for the first time.

"Is that him?" she asked, clearly stunned.

I smiled, waving him over. "Yep, that's him."

Elsie came over to where I was standing and placed an arm around my shoulder. "Oooh, Molly, you owe me big time!"

I rested my head against hers and laughed. "Do. I. Ever."

ABOUT THE AUTHOR

Jill Revak is a member of Minnesota Lakes Writers. She lives on a hobby farm with her husband, two children, one dog, one goat, nine horses, and an abundance of barn cats. Click here to visit her website at http://jillrevak.wordpress.com.

Jill also has a short story published in the *Romancing the Lakes of Minnesota ~ Summer* anthology. Available in print and digital format wherever books are sold.

CARA'S SWIM

Kristy Johnson

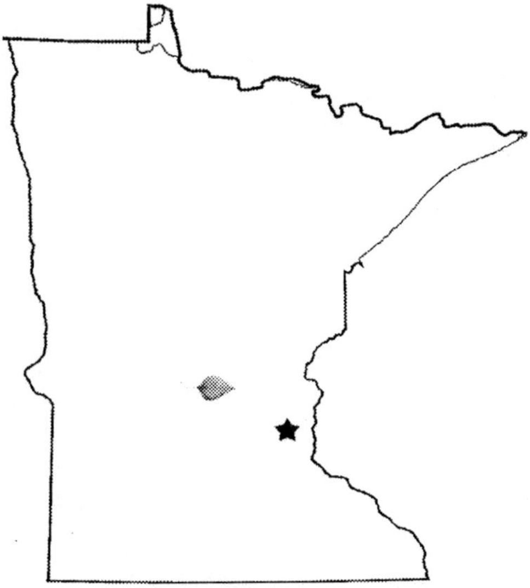

Lake Sylvia, Annadale

It was a glorious late September morning, on the golden shores of Lake Sylvia, in Annandale Minnesota. I was sitting on the dock enjoying the last few sips of coffee when I could sense him approach. I still can't believe it, me, struggling author, Cara Waters and Josh Matthews! Our first kiss had been surreal, it was the fourth of July and we had taken the camp pontoon out on the lake to watch the fireworks with the rest of the lake's residents. There were hundreds of boats surrounding the point near the camp, the sounds of laughter mixed with muffled voices, radios blaring, Chinese lanterns floating silently about us, mixed with roaring booms and bright flashes of fireworks. Josh pulled me in close and kissed me, it was amazing. The thought of that kiss, sent a warm flush through my body. But now the calendar was kissing October, the dark green leaves of summer were replaced by brilliant yellows, oranges and reds and the camp would be closing for the season. I wonder if that means our relationship would also be closing for the season too. Had I just been a fling for Josh? Someone to pass the off hours with? Thinking back on the summer and all that occurred, it really didn't matter what Josh's motives were, I had enjoyed him and our time together.

Josh, who was a counselor at the camp, would be leaving to return to his life in the Cities, while I would stay on at camp Chi-Ro and oversee the renovations. The camp was going to become a year-round facility; catering to families in the summer and adult retreats in the winter. I knew the position was going to be busy in the summer with all of the visitors, but the off season would be more part time and allow me to write. My novel was half finished and my editor was chomping at the bit to get it. With all the distractions at home and my financial disabilities, it was very hard to focus. So, when the position at the camp was offered to me, it was a logical choice, Josh was an added bonus.

Josh's warm lips brushed the nape of my neck as he whispered in my ear, "Good morning beautiful."

I tilted my chin up to him with a smile and anticipation of another kiss, but was disappointed when he continued. "Sorry to be the bearer of bad news, but that contractor, the one who was passed over, is here and he wants to talk with you. I tried to head him off, but he's relentless."

"Gus, is here again?" I asked with a frown and disappointment that my morning was going to be filled with Gus Walberg instead of Josh Morgan.

I could tell Josh wasn't happy either when he replied, "I'm afraid so. Don't worry Cara, I have your back."

Smiling I took his hand as he helped me up and we headed for the camp's cramped little office. The camp's owner, Ozzie Solem, knew Gus from the old days when they worked together on the dance hall at Bridal Beach Resort. There had been some sort of scandal and falling out between the two of them so Ozzie decided to use a different contractor from town. Norberg and Sons were scheduled to start work October first.

Gus, was stomping about the cramped little space filled with souvenir t-shirts, sunscreen and assorted candies. The teenage girl behind the counter looked like a trapped little rabbit wishing she could bolt before the wily fox gobbled her up. Gus saw me though, and he bee-lined out of the office and straight towards me. Instead of going to meet him I stopped where I was and tried to make myself as large as possible. Head high, shoulders back, eyes taking him in watching for serious signs of trouble. Gus was yelling at me as he stomped up to where I stood, "You just have to let me do this project Miss! I know my bid was lower than old Norberg's, besides, I'm a better contractor than he is. Truly I am. This job is mine. I need this job!"

"I am truly sorry Mr. Walberg, but this wasn't my decision, it was Mr. Solem's. I told you this the last time you stopped by and when I spoke with Mr. Solem, he stated his decision was final."

"You don't understand, Miss!" He was shouting at the top of his lungs now, drawing attention from the few remaining campers. He even took another step closer to her allowing small droplets of spittle to splatter my in the face.

Refusing to give up my ground, I stood up taller, and elevated my voice and put all the authority in it I could muster. "I am sorry sir, but the decision is final and now I must ask you to leave. If you fail to comply or if you return the police will be called and I will have you arrested!"

Gus was only taken back for a moment and then he leaned in closer and in an ice cold voice that made January seem tropical said, "You'll be sorry for this," Then turned to leave, stomping and muttering as he went.

As the gravel flew up from Gus's tires, Josh touched my arm, and then pulled me in close, whispering into my hair, "You did great. I don't think he'll be back."

"I hope you're right, because in a couple days I will be here all alone."

"The contractors will be here," he replied soothingly.

"Only during the day. Night time will be all me."

I couldn't see Josh smile, but I knew he was flashing those pearly whites and was up to something when he said, "We will just have to have special check-in times over Skype."

"Oh, we will, will we?" I replied flushing a bright pink.

* * *

Josh was getting into his pickup for the third time and I was fighting off tears. This was finally goodbye.

I leaned into the open window for one last kiss, and Josh never one to disappoint me obliged. "Don't worry, this isn't the end. You'll have a few days off and so will I. The Cities aren't that far, just a quick hour and half drive. You'll see." Josh said with a smile.

Determined not to cry, and because I still believed this had been one of those off beat summer romances said, "I know, besides we always have some of those video chats you're always tantalizing me with."

Smiling and with one more peck on the lips he said, "That's right, I'll call you." With a wink of his eye, he was gone.

I stood there in the driveway for a while allowing the darkness and the silence to envelope me. I couldn't believe he was gone. Actually, I couldn't believe everyone was gone. The camp was eerily quiet. A sense of unease crept into the corners of my mind. This was ridiculous. I just wasn't used to the camp being so quiet. I finally decided to return to my cabin, when a loud noise scared me to death. Turning to face the noise I thought of Gus. I thought he was finally here to make good on his promise, I laughed out loud when I realized what was making all the ruckus. It was a family of raccoons working feverishly to break into the garbage cans. Good thing they were all secured or I would have a big mess to clean up in the morning. I made it the remainder of the way to my cabin without incident and as I locked the door behind me, a lone loon eerily called out in the night. It too did not like being alone and my sense of foreboding returned.

* * *

Frank Norberg and his four sons: Frank Jr., Sven, Cal and Joe, were at the camp bright and early the next morning. They were going to lay out their plans for me and start work on the new office and manager quarters. They wanted to get that building done first, since my cabin was not winterized and I would need a new place to live before the real cold set in. I'd had the staff pack everything up before they left and it put in the shed. The shed was the only building not going to be renovated, so as much as possible had been put in the little outbuilding.

The Norbergs were hopeful that the cabins could mostly be salvaged. The cabins contained a lot of character, that Ozzie wanted to preserve, but he also wanted his adult guests to be comfortable by providing them with modern amenities. Ozzie's dream was to cater to guests looking for long weekend getaways. The type of people he wanted to attract were creative types: scrap-bookers, writers, quilters or the outdoor enthusiast: ice fisherman, cross country skiers, etc. People needing some time to regroup and rejuvenate, so they could face the many challenges of the modern world. Months had gone into the planning so that there would be well equipped workrooms, fish cleaning areas, or just a nice warm lodge to relax in.

"Cara, I just really want to assure you, your new quarters will be done before it gets real cold," Frank was saying. "It's October, which gives us a good six weeks before any real weather sets in."

"I have faith in you guys," I said with a small smile. I hadn't given a thought about cold weather until this point and I realized that I didn't have any warm clothes with me. I'd have to make a trip home to get them. Maybe I could see Josh then. I would have to plan a trip to go in a couple of weeks. I didn't want to appear needy and go too soon. How long should I wait I wondered. "Huh?" I responded, being jolted out of my thoughts by Frank.

"I just asked if you have any questions or concerns," Frank repeated.

"No, but I do have to tell you about Gus Walberg. He's shown up here a few times. He is very angry that he didn't get the contract. He made threats, so you should be on the lookout for him."

Frank's face changed and Cara had a hard time reading the expression that was there. "Don't you worry about Gus. We know how to take care of him, but if he comes around while we aren't here call 911. Don't try to handle him; it's not part of your job. Do you understand?"

"I do," I said nodding my head trying not to let the concern in Franks voice leave a notch of fear in my head.

"Good, now I best get those boys workin'".

* * *

Over the next few weeks, the project proceeded smoothly. I was happy, Ozzie was happy and Frank kept prattling on about his schedule. His boys humored him and would always respond with "You got it Pops," and they would keep working on the task at hand. There were times when someone was a little perplexed about where they had placed something or something was already torn apart and no one knew who did it. It was odd. I was not immune to this phenomenon, because often times when I returned to my cabin I would notice things moved about or out order. I shrugged it off as being too absorbed in my writing or being distracted by Josh's absence.

We had video chatted several times and our calls lasted for hours. We just fell into conversation. Even though it was nice and I felt very comfortable talking with him about everything, I still felt like it was the tail end of a summer romance. No one ever carried their summer romance into the fall. Yes, the fall was full of vibrant color and warm sunny days, but in all reality it was just the death roll before the cold dark hand of winter finished it off. But the reality was I was in love with Josh. I had been since our first kiss, I just wasn't going to be the one to spoil whatever it was we had going with a blurted out "I love you". Nope, wasn't going to be me, but I would try to see him when I went to the Cities to get my winter clothes. Well, it was now or never, I could just go and not try to see him at all, but then I would never know for sure. I took a deep breath, opened my laptop and began pressing keys in order to make the call.

I clicked on Josh's name from my call list and my computer immediately began chirping out a series of tones, signaling that my computer was reaching out to connect with his. He was on-line and his smiling face appeared on my screen.

"Hello, gorgeous!" he announced. "I wasn't expecting you to call until later."

After a little bit of chit chat, I finally got to the purpose of my call. "I have to come to the Cities on Saturday to get some of my winter clothes," I said pausing to see if he would suggest getting together.

"You do?" he asked with a wry smile.

"I do," I said smiling back. I was beginning to feel like an awkward teen age girl talking to a boy for the first time.

There was a long moment of silence, as we each sat looking at our computer monitors, waiting, smiling, imagining until finally Josh chuckled and said, "I sure hope I'm your first stop."

I smiled with relief, "I was hoping you would say something like that."

"Do you know about what time you'll leave?"

"I should be able to leave around 3:00 P.M. Frank has a couple of things he wants to go over with me before I head out. I plan on spending the night at home and then returning here sometime Sunday."

"Hmmm, an overnight stay. Finding winter clothing is sounding better already."

"I think you have a dirty mind," I said playfully.

With an evil laugh Josh said, "Are you just figuring that out now?"

"No, I guess I already knew that."

"See you Saturday," he said.

I smiled and said, "Goodnight, see you Saturday."

* * *

Saturday could not come fast enough for me. Josh and I firmed up our plans over the next few days. I would meet him at Kinkaid's in Bloomington for dinner, by 5:00 P.M. I thought it was a little fancy, but he said we'd never had a real date so he was making it up to me. Who was I to argue?

Trying to finish things up with Frank was another matter. He was prattling on again and it was now 3:15 P.M. Finally I said, "I am sorry Frank, but I really need to go. I need to be in Bloomington by 5:00 P.M."

Frank looking surprised jokingly said, "Why do you have a hot date?"

Blushing I said, "Well, yes, I do."

With hearty laughter he said, "You had better get going then. This can wait until Monday. It's about time you got out of here and had some fun."

"Thanks Frank," I said still blushing and sporting an ear to ear grin. I turned, and ran to my little cabin, so I could finish packing up and hit the road. I was going to have to step on it to make up a little time. I heard Frank and his sons packing up for the day. I smiled because I knew their families would be happy to see them too. This project was taking a toll on all of us. After a quick shower, makeup and hair, I was ready and only 45 minutes behind schedule. I sent a quick text to Josh to let him know I was delayed. I heard Frank and his sons leave in their trucks leave as I was shoving my laptop into its case. With a quick look around to see if I had everything and one more mirror check, I was headed out the door.

I locked my cabin door and turned to see four flat tires on my car. I dropped my overnight bag in disbelief, just as I did; I heard a guttural sound behind me.

"Bitch," he enunciated each letter drawing them out so each letter sounded venomous.

It was Gus! He was coming at me; he had something in his hand. What was it in his hand? A knife? No, it was a crowbar! He was swinging it at my head. Without thinking, I swung my backpack up to protect my head. The crowbar crushed my laptop and glanced off my arm. I screamed in pain. All my work down the drain, but it didn't matter, I had to get away.

Gus yelled in frustration because he had only administered a glancing blow, he screamed obscenities at me, words I couldn't distinguish as my mind raced with what to do. Without really thinking, I decided to go on the offense. I ran right at him, caught him with my good shoulder, knocked him out of the way, and continued running. I knew it was only a glancing blow and that he would recover quickly, but what choice did I have? I needed to hide, to get away, to do something.

"I'll get you!" he bellowed followed by yet another string of obscenities.

I could hear him scramble to his feet and begin the pursuit. Where to hide? The first thing that came into sight was the boathouse. There were lots of things in there I could use to defend myself. Trying not to give myself away, I cracked open the old door and scrambled inside. I bolted the door behind me, but I knew it wouldn't last long if Gus decided to get inside. The boathouse was a rotten old building that was going to be torn down, but it would have to do. I managed to find an old oar I thought could be used as a weapon, so I sat in the dark corner, cradling my injured arm and waited for my destiny. It didn't take long for it to find me.

Gus was pounding on the door and shouting, "I know you're in there you little bitch! I told you I was going to come for you!"

I clutched the oar as best I could and stood up. I wasn't too optimistic, but I would not go down without a fight. Gus Walberg was going to have to work hard to kill me.

Just as I had gathered my resolve the door gave way and Gus came barreling through the doorway with a triumphant, "I got you now girly!"

I smacked him as hard as I could with the oar, he lost his balance for a moment and I drew back to hit him again. With my injured arm it was hard to maintain control over the oar, but I had to try. Gus was ready for the attack this time though, and he grabbed the oar with both hands and swung it as hard as he could. This sent me sprawling, and I landed with a hard thud on the floor, my head hit, and things went dark for a moment. Do not lose consciousness I thought to myself, stay awake, breathe, don't give in.

I could hear Gus laughing as he bent down, stroked my hair and whispered maniacally, "I told you I would get you."

He stopped then, and cocked his head and stood up. He was listening for something. I heard a distant voice calling my name, without thinking I muttered, "Frank?"

Gus kicked me in the stomach and venomously seethed "Shut up!" and then he was gone.

I could hear him lock me in. Trapped, I was trapped! My brain was mush from hitting the ground, but I had to think. Think of how I was going to get out of this and poor Frank. He didn't know what he was walking into. How did he even know to look for me here? Slowly I began to turn myself over; lying on my back, I begin to take stock of all my bumps and bruises. My head was bleeding and I am pretty sure I have a broken rib, but I need to get out of here before he comes back. What to do? Lying here on the cold dark floor, my body aching and my head throbbing I begin to realize that there is a cold breeze blowing on me. Hope sparks in my being, as I try to distinguish where the breeze is coming from, because I know it is my way out. Making my way to my hands and knees, stopping to gasp for breath and my head to stop spinning, I carefully make my way around the dark shed until I find the source of the breeze. Two boards are rotten and slightly pushed in. Some of the kids must have found their way in here during the summer months for a little privacy. I use my legs to push the boards a little further apart so I can sneak through, but what then?

There are shouts in the distance, then silence. I hesitate wondering if Frank is ok. Was he able to take care of Gus? Am I saved? And then I hear it.

"He won't be able to save you girly! But now we will have more time together." And with that, Gus began to laugh a cold evil laugh that was getting closer.

* * *

No more time for contemplation, I slipped off my shoes and stepped into the cold icy waters of Lake Sylvia. Josh and I made the swim to Bulls Island from the point several times a week. It was one sure way we could be alone during the busy summer months. We had left towels and a little blanket on the far tip for their comfort and I was counting on the fact that they would still be there now. The only problem with this plan was I had never made the swim with a broken bones and in icy cold water.

I walked out into the water as far as I could silencing the gasps welling in my throat from the cold. This was my only option. I just knew it. Gus would never think me crazy enough to go to the island. He would look for me on the shore or at some of the nearby cabins. I could hear his rage as he realized I was gone and then he began searching for me. Quickly and as quietly as possible I made my way through the cold dark water to the tip of Bulls Island. I had never been this cold, but my survival instinct was in full bloom. I wanted to live.

Once my feet touched the slimy bottom of the lake I stood up and inched my way toward dry land. There was a path that leading to the other side of the island, well-worn from Josh and me, along with countless other trespassers. Hopefully our supplies would still be there. My mind was getting duller, whether from the cold or the blow I had taken, I didn't know. I just knew I needed to keep moving. The branches and brambles tore at my clothing, my skin, and my hair. I was sure I was making enough noise to wake the dead let alone attract a crazy man. But then I was there, the spot Josh and I had shared so many times over the summer months. I searched for our little stash in the darkness. Still here. The flame of hope sparked brighter as I dried myself off, trying to get the blood flowing again. Then I wrapped my feet in the other towel and snuggled in the blanket. I was so incredibly tired, I knew I needed to stay awake, and I should move a little, but I needed to rest, if only for a minute.

* * *

I woke briefly to Josh's voice, felt him lifting me, reassuring me. This was a nice dream. I think I will go back to sleep for a while and closed my eyes. The next time I opened my eyes I was in a very bright room and to my amazement I was warm! Oh, so warm. It felt so good, I will never take being warm for granted again. I looked around the little room and was surprised to see I was in a hospital room. How had anyone found me?

My eyes were still trying to focus when I realized there was a form sitting in a chair with its upper torso sprawled over the foot of my bed. "Josh?"

His head popped up immediately, "Oh, Cara, you gave me such a fright. What were you thinking going into the water?

Very dryly I answered, "That I wanted to live."

He chuckled a little at that, "You have a funny way of showing it."

"How's Frank?"

"He's got a nice bump on the head, but he'll be ok.."

"What happened? How did you find me? What about Gus?"

"One thing at a time," he said, standing up to stretch, muscles rippling under his shirt. I hadn't noticed those, during our video chats. "Well, I got worried when you hadn't called to tell me you were really on your way, so, I called Frank. Frank drove over to check on you and was blindsided by Gus. Frank failed to check in with his wife so she called the sheriff. The sheriff shot and killed Gus, when Gus tried to do the same to him. In the meantime, I couldn't wait so I started driving. I think I broke every traffic law there was to get to the camp. We were searching everywhere for you when a deputy followed your tracks to the edge of the lake. No one thought you would do a crazy thing like swim over to Bulls Island at the end of October, but I had to be sure so we found a boat and went to our spot. There you were curled in a ball, looking like hell."

"Felt like hell, too," I interjected.

"Yeah, well it was a good thing we found you," he replied angrily.

I let it slide because I was so grateful to be alive and I still had questions. "Josh, do you know why Gus did it? I mean why he tried to kill me. It was only a construction contract and it wasn't even up to me."

"Well," Josh said before taking a long deep breath and then releasing it, "it goes back to when Frank, Ozzie and Gus were working on the dance hall at Bridal Beach Resort. They were all in love with a young lady named Anna Bjorkstrand. The three of them, all vying for the young lady's attention, but she only had eyes for Ozzie. Frank took it all in stride, but Gus he got angry, really angry. Then Anna disappeared. Ozzie was heartbroken. There was a big scandal about why she disappeared. All three men were questioned at length. Fingers pointed at Gus, but law enforcement couldn't prove a thing. So, Anna Bjorkstrand disappeared into the history of Lake Sylvia."

"Oh, how sad," I said, "but what does that have to do with me?"

Josh looked at me with concern written all over his face, "Are you sure you want to hear this now?"

"Yes, I'm sure," I replied very confused.

"Well, when the sheriff was trying to piece things together they found several pieces of siding missing from your cabin and in there was..." Josh paused and looked at me.

I could not read his expression so I said, "Go on."

"There was."

"There was what? Just go ahead and say it, Josh," I was a little frightened now, my imagination running wild.

He sighed in resignation, "There were skeletal remains and they believe them to be Anna's remains."

I gasped, not prepared for this revelation.

Josh continued, "From what Frank and Ozzie said, you look a lot like Anna did back then. They think Gus had been haunted for years because he killed her and stashed the body in the camp while it was being built. He figured somehow you, I mean Anna had come back for retribution. He also knew that because of the renovations the remains would be discovered, and an investigation would be launched. He was sure he would finally be brought to justice."

He just sat there looking at me then. I sunk into my pillows, deep in thought as I processed the whole story. Josh gave me time and when I finally looked up he was staring at me a with a fire in his eyes I hadn't seen before. My insides stirred and I started to cry. The revelation of how close I had come to death finally struck home, I just couldn't help myself. Josh sat on the edge of my bed and pulled me close. He just held me and let my tears fall into his chest. "Thank you," I said, "Thank you for telling me, thank you for finding me and thank you for being here now."

He lifted my chin and smiled at me and said, "That's what we do for the people we love." Then he kissed me.

ABOUT THE AUTHOR

Growing up and attending the university in Bemidji, Minnesota, Kristy Johnson now resides in Jordan, Minnesota with her husband, two boys, two dogs, twelve chickens and a cat. *Cara's Swim*, is Kristy's second short story. Her first short story was published in Romancing the Lakes of Minnesota – Summer anthology in 2013. It is available in print and digital format wherever books are sold..

She is working hard to have her first full novel published in early 2015.

When not writing Kristy can be found taking photos for her company Fotonic Images, LLC, which specializes in a wide variety of photography, including portrait, sports and event photography. To learn more about Kristy and her publications you can visit her at:

www.WildhorsePublications.com

www.facebook.com/WildhorsePublications

www.amazon.com/author/KristyJohnson

www.twitter.com/FotonicImages

CUP A' JAVA

Ingrid Anderson Sampo

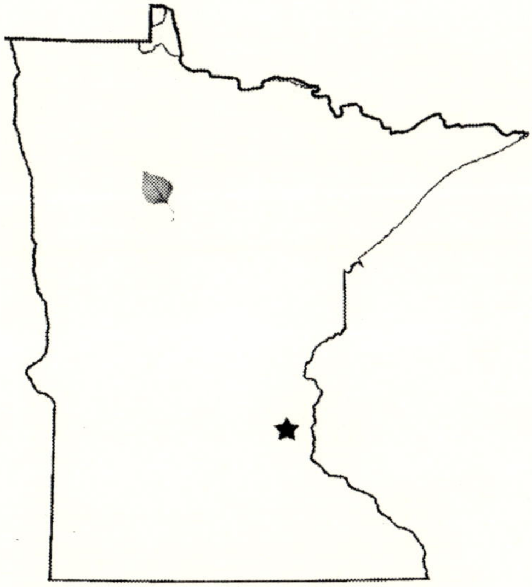

Big Moose Lake, Bemidji

~~~ "In 1896, the Village of Bemidji was incorporated and had a population of a few hundred. The Norwegians that settled there comprised 15.9 % of their population, who were fans of the great outdoors. It is the first city on the Mississippi and the home to the legendary Paul Bunyan and Babe the Blue Ox." ~~~

"Smitty." The greeting rang throughout the Cup 'a Java Cafe. Table upon table, and booth upon booth of red and white checkered tablecloths danced about the café as if it were an open invitation for one grand polka party for the citizens of Foulwell.

The effect was warm and welcoming, aided and abetted by the log cabin look outside and the wooden rafters within, pitching a tent above the customers' heads. Upon entering the Java, newcomers craned their necks to take in the rustic splendor. Blending in was out of the question.

The usual townsfolk congregated in the morning—retirees to begin their day. The working stiffs for their coffee breaks. All the Java regulars drinking their morning brew knew Smitty, the little old man, who walked with a limp. His once night-black hair was now as gray and sparse as his paunch was round.

Too early to layer, he'd thought as he'd dressed for his morning cup of the day's incentive to get up and join the world. It was autumn in northern Minnesota, and Foulwell's weather was unseasonably cold. "Foulwell, perfectly named—things can get fouled up around here." Smitty had complained to a friend when the lottery ticket he'd purchased, with a loon on it for good luck, had failed to come through for him.

Foulwell may have seemed cursed by its name. Its natural beauty made up for any negative perception. Flanked by pine forests on the north and south, Foulwell's easterly quadrant merged into a lake with a graceful coastline and quaint coves. Shining emerald in the summer, Big Moose Lake morphed into a brilliant blue when temperatures plummeted in the fall. All this was a harbinger of the coming winter.

Today, however, was not foul because it was bursting with

possibilities—Smitty was about to explode with the news he bore. The retired town blacksmith, one of the last living in Minnesota, found it difficult to restrain himself from prematurely upchucking the prime morsel of gossip he'd wolfed down on his way to the coffee shop. Miller, Smitty's informant, had pounced on him with the breaking news.

"Hey, everybody. Have I got a story for you," Smitty called out as he ambled to the counter, his rolling gait interrupted by a pause and jerk and then another roll, pause and jerk.

Sylvia was a mousey-haired bit of a spinster—still a maiden lady as they called single women in Foulwell. She perched on the third stool and nodded her head with an enthusiastic, "Hey." She lifted her incongruously large hands in salute. Everything else about her was small, although as she aged she was thickening about the middle. Her salt and pepper hair made one assume she was similar to Smitty in age, but she moved with the ease of youth and her dark eyes glowed with health. At times, she was almost nice-looking. Good German stock, Smitty, the Swede, had admitted.

"Weather got that gimpy leg acting up?" Sylvia's voice held a note of concern.

"Oh, yah. I betcha the leg will be as good as new tomorrow. Heutemyteu." Smitty echoed his late wife Sigrid's favorite Norsk exclamation. "Today's another story. It's that dang blast-it cold wind. September's too early for that. I even saw frost on the last of the tomatoes. Ding blast it, if Big Moose Lake isn't turning blue. You know what that means—colder weather ahead."

Sylvia rolled her pen between her fingers and palms, producing a clicking sound as the pen made contact with her rings. It was a habit, aggravating fellow workers and coffee-goers. She screwed up her face in thought. "Wonder about that wooly-bear caterpillar. It's probably extra-furry this year. We're due for a bad winter." Sylvia hunkered down, placing her toes on the ledge in front of her and shoved herself forward on the stool.

"Sven over in Geranger, you know over there near Big Turtle Lake, spotted a wooly just last week. It was as hairy as my neighbor Bertram Lunde's back when he peels off his shirt to mow the lawn, come summertime." Smitty paused quickly for air, not wanting any interruptions. "The wool was half an inch long. According to Sven's scientific chart, it's gonna be a bone rattler of a cold winter. Five, maybe six months long."

His report met with several uff-dahs.

Scowling, Smitty sighed. He still had not had a chance to share his news. It seemed to him everyone in Cup a' Java was determined to keep a lid on his gossip. Amazingly, Sylvia turned out to be his salvation.

"What else's new?" Sylvia remarked. "You're still fairly foaming at the mouth."

Smitty could not hide his surprise. Sylvia never asked about his news. She objected to his rumor mill, accusing him of slander. "You're defaming the reputation of half the upstanding citizens of Foulwell," Sylvia had said.

Joan, Cup 'a Java's only waitress, refilled Sylvia's cup. "Have another cup of joe. You *need* a caffeine jolt." Joan appeared to need more herself, as Sylvia's dislike of gossip had slipped her mind, Smitty mused.

Smitty's shock over Sylvia's apparent interest in his choice bit of news failed to hold him back. Standing to demand attention, he took in the room with his gaze and prepared to project his voice so that Evan in the far corner of the room could hear him. Smitty drew in a super-sized gulp of air, determined to milk the moment for as much drama as the locals would allow. Looking directly at Sylvia, he said, "Remember that good-lookin' Jarvis girl? What was her name? Lucille. Ahhh, Lucy. Would you believe she's Frieda's sister?"

"Asking back-to-back questions and answering them yourself. You're at your peak of gossip form." Coffee pot in hand, Joan smiled, shook her head and poured Smitty another cup of coffee.

"How could *I* remember the Jarvis girls?" Sylvia interrupted. "I was typing work requisitions at the Cure-All Body Shop in Sverdrup when the Jarvis girls were wearing training bras."

"Smitty, where's your memory *going* these days?" Joan joked good-naturedly as she gestured grandly with the coffee pot at a dangerous angle. It was one inch short of releasing a deluge of caffeine down Smitty's back.

"Out to lunch." Sylvia chided, click-clacking pen to rings once again in a state of extended animation.

"Anyway, as I was saying *when I was interrupted.*" Smitty cleared his throat, "Lucy's in town, and Jacob Miller spotted her keeping company with Lars Deiserud. Lars and Lucy were a hot item in high school back in the sixties. Seems the both of them forgot they're now married to other people." Despite its gravelly quality, Smitty's baritone fell softly on one's ears and with a bit of a swing, reminiscent of a good polka. One was apt to be marked forever with the trace of a brogue if you had Smitty's credentials. He was of Swedish descent, grew up in the 1940's in northern Minnesota, and lived there the remainder of his life.

Joan set out with another pot of coffee of the Scandinavian variety, fortified with eggs giving it a stick-to-your-bones quality. The richness of the brew's aroma drifted down the line at the counter.

"Who was a hot item?" Joan inquired, her eyes growing larger in question. Not long ago, Smitty had given her an off-handed compliment, stating her eyes were the color of the Java brew and set off her fair skin nicely. Many of the men in Foulwell considered Joan still a handsome woman, despite creases that fanned out from her eyes, proof she was a hardworking, hard-smoking woman.

An objection sang out from the corner booth, where handsome Evan, the town's most eligible bachelor, sat in his usual corner booth. "I don't want to fill Joan in on the details. That would be giving you, Smitty, the satisfaction of repeating your choice bit of slander."

"Is not," Smitty sounded like an aging six-year-old as he scratched his balding pate. Whenever he felt misunderstood, his hand inevitably found its way to his head. "They were in his car, all a 'snuggled up. I wouldn't be surprised but I hear they drove out to Big Moose Lake and that parking spot on the lake's south side."

Sylvia rose to her feet and loomed menacingly above Smitty, who had returned to his stool. "It is slander you're talking as sure as I'll be an old maid 'til they place me in the ground. Lars is the most upstanding man in town, which is more than I can say for you." As if adding an exclamation point for emphasis, Sylvia rolled her pen between her fingers, click-clacking her rings.

"Now, now," Joan retorted. The Java regulars knew Joan worked almost as hard as Java's resident diplomat as its congenial, diligent waitress.

Smitty turned to Joan with a soft smile on his face. He couldn't help but recall the drama in Joan's past life. How Joan's husband had abused her and how Joan had threatened him at gunpoint the day he left. Smitty was the only one she took into her confidence. Smitty felt grateful that Joan recognized there were some things sacred to him that he would never tell another soul.

Turning back to Smitty, Joan stood her ground and argued her case concerning Lucy Jarvis. "That youngest Jarvis girl was always sweet and good. Some folks mistook her lively personality for flirtation. My uncle had a case on her. He'd say, 'She's the prettiest little thing; coppery hair and green eyes that can look into the heart of you.'"

Leaning forward like a trial lawyer completing her summation, Joan said, "Smitty, she never went after anybody else's man." She deposited the coffee pot on the warmer with a thump.

"Well, people change." Smitty was not about to back down.

"Harrumph," Sylvia snorted. "They do if it suits your story. Lars is as devoted to his wife Phoebe as any husband could be."

"Time will tell. *I'm* keeping an eye out."

"I bet you are," Evan called from the corner.

Scratching his head, Smitty cast a defiant glance across the Java. "And if you're so set on proving me wrong, watch what comes around. It'll spice up your lives, sure as the wooly bear's hairy." He grew quiet as he listened to the chatter of the other regulars and chimed in with a "yah sure."

* * *

Deep in thought, Evan had grown quiet. Little did any of the Cup 'a Java regulars know, but Evan had a love of his own. She was far away to make the relationship easier to keep secret. With Smitty's rumor mill and Jacob Miller as informant, Evan was not about to let slip any news of his relationship.

They had met two months ago at the University of Minnesota–Bemidji. Evan needed to do some research on his family at the library. He signed off the computer and before he reached the printer for the search results he had printed, he was knocked to the floor. Evan blinked and looked up into the most glorious, deep brown eyes with flecks of gold. Skin the olive most Minnesotans only achieve mid-summer.

"Oh please, sir, I'm so sorry." The woman had sensuous lips and a husky voice. She was in a rush to check out a book before the library closed. "Are you all right?" she stroked his forehead and took his pulse. Justine was a nurse from Bemidji's North Country Regional Hospital. She insisted on treating him to dinner.

They made their way to a steakhouse not far from the campus. Despite their attraction for each other, their food choices had been a turn-off with Evan ordering his rib-eye steak medium rare and Justine's well done.

Evan expounded, "You know, when you order a steak well done there's no control over burning the blame thing—at best it will be dry and tough as shoe leather."

Justine responded with a glare, and when the steaks were served, she cried out in disgust at Evan's steak. "It's fairly oozing blood," she said with a look of horror.

Luckily, the conversation took a turn for the better.

"How's the arm?" Justine inquired

"Oh. I think I'll survive. Nothing broken," he said with a smile.

Moving closer to Evan, Justine gazed deeply into his eyes and asked in a sultry voice, "Is your wife going to wonder where you are?"

"Oh no, I'm not married."

"Really, I can't imagine you still single. Divorced?"

"No, never married."

"Someone broke your heart and you never recovered, right?"

"Nah, not really. Guess I've never met the right one." Evan's voice hung on the last phrase.

Before the evening ended, Evan drew Justine close and asked for a date for the very next day.

From then on, it was a Monday through Thursday evening tryst. Either at the tiny diner near Justine's home. Or she would cook a meal for Evan at her own home—that at times, grew cold or burned beyond recognition when they became lost in one another's arms.

Evan felt at ease with Justine, and at the same time, fully alive. She was warm and loving and made him laugh. She lived in the tiny hamlet of New Oslo, not far from Lake Bemidji, some 40 miles from Foulwell. Justine was 15 years Evan's junior, flirtatious, light-hearted and lovely. Justine was irresistible to Evan. He was convinced that she was everything he needed.

On a date the night after they met, they ate at what came to be their favorite diner. After dinner, Justine invited Evan into her home.

Small, warm and inviting, like Justine, Evan thought.

It was 2 a.m. by Evan's watch when their talk of past relationships started.

"My high school crushes were just that –nothing serious—nothing hurtful. But in college. Wow, I fell for Randy like the snow in last April's blizzard. And it hurt more than my backside when I slipped on the ice the very next day.

"I learned the hard way not to trust the flirty, charm your socks off type of guy. He could lie convincingly, as I learned when I ran into him with another woman, his fiancée."

Justine's lovely eyes lit with anger. Evan could feel its power. But soon he was drowning in their glorious brown beauty once again.

"What about you?" Justine asked.

"Oh, a few here and there. Nothing that lasted too long. When women start making marriage noises, I run scared. I guess some would call me a commitment phobic." He looked down in embarrassment, shrugging his shoulders.

"But with you, it feels good, right," he admitted. "You make me happy." He couldn't believe what he had just said. Something about Justine drew him out and tore down all his defenses.

That night ended with a long, sensuous kiss, that stayed on Evan's mind all the way home and lingered in his memory throughout the next day.

He had to see her again the next night. She cooked for him in the tiny cabin. Somehow it was the most elegant looking home Evan could remember, partly because Justine was there, and he admitted, she did have great taste. The décor was casual yet quality – fine oak in the coffee and end tables as well as the dining table that doubled as a kitchen nook. With a green color scheme throughout her home there was no doubt in Evan's mind. His first gift for Justine had to be green. Usually buying women gifts was daunting for him. Why, he asked himself, was this different? Because he felt at peace and safe with Justine, and at the same time, excited and aroused more than he had been in years.

They lingered over merlot after "the best lasagna dinner ever made."

"Now, you're just saying that," Justine teased.

Watching a movie from the cozy green sofa, they snuggled in each other's arms and soon were lying side by side, smothering each other with long, wet kisses.

The next dinner date at Justine's drew them into conversations about their families, growing up and how those years shaped the people they had become.

Not surprisingly, Justine grew up in a large, loving family. "No wonder you are so outgoing and well-adjusted. I envy you." Evan once again opened up to Justine like he had with no other woman.

"I guess I just took my family for granted. I assumed everyone had a great family and happy childhood." Justine's head rested on Evan's shoulder, his arm wrapped around her, as they sat side by side on Justine's sofa.

"I knew my folks loved me, but we never really said it. We weren't huggy. I guess that's why I'm slow to warm up to people. Except you, I always feel good with you—always." Evan's voice trailed off and he pulled Justine close. Their kisses passionate, slow and long.

Some twenty minutes later, Evan said, "I have to be up early tomorrow. I better head for home. The boss called a pre-work breakfast meeting."

"Why do you have to leave?" Justine gave him a longing look and pulled him to her. "Please stay."

* * *

Entering the café, Smitty appeared less bent on gossip than the previous day when he spun his tale about re-united high school sweethearts. North woods timbers loomed above in the peaked rafters. Sundry remnants of wildlife peered menacingly from their perches. The head of a moose met the astonished gaze of a visitor. A loon appeared to be landing and about to settle on old Smitty's head. An open-mouthed bear on the opposite wall looked as if he were about to devour Evan in his corner booth.

Evan called out to Smitty, "I obeyed your orders. Found out about the auburn-haired beauty."

"Oh yeah?" Smitty failed as miserably at concealing his delight as he had the day before when he flunked his attempt to hold his temper.

"Lovely red-haired Lucy's here to visit Frieda, but Sis won't see her. Seems there's a bit of a tiff. The two haven't spoken a word for a good six years."

"No," Smitty sat stunned, but recovered his voice and made his way to Evan's booth. "But that doesn't prove a thing. She's playing around with Lars to pass the time 'til her sister comes around."

"Namen, you're a stubborn old goat." Evan borrowed one of Smitty's Scandinavian phrases and threw up his hands in surrender. But a smile caught the corner of his mouth and his hazel eyes danced a jig in his shaggy face. A three-day growth crowned his jaw making him look older then his forty-four years. As mechanic for the corner gas station, Evan was called upon for assistance by those less mechanical than he. Frequently these were unattached females who found his dancing eyes intriguing.

"Now boys, calm down, let's keep it a friendly disagreement." Joan approached the two with her brew of the day, rich Sumatra. Today was the kick-off of the cafe's coffee-du-jour, rotating blends for each day of the week. A few of the old-timers shot angry glances at the specials' blackboard as they entered the log vestibule, walked past the wooden benches and the Velkommen sign. Jacob Miller had barked, "This is a sorry day. Cup 'a Java's yielding to the tactics of the coffee chains."

Joan placed her free hand on Smitty's shoulder, feeling the scratchy flannel. "You know, you and Evan could both be right. If Frieda's so stubborn, there may be some time for fun, should we say, on the side."

Evan's face registered shock. "Joan, I knew you were a diplomat, but not at such a cost. Saint Joan, turned gossip."

"She's got some spunk. Nothin' better in a woman." Jacob Miller had remained silent after his initial shock over the coffee-du-jour. Now animated, he nearly spun around in full circle on his stool.

"Look who's the expert on women; the German bachelor farmer, retired to hobby farming." Evan returned to the fray, casting his gaze toward Jacob. Evan looked as if he was pitching a fast ball, and Jacob was batter up.

"And who's talkin'? The most eligible bachelor in town," Miller fired back, swinging his arm at Evan like a batter hitting a homer.

Looking younger than Smitty, Jacob Miller had a thick pate of gray hair and a lean body that moved with ease, not troubled by Smitty's rheumatism. "I'm the one who passed the news to Smitty in the first place," Miller bragged with a toss of his head. "Saw them in Lars' car, driven' through the rain from Frieda's house. They were headin' back to Shaw's, where Lucy's stayin'."

"That explains it. He was being polite, offered her a ride in the rain." Returning from a brief side trip into gossip territory, Joan was back on her usual high road, speaking the truth and finding the best in people.

"Gave him an excuse," Smitty chimed in.

"I give up on you." Joan waved Smitty off with one hand and carried Java's coffee pot in the other. Despite a shuffle in her step, she moved quickly toward the new customers who had just seated themselves. Joan was plagued by what she often referred to as "waitress dogs. That is, arches falling faster than the snow` during the '91 Halloween blizzard."

Her face a giant question mark, Joan stuttered, "Wh-Why h-hello." Lars Deiserud sat beside a woman with the greenest eyes Joan had ever seen and auburn hair done up in a twist.

Fumbling with her coffee pot, Joan stammered, "M-may I-I help you?"

"Coffee and donuts for me and the pretty lady," Lars said. A wiry bit of a man, Lars was almost entirely white and blue. Huge blue eyes shining like crystal, hair so white, it was nearly transparent, and the pasty skin that comes with approaching age. But his step was that of a basketball star executing a rebound, and his eyes glinted with the passion of the young.

"Remember Frieda's younger sister, Lucille Jarvis, now Moore?" With a wave of his hand, Lars included every customer in the Java. "Lucy, this is Joan Lowry, Smitty Lundquist, Jacob Miller and Evan Stone."

Miller was the first to recover, saying with a turn of his head, "Oh, yes, Lucy, how are you?"

"Great. Well, not really. I know I've just met many of you, and it's the first time I've seen the rest of you for some time, but to tell you the truth, I'm down, and I need to vent."

"Don't hesitate to share. That is, if you want to. We'd love to help, if you'd like." Joan struck a chord half way between curiosity and empathy.

"I came here to settle this feud between me and my sister once and for all. I can't for the life of me remember what we argued about. She won't see me. Ran into Lars the other day as I was coming back from one of my attempts to visit her. She wouldn't answer her doorbell, and I know she was there. It was raining cats and dogs, and Lars was nice enough to bring me back to Shaw's. And then who should I run into this morning on my way to Cup 'a Java, but Lars. It was serendipity. You do have a way of cheering me up, Lars, and saving me a few steps."

"Serendipity. *Must be*," Smitty said.

Lucy seemed oblivious to his jibe. "Anyway, in spite of Lars' attempts to cheer me up, this whole thing has gotten me down. I could use some friendly advice. You know how stub…I mean, determined Frieda can be."

"Listen, I figure you probably weren't to blame. But a note of apology might be a nice gesture." The regulars sat stunned. Joan usually remained neutral in matters like this. "Matt, the grocer's son, could deliver it with Frieda's order. Barker's always deliver her groceries on Tuesdays. And it's Tuesday. It's serendipity all over again."

"What a wonderful idea." Lucy bounced on her stool, her auburn top knot looking as if it was ready to leap from her head.

"You're a life-saver, Joan. I'm writing her note now. I can drop it at the grocery on my way to Shaw's. There's something magical about this town. When you need help, there's always someone there for you. You don't find people like this most places—like you, Joan. I have half a mind to move back here."

"Nae, that would be grand," Lars lilted. In times of high emotion the Scandinavian phrases from his childhood would return to his vocabulary. Clapping his hand on the counter top, he added, "You would be more than welcome." His crystal-blue eyes danced in time with Lucy's topknot as he curved his arm around her.

Smitty looked knowingly at Evan in the corner, then Joan, and finally, Miller.

"Well, I best be going." Lucy alighted from her stool with a new energy. Lars moved a bit slower, extending the moment for as long as possible.

"Lars, you go home to Phoebe. Barker's is only a block away, and then I'll stop over at the bakery to see Sonja. It's been ages since we've had a good talk." Lucy nearly skipped toward the door.

"Ohhh, but I'll take you," Lars insisted.

"No—you go home to *Phoebe*."

With that, Lars paid the bill against Lucy's protests. Joan peered triumphantly at Smitty and Miller.

After the door closed behind the two, she said, "Now see this proves what I said; Lucy's such a sweet, open person."

"Especially with Lars?" Scratching his head, Smitty rose from his stool and began to pace. "Naedah, when Lars put his arm 'round Lucy, he moved faster than Joe Strom cleans up on us in a poker game."

"That doesn't prove anything other than filial affection."

"You been readin' your dictionary lately, Joan?" Smitty's eyes sparked.

"Smitty, you madden and delight a person all at once." Dropping her shoulders, Joan turned to refill the coffee pot, and slammed it down.

* * *

Evan started. He had been daydreaming about Justine and the last night they spent together. Thinking of Justine caused Evan's heart to nearly burst with joy. She had admitted she loved him. He couldn't believe it. This beautiful woman in her late 20's loved him—a forty-ish, bachelor grease monkey.

After dinner, they had snuggled spoon-fashion on the sofa as they watched an old movie. It was becoming a habit. Evan discovered he enjoyed classic movies as much as Justine. As usual, they became distracted, kissing passionately. Before they knew it, the movie's end credits were rolling, and the final music score startled them. It was then Justine breathed her declaration of love.

Evan had always had difficulty saying those three little words. Now they were as natural as cheering on the home team at a football game. He took a deep breath and stated, "I love you, Justine. Totally, completely. I'm forever grateful you ploughed into me at the library!"

Justine smiled, giggled and added, "Best accident I ever encountered. You'd think I planned it all and lay in wait for you." A devilish look crossed her face, almost leaving Evan wondering at its truth. Don't flatter yourself, he silently said to himself.

She leaned forward and murmured, "I love you." He drew her close. This time their kisses were hard, demanding and desperate. Their love, a fire, their kisses fueling the blaze. As a second movie moved well into its plot, they moved slightly apart, holding each other, gazing into each other's eyes until the end credits ran again.

* * *

A chilling blast of wind hit those hunkering around Java's counter the next day. Smitty slammed the door and hobbled up to the counter, clutching onto its edge and pulling himself up onto the stool for his morning coffee.

Sylvia could feel a giggle tickling her soul. Smitty's limp reminded her of the Norwegian two-step Smitty and his late wife, Sigrid, had perfectly executed last year at the Northern Lights Syttende Mai Celebration. Smitty had conceded his Swedish heritage to his wife's Norsk for the Norwegian Independence Day event and the dance that marked the May 17 celebration.

Sylvia remembered Smitty before his wife passed away—not as outgoing, but what he had lacked in exuberance and charm, he had made up for in a state of contentment and a noticeable lack of gossip. Sigrid had been everything to Smitty. Nearly always in Sigrid's shadow, Smitty was quiet, except when he was enjoying her stories or jokes. He had been withdrawn the first few weeks following his wife, Sigrid's death. He stayed in his home in solitary confinement for three weeks. On the third week, he emerged with a spring in his step, more talkative than before Sigrid's death, and with a new bent toward gossip. It was as if Smitty had undergone a bizarre personality transformation. As if he had assumed Sigrid's self. Smitty began storytelling.

Sylvia was concerned about Smitty. Was all this drastic character change about to come crashing down upon him? Would he enter his dark night of the soul? She would rather put up with Smitty's gossip, even if it was a type of denial. She had to admit that Smitty's gossip was entertaining. It did add a bit of drama and adventure to life. She decided, gossip had become his coping mechanism. So ran Sylvia's thoughts and her pop psychology as she evaluated Smitty and his psyche.

Not so long ago, Sylvia made a significant discovery. The Java customers had become her family. Sharing each other's ups and downs bonded them in relationship. She realized it was not so altogether different for Joan, Smitty and Jacob Miller. Evan was another breed, born to be a loner, Sylvia thought.

So Sylvia's life offered a type of order on which she thrived. Daily she stated to herself, 'To thine own self be true.' If it was good enough for Shakespeare, it was good enough for her.

* * *

Turning toward Smitty on the stool beside her, Sylvia left her thoughts behind and re-entered the day's reality. "Bad day for the leg?" Sylvia's question was punctuated with a click-clack as she moved her pen across her ringed hand. Her face was painted with concern, along with a bit more make-up. Sylvia was using noticeably more cosmetics since Lucy had re-entered their lives.

The standard had been raised."Uff dah, that cold norther is blowin' again," Smitty said on day three of his steamy tale of Lucy and Lars. "But there are more interesting things to talk about than my gimpy leg.

"Like Lucy Jarvis?" With coffee pot in hand and a teasing grin, Joan volunteered for battle. "Well, yah."

"Well, duh." Needing no more encouragement, Smitty called out, "Anybody see Lars or Lucy this mornin'?"

"No-o-o." The smile erased itself from Sylvia's face as she swiveled on her counter stool. Not present during Lucy's first visit the day before, Sylvia had been filled in on the details by the Java regulars first thing that morning. She was concerned that Smitty's tall tales were entering the realm of controlling others' lives and possibly their destinies.

As if on cue, Lucy floated through the doorway and announced. "I have wonderful news."

"Sit down, tell us all about it." Sylvia patted the stool beside her. "By the way, I'm Sylvia—missed you the other day."

"Yes, let us in on *all* the details," Smitty commented. Sylvia slugged him in the gut with her elbow.

You worked a miracle."Lucy hugged Joan, coffee pot and all. "Frieda called me at Shaw's not more than an hour after I left Barker's grocery. In minutes, I was sitting at Frieda's kitchen table. We talked about everything under the sun. We talked about the weather; the state of things; ladies' aid meetings, for goodness' sakes. We even admitted how far we've moved into the computer age, or not. Turns out, we both just bought our first tablet. Heck, we talked about live husbands versus dead ones, which is better."

"What did you decide?" Sylvia asked. Smitty elbowed her.

"Both have their pluses and minuses." Lucy giggled. "And best of all, we reminisced about family and friends."

"Any gossip?" Smitty asked unabashedly. Sylvia stomped on his foot from under the counter and he cried out in pain.

Ignoring Smitty's comment, Lucy continued, "Things were so easy between us, like we'd talked every day for years. Nothing was said about our set-to until the very end. Like me, Frieda couldn't remember what our bickering was about. All these years of silence for nothing. Oh well, they're over now, thanks to you."

Reaching forward to grab Joan in another bear hug, Lucy upset her coffee cup and nearly burned Sylvia, who leapt from her stool just before the Columbian deluge.

"Uff dah," Lucy squealed. Hiccoughing with laugher, she initiated a veritable chain reaction of guffaws and giggles that fell like a set of dominos from one end of Cup 'a Java to the other.

Smitty was the first to escape the laughing fits. "Oh, Lucy, you're still one of us—down to our silly Scandinavian ways. You know, there is no English word that can compare, that has the exact meaning, or the power of a good uff dah."

"You're all such dears," Lucy remarked, "so concerned about Frieda and me. And Joan, how can I thank you enough?" Joan stepped back, bracing for another hug, certain to drown the lot of them in coffee this time.

Viciously clacking pen against rings, Sylvia glared at Smitty with a look wielding the power of a left jab. Ducking his head, he reeled back as if from a blow

"Glad to be of help," Joan patted Lucy's hand. "Just took a shot in the dark with the note idea. Who would have thought it would work? You and Frieda are talking again—that's what counts."

"Oh, yes." Lucy looked as if she were hundreds of miles away. "I guess I'll enjoy a day or two more with my sister and then be heading home to Wally. He's due home from his business trip by then. And he'll be lonely. Actually, I am already. We've been married forty years next month."

Four pair of eyes turned toward Smitty and four knowing smiles greeted him.

Ignoring them, he raised his coffee cup in toast. "To Wally and Lucy, may they be together another forty."

Saluting Lucy with her coffee pot, Joan announced, "In honor of Lucy and Wally's fortieth, coffee's on the house." Joan hadn't been this animated since the New Year's party three years ago when she was snockered, an unusual event for her.

"When do we get to meet 'ol Wallace?" Miller said.

"You can all meet Wally next time we visit Foulwell." Lucy turned back and forth on her stool.

Nearly all of Foulwell made their way to Cup a' Java, where the celebration of Lucy's anniversary continued. The word was out, once Jewel Wold delivered a decorated cake from the Lil' Bit 'o Heaven Bakery with Lucy and Wally's names written in Jewel's signature scrawl. Jewel made a grand entrance as she tossed a gallon of confetti about the room. Joan, who had called in the cake order, served it with great fanfare.

* * *

Noticeably aloof and resistant to the Java-wide gaiety was Evan. Smoldering in the corner, Evan had been inconsolable—even his dog had been unable to cheer him. Justine and he had words. Like Lucy and Frieda, he couldn't remember what it was about. But, he remembered distinctly her command to "get out." He knew she could be feisty, but he had never before experienced her wrath with the finality of that outburst.

What could he do? Apologizing for whatever made her upset? Doggone if he could remember what. She'd be angry about that too—that he couldn't remember. And then he had a flash—that was it—she had often accused him of not listening! He would call her, apologize and beg her for a callback and a chance to visit and make it up to her.

Slowly he made his way to the door unnoticed and made the call from his car. Justine answered and before he could apologize, she did. He was doubly thankful. She had a change of heart, and she shared the reason for the disagreement. She had hinted about their relationship moving toward a commitment, and Evan had only responded with a slight smile.

Truth be told, Evan thought, he was shocked and couldn't speak. Now he was grateful he hadn't apologized for not listening!

He recovered from surprise more quickly this time, explaining his shock the night before. "I was numb—I couldn't believe that wonderful, gorgeous, younger you could love an old grease monkey like me."

"Oh Evan, don't ever say that. You are one of the most intelligent and definitely the sweetest, most loving men I have ever had the pleasure to know."

The night of reconciliation was the most special they had shared yet. Holding each other and talking long into the night of what they cherished about each other and dreaming about the future.

* * *

As Smitty loped into Cup 'a Java the next day, he barely missed taking a header as his feet hit a puddle of peanut shells, the appetizer of choice at the Java. Customers were encouraged to toss the shells as they ate. Gesturing wildly, with a red flush about his face, Smitty rushed to the counter with no noticeable limp. "They're gone. They've disappeared, both Lucy and Lars, together. What more evidence do you need?"

"How do you know that?" Sylvia bucked Smitty's claim like a bear outwitting his hunter.

"Lars Deiserud's car is gone. Miller saw him leaving the house 'bout six this morning. And Jewel claims Lucy left this morning too. That's not a coincidence."

"Could be," Evan said in a deadpan voice from the corner.

"It doesn't prove anything." Joan lifted the coffee pot from its warmer. "Smitty, you are an old curmudgeon and gumshoe of the worst kind, guilty of meddling in the first degree. Just like in those old 'B' movies."

Miller thrust open the door, letting in a northerly that ruffled the feathers of the loon overhead. "You know, Lars' brother, Jonas, had a heart attack. Lars got a call in the wee hours of the morning and took off at sunrise for Bemidji."

Smitty pounced on Miller. "What have you heard about Lucy?"

"Lucy? I don't know."

"Smitty claims Lucy and Lars left town together." Sylvia raised one eyebrow higher then the other. Shades of Joan Crawford in a classic movie. The Java regulars teased her about this habit. They called her "Joan C."

"Why should Lucy go see Lars' brother?" Miller said.

"Exactly, but you know Smitty." Sylvia's voice trailed off.

Evan left his corner booth. And with a knowing smile, said, "Ran into Lucy last night. She'd gotten a call from her hubby. Wally got home early and pleaded with her to leave for home ASAP. Shaw's were just about to drive her to the Sverdrup bus station."

"Why in the heck didn't you tell us earlier?" Sylvia demanded.

"Couldn't get a word in edgewise." Evan chuckled.

Smitty inhaled a gasp of air and the muscles about his jaw tightened. "Lucy's call from Wally doesn't prove a thing." Without a second's hesitation, he said, "Besides, did you hear about Olive Strand? Seems she's taken up with the postmaster over in Dyarsville, and her husband's funeral just last month. Not enough time for the daisies to grow over his grave."

Smitty didn't get the last laugh or shock value from his ready-made Java audience. Evan had disappeared, making his way to a parked car just outside of the Java.

Now, just as Smitty ended his newly devised piece of gossip, Evan started his own. He and Justine walked into the Java. With his arm around Justine, Evan swept the room with a smile and cleared his throat. "Everybody, I want you to meet my fiancée, Justine."

The upshot of Evan and Justine's special evening had been Evan asking Justine to marry him. It happened before he had even had time to consider how he would word or carry out his proposal. Talking long into the night, they decided they would be married soon in a simple, small ceremony. The two of them, a justice of the peace and as witness and groomsman, his brother, who lived near Bemidji.

Cup a' Java had never been as silent for as long a time as they had following Evan's announcement. Finally, starting with Joan, one after another Java regular began to clap. Soon all of the Java brethren were applauding wildly. The moose above Justine's head appeared to beam down at them with approval.

ABOUT THE AUTHOR

Ingrid Anderson Sampo has had eight short stories published: Incident at the Tom Thumb and The Long-fingered Woman in Lakes Alive magazine; and Crimes of the Heart, American Geisha, Sleight of Hand, Daisy and Nordic Craftiness in the Rockford Review magazine. She also has a short story "Loon Racing" that was published in *Romancing the Lakes of Minnesota ~Summer* anthology.

She has authored two novels that are progressing toward publishing—historical fiction about Priscilla from the New Testament, and a road trip story about a Grandfather and Grandson experiencing adventures, telling tall tales and learning life's lessons.

She has studied under authors Faith Sullivan, Jonis Agee, Mary Sharratt and Alison McGhee at the Loft Literary Center, Minneapolis, MN; and has attended the Annual Minneapolis (MN) Writers Workshop Conference, Bloomington (MN) Writers Festival and the Flathead River Writers Conference, Whitefish, MT.

Ingrid earned a Bachelor of Arts degree in English from Concordia College, Moorhead, MN, has taught English literature and writing, worked in community relations and communications, and is currently a Fund Development professional planning appeals, capital campaigns and writing grants.

FISH FLIRT TOO

Peg Pierson

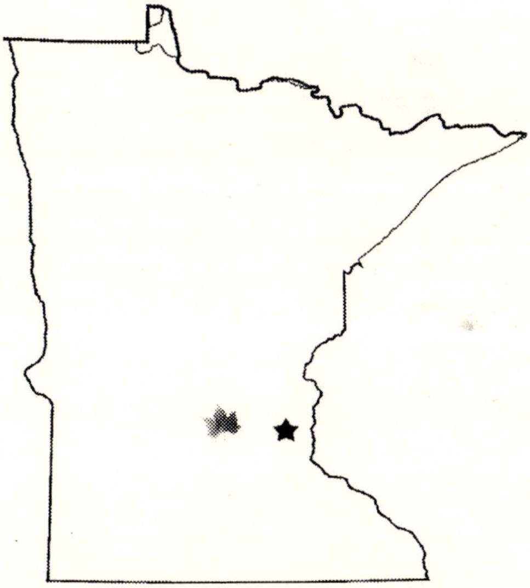

North Long Lake, N. Long Lake

"People are going to notice, you know."

"No. They won't."

"Uh, yes, they will. Folks notice stuff like this."

"I won't be gone long, Sven." Hans said tightening up a bolt.

Sven rolled his crystal blue eyes. "No numbnuts, not you leaving. I'm talking about the people up there." He pointed upward and circled his finger for dramatic emphasis. "The topsiders will notice a gaping hole in the middle of their frozen lake."

Sven shook his head as Hans completely ignored him.

"Seriously," he continued crossing thick arms over his bare chest, "they're Minnesotans not Kardashians. Trust me, they will notice."

"There! Done." Hans beamed at his invention. "This Portal Keeper will keep this spot in the lake from freezing over in winter, Sven." He smiled brightly. "It's only October. I'll be back in a couple of days. This is just an emergency backup plan. So, you want anything from top side?"

"No, thanks. I still have all the crap you brought back last time." Sven bit his lip. "Hoarding is an illness. You know that right?"

Hans covered the device with pondweed. "Okay. Well I'll see ya in a day or two." He waved goodbye, started off, then whipped back around. "Remember, don't tell anyone."

Shaking his head Sven said, "I got ya buddy. But don't bring back any more souvenirs." He made water quotes with his webbed fingers. "Your apartment already looks like a friggin' shrine to the top siders."

Hans gave his friend another wide grin, showcasing dazzling dentition worthy of a Crest White Strip commercial, then sped off, his tail fin a blur at warp speed.

Sven bobbed in the wake, "Wait! Grab some more of that Tater Tot Hot Dish!" Shrugging, he swam off hoping like hell that Hans wouldn't get caught. And that he might bring back cheese curds.

* * *

Savanah welcomed October with open arms. It felt like an old friend come to visit. A friend that let you relax, be yourself, maybe even be a little lazy now that the tourists had all gone back to the Twin Cities. Like most residents of North Long Lake, she welcomed summer and all that came with it. Sure, it was noisy and hectic, but being a part of something people loved and looked forward to all year…was intoxicating. But like any good party, it had to end, and when it did, left the thirty two year old inn keeper feeling somewhat hung-over and ready for a really long nap.

The horizon glowed auburn when Savanah stepped onto the back porch of her bed and breakfast, The Escape. A glass of unoaked chardonnay in hand she nestled into her favorite porch chair and she inhaled the cool night breeze off the lake.

With only one room occupied, and it's guests out for dinner at the Blue Ox Bar and Grill down the street, Savanah slipped off her shoes and kicked her feet up onto the wood railing. Taking a long sip from her glass, she reveled in the peaceful moment, listening to the waves lapping in a soothing rhythm against the shore.

She treasured her little rustic Inn. It had been a dilapidated ruin of a resort before she and Ryan painstakingly renovated it. Closing her eyes, she pushed back the sorrow that threatened to obliterate her solitary cocktail hour. She repeated the prayer that had become a ritual over the past six months begging God to help her fight. To help her hang on to what she had worked so hard for.

A loud splash sounded off the shore, startling Savanah out of her reverie. Setting down her glass she slipped her shoes on and bounded down the porch steps toward the lake.

Gold and burgundy leaves crunched under her feet where a track of wet foliage led up the embankment, then disappeared under the wood framework of the deck.

Savanah considered running back into the house to get Ryan's gun. A rabid or injured raccoon was nothing to fool with, but curiosity won over the niggling fear. Creeping closer she peered under the house.

It was *so* not a raccoon.

* * *

"Hi. My name is Hans. I like your gnome," said the naked blond man holding Savanah's red hatted yard fixture.

The innkeeper didn't know if she should scream, laugh hysterically, or cease and desist her relationship with chardonnay. "Uh, excuse me. What are you doing under my porch?"

Hans smiled and Savanah felt her stomach flip. His eyes were spectacular. They were like nothing she'd ever seen, so bright, so blue; they sparkled in the shadows.

"I think I twisted my ankle." He gave an apologetic shrug with his enormous shoulders.

Savanah swallowed and took a moment to recall how to speak English. "Why are you naked?"

"I was swimming."

"Do you always swim naked?"

Hans paused thoughtfully, then nodded. "Pretty much." He set the gnome aside and started to crawl out from under the deck. Wincing, he drew in a sharp breath.

"Can I call someone for you? Maybe you need to see a doctor?"

"No, no." Hans kept coming, revealing more and more bare flesh and sculpted muscles. "I'll be fine." He grimaced. "Not from around here, nobody to call," He said biting the words out.

Savanah backed up allowing Hans to emerge. He was 6' 4" at least, with flawless pale skin, a tapered waist and manly parts worthy of serious bragging rights.

"Well, I'll be going." Hans started to limp off toward the shore, making faint mewling moans with each step.

Staring at his impeccable backside, Savanah decided tonight would be the perfect night to become a Good Samaritan. With a sigh and a shake of her head at her questionable judgment, she trotted after him, turned him around and marched him into her home.

* * *

Gazing down at his swollen ankle Hans felt very, very guilty. All he needed to do was slip back into the lake, transform, and then walk back up the shore right as rain. He'd done it a dozen times. Switching to legs was *always a* bitch.

But when the beautiful human peeked under the structure….well, he had to get to know her. Sure, it was dangerous. Communicating with land folk was prohibited. Mermaids, as the top siders called their kind, pre-dated air breathing communities by a thousand years, so needless to say there was a bit of a prejudice concerning the mental capacity and trustworthiness of the human species. Hans understood this. After all he had seen The Real Housewives of New Jersey.

Hans however liked the land folk. In fact, he was fascinated by them. Most people were very friendly and very helpful. He really didn't believe they were that dangerous. At least not the beautiful brunette Innkeeper.

A knock on the bedroom door drew his attention. Savanah, as she had introduced herself, poked her head in. "I found you a robe to put on." She pushed open the door and walked to the bed, "It's the only thing of Ryan's that will fit you." Her eyes surveyed the length of his body under the quilted duvet. She licked her lips and quickly looked across the room. "I'll run into town later and pick you up some sweat pants or something." Again her tongue darted out around her very plump lips.

Hans tipped his head to the side. "Why do you keep doing that with your tongue?"

Savanah's face flushed crimson and her dark lashes fluttered. She tossed the robe at Hans and sprinted back to the door. "I'll go get you some aspirin for your ankle."

"No! Don't leave," Hans threw back the covers and wobbled fast enough to stop her.

"Aw!" She sucked in a breath, "Robe!" Her eyes scrunched shut. She pointed to the bed. "Robe, robe, robe!"

Hans rolled his eyes. Top sider females, in his limited experience, generally enjoyed a naked Hans. But to be accommodating he shrugged on the purple and gold garment.

"Thanks." Savanah said, peering through squinty eyes. She grinned. Then she covered her mouth laughing. "I will definitely go get you some clothes."

Hans glanced down noticing the Vikings logo. He grinned at Savanah. "How did you know?"

The front door chime rang out. "Sit down," she said shooing him back to the bed. "You're going to hurt your ankle. I'll be back."

Hans did as he was told. He really wanted Savannah to like him. She looked so cute when she fluttered her lashes. And when she licked her lips.... He wished he had more time to stay and get to know her better. But he just couldn't. Sven was right. He couldn't keep coming ashore. Even though he wasn't happy in the world under the waves, it was his home.

* * *

Savanah drew in a breath at the sight of her nemesis standing in the lobby of her Inn. As usual Nancy Gunderson appeared to have walked off the cover of Vanity Fair. She smiled tossing a cascading lock of shiny blond hair over the shoulder of her Michael Kors suede jacket. On the surface she appeared nearly royal, but Savanah thought of her more like a sinister shark, lurking around waiting to take a bite.

"Good evening, Savanah. You're looking…a bit tired. It must be so taxing having to run this place all by your lonesome. Poor baby. Oh well, it won't be long till that problem is solved."

Savanah silently counted to ten to keep from dashing over and strangling her stepdaughter. "Hello, Nancy. How not-nice to see you. What do you want?"

"So crass. I really will never understand what Daddy saw in you."

Heat swept Savanah's body. Through clenched teeth she said, "Get the hell out of my home you selfish little witch!"

Nancy stepped closer and crossed her arms. "Your home? That's not quite accurate now is it?"

"This is my home. It was your father's home. It's nothing more to you than real estate." The back of her throat stung, threatening tears. "He left you everything else, Nancy! This place is all I have left. Your father loved me and he loved this hotel. He loved you too, though I don't know why. You never came to visit. You never even sent a Christmas card."

Nancy paused, then opened her purse and drew out an envelope. She cleared her throat. "I stopped over personally to bring you this." She stepped over to the little front desk and laid it down. "It's official. I take possession of the land and the building in thirty days. I'm going to be out of the country for a while. I'll be back at the end of the month."

Tears welled in Savanah's eyes. "I'm not giving up. This isn't over."

"Oh, it is over." Nancy smiled, turned on the heels of her Prada boots and was about to exit the premises when Hans stormed in from the bedroom, the Vikings robe just barely covering his bits and pieces.

"You are a mean, mean female!"

Nancy drawled, "Well, Mrs. Gunderson, I see the hotel isn't the only thing tiring you out."

Savanah sputtered. "I was… I helped…his ankle..."

Hans limped over to Nancy and shook his finger in her face. "You get out of here. Savanah doesn't want you here, and this is her house, no matter what you say."

"Eloquently put." Nancy pinned Hans with a suspicious stare." "Hmm.

You surprise me Savanah." She turned and walked briskly to the door. "See you in a month."

Mini waterfalls of tears cascaded down Savanah's flushed cheeks. She'd lost her husband and now she was losing her home. Hopelessness swept through her. Despite the fact that the hottest man she'd ever seen stood half naked in her lobby, Savanah felt completely and utterly alone.

* * *

"I told you, Hans swam over to Lake Michigan to visit a friend." Sven brushed a clown fish away trying to assume a nonchalant demeanor.

The Official snorted. "Geez, Sven, are you a terrible liar." With a swish of his tail he entered the dwelling and scanned the room. "You're the only friend that half-wit has." He swam up to the younger merman. "So really. Where is he?"

Sven was indeed a terrible liar. If you needed a patsy at a poker game he was your merman, but luckily for Hans, Sven had been covering his tail for years.

"Look." He put his webbed fingers on the Officials shoulder, and shook his head. "You got me. It's not a friend he is seeing. It's some doctor he found on internettingahuman.com. He's off again on a wild guppy chase to become a top sider."

The official gave him a long cold stare, making Sven's stomach swirl. He loved Hans like a brother but the frequency of these visits were getting out of control. Sven made his mind up right that moment. Hans had to get his fins out of the clouds and back in the sand where he belonged. His peculiar passion for all things top side had been tolerated when they were kids, but now they were expected to be responsible members of the community. And that did not include swimming off to forbidden shorelines to collect crap. Although Sven would miss the Tater Tot Hot Dish and cheese curds.

The Official bent over and barked out a laugh. "That dolt. I know he's your friend but seriously? Humans are nothing but heathens. They kill each other; they're ruining their own habitat, and please, Duck Dynasty?"

Sven put his finger on his chin. "True. But they are making progress. They're building smart cars, passing gun control laws and clearly you missed Game of Thrones. Dude, you need HBO."

The Official said, "Tell you what, Sven. I'm going to let this go. But if I catch Hans anywhere near the surface again, or wasting time with these crazy schemes, I'm going to have him locked up. The humans are dangerous. We can't take a chance on being discovered. Again."

* * *

Guilt from deceiving the beautiful, tearful female twisted Hans's normally carefree attitude. He couldn't keep milking an ankle sprain when she was about to lose her home to the really mean, but very pretty, blond lady. There had to be something he could do. He had to. What that something was he had absolutely no idea, but first things first.

Grabbing Savanah's hand he led her over to a small green loveseat. He pushed her down gently. "You sit here for a minute and uh…" he snatched a box of Kleenex from an end table and put it in her lap. "I have to go outside and check on, I uh, need to just…go find my wallet!" Hans sounded very relieved to have come up with an excuse to go outside.

Savanah blew her nose then gave him a quizzical look. "You came here naked, Hans. You did not have a wallet."

Humans. They notice everything. Hans thought as he came up with, "You're right." He hit his forehead with the heel of his hand. "What was I thinking? I meant I need to check on your gnome."

"My gnome?" Savanah slumped back on the couch. "Whatever. Just go do whatever it is you need to do. I should be used to not getting the truth from people."

Now Hans felt really bad. Thoughts of escaping to heal his ankle jumped ship. He tightened the silk belt on his robe and sat down next to her, his thigh brushing against hers. "Why do you say that? Do people not tell you the truth? That's not very nice."

She snorted a soft laugh. "Where are you from anyway? Sesame Street? I guess I do sound jaded but lately things have not been going my way."

"What happened? Did that Nancy lie to you? Is that why she is trying to take this Inn away from you?"

"Actually, her father lied to me." She plucked another tissue from the box and wiped her nose, which was starting to turn red. "Ryan, my late husband, is Nancy's father. He was a lot older than I am but I loved him. I didn't care that he had money. Neither did he actually, he worked his fingers to the bone refurbishing this place."

"We did it together. He called it a labor of love. Then he got sick. I had signed a pre-nup, so he promised to change his will so I would get The Escape. I believed him." She got up and paced the hard wood floor. "But after he passed Nancy found some clerical error, so because of some legal mumbo jumbo, it looks like she'll get every dime. Including my Inn."

This was way too much information for Hans to digest on an empty stomach and a sore ankle. He stood up and purposefully limped over to Savanah.

"Savanah. I promise I will never lie to you. I am very hungry and my ankle hurts. I'm going outside now to fix my foot in the lake and then I would very much like to go somewhere to eat some food."

* * *

The waitress at the Blue Ox Bar and Grill tapped her pen on her pad and pursed her lips. Hans pointed at the plastic coated menu again, "Can I get gravy on cheese curds? What about on the walleye? Oh wait I don't want fish!" He chuckled and winked at Savanah leaving her even more confused about this super-hot, yet somewhat ditzy man.

"Sir, I will put gravy on the chocolate lava cake if you want, but we're getting ready to close so…"

"Oh! Sorry." He appraised the menu once more, placed his order, then smiled broadly at Savanah. "You should have ordered more food. A salad isn't very filling. Are you sure you don't want a hamburger or something? I love hamburgers, especially with cheese and pickles and-"

"Hans!" Savanah slammed her palms on the tabletop. "Enough about the damn food. How the hell did you heal your ankle? It was swollen and turning purple." She peered under the table again shaking her head, then rose up and scrutinized the man shoveling popovers into his mouth at lightning speed. Something wasn't right. She couldn't deny her attraction to him. Ryan had been gone for almost a year and Hans's beautiful physique and dynamic blue eyes made her bloodstream tingle. Yep. He was yummy. But even if she could explain away his strange naked arrival under her house, nothing could explain his miraculous recovery from the injured ankle.

Their food arrived and Han's dug in ferociously. Savanah pushed cherry tomatoes around on her plate. "So, again. How exactly did you fix your ankle so fast? And without medical attention?"

Hans acknowledged the question with a nod, continuing to chew, then through half a mouth full of food answered, "The ah…lake has um, homophobic qualities."

Savanah narrowed her eyes and set down her fork. "You're telling me North Long Lake is anti-Gay?"

Hans scrunched his brows. "Noooo. It's got you know, homemade ways to heal stuff."

"Homeopathic." Savanah stated.

"Ya. That's what I said, isn't it?" Hans washed down his last bite of food with a long pull off his Grain Belt beer.

"Well, no but…Hans, no lake in the world can instantaneously cure anything. Please. Tell me what you really did? Were you faking it? Did you for some crazy reason put a bunch of makeup or something on to look like you were hurt? Then washed it off?"

The waitress stopped at the table laying down the check as she asked, "Can I get you anything else?"

Hans drained his beer without noticing. Savanah smacked her lips, pulled out a card and handed it to the waitress who ran it with warp speed before wishing them a nice evening. Savanah gathered her purse and her jacket. "Let's go. You can keep the clothes we bought. I'll take you back to the house. You can call a cab and find another hotel."

Walking to the car Savanah bit back tears again. She needed to concentrate on how to fight Nancy and save her home. Mr. Deliciously Deceitful needed to hit the road. Too bad because despite his unwillingness to be truthful, he did seem like a genuinely sweet man. And seriously, breathtakingly, handsome.

* * *

The ignition rumbled to life and Savanah pulled out onto the two-lane highway. She stepped on the gas, tires squealing.

"Are you mad at me, Savanah?" Hans asked.

"No, Hans, I'm not mad. I'm sure you have a good reason for not telling me the truth."

He grunted. "Boy do I."

"Urgh! Hans! That is just rude!

The headlights from the passing cars traveled by quicker than Hans liked. Cars were not his favorite thing. They were loud and fast. And they had accidents.

No sooner had the thought popped into his head, it happened.

Savanah screamed. She jerked the car to the right. Hans's body strained against the seat belt. Everything spun. A thundering bang slammed him again against the cars restraints, and as quickly as it started, it was over.

Hans looked through the cracked windshield. The car had hit a tree, leaving the hood pretty smashed up, but that wasn't what sent an electric wave of fear through his veins.

Savanah's head lolled forward, a cut on her forehead slowly dripped crimson. "You okay, Hans?" She mumbled.

He hated seeing her banged up, but that wasn't what scared him.

Screams cut the night air. A car was sinking into the murky depths of the lake. Hans tore off his seatbelt, scrambled from the car and ran to the shoreline.

A young girl stood knee deep in the water screaming and pointing to the slowly descending vehicle. Hans gripped her arms, bending down to meet her eye level. "Is anyone still in there?"

"My mom and my brother."

Hans jumped in the water.

* * *

A gust of cold night air brushed Savanah's cheek. The passenger seat was empty, the door ajar.

After a deep breath and a quick self-assessment that seemed pretty ship-shape, she scooted out of the car. She followed the sounds of splashing and arguing to the shore of the lake.

At the edge of the water two kids were huddled together, shouting at Hans, who was waist deep in the lake, lip-locked with an unconscious woman lying in the surf.

"You're not doing it right!" The boy shouted.

"It's two breaths and then chest compressions." His older sister added.

"No, no, no!" The boy said shaking his wet head. "You only do the chest thing now. No mouth breathing stuff."

Savanah closed the distance quickly. Clearly the big lug needed her help. When she approached he looked up, his golden hair wet and clinging to his chiseled jawline. Their gaze locked and Savanah couldn't read the odd range of emotions swimming in his eyes. His eyes glowing with a mysterious sapphire radiance that enticed her very soul.

"Savanah!" he shouted, "Call 911! Hurry!"

She snatched her cell phone from her pocket and made the call. When she looked back again the woman had sat up. She was coughing and tugging her children to her.

Hans was nowhere in sight.

Savanah scanned the dark waters. The moonlight betrayed his escape, capturing a perfect view of his luminescent tail fin as he swam away.

* * *

Savanah lay awake staring at the ceiling. She'd been reviewing the night's events over and over trying to come up with some explanation, other than the one she struggled to believe. Deep in her heart she knew it was true.

The family Hans had rescued only remembered a big blond man jumping in the water to save them. They hadn't noticed anything strange. They only wished they could have thanked him.

A soft rap on the sliding glass door to her room broke her reverie. The porch light showed the shadow of a tall figure. Fear flashed but faded.

She realized who it had to be.

Throwing off her covers she ran to the door slinging it open. Hans stood, stark naked, dripping wet, holding a large canvas satchel.

"Hi. Sorry I'm naked again, but here's a bag of gold so you can buy your Inn back from Nancy." He handed the bag through the doorway. Savanah grabbed it with both hands, nearly dropping it from the weight. "I know you're mad at me so I'll go now." Hans turned and started to walk away.

"Wait!" Savanah dumped the bag on the carpet with a thud. "Please don't leave, Hans. Come inside."

He craned his head back over his shoulder. "You sure? I thought you were mad because I couldn't tell you the truth about my ankle."

"It's okay. I figured it out myself. I'm not mad anymore." She stepped out onto the porch and touched his arm. "You're a mermaid. That's why going back in the lake healed your ankle. Right?"

Hans slowly turned around. "Are you going to kill me? Or do painful medical experiments on me? Or trap me in a tank and sell tickets to other humans? I really, really don't want to-"

Savanah threw her arms around his neck, stopping his rambling with a kiss.

A kiss, deep as North Long Lake and as promising as the dawn blooming in the sky above it.

* * *

"Do you want Swiss cheese or cheddar on your sandwich?" Savanah asked Hans who entered the kitchen garbed in jeans and a flannel shirt. He snuggled up to her back and nibbled sweet kisses behind her ear.

"Can I have gravy?"

Savanah smiled. "If you keep putting gravy on everything you're going to look more like a whale than a mermaid."

"Merman! Merman!" Hans shot back in his best Derek Zoolander impression.

"That's another thing. You can't just watch Netflix all day, your mind will turn to mush."

With a low chuckle Hans said, "Too late."

Savanah turned her back on lunch giving Hans a scowl. "I hate it when you put yourself down like that. You are smart and generous and brave. So shut up and grab us some tea. I want to finish eating before Nancy gets here."

Hans was giddy with excitement to watch Savanah surprise Nancy, but he couldn't ignore the nagging voice in his brain.

He needed to go home.

It had been almost a month since he'd seen Sven. He promised to be back in a couple of days, not weeks, but being with Savanah was a dream come true.

Every time he started to tell her he had to leave something wonderful would happen. They would go for walk on the shore, autumn leaves blowing in her hair, or cuddle on the couch watching TV, or something in the Inn would break. That was the best! Well almost the best thing because making love with Savanah was spectacular, but seeing her face light up when a broken door knob got fixed, or he got the washing machine going again, well, that topped the list. For the first time in his life he was needed, appreciated and loved.

Going home not only felt sad. It felt wrong.

* * *

Savanah couldn't wait for Nancy to come in the door. She ran outside and met her as she stepped out of her BMW.

"Hi, Nancy. No need to come any further," Savanah said grinning like a Cheshire cat. "I sent a check to your attorney buying you out. I'm really sorry you had to waste your valuable time coming all the way out here to the boondocks. Poor baby. Oh well, that problem is all solved now. You don't ever need to come back."

Hans wrapped an arm around Savanah's waist, he raised his fingers wiggling them at Nancy, "So, buh bye." He winked at her then kissed Savanah on the cheek.

Nancy slammed the door of her car closed and strode over to the couple. She tilted her head curiously at Hans, then placed her hands to her hips addressing Savanah. "I know about the money. Too little too late though. I already bought all the properties on both sides of this wreck for a mile. I'm bulldozing everything and building a brand new luxury resort. In between cleaning and cooking for your pathetic guests you should check your bank account. I never cashed the check."

Shock and disbelief slammed Savanah like a lightning bolt of anguish. She stammered, "But…You…Uh…No!"

A deep voice suddenly drew all three of them to look toward the dock. Waving frantically, a blond head and muscled torso bobbed in the water calling Hans's name.

In unison they all bolted toward the small wooden pier. Hans reached it first. "Sven! What are doing here?"

"You'll see. Just wait, numbnuts. You owe me big time." Sven lifted himself from the water transforming his brilliant green tail to legs.

Nancy whipped around and started back to her car at a brisk trot. Sven shot after her. "Hey. Hold on there you." He caught up with her as she reached the BMW. "Nice to see you again, Nancy."

"Sven." Nancy coolly replied, flipping an errant blond curl over her shoulder.

Together Hans and Savanah said, "You two know each other?"

Sven grinned at the couple, "Okay you two are just adorable." He shook his head showering them all with water drops.

"Watch it you stupid guppy!" Nancy hissed brushing the lake water off her designer suit like it was acid rain.

"What's the matter? Afraid you might transform right here in the driveway?"

Nancy shot Sven a menacing stare. "Get out of my way. I'm leaving." She reached for the door handle but he plopped his very bare butt on it.

"Okay." Savanah crossed her arms. She felt like she'd had a big helping of crazy for lunch instead of a turkey sandwich. "Somebody tell me what the hell is going on?"

Sven tipped his chin up and let out a whistle. Loud splashes of water drew all eyes to where three more naked men were walking up the shore.

"Sven." The Official stated striding ahead of his two aides, his bare feet crunching the dried leaves. "Hans," he nodded toward the only clothed man in the crowd, "Well done. We've been searching for this fugitive for years."

Nancy's usual panache cracked and panic blossomed across her face. She made a break for it. Sven snatched her back, drawing her into a tight hug flush against his body.

"You won't get away with this!" Nancy growled straining against Sven's steel grip. "I'm not going back."

"Oh, yes you are my dear." The Official said motioning for his men. They flanked Nancy each grasping an arm. Sven released her. "Thank you again, Hans. Remember, we will need an update every month about any other suspicious events. Your Portal Keeper will work perfectly during the winter months." He gave Hans an approving nod. "Ingenious device. And brilliant espionage. I didn't know you had it in you."

With that, and Nancy swearing up a storm of nasty threats, the Official and his men marched back into the lake. After one last howl from Nancy, and a brilliant splash of colors from their tails they disappeared underwater.

"Well, I'm outa here," Sven said, trotting after them. He pulled up, looking back over his shoulder. "Unless you have any Tater Tot Hot Dish lying around?"

"Wait!" Savanah and Hans said in unison.

Sven turned, rolling his eyes. "Seriously you two are ridiculously cute."

Hans said, "I'm confused."

"Ditto." Savanah added. "What the hell just happened?"

"Well, when Hans came back to get the gold for you he told me the whole story. He described your stepdaughter and I just knew it was Nancy the Night Bandit."

"But how could Nancy be a mermaid?" Savanah asked. "I was married to her father. I'm pretty sure I would have noticed if he had a tail?"

"He was her stepfather. Nancy's mother was a mermaid. And a thief. She covered up Nancy's true nature hoping they could both profit from Ryan Gunderson's wealth."

"Wow." Savanah said softly. "This is a lot to take in."

"Hey." Sven clapped his hand on her shoulder. "This is a good thing for you. Now you can petition her claim on your late husband's estate, including The Escape."

Hans grabbed Savanah's waist and lifted her into the air twirling her in a giddy rush. "Yeah! The mean, mean female can't have your Inn now."

He kissed Savanah, set her back down then tilted his head at Sven. "But what about the Official? What was he talking about? What reports?"

Sven said, "You're my best friend. I could tell you were head over fins in love with this topsider so I came up with a plan. I told the council you were an undercover agent, you had located the fugitive Nancy the Night Bandit, and that with your Portal Keeper in place you could make regular covert reports on the human world."

"That's pretty impressive." Savanah said.

"Ya." Hans agreed. "How can we thank you?"

"How about you two live happily ever after?" The handsome merman said with a grin. His blue eyes sparkled. "But in the meantime, I sure could use some Tater Tot Hot Dish."

* * *

Epilogue

"Hey, Ole?"

"Ya, Lars."

"Don'tcha think whoever made this here hole is gonna notice?"

Ole dropped another line. Ice fishing was his passion. He didn't much care who made this wondrous hole that never froze over. He'd caught more walleye in two days than he had all last season.

"Lars! I got a big one!" Ole pulled up.

"That's a big one alright there, Ole."

The fisherman gaped. A naked man grabbed the lure, tossed it on the ice and emerged from the lake.

"Hi. My name is Hans. I like your tackle."

The End

ABOUT THE AUTHOR

Peg Pierson is a full-fledged Fang Fanatic and slightly deranged Halloween Enthusiast, with a closet full of plywood coffins, an assortment of plastic dismembered body parts, and of course..skeletons.

Her debut novel, *Flirting with Fangs*, received rave reviews. Coming soon, two more paranormal comedies, *Flirting with Faeries*, and *Flirting with Fins*.

She lives in Minnesota and is busily typing away on a new paranormal comedy. Along with vampires, she loves her family, pecan kringle, and a good laugh.

She loves hearing from readers!

Please visit her at www.flirtingwithfangs.com.

FOR THE LOVE OF BERTHA

Ann Nardone

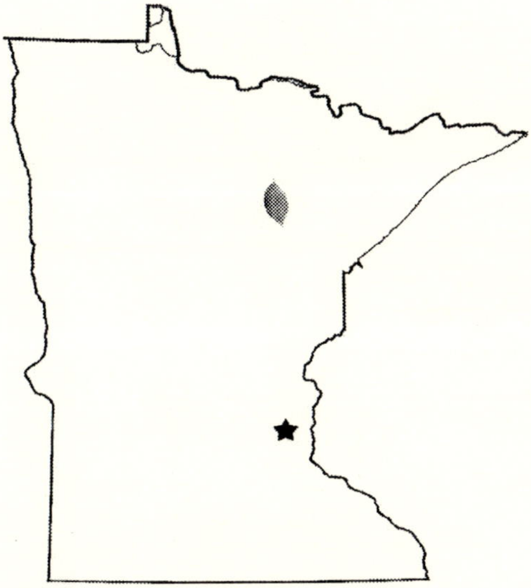

Trout Lake, Coleraine

I parked the car on the dirt road outside the entrance to Lakeside Cemetery. This would be the perfect place to be alone. As I went through the gate, I took note of the clearly marked sign, forbidding entrance after dark. I looked up at the sky. The sun has hanging low, shining painfully against the sapphire background. I had an hour, maybe.

In high school, I was known as the kind of girl who hung out in cemeteries. It fit my draped black clothing and deep purple lipstick. When I had gone up north to Itasca College, I was looking for a place where I would not be known as anything at all. I had considered school in a city, where I could get lost in a sea of strangers. Now, looking at the orange and crimson-topped trees that surrounded me, I knew why a small town was a better place to disappear to.

The sunshine fell on my back and a sweet smell hung in the air. The scent, of course, was the decay of fallen leaves. Here in this spot it was the perfect reminder that these warm days were numbered and bitter cold would soon set in. I wandered among the stones, looking for the oldest and the newest, checking the last names for interesting patterns in the family groupings. Then I turned down towards Trout Lake and something odd caught my eye.

It was one grave, standing by itself on the lakeshore. The sight of it struck me with a strange loneliness. Living alone was one thing, but to be alone even in your final resting place seemed somewhat sad. Drawn to it, I walked down the hill until I was in front of the desolate spot.

The pale stone was weathered, with a few chips missing from each corner. I dropped to my knees and ran my fingers over the letters, which were no longer sharply indented. Bertha Mylard was buried here. She had died in 1910.

Somewhere behind me, leaves were crunching under a pair of feet. A shiver ran down my neck and just for a second I was afraid to turn around. I took a deep breath and glanced over my shoulder.

The young man walking down the hill toward me was decidedly un-ghostly. He was maybe a year or two older than me, slender, dark-haired and cute in a hipster sort of way. He wore jeans and a button down shirt. A camera on a black strap was over his shoulder. I should have been afraid to see a strange man approaching me here in an isolated graveyard, but I wasn't. Coleraine, Minnesota was not known for random crime. Anyway, he was not a total stranger. I had seen him before.

"Are you waiting for it to move?" He gave a friendly wave.

"Move?"

"That's how the story goes. After dark, Bertha's grave moves. Sometimes it glows."

"Really?"

"That's what they say, at least." He put his hand up to his forehead and squinted. "Do I know you? You go to Itasca, don't you? You work in the bookstore."

It seemed funny that he would know me now. I had never seen him even look my direction while he was going around campus.

"I'm Nick. Nick Capeletti."

I already knew his name, his first name anyway. I had heard it called out to him as he passed by many times.

He stood there looking at me as if he expected a response.

"My name is Melinda."

"Pretty name."

What does someone really say to that? "Thank you" didn't make sense to me. I wasn't the one who picked it.

"Is that why you're here?" I decided to let the name comment go. "To see the grave move?"

"No," he smiled. He had straight white teeth, and dimples I had not noticed from a distance. "I'm on the committee for the Halloween carnival. You know the one we're having at school to raise money for the food shelf. I thought I'd snap a few pictures of Bertha's Grave and put them in the ghost story booth to give it a little local color."

I was still kneeling, looking up at him, but the sun was behind me, giving me an advantage. "I see."

"Have you thought about volunteering? It's for a good cause and it would give you chance to meet some people, make some new friends."

I did love Halloween. Maybe they could use a fortuneteller. I knew how to read palms and do Tarot cards, a lingering trace of my Goth girl days. "I would but I'm really busy. You know, school, work…"

"Sure. I know how it is."

He still stood there. Maybe he was waiting for me to leave so he could take the pictures. I was about to get up when crouched down beside me, one knee just above the ground.

"So, you don't know the story. You're not from here, are you?"

"No." I hadn't expected this guy to come along and ruin my peace and quiet but I was too curious to let it go. "What is it?"

He stared at me with his deep, dark eyes and lowered his voice. "A little over a century ago a woman named Bertha lived in a little shack in the woods just outside of Coleraine. She was strange, kept to herself, and after a while, people around town started to say she was a witch. She was even suspected in the disappearance of several children. Eventually, she died. Thing was, no one wanted her buried next to their loved ones. So they put her here, by the lake. That way no one would ever have to be near her. And, since according to legend, spirits can't work their powers across water, they wouldn't have to worry about her haunting the town.

"Before long, they realized Bertha wasn't at rest. People would come to the cemetery one day and then return a few days later, and find the grave was in a different place. Like it moved on its own. Sometimes they would come here after dark and see the headstone lit up, as if it was glowing. There have even been reports of an old woman in black walking along the lakeshore. If you look at her, she suddenly disappears."

"Do you believe any of that?"

He smiled again. "Nope. That's just the story. I imagine Bertha was some creepy old lady. Not a real witch."

"She wasn't old."

"What?"

I realized I had been speaking so quietly he couldn't hear me, even in the silence of the graveyard. "She wasn't old. Look at the dates. She was thirty-eight."

"Huh. I never noticed that."

"Have you been here before?"

"When I was in high school. I think every kid had to check it out at least once."

I had to ask. "Did you see anything?"

"Oh, I got the hell scared out of me. We were standing around, right in this spot and suddenly we saw a ball of light shining from up behind those trees, just kind of moving back and forth."

I waited, not sure, if he was messing with me.

"It was a cop with a search light. We were trespassing and I thought I was going to get arrested. Ghosts, I could handle, but having to call my dad from jail would really be scary."

I smiled because he expected me to find that funny. How could I explain there was nothing funny about this woman, mocked and scorned even in death? I looked back at the headstone. Now I could see the broken spots at the edges were not from weather but human hands. "Do you know who she was? I mean, really? What is the real reason she's buried here all by herself."

Nick Capeletti shrugged. "Never thought about it."

One cue, he pulled his smart phone out of his pocket and punched a few keys with his thumb. I let my eyes and my mind drift. The setting sun hit the headstone and it really did seem to glow. That mystery solved, at least.

"OK, I got something," he said without looking up from the screen. "A lot of people were buried right around here, initially, but they were moved about 80 years ago because being so close to the lake caused a flood risk."

"They moved everyone but her? Why was she left?"

"I couldn't find anything."

"I wonder." It was the sort of thing people say, but I meant it. ""Don't you? If you don't believe she was a witch, what do you think she was? Why did she deserve to die an outcast?"

I waited for him to tell me it didn't matter, there was no reason we should care. "That's very interesting. I never thought about it before but you're right. Maybe we shouldn't just tell the ghost story. Maybe we should tell the real story, too."

I rolled my eyes. "That will make a fortune for the food shelf."

He laughed again. "Right. I like the idea anyway."

The sky over the lake had turned pink and orange and light around us had dimmed. "We'll be breaking the law in about five minutes," Nick said.

I stood up and brushed the dried leaves off my pants. He seemed to be waiting for me.

"If you don't mind me asking," he said as we walked up the hill, "what were you doing here?"

I might have minded a little. "It's pretty and quiet."

He nodded like he understood. "Well, I'll see you later"

Another stupid thing people say. Though I guess he would. It was a small town and a small campus. Maybe next time he passed by me he would say hello.

* * *

During the next week I thought a lot about Bertha. I tried a more extensive internet search. It turned up the same legends Nick had told me about, along with something about sticking a knife in the grave and a hand reaching up out of it. I did learn that city officials had once removed Bertha's headstone over concern about vandalism. It was returned eventually but not before adding one more indignity to the dead woman. I could not find a single thing about Bertha Mylard, the real live person. Whatever she had done to be branded a witch remained a mystery.

Over those days I also thought about Nick Capeletti. I'd seen him from a distance, always with people beside him. Sometimes they seemed engaged in serious conversations, other times they were laughing. When I would see him with a girl, I'd look away. Silly, I know.

The weather had stayed warm most of the week, but on Friday it turned cold and rainy with a sky so dark Bertha's grave could have moved at noon. I was in the cafeteria, sipping a latte and staring out the window into the gloom when I heard my name called. Who else could it be but Nick?

He stood next to my table wearing a dripping hoodie. His damp hair was starting to curl under the humidity. He was not my type at all, but, really, he was very good looking.

"I found something!" He took the empty chair next to me, turned it around and sat straddling it. The grin on his face showed he was pretty pleased with himself. "I kept thinking about what you said."

I just stared at him, not sure what he was talking about or what I was supposed to say.

"About Bertha. About what her true story might be."

"You…you're still thinking about it?"

Something fluttered in my throat. He thought about something I said. For a week. This must be what it feels like when a man surprises you with flowers.

"So it occurred to me Coleraine is a really small town and a good piece of the population is made up of people who are old and whose families have been here generations. Someone must remember something they heard from relatives, right? So I talked to my grandparents."

"They knew something?" I was starting to catch his excitement.

"Well, no, not at first. Then yesterday my grandma called me up." He leaned forward. "There is this lady who lives at the same place as my great-grandmother. Her name is Mrs. Kovich and she is literally a hundred years old. She lived her whole life here and get this: her family was really into keeping diaries. She's got them going back for years."

"Did any of them know Bertha?"

His face fell a little. I hadn't meant to slow down his enthusiasm. "I don't know for sure. But I called the home and the nurse said she can have visitors. So why don't we find out?"

* * *

Nick picked me up at my dorm the next morning. I had taken more care than usual getting ready, putting on normal make-up and fixing me hair. I told myself it was because I wanted to look presentable for the old lady. When I got into Nick's pick-up truck, he said, "You look nice."

We found Mrs. Kovich sitting in a wheel chair in the day room, eating a cup of gelatin. She looked as though someone had draped a skull in cracked leather but there was life in her pale blue eyes.

Nick and I sat on either side of her, instead of directly in front because the nurse told us she would be able to see us better that way. He introduced us and gave a quick explanation of our mission.

"I don't remember yesterday or last year," she said with a rusty laugh. "The farther you go back, the more I remember. Sometimes I find myself drifting back through it all. Good times and some bad ones. But even I am not old enough to remember 1910."

"No, ma'am, of course not," Nick looked a little embarrassed. "We just thought you might have heard about someone, an old story maybe."

I spoke for the first time. "We are interested in a woman named Bertha Mylard."

The wrinkles on her forehead deepened to trenches. "Bertha. Yes. That name does ring a bell." She stared off into space for so long I thought she had forgotten we were there. When she spoke again, her voice was stronger. "I'll show you what I have. Take me to my room."

Mrs. Kovich's room was stark, the only personality coming from a wall decorated with children's drawings and family photos, suggesting she had lived to see great-great-grandchildren.

With a shaky hand, she motioned for Nick to open the metal wardrobe across from the bed. Instead of clothes or blankets, like I would have expected, it was packed with boxes, some wooden, some cardboard.

"Turn on the TV for me, and then you can go through anything you want. It's just a bunch of old junk."

The boxes were stuffed so full I wondered how she got them closed. There were photos, letters, old journals, and post cards. At first they seemed to be packed in at random but before long we found a pattern that let us locate the oldest things, those predating Mrs. Kovich herself.

We sat on the cold tile floor, letting the smells of must and dust overpowers the antiseptic. Whatever was playing on the television didn't register with me, as I became lost in the past. Some might consider Mrs. Kovich's collection old junk but I knew it was treasure. Nick seemed equally engrossed and for an hour, we didn't say a word. Then I found the first reference to Bertha.

It was in a diary written by a young girl named Greta, who must have been Mrs. Kovich's mother. The reading was hard, the old ink badly faded. Her words spaced tightly together and additional entries were written in a circle around the pages. Paper was scarcer in those days. But, with effort, I made it out, reading twice to be sure. I tapped Nick on the shoulder and read aloud.

"'Four of us girls- Marta, Clara, Ellen and I went berry picking today. Saw Bertha on the way and asked her come with us. She said no of course. Such an odd duck.'"

"Not exactly witchcraft," Nick said.

No, it wasn't. I was just being different. We read on.

Nick moved closer to me so we could use two sets of eyes to scan the old pages. I tried to ignore the jolt of electricity I felt when his shoulder touched mine. Soon I was lost again in this other world.

From across the decades Greta filled me with stories of life playing out in the harsh north woods. She told of church picnics and 4th of July parades. She dutifully recorded births, marriages, and deaths. She knew whose husband was a drunkard and whose daughter was fast. There were sweethearts courting and friendships forming. Most of Coleraine's citizens made her journal. But, references to Bertha were few.

"Listen to this," Nick said, his breath close to my ear. "'Dance at the village hall on Saturday. Danced a polka with Harold Iverson. He asked if Bertha were coming. I had to laugh. Bertha at a dance!'"

"Do you think she had a romance with this Harold?"

But, a few pages later told of Harold's wedding to someone else. Life seemed to go on for everyone but Bertha. When we came to the page that made a brief mention of Bertha's death, we almost stopped reading. The nurse had taken Mrs. Kovich down to dinner and our own stomachs were growling. Somehow, though, I wasn't quite ready to stop. It was a good thing, too. Bertha got one final mention.

"Saw Harold Iverson today. He had been working on the docks in Duluth and just returned. When he asked after Bertha, and I told she'd passed, he looked quite stricken. Honestly, a man who had lost his own wife in childbirth should be accustomed to death!"

We said out goodbyes to Mrs. Kovich. She asked us to visit her again, and we said we would. I wasn't sure if she would remember us. She seemed to be drifting off into her far away memories again. I wondered, if I live as long as she has, will I have any memories I'd want to return to?

"That was kind of cool," Nick said as we got into his truck. "But it ended up being a bust. We didn't really learn anything about Bertha."

"Yes, we did." An idea came to me. " Can we go out to the grave?"

"It's getting dark."

"I'm not scared of ghosts."

"How about cops?" I could see his grin lit up by the dashboard lights. "All right. For you, I'll risk it."

We slipped through the cemetery gates. The skies had cleared and a full moon shined down, making the frosty grass sparkle. We didn't talk as we walked down the hill. I wished I had a flower but there were none growing this late in the year. Instead, I picked up a maple leaf and when we reached the grave, I laid it down.

The grave wasn't moving, it wasn't glowing, and if Bertha's ghost hovered around, she wasn't going to let us see her.

She wasn't a witch," I said, my voice cutting through the silence. "She just didn't know how to fit in. People didn't have anything against her at first. They just couldn't get to know her. I guess, after a while their imaginations sort of filled in the blanks."

"It's not a scary story, just a sad one." I could see Nick's breath following his words. "I don't think Bertha should be used as a prop in a Halloween carnival."

No, she shouldn't. She didn't deserve to the villain in a ghost story. I looked out at the moonlight dancing over Trout Lake. This was not a scary place. It was beautiful.

Still, I could almost believe it was haunted. It seemed like Bertha had drawn me to her. We were kindred spirits. There was a lesson I could learn from her.

"Speaking of the Halloween carnival…"

I could see his smile under the bright moon.

"I might be able to do it after all. It is a good cause and I would like to make some friends."

"That would be great." He reached out and took my hand. It felt so warm, like it was thawing me out.

I felt a strange thrill that made me happy and scared at the same time. But, I was not going to let life go by without me.

I put my arms around his neck and kissed him. It was quick and I pulled away, embarrassed.

"Melinda," he pulled me back. "I've wanted to do that since the first time I saw you here. But I didn't think you wanted me to."

"Now you know."

He kissed me and if the tombstone had moved, I would not have noticed.

ABOUT THE AUTHOR

Ann is a graduate from the University of St. Thomas and Hamline University in St. Paul, Minnesota. She works a variety of seasonal jobs, while raising a family and pursuing a writing career. She lives in Farmington Minnesota.

Ann also wrote a short story "Putting Demons to Rest" that was published in *Romancing the Lakes of Minnesota - Summer* anthology, which is available in print and digital format wherever books are sold.

GHOST LIGHT

Rachael Passan

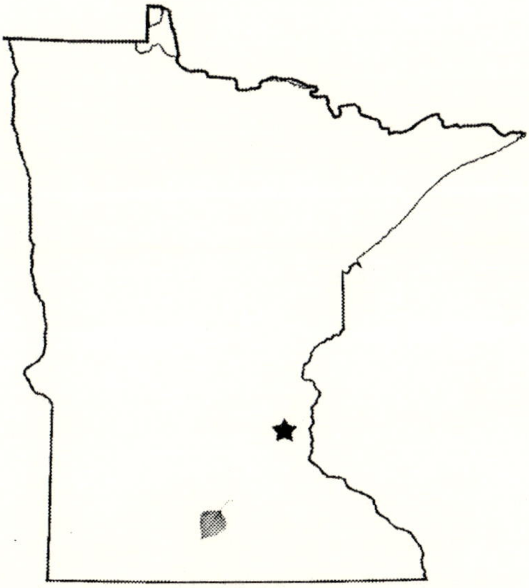

Eagle Lake, Mankato

"There's no such thing as ghosts, you know."

If Lena Kaminsky received a dime – even a nickel – for every time she heard that expression in her life, she would not be struggling to gain tenure as a professor of paranormal psychology. Well, she'd still be trying for tenure, but it certainly wouldn't be as much of a struggle.

Lena arrived at the Majestic Theater in the heart of Mankato, not more than a few blocks from her Minnesota State University office, near the lunch hour on this brisk fall day and dropped her backpack of equipment at her feet. The front doors were solidly locked and there was no response to her knocks. She walked around the building and found the stage door in the alley running alongside the theater. She knocked but again no response. She removed her gloves which she thought might be muffling her raps and tried again. After a fourth round, the door finally swung outward and she had to jump backwards to avoid being hit.

"Sorry, we're not open for business," the man said quickly and began to shut the door.

She grabbed the stile. "Eli Hunter?"

He stopped and leaned against the doorframe, blocking her entrance. "That's me."

When she learned the Majestic had been sold to Eli Hunter, who ran his own New York architectural firm, she expected to meet a middle-aged man in an immaculately tailored suit, maybe with a hint of gray at the temple. Or, since the only architect she could name was Frank Lloyd Wright, she imagined him wearing a flamboyant cape and pork pie hat. This man who stood in front of her was tall – much taller than she, probably six-three to her five-two – with dark, wavy hair which could have used a trim about three months ago. He wore jeans and a white button-down shirt with the sleeves rolled up past his elbows. A plain navy tie was loosened and his collar buttons undone.

"I'm Lena Kaminsky."

"Nice to meet you but, like I said, we're not open." He moved to close the door again, but she kept a firm grip on the door.

"You were supposed to receive a letter from the university about my research?"

Realization dawned on his face. "Right, the ghost hunter."

"Paranormal investigator," she corrected.

"Well, c'mon in before you let all the cold air in and the ghosts out." He held the door open wider. She scooped up her backpack and ducked in.

She followed him to the stage area, the heels of her boots echoing in the empty theater. The main auditorium, which should have included row upon row of upholstered seating, was deserted and the faint smell of recently laid carpeting hit her before she noticed the deco pattern now covering the auditorium floor. The stage was lit by a single bare bulb in a wire cage mounted on a tall pole, powered by an electrical wire leading to the wings offstage. Scaffolding surrounded the stage's proscenium arch to clean and/or repair the decorative molding, but was conspicuously void of workers.

"Everybody still at lunch?" She dropped her bag to the floor.

"The project ran out of money a couple of weeks ago. I have three volunteers, but I don't have anything for them to work on right now, so I told them to go home. I hope you don't mind working in an empty theater. C'mon, you can stow your things in my office."

He led her through the empty auditorium and into the main lobby which also had newly laid carpeting. A curved staircase led from the lobby to the upper balcony and past a plain gray door, concrete steps took them another floor above to utilitarian offices overlooking the MSU parking lot near the Taylor Center, the university's sports complex.

On their journey, she asked questions about the theater or about the renovations, but was greeted with one-word responses or silence.

Like the rest of the building, furnishings in his office were scarce. A large, ornately carved mahogany desk, with papers and rolls of architectural drawings covering the top, took up most of the space. The only other furniture was his desk chair and a four-drawer wooden filing cabinet, on top of which was perched a Keurig coffee maker. A small garbage can held the remnants of numerous K-cups. Either he had no one to empty the garbage or he was a major coffee drinker. Or both.

"What's behind the door across the hall?"

"The old projection room. Want a coffee?" he offered as he inserted a cup into the machine.

"No, thank you."

"Well, if you do, you'll have to bring your own mug."

"I'd like to take a moment to explain how I conduct my research."

"No offense, Ms. Kaminsky---"

"*Doctor* Kaminsky."

"*Doctor* Kaminsky, but I think your theory about ghosts in this theater is just…"

Oh, please do not *say "nonsense."*

"…a bunch of mumbo jumbo."

Just as bad.

"But I'll be honest with you." He leaned a hip on his desk and folded his arms across his chest. "For all I care, you can be researching Jack the Ripper or the Bermuda Triangle. The bottom line is: I allow you access to the theater for a week, two at the most, and the university has agreed to give me additional funding for my renovation."

"You don't believe in ghosts?"

"There's no such thing as ghosts, you know."

"And yet, many theatrical practices are based on the idea of ghosts. Your ghost light, for example. Every theater is supposed to have a light burning on the empty stage because the light is supposed to keep ghosts away."

"It's actually more a question of safety," he countered. "The backstage area can be cluttered with props and set pieces and someone could get hurt trying to find a light switch. But if the light is meant to keep ghosts away, maybe you'd like me to turn it off."

"Or, as you know, many theaters are closed one night a week, usually on a Monday. There are, of course, differing opinions on why this is but the most commonly held belief is because having one night without a performance keeps the ghosts of the theater subdued by not having so much activity. Some even have postulated the ghosts use the dark night to perform their own plays."

"Most theaters are dark on Mondays," he explained, "because actors are limited to eight performances a week. And, if you count matinees, they usually have three performances over a weekend, so they need – or want – a day off."

"Yes, I suppose it could be considered another explanation. But perhaps I will be able to change your mind. Old buildings like this one can often be goldmines of paranormal activity."

"What got you interested in haunted theaters?"

She wasn't about to tell him about her own paranormal experience, seeing the spectral image of her beloved grandmother. But that's what sparked her lifelong passion.

"I grew up in Eagle Lake, not too far from here," she began.

"Really? Me, too."

She was pleased they might find some common ground. "My grandmother loved this old theater, although back then it was a movie house."

"Wasn't always that, was it? You see, I've done a little research of my own on this old place. In fact, the original building was a saloon, although some accounts list it as a brothel and gaming house. That building burned down – with no casualties – in the late 1890s and the lot remained vacant until the Majestic Theater was built for live productions, mainly vaudeville performers who weren't as popular as those acts playing on the Orpheum Circuit. By the 1930s, the Majestic had been converted to a movie theater and, during World War II, served as a USO – kind of the Midwest's version of the Hollywood or Stage Door Canteen – and, later, it became primarily a movie theater with limited live productions."

"I'm impressed."

"And, when multiplex auditoriums were being built with Dolby stereo and Surround Sound, the old girl went to ruin."

"Until you bought it last year."

"Guilty as charged. I hate to see grand buildings like this torn down for another parking lot."

She was well aware of a small portion of the funding to rehab the building came from the University's Theatre Department which, for its small contribution, would be able to use the refurbished theater for its live student productions. But there were numerous University and city administrators pushing to build a parking structure.

Eli sat at his desk and shuffled through papers without looking up at her. "So why are you so interested in any ghosts that might be hanging around? That letter of introduction from your department chair said you're doing some research into haunted theaters."

"Actually," Lena explained, "I've done several studies this summer on theaters throughout Minnesota. The Majestic will be my last one."

"Well, I'll be honest with you, Doc. I've been working on this place for months, days as well as nights and often alone here in my office. And not once have I heard, seen or smelled anything that resembles a ghost."

"Smelled?" Lena didn't get that connection at all.

"You know, like in the movie *The Univited*? The smell of mimosa signaled the ghost was present? You see, I came here a lot myself when I was a kid, especially when they used to show the old classic movies. Hell, my Boy Scout troop would meet here sometimes. So, even though I don't think you're going to find any evidence for your research here, you are welcome to snoop around all you want."

"I do not 'snoop,' Mr. Hunter."

"Eli."

"I conduct scientific research, *Mr.* Hunter," she said, emphasizing the honorific. "And, if you don't mind, I would like to get started as soon as possible."

She was a spitfire for damned sure, Eli thought. He didn't know what a ghost hunter should look like, but he would have pegged this one as a cheerleader, especially with her long blonde hair pulled up into a ponytail. Her manner of dress, however, was more severe and typical of a formal college professor – a black pant suit. She was so short, it was hard to picture her standing in front of a class – she'd be hidden behind the lectern.

When he first got the letter from the chair of the psychology department *telling* him - not *asking* him – she'd be coming to do this research, he thought it was a joke, something his volunteers had concocted because they insisted the place was haunted. But every old building creaked and settled – it didn't mean it was haunted.

And, when he went to the chair's office, the man claimed to know nothing about the letter. When Eli threatened to file a complaint with the President's office, the chair finally agreed to token funding as a kind of peace offering. He'd get his money when Kaminsky found (or even if she couldn't find) her ghosts.

Even leaning against the desk, he was a head taller than Kaminsky and resisted standing to his full height, but looked down at her and square into those hazel eyes. "Show me some proof and I'll concede there are ghosts."

"Thank you. I'll need access to all areas of the building and, if possible, I'd like access in the evenings."

"One of my volunteers still has my extra set of keys, but I can get you another set by tomorrow. And you're welcome to go anywhere you like except the fly loft."

"Why can't I go up there?"

"You can go up there, but I insist, for safety sake, no one goes up there alone. If you were to fall, it's a long way down."

"Well, as long as you're here, perhaps we can go there now?"

She was determined, he'd give her that, but he had an appointment at the bank. "Unfortunately, I have an appointment this afternoon, so we'll have to postpone the catwalk until later today or tomorrow. Do you think someone may have fallen and their ghost haunts this place?"

"I suppose most people think specters remain in a location because of sadness or tragedy. But, in most of the cases I've investigated, most seem to stay because it was a place which gave them pleasure during their lifetime. In one theater in Memphis, there have been reports of the spirit of a young girl who likes to sit in one particular seat in the balcony. Anyone who's sat there complains of being tickled until they have to move. And, another theater I studied in Duluth----."

He didn't have time for another lecture. "I'm going to be late for my appointment. I should be back by three o'clock, but if you need to leave earlier, go out the stage door where you came in and make sure the door closes behind you – it'll lock automatically."

"I'm ready to begin right away." She hefted her patterned backpack.

If she wanted to be taken seriously as a ghost hunter, she might want to rethink the big pink flowers.

* * *

On her initial walk-through of the lower level, the darkness didn't bother her. Her camcorder was equipped with night vision, illuminating the hallway without light.

She was very glad she kept her coat and gloves on. Hunter was obviously saving on the heating bills and this hallway felt colder than the outside temperature.

She walked slowly down the corridor, making sure her full spectrum HD camcorder kept both the hallway as well as the electromagnetic frequency meter, held in front at arms' length in her other hand, in the frame. The EMF meter displayed a range of multicolored lights in the presence of a spike in electromagnetic surges, indicating activity or communication from spirits from the other side. On the left was green, but it would change up to five colors to the final red, indicating more than twenty mG, or milliGauss.

On the stage level, and in Hunter's office after he left, the light indicator was solid green, but as soon as she came down to this lower level, where the dressing rooms, green room and costume shop were originally located, the mG began to rise. Keeping a careful eye on the camera and watching to make sure she wouldn't run into anything, she called out to any potential spirits, keeping her voice soft and pausing slightly between sentences in case anyone wanted to answer.

"Hello there. Is anybody in here? I hope you don't mind my being here. I'm just conducting a little research. If you're here, can you identify yourself?"

She stopped and listened. 2.5 mG.

"Are you in here?" She turned towards a door on her right. She had to put the EMF meter in her pocket in order to turn the doorknob. With the door slightly ajar, she pulled out the meter. Still 2.5 mG. Nobody in here, but she'd come back later.

Three more rooms and, with each one, the EMF began to flicker, moving into the next color range. She continued down the hallway. There was one last door at the end of the corridor and, with each step, the EMF flashed closer to red, mimicking her accelerating heart rate. She was within five feet of the door. The red light was glowing brightly.

"Are you there, in the old costume shop?"

She jumped slightly when she thought she heard a muffled reply.

"Did you say something to me?" She pocketed the EMF and stepped closer.

"C'mon in!"

She opened the door and her heart sank.

* * *

There were three of them – two men and one woman, all seniors – seated around a small card table surrounded by dress mannequins, probably the old costume shop. They were all involved in a card game.

"Mr. Hunter said no one was in the building."

The older woman was the first to speak up. "Please don't let Eli know you found us here. With all the construction going on, Eli doesn't think it's safe for anyone to be here. But we can play uninterrupted and we're not bothering anyone. I'm Laverne, by the way. Two cards."

Lena was never good at guessing ages, but they all looked somewhere between sixty-five and seventy years old. Laverne was lean, wearing a periwinkle flower-patterned dress with perfectly coiffed hair, even if both hair and dress were slightly out of style.

Max, to Laverne's left – Lena's right – was rumpled, balding, in shirt sleeves and suspenders. He chomped on an unlit cigar. "Gimme three."

Across from Max, the other man was, by contrast, very dapper in appearance, with a buttoned vest over a slightly protruding belly, and was introduced as Patrick. He ran a manicured finger across a trim moustache. "Dealer takes one. What do you bet?"

"Poker, huh?"

"Do you play, Dearie? I'll bet three," and Laverne tossed three matchsticks into the small pile in the center. "Our fourth hasn't been coming lately."

Grandma Stasya adored playing poker and could get lost for hours on end in games with friend and neighbors. She taught Lena how to play and to spot the "tells," the body language indicating what a player has. Someone covering his mouth, as Patrick was doing now, often indicated they held a weak hand.

"You must be Mr. Hunter's volunteers."

"You might say we are working in more of an advisory capacity," said Laverne. "We all worked here at one time or another."

"I used to run the light board," said Max, seeing and raising the bet by two. "Laverne ran the costume shop here. Only Patrick over there wasn't on staff."

"Not an employee of the theater *per se*," Patrick countered, with the slightest trace of a British accent, long subdued by years of living in Minnesota. "Call and raise you five – although I found myself in attendance nearly as frequently as my compatriots."

"Patrick was the theater critic for the paper in St. Paul," Laverne explained, splaying her cards in front of her. "Full house, ladies over deuces. Read 'em and weep."

The two men threw down their cards in disgust. Laverne swept the matchsticks into the mound in front of her and picked up the cards to shuffle. "Deal you in for a hand? No money, just matchsticks."

"What a wonderful phrase." Patrick began arranging his matchsticks into piles of ten. "'Advisory capacity.' He repeated it in varying intonations, one grander than the next.

"I'd love to talk to all of you about the theater in its heyday," Lena said, fumbling through her bag for her notebook.

Laverne began dealing the next round of cards with an experienced hand. "This was one of the loveliest theaters in the Midwest. And, I think I can speak for all of us, when we found out Eli planned to renovate, we agreed we should stick around and give him a hand whenever he needs it. Are you helping him out with the renovations? I hope you're the new liaison from the Community Development Office. I was not very fond of your predecessor. She was a… What'd you called her, Patrick?"

"A 'twit,'" Patrick supplied.

Max continued, obviously in agreement. "Said they should take a wrecking ball to the old girl. Couldn't understand the value a theater like this gives to the community. Hope you have a more open mind towards the Majestic."

"I'm actually conducting research on paranormal activity in this theater."

"Ghost hunter, huh?" Max tugged on one suspender. "Never had one of them 'round here before."

"I prefer Paranormal Investigator. Have any of you ever witnessed any unusual activity?"

"There was an experimental production back in '69," Patrick offered. "A lot of strange goings-on. It was a very odd play, indeed."

"She means ghosts, you old coot. Right, Dearie? Five card stud, nothing wild."

"As I came down the corridor, my equipment was displaying high EMF readings." And then she had to explain the significance of EMFs to the three questioning faces.

"Electromagnetic field, huh?" Max checked his hand, keeping his cards close to his body. "Might have something to do with the wiring leading to the university transformers. When they upgraded their system, the new wires run right under here."

"And I'm getting cooler temperature readings at this end of the corridor, too." She explained how spectral presences are sometime detected by changes in temperature.

"Damn HVAC system never did work properly," Max complained. "Hasn't worked in years. Cold always went on when you wanted heat and heat when you wanted cold. Maybe they're throwing off your ATFs."

"*E-M*-Fs," Laverne gently corrected him. "Oh, my heavens, yes.

Working down here in the costume shop, sometimes, we'd have to wear mittens in July. Do you think Eli will finally be able fix it?" Laverne's slight smirk, her "tell," indicated she had dealt herself a pretty good hand.

In-between hands of poker, the trio turned the tables and interrogated her. Patrick wanted to know how she became interested in ghost hunting. Max questioned her on her investigative methods and was fascinated by all her equipment and how each piece worked. Laverne, like a doting grandmother, was more interested in her marital status and whether she was "seeing" anyone.

Even though Lena was able to investigate other areas of the theater, she never got readings as clear as those in the costume shop. Max helped her position a couple of motion detectors and electronic voice phenomena recorders, asking her detailed questions about how the EVPs worked and what she might expect to find on them. Hunter gave her strict warnings about no one going to the fly loft alone but, before she could warn her helper, Max scampered up the spiral staircase in the stage wings with a practiced step.

A few hours later, Max led her back to the costume shop to pick up her gear. Without a third or fourth card player, Laverne and Patrick were now playing *Switch*, another card game Patrick described as a British version of *Uno*.

"It's getting late," Laverne checked her watch. "And Eli's not back yet."

"I do hope nothing was amiss with his appointment," Patrick chimed in. "But, as he has not yet returned to work and it is nearly five o'clock, I fear they may not have provided him the necessary support."

"Damn banks," Max grumbled, pulling out the unlit cigar stub from his pocket where he had stashed it before and jamming it into the corner of his mouth. "Never could trust them after the Depression."

"Oh, don't listen to him," said Laverne. "But poor Eli has already used up the funding the Theatre Department gave him."

"The carpeting was far more expensive than he originally estimated," added Patrick.

"But don't you think it looks lovely?" Laverne asked Lena, but didn't wait for her response. "He's hoping to get funding for the next phase of the renovations."

"Which would be what part?" asked Lena. These three obviously had a great love of this place.

"Perhaps you noticed the art deco frescoes around the proscenium arch," Patrick continued. "The originals were done by Emmanuel Briffa. And the Majestic was one of the last theaters remaining in the United States to house his work before he moved to Canada in the early 1920s."

"I've actually heard of Briffa." Lena remembered the name from an undergraduate art history class. Briffa was one of the most sought-after theater decorators in the early days of the great movie palaces. "Some of the theaters he worked on in Canada are listed as historic landmarks."

"Now there's a girl who knows her history!" Patrick applauded. *"Brava!"*

"If those frescoes are so special," mused Laverne, "Eli could get this old girl listed as a historic landmark and if he got that, maybe he could apply for a grant. They explained how Eli had already used up the funding provided by the university's Theatre Department and was trying to secure another loan from the bank to help pay for the next phase of restorations, specifically, the refurbishing of the elaborate frescoes around the stage's proscenium arch. The originals had been done by the artist Emmanuel Briffa, and the Majestic was one of the last theaters remaining in the United States to house his work before he moved to Canada in the early 1920s.

"I've heard of Briffa," Lena said. "Now there's a girl who knows her history!" Patrick applauded. *"Brava!"*

"If Eli could get the Majestic listed as an historic landmark," Laverne mused, "maybe he could apply for grant money to help him with the restoration."

"Didn't he fill out some kind of paperwork for the grant?" Max asked his cronies.

"He started it, I believe, at the point when he began this venture, but I don't recall it being mentioned since," Patrick replied.

"I think I know someone who might be able to help us," Lena offered, quickly correcting "us" to "Mr. Hunter." During her Ph.D. research, she had investigated theaters in and around the District of Columbia and dated a young man who worked for the National Trust for Historic Preservation. They remained friends and he was now working with the Trust's Western Field Office.

"That's a marvelous idea!" cooed Laverne, as she took Lena by the arm and the trio began walking her out of the costume shop, all talking at once and she was unsure who was saying what.

"Is there still time today to contact your friend at the National Trust?

You should do that as soon as possible."

"Won't that be wonderful when this place is a deemed a landmark?"

They were all talking about what improvements could be made with additional grant money. Before she knew it, the trio had led her to Eli's office and were helping her with her coat and guiding her back down to the stage level.

"I think Lena should be the one to give Eli the good news, don't you think?" asked Laverne of the others.

"Indubitably," agreed Patrick. "You can have that honor."

"He's probably at his favorite 'thinking spot," added Max.

"Oh, yes," agreed Laverne. "He often goes to the Vetter Stone Amphitheater at Riverfront Park. Do you know where that is, dear?"

Max supplied directions even though she didn't need them.

"Oh, yes," added Laverne, "and the poor boy is probably cold – I don't think he had more than a thin jacket on him when he left."

"If you really want to stay on his good side," offered Max, "you might want to stop off and pick up a coffee for him." He mentioned a nearby coffee house a few blocks away from the Amphitheater he said was Eli's favorite.

Before she knew it had happened, her coat was buttoned, her gloves placed in her hands, and she was ushered out the stage door in the alley and the door firmly shut behind her.

* * *

Eli sat alone in the last row of the theatron, or seating area, of the amphitheater overlooking the Minnesota River, although the view of the river was obscured by lush landscaping, giving it a woodsy backdrop.

Now, towards sunset, a pink glow filled the theatron.

It was a place he could sit and think, even though the only thing he could think of now was how cold the limestone slabs can get as the weather starts turning cold. Without the sun, and without the lawn chairs people would normally bring with them to the venue, the cold seeped through his wool slacks.

No money to continue the restoration. The bank said "no" to additional monies and "no" to extending the existing loan. All he'd heard for the last few weeks was "no."

Even he said "no," to her ghosts. But what harm was there in opening the theater to paranormal research? Maybe she could find a ghost who knew where to find a hidden treasure stashed somewhere in the building's rafters to supplement what little he had.

"You must have a 'thing' for empty theaters, huh? First the Majestic, and now the amphitheater?"

He jumped at the unexpected voice behind him. A gloved hand extended a large cardboard cup to him from his favorite coffee place.

"Thanks," he said as he took the cup and motioned for Lena to sit beside him.

"Didn't mean to scare you. I thought you'd hear me come up behind you."

"Lost in thought, I guess. You know this place?" he said after a satisfying gulp of the warm liquid, indicating the coffee house logo on the paper cup's cozy. He guessed she noticed the Keurig in his office and the piles of discarded K-cups to discern his coffee addiction.

"Lived here for five years and only found out about the coffee house today. I'm not much of a coffee drinker, but this apple caramel cider is to die for. I'm going to have to go there more often."

"Find your ghosts?"

"Nothing just yet," she sipped thoughtfully at her drink. "I'm still in the information gathering stage. I set up some equipment this afternoon. Hopefully, there will be something to look at tomorrow."

She noticed he now listened with interest as she described all her devices, how they were set and what kind of information they might yield.

And his eyes grew wider when she talked about the Briffa frescos and how her friend at the National Trust, when she called him this afternoon, was *very* interested in helping to expedite the paperwork to declare the Majestic a historic landmark.

"I also know a couple of the professors in the Art Department – I bet they'd love to help you work on the restoration. Professor Franciscono always says his students ask for extra credit assignments, so you can expect a lot of students to come by asking if they can help out. Can hardly say 'no' to free labor, can you?" Eli might already have Patrick, Max and Laverne, but she was sure he would welcome some younger people on the crew as well.

"Thank you."

"Oh, it's nothing. You're giving me access to your theatre – the least I can do is buy you a cup of coffee."

"Not the coffee. You probably saved the Majestic."

Pink rose in her cheeks and she turned away from him. "You really love the place, don't you?"

"When I got my architecture degree, I wanted to preserve great old buildings like this rather than tear them down for something new. As a kid, my family would always drive to Mankato every weekend to see a movie – my dad was a huge movie buff. Spent nearly every Saturday at the movies and, as I got older, found I was studying the building more than the movie."

"Me, too. I mean, my grandmother would always take me to the movies as a special treat whenever she visited Mankato on the weekends from Eagle Lake."

"Who was your grandmother?"

"Stasya – her real name was Anastasya, but we always called her Stasya – Kaminsky."

"Kaminsky," he ruminated on the name and it bounced around his brain until the image of a sturdily built Russian woman solidified. "The lady with the ham radio?

"W-Oh-S-G-P," she answered with Stasya's call sign, mimicking the older woman's thick Russian accent.

"Oh, yeah, all the kids in the neighborhood knew her. She'd always let us play with her radio. Because of her, I got my Boy Scout radio badge."

Lena smiled nostalgically. "My great grandfather – Stasya's father – was one of the area volunteers for Civil Defense during World War II. He was responsible for radio communications in case of emergency. Stasya, along with her four brothers, learned from him. Even when they no longer needed the radio for emergencies, she used it as her own personal party line."

"Yeah, she was a nice lady," Eli continued. "She'd take you to the Majestic?"

"Every weekend. She never went to any other theater except the Majestic – said it was 'special'."

"And you still think there are ghosts happy to stay at the Majestic?"

"I think any spirit could love the place as much as you do."

An awkward silence hung between them. She was about to get up to leave when he suddenly stood.

"Hey, you're starting to turn blue. Since you bought me coffee, as well as helped to save the Old Majestic, the least I can do is buy you dinner, but I'm a little light on funds. Pizza okay?" He offered her his hand.

"Pizza sounds great. I know a place on Front Street." He noticed, as they walked to the parking lot with his hand in hers, he didn't feel nearly as cold as he had a few minutes ago.

* * *

Over the next few days, Lena helped Eli complete the mountains of paperwork to help the Majestic gain historic landmark status. Lena's friend at the Trust was coming out next week to talk about the next steps in the process and put Eli in touch with the Development Office who would help him find grant money. Eli, in turn, helped Lena place motion detectors and view video footage taken with the full spectrum camcorders, changing positions each night with no results.

At the end of the week, he was nearly as anxious as she when he presented her with the voice-activated recorder he said he found the night before on the catwalk above the stage. She could barely contain her excitement when she noticed that something was recorded. After a week of nothing but blank tapes, she was giddy at the prospect of some evidence of spectral presence. She tapped her fingers nervously on the Eli's desk waiting for the tape to rewind.

The EVP was full of static, typical of these kinds of recordings because of air circulation or just the sound of the tape reels moving. She listened for a few minutes, rewinding every so often if she thought she heard something.

"Nothing, huh?" Eli made himself another cup of coffee and popped in an apple cider K-Cup for her, using her purple and gold Lady Mavericks mug.

She sighed and pushed the recorder away, still playing nothing but static. "Nothing. Guess the whole investigation was a bust."

"Wait a minute." He placed his own mug on the desk, his brows furrowed. "Play that part back again."

She let the tape rewind for a few seconds and he leaned closer, concentrating on the sounds.

"Go back further." She did as he asked. "Don't you hear it?"

"Hear what?"

He grabbed the recorder and played with the controls, playing back a section. "Listen."

She, too, leaned closer so they were nearly bumping heads.

"It's just some clicking. Probably the water pipes in the ceiling. Or the building settling."

"That's not just clicking – I think that's Morse code." He grabbed a piece of paper and pencil from the desk drawer and, furiously, began writing. After a few minutes, he showed her the message. Even as he handed it over, she could see he didn't believe what he wrote.

T-H-A-N-K-Y-O-U-F-O-R-S-A-V-I-N-G-O-U-R-T-H-E-A-T-E-R-D-O-N-T-S-E-R-V-E-C-H-E-A-P-C-H-A-M-P-A-G-N-E-A-T-T-H-E-G-R-A-N-D-R-E-O-P-E-N-I-N-G

Thank you for saving our theater. Don't serve cheap champagne at the grand reopening.

Lena just stared, first at the paper, then at him and laughed. "You made it up, didn't you?"

"Scout's honor." He raised the three-fingered scout salute. "That's what it said."

"Then someone is playing a joke on us. It's probably Max. He could have tapped out the Morse code when he placed the recorder on catwalk."

"Who's Max?"

"You know, Max, the bald guy who used to run the light board. He's always playing cards with Laverne from the costume shop and Patrick, the theater critic."

"Who are you talking about?"

"Patrick, Max and Laverne. The threesome who are always playing cards in the costume shop? Your volunteer crew."

"The only volunteers I had are Bob, Craig and Henry and they haven't been around for weeks."

* * *

Down in the costume shop, Laverne was scooping her matchstick winnings from the center of the table when the form of another elderly woman appeared at the table.

"Stasya!" Laverne exclaimed, "We were wondering if you were going to come back to the game."

The short, plump Russian woman took her place next to Max at the card table and pulled a pile of matchsticks from her handbag to place in front of her. "I vouldn't vant Lena to see *me* vile she vas poking around da tee-a-ter. You should know I vould come back – who else vould I play cards and *kibitz* vid?"

"Looks like your plan worked, Stasya, my darling girl," said Patrick as he shuffled the deck. "I always thought Eli was such a nice chap, although sometimes a bit too somber. Glad to see him lighten up a bit. And you've come back at the perfect time. I've heard rumors John Barrymore might come next Monday to perform scenes from *Hamlet.* I did so love his *Othello* last year."

"He's alvays so serious – Eli, I mean, not dat actor – even vhen he vas little boy. Too much verk and little play. He need a nice girl, like my Lena. I alvays wanted her, too, should find a nice man and settle down."

Laverne cut the deck into three piles, recombined them and handed the cards back to Patrick who dealt the next hand. "Your plan was marvelous, Stasya! I've seen Lena and Eli going out to dinner every night this week. But I still don't understand why you had to use Morse code."

"I couldn't just talk to dat recorder machine ting she got dere – Lena vould hear my accent. I taught Eli dat code vhen he vas little boy and I knew he vould remember how to read it. And I vant to tank you all for your help – I could not have done dis vid out you all. Laverne, you gave me the idea."

"Well," Laverne preened, "I do have to admit doing something similar for my granddaughter and her now-husband a few years back – I'm expecting my third great-grandchild next spring, doncha know."

"And Patrick, you wrote dat letter from da Dean."

"That little dilettante always claimed to be 'too busy' attending fund raisers for his precious research projects to write it himself. Couldn't be bothered with the preservation of such a magnificent building as the Majestic. But it was Max who convincingly copied the man's signature."

"Easy enough when the signature ain't nothing but a scrawl." Max stopped Patrick from dealing the cards. "I think Stasya should have the first deal, this being her first day back."

"An excellent idea," Patrick agreed and he handed over the cards with a flourish.

"Tank you, Patrick," Stasya said as she accepted the cards and fanned the deck with a practiced hand and dealt each player five cards, all face down. "All right, gentlemen – and lady – da game is *Califor-nee-ya Low-Ball* – lowest hand vins and da joker is vild."

ABOUT THE AUTHOR

Rachael Passan works as head of the fiction collection in a Chicago-area library. For her work with Readers' Advisory, she is honored to be a two-time winner of the Northern Illinois Librarian of the Year award and recipient of the national Librarian of the Year Award from the Romance Writers of America.

A long-time television/movie aficionado, she's been published in non-fiction and has been a contributing author to two editions of the Museum of Broadcast Communication's *Encyclopedia of Television* (1997 and 2004). She is currently working on a paranormal mystery series featuring the ghost of a 1940s Hollywood leading man.

Rachael also has a short story published in the *Romancing the Lakes of Minnesota ~ Summer* anthology. Available in print and digital format wherever books are sold.

KNIGHT OF THE WITCHING HOUR

Christopher Edmund

Devil Track Lake, Grand Marais

Caden Lee Wester flicked the kill switch on his old hand-me-down motorcycle and flipped out the kickstand, resting the bike gently on the rocky ground. He unstrapped the worn leather belt of his scuffed half helmet and hung it from the handlebar. He breathed in deeply as he rotated the stiffness out of his neck and took a moment to soak in the setting sun. Devil Track Lake's beauty never ceased to amaze him. Well worth the long ride to Minnesota's north shore. With some reluctance, he pulled himself from his saddle and went about setting up his campsite in the usual spot near the shoreline of the gently lapping lake.

The last of the day's light faded behind the trees as he pounded the final tent stake into the ground, giving it an extra tap for reassurance. Caden zipped up his leather jacket as crisp autumn air moved in from the lake. He stood awhile longer and watched as the stars appeared one-by-one, then two-by-two, then ten-by-ten. The night sky was clear, and it soon gave way to the vibrant colors of the aurora borealis, which danced across the sky in transcendent colors of green and blue fire.

The drifter found himself so lost in the solitude of his surroundings that he didn't even see the woman sneak up on him.

"Holy shit!" He jumped backwards in a defensive stance at the sudden sight of the stranger. After the initial scare subsided, he rubbed his eyes and blinked.

She was still there.

"Where the hell did you come from?"

"Please help me!" She cried, terrified, fully collapsing in his arms.

Her sudden plea triggered an involuntary instinct in him to comfort her and he gave in to her embrace momentarily, consoling her trembling body. Her presence in his arms felt oddly satisfying and enchanting before he came to his senses and pushed her away, a tinge of embarrassment flushing his face. "Who are you? Help you how?"

She looked at him with big round green eyes filled with starlight and sky fire. "I'm Lilte. I managed to escape… but she's after me. The Witch!" She spoke fast between heavy gulps of air. "Please help me, you're the only one who can! Will you take me with you? I don't care where, just as long as it's not here."

He smirked. "A Witch, you say?" *Whoever this girl is, she's clearly nuts.*

"Yes, the Devil Witch!" Her brow scrunched in anger at the sight of his disbelief. "She'll awaken soon. Please, we don't have time for me to try and convince you. You're just going to have to trust me."

Caden scratched his matted brown hair and shifted uncomfortably. "Look, Lilly…"

"Lilte! Lil-tee!" she huffed.

"Lilte, sorry. I don't know what you want me to do about this, uh, supposed *Witch*, but I think you might have the wrong guy here." If life had taught him anything, it was that people were hardly what they seemed, and now this possibly insane woman wanted him to just take her word for it? *I don't think so.*

She stood before him, vulnerable and alone, dark hair spilling over slender shoulders and subtle frame. She glanced around hopelessly at the isolated location.

He felt a pang of guilt and sighed. Something about this woman caused his instincts to scream in warning, but his heart felt some sort of empathy for her, whether he wanted to admit it or not. *It couldn't hurt to at least hear her out. What's the worst she could do to him? If she was after his money, she'd be disappointed.*

He stroked his scruffy face and glanced towards the gravel road. "There's a lodge about a mile from here. I can take you there if you'd like. Do you have someone you want to call? I'll just grab my phone from my tent. Sometimes I get a trace of a signal up here on clear nights like this." *So much for a relaxing evening.*

She simply grinned.

What is with this woman? He shook his head.

He walked over to his tent and attempted to unzip the fly, cursing under his breath as it snagged on the fabric. *Cheap shoddy product.* The zipper wouldn't budge. In fact, upon closer examination in the faint light, the metal seemed to have fused to the fabric. *The hell…*

A low grumbling sound shook the tent from the bottom upward, like a shiver running along a spine.

Caden stood silent, his hands hovering over the tent in absolute stillness. "Did you just see that?" He took a few paces backwards.

The tent *growled* at him.

Caden Lee Wester had seen some *shit* in his travels, but never this.

The tent groaned as it puffed out, the elastic poles stretching to breaking point, then snapping into place like bones, bringing to life a monstrous form.

Upon its full awakening, the tent broke free from the ground. The zipper split, revealing a gaping maw of darkness and fine razor sharp teeth.

"What the crap!" He fell on his back and used his arms to scamper backwards frantically. The stakes ripped from the ground and flailed through the air with blinding speed. He felt a sharp sting as one of the stakes struck his cheek, leaving a bright red gash in its wake. *Did my tent just try and eat me?*

Caden scrambled backwards until he was able to pick himself off the ground, took Lilte by her hand as she stood awestruck, and made a mad dash to his motorcycle. He mounted the seat in one fluid motion and felt small hands wrap around his mid-section as Lilte pulled herself up behind him. He turned the ignition. The bike rumbled to life with a *strange* noise that caused him to pause. *She may be old. But that's not like my baby at all.* As he revved the throttle, the bike stirred as if it were thunder in the distance—but moved forward at a sluggish pace.

"Come on, now's not the time for you to break down!" He kicked at the side of the bike with his boot and felt a burst of power churn through the engine. It took all he had to keep the front wheel on the ground as the bike tore through the rocky terrain as if it were paper-*mâché*.

"Hold on!" he shouted, attempting to steer the bike towards the gravel road. He chanced a glance behind him and saw the tent stumbling after them in a haphazardly attempt; still very much alive. *Alive? Why is my goddamn tent chasing me?* He started to wonder what was in that secret sauce at the café he had stopped at on the way up.

The bike suddenly skidded to a halt and turned sharply digging the back tire in, sending a flurry of rock and dirt through the air. He clung to the handlebars with all of his strength.

They were facing the lake again—and the tent *monster-thing*. *Fantastic. Now my bike is turning on me too.*

The headlamp flickered orange and began puffing a deep sooty smoke.

"This can't be good."

The engine of the bike began to heat rapidly beneath him like a hot iron.

The leather seat and metal frame shifted and groaned beneath him, twisting and transforming into *flesh.* As the motorcycle, *or what was left of it*, lurched towards the tent, it expanded into a great winged beast covered in scaled-hide and boney spikes. It released a terrifying roar unlike anything he had ever heard in his life.

He placed his hands on the woman's, still tightly wrapped around his abdomen, and leaped from the back of whatever his bike had become just as the monstrosity flapped its wings and began to lift into the night. The two tumbled to the ground in a tangle of limbs, but managed to land without injury.

Before his eyes, his bike—or what remained—now soared through the sky, spewing bright orange flames. He blinked. "Is that a dragon?"

The tent lashed out at the dragon with flailing cord lines and snapping teeth, but it was a failed attempt. The fabric-like skin quickly caught fire, sending flames leaping brightly into the night sky, yet it continued to fight well into its death throes, spreading flaming chunks of tent-flesh across the landscape.

Caden remained frozen in place, watching the battle unfold until Lilte shook him out of his dazed state of mind.

"I was too slow, she's waking. Her magic is turning these objects against us. They're weak though, she hasn't fully awoken yet. We have to run! Right now while her creations are confused and fight each other."

Caden forced his eyes away from the scene and focused on the intensity in Lilte's eyes. He nodded in determination.

They ran for several minutes, taking cover in the thick overgrowth of birch and pine that covered majority of the shoreline. In a small clearing next to a large, flat boulder, he paused a moment to catch his breath. "Listen. I think we lost it, I don't hear it anymore."

"Not for long, the Devil Witch's dragon won't stop until it finds me."

"My bike…is a goddamn dragon. A make-believe creature from children's books. What the hell? Who are you? Is this all the Witch's doing? It's time to give me some answers."

"I know it must all feel very strange, but believe me, it's real. This is really happening. Right now." She paused. "What's your name, sir?"

"Caden."

"Caden," she repeated his name, as if trying it out. "Thank you for saving me, but as I've mentioned, we're not safe yet."

"What do you mean *we*? I thought it was you the Witch wanted. I've got nothing to do with any of this. I just came up here for one last relaxing getaway before the snow falls."

"As my knight and guardian, the Devil Witch will try to eliminate you as well."

"I'm sorry, your knight? As *I've* mentioned before, you've got the wrong guy. I don't want anything to do with this fantasy tale. I was perfectly content to relax beneath the stars tonight."

"Relax or brood?"

His temper flared. He narrowed his eyes at her. "It's none of your business why I was here. I wasn't in danger of being devoured by my tent or burned to a crisp by my motorcycle until you showed up."

"No, my guess is you were doing a fine enough job self-sabotaging yourself on your own." She took a defiant step forward. "I know that look in your eyes. The loneliness. You're hollow inside. You've lost something, or someone, haven't you?"

Caden was a bit taken back by her all-too-revealing reading and tried to look away, but she followed his gaze. *She's right, if not a bit creepy.* "How do you know any of that?"

"Please. It's obvious," she brushed it off casually. "You're not as stone-faced as you think you are, you know."

"It was a long time ago," he admitted. *As if that somehow made it better.*

"Time heals all as they say," she said sarcastically.

He laughed. "What a load of crap."

She flashed him a quick smile, and for a moment, he felt a hardened piece of armor around his heart chip away. This woman, whoever she was, held some kind of sway over him he couldn't figure out; but he also found it oddly satisfying and far too easy to give into. Caden turned his head quickly as he felt a blush of color creep up his face. He cleared his throat and straightened his shoulders. "Right, anyway. We can't go back the way we came, and the woods end well before the lodge. We'd be exposed out in the open." He sat down with his back against the boulder and tried to sort things out in his mind.

"Might I make a suggestion, sir?" Lilte said softly.

"If only we had something to use against them. Everything was back at my camp."

"Caden." She tried again, placing her hands on her hips.

He buried his head in his hands out of frustration. "I'm helpless against this."

"Caden!" she shouted, pointing to the top of the boulder.

He raised his head wearily and turned to see what she was pointing at. A sparkling light caught his eye and he stood up to get a better view. Stuck into the rock, a sword made of white diamond glimmered beneath the starlight.

He squinted. "Is that a *sword*?" *I really am in a fairy tale.* The sword brought back childhood memories of when he used to pretend he was a knight, rescuing the princess from evil's clutches. The sight awakened a dormant feeling of heroism and adventure, long forgotten.

"Orion's Blade," Lilte gasped. "Caden, this weapon is no ordinary sword."

He snorted. *Ordinary, now there's a word that's lost all meaning.*

"This sword is legendary! Said to have been forged and wielded by the Celestial Beings. Its crystal is immune to spells, indestructible, and impervious to flame. It is bound by the stars themselves!"

"Perfect!" He placed his palms around the grip.

Warm.

He tested the resistance and felt the blade budge beneath his tug. "Well, here it goes." He leaned back with one foot against the stone and pulled the sword from the rock in one swift motion.

As the blade slid from its home, the boulder separated like liquid. Residue clung to the crystal blade, and as he raised the sword above his head, it ran down its length and covered his body. His initial reaction was to shake it off, but as fast as it happened, the liquid hardened, leaving him encased in crystal plate armor. The remaining liquid that was once the rock, pooled on the ground into the shape of a crescent shield with a mirror polish.

Caden turned to Lilte, and watched as swirling white light danced around her body, weaving through her arms, legs, and hair, materializing a gown of silken white brilliance that fit her form immaculately.

"Don't you know it's impolite to stare," she mocked, flipping her raven hair to one side.

"I'm sorry." He found himself lost in her emerald eyes and tracing the curvature of her body. "You're beautiful?" He said it in the form of a question.

"You don't look so bad yourself," she bit her lower lip, eyeing him up and down. "A true knight of the realm."

Caden checked himself. From head to toe, he was encased in pearlescent crystal armor. Attached to his back, a navy blue cloak trailed, embroidered with the constellations of the stars above. His shield, which he strapped to his left arm, was in the shape of a crescent moon and shone with the same brilliance. In his right hand, he held the crystal sword known as Orion's Blade.

"Magnificent," Lilte breathed the words.

"I look ridiculous," he said. "Is all of this really necessary?"

"The Celestial Beings must believe so; otherwise their power never would have revealed themselves to you. Caden, the magic has chosen you to play the role of the Seraphic Knight. That's not something to be taken lightly. The Seraphic Knight has remained dormant for centuries! The magic of the stars only makes itself available to someone of pure heart who finds themselves trapped in a dire situation."

Seraphic Knight? Orion's Blade? Celestial Beings? It's like I'm living in her make-believe world. Well, at least I don't have to ride a goddamn unicorn into battle.

He looked deep into the blade, finding his reflection among faint swirling nebula and twinkling stars. Sadness stared back at him with hollow eyes. "I'm no knight though." He turned his back to Lilte. "I'm not the hero you think I am, and I'm definitely not pure of heart."

She placed a small hand on his shoulder. "Caden, you are. You need only look deep enough to find it. I believe in you, isn't that enough?"

He shifted away uncomfortably. "I'll just let you down too. I let everyone down. I'm damaged goods, Lilte."

She turned him around. Her eyes glistened with the light of the stars. "You're here now though. You're here for me. And I'm here for you."

"Lilte, I…" He didn't finish.

The dragon burst into the clearing with incredible force, splintering wood and tree in a path of destruction. Caden pulled Lilte into his arms and raised his shield as a fireball came hurling towards them. The shield deflected the burst of flames, spewing fire upon the clearing.

"Are you okay?" He shouted behind him.

She nodded.

He grabbed Lilte's hand and ran for the tree line, dodging fireballs as they slammed into the rocky soil on all sides like grenades.

The dragon was faster.

Sending a wall of fire to enclose them within the clearing, the dragon had trapped its prey. Caden attempted to double back, but came face-to-face with the beast. The creature swatted with one massive hand covered in iron-hard scale, knocking him to the ground with bone-crushing force. He felt Lilte's grip loosen from his own as his vision blurred. Between glimpses of darkness, he saw the creature standing tall before him. It roared triumphantly, and tamped its enormous foot atop Caden's body, pinning him between its claws.

As Caden drifted through reality and dream, he thought he heard his name.

So distant; so faint.

He struggled to remember where he was. *Who am I? I'm so tired. This is what I wanted, isn't it? For the pain and the heartache to stop. This is what I wanted. But I'm alone.* He felt himself sobbing but couldn't tell if it was real or only in his head. *I'm always alone.* He thought he heard his name again, like a whisper carried on the wind.

"Caden…"

His world became a white blanket. Nothing else existed, only his thoughts and the strange voice in the distance. He heard it again, and attempted to reach out with his hand, but felt nothing but emptiness.

"Caden, you're not alone."

The voice jolted through his body like a lightning bolt, and suddenly he recalled. The strange woman who found him on the beach; pleaded for his help, and brought him to this state of being. *Lilte, her name was Lilte.* He remembered. But where was she? In the center of his vision, a tree materialized. A great, old oak tree gnarled with age. It stood before him, towering high into the sky like an impervious sentinel.

"You don't have to be alone anymore," Lilte's voice came from behind the tree.

"Where are you?" He ran around the tree trunk searching for her, but the tree continued in an endless loop. Around and around he went, the same bark and branches facing him wherever he moved. He grew frustrated. "I can't find you. Lilte! Where are you? I don't want to be alone anymore. I want to find you. I want to help you!" And then suddenly she was there, standing before him with a smile on her face.

"I knew I was right to believe in you, Caden."

His washed out world, the tree, and even Lilte vanished before his eyes and he found himself back in the clearing, staring up at the behemoth. Its crimson eyes bore down on him like two pits of hell. Its nostrils flared, puffing black smoke into the night.

With renewed inner strength, Caden reached for his sword resting just a few inches from his hand. He groaned against the pressure of the dragon's talons as they pressed into his ribs, but then felt his fingers graze the pommel of the weapon.

His hand wrapped around the sword grip and he brought it before him to slash wildly at the scaled-hide of the beast. "You can't have her, Witch!"

The dragon lurched backwards, stumbling long enough for Caden to break free. He scanned his surroundings and quickly saw Lilte collapsed on the ground only a few feet from where he was. *I won't let you hurt her.*

Anger, frustration, and bitterness that he'd kept bottled up for years as he drifted through life aimlessly suddenly came pouring out as he howled in rage at the dragon. He slashed back and forth like an insane man without any sign of grace or having ever used a sword before. In his blind frenzy, he couldn't tell if his hits were even landing, but the dragon grudgingly gave up ground, so he kept at it. The hilt of the sword grew hot within his grip. The blade burst into bright blue flames along its edge. The sword led his hand as if it had suddenly become sentient. He felt his arm pulled in wide, controlled sweeping arcs sending the dragon reeling backwards in pain as the blows struck through flesh and bone. The blade then plunged itself forward, straight into the monster's exposed chest. The dragon howled in agony and toppled upon the earth with a ground-shattering thud.

Caden withdrew the blade and watched as the magical beast dissipated into the night, leaving behind a mangled, scratched and broken motorcycle. Nothing more than a heap of parts. The flames surrounding the clearing immediately extinguished.

Caden ran to Lilte and knelt beside her, cradling her head in his lap gently. Her eyes fluttered open.

"Sorry about your motorcycle," she said.

He caught himself laughing. *It felt good to laugh.* "I'm just glad you're safe, Lilte," he said heroically.

"I knew you could do it," she sat up, taking in the damage done. "That was only one of the Witch's spells though. She will continue to hunt us as long as she has my emblem."

"Your emblem? I don't understand."

"My mother's ring. As long as the Witch is in possession of it, she'll always hold sway over me. It binds a pact my mother made with the Devil Witch centuries ago. My mother was fleeing from someone or something, I'm not sure what. I was only a child at the time."

"Wait, wait, did you say centuries?"

She nodded. "The magic of this area has strange effects on time. The outside world passes by much faster than it does in the Witch's realm. The Witch came to my mother when her strength had all but exhausted and offered her help. For a price. All my mother asked, was that I might go on living. However, the price was me becoming the Witch's servant. I would not be allowed to leave her realm. To keep me bound to these terms, the Witch infused my mother's ring with the pact."

"And you didn't think to grab the ring when you made your escape?" Caden frowned.

Lilte glared at his tone.

"She keeps it closely guarded on a chain around her neck. I can't even go near it. She has a warding spell placed on it making it impossible for me to touch. You on the other hand, with the power of the stars coursing through you, would be able to break the binding. I'm certain of it! You will help me, Caden, right?"

Something had awoken inside him in that battle. A feeling that left him invigorated. He had purpose again, and he wanted to hold onto it with an iron grip. He stood, sheathed his blade to his belt, and offered her his hand. "Where do we find this Witch?"

"One small thing I forgot to mention," she said evasively as they walked along the shore of the lake. "Are you good at holding your breath?"

I don't like where this is going.

She twiddled her fingers and dug her toes into the sand in a cutesy, innocent manner. "The Witch sort of lives in a cave beneath the lake."

Of course she does.

"Beneath the island on the western end of the lake. We'll have to swim."

He grimaced. The thought of swimming in open water in the middle of the night with a wicked Witch flinging magical monsters at them around every corner didn't bode well in his mind.

"I have an idea. Come on, follow me." He ran along the shore, his blue cloak trailing behind him. He retraced their flight from earlier and came upon the scorched ground of his campsite. He eyed the remnants of his tent cautiously before approaching. Determining the monster thoroughly lifeless, he took Lilte's hand and led her to the water. Shrouded in overgrown weeds, an old rickety dock remained almost hidden to the naked eye. Tied to the dock was an even older canoe that someone had long forgotten about. "There's a reason I always come to this campsite. It has its perks."

"Does that thing even float?" she glowered, taking in the half-rotted wood hull.

He shrugged. "Seems to be floating just fine right now. Though..." Skeptical, he pulled his sword from its sheath and tapped the wooden canoe. A hollow echo greeted him back and he sighed his relief. *Not going to eat me.*

He helped Lilte into the canoe and noticed her brow scrunched in thought. "What is it?"

"I was thinking, remember when I mentioned the sword repels magic? Well, as soon as you made the killing blow against the dragon, the spell reverted! If my understanding is correct, that means as long as it's with you and touching whatever object is in question, the Witch's spells will be negated."

"Hmm, I suppose that makes sense. Like when I checked the canoe just now. If the Witch were planning on turning it against us, the sword must have blocked it."

"Exactly! You know, we make a pretty good team. Caden and Lilte, adventurers extraordinaire!"

He smiled faintly, untied the frayed cord anchoring the little boat, then pushed the canoe into the water, jumping in as it cleared the docks, careful not to tip it in the process. Resting his sword and shield in the base of the hull, he picked up the oars and began pushing into the open water.

The water was serene. The air still. The only sound the gentle dipping and rising of the oars. Caden looked up at the sky, the Milky Way clearly visible, spanning the night sky with dazzling brilliance.

"Lilte," he looked at her sitting across from him in the canoe. She was busy studying the night sky as well. "If this works, and we free you, where will you go?"

She turned her head to him, "I haven't given it much thought, I guess. There's so much of the world I haven't seen. I want to explore it all. I want to experience life and all it has to offer. I am beyond thankful for my mother's sacrifice, but I can't remain bound here any longer. Caden, will you explore the world with me when I'm free?"

"I've experienced life, Lilte. Lived through all of the heartbreak and the shattered dreams, all the disappointments and short fallings, all of the pain and suffering. If you ask me, what you have here isn't so bad."

She shook her head, "You don't understand. All those things you've listed, sure, they are devastating, but you've endured them all. You're still here right now, talking to me. You know why that is?"

He shrugged, looking away from her.

"Because you have a strong heart, Caden. It's the reason your thoughts weigh so heavy on your shoulders, why you have such a hard time accepting who you are, and what you're capable of. It's not a bad thing, Caden. It's wonderful."

"I think you presume too much."

She placed her hand on his, forcing his gaze on her. "If anything, I presume too little. I've seen who you really are."

"Lilte…" He wanted to say more, but suddenly felt the oar stick to something in the water, scattering his thoughts and any moment they just shared.

The oar refused to budge. He pulled and wiggled at it, but to no avail. The boat came to a standstill on the open water.

A tentacle lurched from the water, wrapping itself around the oar, pulling it down.

"Oh no you don't!" Caden fought back, causing the boat to rock violently. "I've had about enough of this night."

Caden reached for his sword, striking at the repulsive oily arm. The beast slunk backwards into the water with a shriek, releasing its grip.

The water bubbled and churned.

"I think you just pissed it off," Lilte said, looking over the side of the canoe.

"It?"

"The Witch's pet."

The lake burst upward in a torrent of water spray nearly capsizing them, revealing a nightmarishly grotesque octopus-like creature.

"Caden!" Lilte shouted, "This isn't just one of the Witch's spells. It's her pet kraken!"

"Pet?" Caden shouted over the roar of waves and falling water. "You've got to be kidding me."

The kraken lifted one colossal tentacle high above their heads.

"Hold on to something!" Caden barely had time to yell as the beast crashed its limb into the water with thundering force, sending a wake high enough to crush the canoe into splinters, but somehow, they managed to keep the seasoned little boat upright and in one piece. *That was too close.*

He brought his shield up before him and held his sword ready. The kraken moved in closer, sending its countless limbs sprawling around the canoe in every direction. Caden slashed at the arms as they threatened to overtake the boat, slicing off fresh chunks of meat with each attack. The monster groaned in fury, and tightened its grip around the small boat, bringing it out of the water entirely.

"Bad kraken!" he shouted awkwardly at the creature. "Back to your sea kennel."

"It's no use," Lilte cried. "It only obeys the Witch's commands. And even then, not always. But she has a way of coaxing it using light."

"Light?" *But it's the middle of the night, where am I going to find a source of light?* Then he remembered how his shield had lit up in the woods against the Dragon.

His shield remained dormant as he glanced down at it.

I don't understand. How had he managed to make it glow before? *What is different this time?*

The kraken shifted its tentacles around the canoe like a snake constricting its prey. The boat creaked against the strain. Caden lunged at its nearest arm, slicing it off, only to have it replaced by another in its wake. *This is useless.*

"Caden!" Lilte shrieked, dodging attacks as they came her way. "If you're going to do something, now's the time!"

"I know! But what?" Without a light source what could he possibly do? As he dodged an attack from above, he noticed his shield light up momentarily as a gap in the wall of slithering tentacles were broken to reveal the stars above. *Of course! Starlight!*

Caden leapt from the tattered remnants of the canoe and clung to the nearest spiked arm of the kraken, riding it upwards as it rose from the waters. Swinging himself onto the back of it, he raised his shield to the sky and watched in amazement as the light filled the shield with its glow. After sufficiently soaking in the light of the stars, he aimed it at the center of the kraken.

The beast gurgled. Caden felt it hesitate. *It's working!*

He raised the shield above his head to recharge while clinging to the tentacle. The illumination spread across the shield as it soaked in the ambient light of the stars once again. He shifted his position around to bear the light of the shield on the kraken's eyes that had revealed themselves. Caden swung himself back into the canoe, maintaining the beam of light on the kraken.

The creature vanished into the depths, lulled by the light.

Lilte blinked at him, "You did it! I have never seen anything like that."

"But now we have another problem," he pointed to the bottom of the canoe. It was taking on water. Rapidly. "Looks like we're swimming the rest of the way."

He pulled Lilte into his arms and pushed away from the canoe as it sunk beneath the surface of the lake.

"Caden, you were amazing."

He could feel her heartbeat accelerated against his chest.

"All in a day's work," he joked. "I am the Seraphic Knight after all."

They bobbed along in the water, gently kicking their feet toward the island. He felt his legs brush against hers. He gazed into her softened green eyes dancing with the reflection of the waves and the stars above.

Despite all the danger that followed this woman around, he felt happiness. True happiness. A feeling, he realized, he hadn't felt in a very long time. Caught up in the momentary peacefulness that had returned to the night, he embraced her in a long kiss.

* * *

As they edged closer to the island, Caden spotted a strange whirlpool next to a rocky cliff face. The water pulsed with a pinkish hue coming from far below the surface.

"Hope you're better at holding your breath than you are at kissing, Sir Knight," she teased.

"Hey, it's been awhile!" he defended, then nudged her toward the vortex. "After you, Princess."

Caden felt the current pulling him towards the epicenter of the gyre. He took one last gulp of air and closed his eyes tight. The water rushed over his head. Down, down, down he went. Losing all orientation, the water spun him around and around.

Then Caden felt hard stone beneath his feet and fresh air against his skin. He blinked his eyes open to reveal a narrow corridor lined with burning torches of pink fire. When he looked up he saw the night sky pin-pricked by twinkling starlight, but distorted and skewed as if viewing them through a glass of water. Caden reached a finger up to touch the surface of the floating water ceiling.

"I wouldn't do that. Not unless you want to go back up."

He retracted his finger, taking her word for it. "This is unreal, Lilte. How is all of this possible?"

"Magic, obviously." Lilte took his hand in hers and led him through the cavern. "This way."

They crossed a set of stone stairs cut straight into the rock that led them up to a mound.

Before them, a hill stretched on for several hundred feet—covered in lush dark green grass wet with drops of dew that glistened beneath a dome of stars. Great oak trees spread their branches high into the ceiling of water and beyond. Flicks of light flitted about the hillside like fireflies, darting left and right, playfully chasing one another.

At the crest of the hill stood a small, worn-down cottage, dark as pitch. A shiver ran down his spine.

"The Devil Witch is in there, I take it?"

Lilte nodded.

"Let's end this now then," Caden drew his sword and shield and started up the hill towards the home. He reached the door in almost no time flat, tried the doorknob and felt it turn. *Unlocked.*

The door creaked open slowly with a push of his hand.

Caden brushed strands of wet hair from his eyes and reached for a small oil lantern he found next to the door. He turned the valve and a small spark of light spread, basking the room in a golden glow.

At the end of the room, a chair faced a desolate, cold hearth. A hooded figure sat in it.

Every nerve in Caden's body screamed at him. *Run!* His mind kept telling him. *Get the hell out of here!*

But instead, he took a step forward. The old floorboards creaked beneath his heavy boots one by one. The figure remained silent.

"Caden." Lilte whispered, but he continued forward.

The knight placed his hand on the top of the worn-wicker chair.

"Caden!" Lilte tried again, but her voice sounded small. "There's something I need to tell you..."

He motioned to her and shook his head. He surged in front of the chair, sword and shield held high.

"What the...!" Caden dropped his sword on the floor with a loud thud echoing throughout the small cabin. "I don't understand."

Before him, the skeletal remains of a woman sat slumped over in dust and cobwebs.

Caden looked up, horror reflected in his eyes. Lilte stood on the opposite side of the room. Tears streaked her cheeks.

"Caden, I wanted to tell you, I just didn't know how." She lifted the silver necklace from beneath her dress. Dangling at the end of the thin chain, a small ring danced in the light of the lantern. "I am the Devil Witch."

"What do you mean, how can you be the Witch? The monsters... the ring, you said you couldn't touch it!" His mind felt overwhelmed with conflicting emotions. He threw his shield to the floor, sending it crashing into an old, rickety table. "You... you played me?"

"Caden, no! Well, not exactly. It's not like that! It wasn't all a lie. It's true the Witch held me here—the old one that is. For years and years, I was trapped in this place. Time passes slower here, but it still passes, and eventually the old Witch succumbed to its calling."

"Couldn't you just leave then? Why all of this? Why the ruse?"

"When the old crone died, it didn't exactly lift the curse. Not completely. The pact my mother made with the Witch was still bound to this ring, but its state was weakened, and I was able to reclaim it as my own. With it, came powers I had never known before. The Witch's own magic was now mine. I don't know if she planned it this way or if it just happened. At first, it took some getting used to, but after a few years, I got the hang of controlling the magic. Getting it to obey my desires. But it was all empty. I was alone. Much like you."

Caden shook his head, "Is this all just a game to you? Am I just your entertainment to pass the time?"

She took a step forward, then retracted her step and hung her head. "Caden, I've been watching you. I know you come to this lake often. I could feel your pain. I felt it as if it were my own, and I wanted to take it away from you. But you had grown bitter." She raised her head, intensity in her eyes. "So bitter! You did nothing but waste away, mope, and sulk. I knew getting under your armor was going to take something special. Something only you could do in the end. I used my magic to trick you into thinking you were saving me, and for that, I am immensely sorry. But you must understand, in the process, you really did save me. You saved me from myself, from who I was becoming, from my overwhelming loneliness."

"I was doing just fine before I met you, Lilte! You don't know me like you think you do. You know nothing!" Caden ripped off the cloak and undid his gauntlet and bracers.

"Caden, no! Don't remove the armor, the magic of this place—"

"What's it matter anyway? I was right to be bitter. All my life I've been manipulated. I'm weak. Unneeded." He unstrapped the shoulder armor and let it fall to the wooden floor.

"Please, don't do this! You're not weak! You proved that tonight. I need you more than you realize. The kiss we shared—that was real, I swear on my life! Please, this world will crush you without the Celestial Beings' magic warding you."

Caden dropped to his knees lightheaded as he removed his chest plate. A crushing, constricting feeling wrapped itself around his body as if he were feeling the entirety of the lake's pressure bearing down on him. He gasped for breath but could find none, "Maybe it's better … this way … anyway. Lilte …"

He felt himself fading into blackness. He felt her hands wrap around him as he collapsed to the floor and into darkness.

"Caden, I love you…"

* * *

Warmth filled his body. Light washed over him. He drifted among clouds.

Caden awoke in his tent alongside the shoreline. The sun was bright and warmed his face through the mesh window. *Was it all a dream? That seemed a bit cliché.* He rubbed at his eyes and emerged from the tent, breathing in the morning air. Parked a few feet away, his motorcycle sat on its kickstand, right where he had left it. He almost laughed. *It really was a dream then.*

Still. The image of that woman was burned into his memories. He recalled the way she felt in his arms, how comforting it had felt, how *right.*

He shook his head, "Just a dream Caden, that's all it was."

Caden packed up his supplies, strapped them down on his bike, and then mounted. Eager to put distance between him and this place. If it really was all just a dream, why did it linger on his mind the way it did.

Lilte. Maybe I was too hard on you.

Truth was, last night, dream or not, was the most alive he'd felt in years. The idea of going home alone made him feel hollow. As if a piece of his soul was being left behind at this lake.

And then, as he placed his hand on the throttle, he saw it.

Dangling from the handlebar, a silver necklace with a ring hung Lilte's emblem.

Caden cradled the ring in his palm, a flood of tears erupting from his eyes at the tactility of it.

Tears of joy. *It wasn't just a dream. She was real, it was all real.*

Standing at the tree line, surrounded by the changing leaves of autumn, stood Lilte.

She walked over to him without saying a word, climbed on the back of his bike, and wrapped her hands around him tightly.

"Where to?" He asked, unable to contain the smile on his face.

"Anywhere, as long as it's with you."

ABOUT THE AUTHOR

Living in the Minneapolis area, Christopher Edmund is a fantasy author and graphic designer. He's written and published "The Last Tide", a story about a Princess beneath the seas, and is currently working on a joint project called "Pendant of Brackenspire", as well as a full length fantasy novel series tentatively titled "Cinder Witch." He has designed several book cover designs, author logos, and social media banners as a side job, and is always eager to take on new clients.

During the brutal winters of the north, he survives by snowboarding--though there may not be any X-Games or Olympics in his horizon, it has become a lifetime passion of his. He enjoys taking trips out west to the Rockies whenever the opportunity arises.

In the summer, He's always looking for an excuse to take a motorcycle trip or adventure. While he might say it helps free his mind and give him time to sort out mangled story plots and ideas--it's really just to take in the scenery.

And of course, what self-respecting fantasy author *isn't* a nerd? With what shred of free-time he has left at the end of the day, he revels in a bit of gaming. Whether it be board games, miniatures, table-top RPG's, or MMORPG's; he's not ashamed to embrace his geeky side.

Christopher also has a short story published in the *Romancing the Lakes of Minnesota ~ Summer* anthology. Available in print and digital format wherever books are sold.

Check out his website at http://www.christopheredmund.net for more information. Like him on Facebook at Official Christopher Edmund and follow him on Twitter at @FantasyEdmund.

MAGIC AT MOOSE LAKE

Diane Wiggert

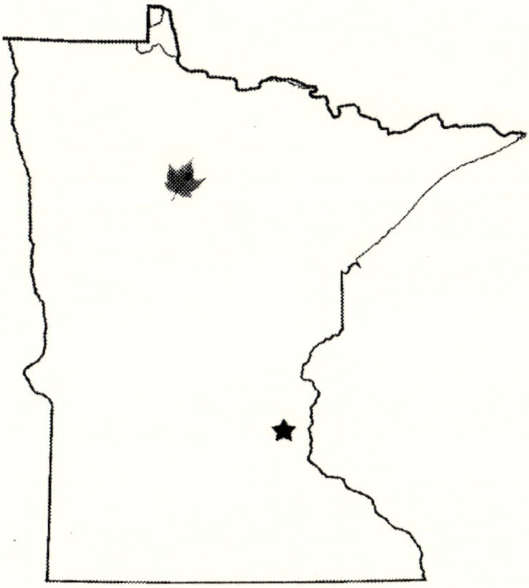

Moose Lake, Bemidji

A scratching sound brought Shelby Maguire out of a deep sleep. Shivering, she pulled the quilt tighter around her neck. Slowly opening one eye she found it was still dark out, but sunrise was near. It took her a moment to remember where she was. She was in her friend Kelly's cabin. Shelby had driven up to the Northern Minnesota cabin last night.

The sound increased in volume and appeared to be moving closer. Reaching for the side table light, she felt something small and soft brush her hand. A scream ripped from her throat, when she flipped the light on and caught sight of a small streak of red fur scurrying across the floor and under the armoire.

She threw off the covers, slipped on her shoes, and ran for the door, running right into a broad camouflaged covered chest. Another scream flew as she lashed out and punched the stranger in his muscular chest.

With a grunt, strong hands gripped her shoulders, "Shelby?" a gruff voice asked, startling her out of her panic.

"Tanner?" She looked up at the face of a man she had known most of her life. "What? What are you doing here?" she stammered, as she stepped free from his clasp. Last time she had seen Kelly's older brother he was engaged to be married and living in Iowa.

He rubbed the spot on his chest that she'd struck and bent over to catch his breath. "Hunting."

"Huh?" She hadn't heard any gunshots yesterday.

He straightened, "I came up here for deer hunting."

"But? It's October?"

"Bow hunting starts early. What brings you here?" His rich brown eyes took in her pajamas and Crocs before resting on her face.

Feeling exposed, she pushed a few auburn strands from her face and crossed her arms over her chest. "Kelly offered me the cabin for a few weeks."

"Oh. No problem, I'll take the couch." He picked up his duffel bag and crossed to the couch as if it was no big deal. "So what scared you?" he asked casually.

"What?" Her unwelcome furry guest was forgotten with Tanner's arrival.

"You screamed. Before you ran into me and punched me in the chest." He raised an eyebrow in question.

"Oh, a squirrel. I think." She felt silly admitting it. "It was too big for a mouse."

"We get one or two in every year. I'll take care of it for you," he said, heading for the bedroom.

She just stood there, her mind blank for a moment. Had he said he would take the couch? As in he was staying?

Not thinking that was a good idea, she turned to tell him she'd leave; after all, it was his family's cabin. She hadn't seen Tanner Burke in years, and now was not the time for a reunion. She needed peace and quiet, not a big handsome man taking up space in this tiny cabin.

Out the window, the sight of the sun rising over the lake made her rethink leaving. It was the perfect place to decompress, and he would be out in the woods all day.

She looked around at the cabin with its 1970's décor. She had her doubts last night as to whether she could stay here for two weeks alone. Nine years of Girl Scout cookie sales and merit badges hadn't prepared her for the wood stove and old-fashion hand-pump on the sink. But when she saw the bathroom with hot and cold running water she had praised Jesus and decided to stay.

Maybe this would work out. They could go their separate ways, and she would have a strong man around to carry in the wood. It was chilly on autumn nights, and she would definitely need to use the wood stove.

"Got him." Tanner said as he came out of the bedroom, carrying a wiggling pillowcase.

Yup, a man could be useful in the woods.

* * *

After Tanner released the furry intruder, he grabbed his bow and backpack and headed for the tree stand. Shelby remembered him as being the strong, silent type growing up. He wasn't a sports kid in the traditional sense. Tanner was an outdoorsman. He loved to hunt and fish, she remembered as she walked outside.

Knowing this made it easier for her to stay in the cabin with him. He would be out in the woods from sun-up to sundown, giving her all the time she needed to figure out what to do about the rat- bastard (aka, Justin Baldwin).

Yesterday, Justin wasn't the only one surprised when a bubbly blonde came into her boss's office and yelled, "Surprise" she recalled.

"Miss Maguire, can I see you in my office for a minute." Justin sat at his desk all business, not looking up as she walked in. "Can you close the door, please."

His eyes slowly made their way up her body, finally meeting hers. They smoldered and heated as they burned into hers. "Are you packed and ready for our weekend?"

"Yes," she tried not to blush, but the thought of her clothing choices for their romantic weekend was making her want to fan her face. She had maxed out her Victoria's credit card and couldn't wait for him to peel the intimate apparel from her flushed and heated body. They had been dating for a few months and she was finally ready to take their relationship to the next level.

Justin started to rise and come around his desk towards her when the office door flew open and a petite blonde burst in like a stripper popping out of a four-foot high cake at a bachelor party. "Surprise!"

"Honey!" Justin stopped mid-stride, running his hands through his perfectly gelled hair. He recovered quickly and moved to meet the blonde with an obligatory peck on the lips. "Wow, and what a surprise it is. What are you doing here?" he said pulling her into a hug.

He locked eyes with Shelby over the woman's head, they begged for her silence, screaming at her loud and clear, *Please don't make a scene.* In that moment Shelby knew exactly who the blonde was.

Mrs. Baldwin was wiggling with excitement. "The house sold. Oh, and I found the cutest craftsmen style home right by the lake. I want to show you, can you take off early?"

"Honey…" before Justin could answer, the bundle of energy that was his wife turned and lit up like Christmas.

"I'm sorry, it was so rude of me not to introduce myself. I'm Maddie, Justin's wife. You must be Shelby, his assistant, I feel like I know you already. Justin's told me so much about you." She extended a perfectly manicured hand.

Nice to know he told someone something, because in the six months he's been here not one word has slipped passed his lips about you. Her shouting tirade was all in her head, on the outside her eyes glazed over and her smile was so fake a blind man could see it.

Justin had barely ushered his wife out the door when Shelby grabbed her purse and was running for her car. Once she was locked inside the car she dropped her head and let the tears and pain overtake her. Pulling out her phone she called her friend, Kelly, to vent.

"I was such a fool," she sobbed.

"Shel, you didn't know," Kelly soothed.

"But the signs were there. You saw them, why couldn't I?" a hiccup broke the steady stream of sobs as Shelby tried to compose herself. "What am I going to do?"

"I'll tell you what to do. You call his cheating ass up or better yet, text him. Tell him you are taking your vacation. After you inform him what a lying, cheating, no-good bastard he is. You need to get away so you can calm down and think." She paused for a moment then continued, "I know, go to the cabin. You remember the cabin?"

Shelby shook her head, forgetting Kelly couldn't see her.

"Yes, that's the perfect place. It's quiet and no one's there right now. Mom and Dad won't mind."

So that's what she did. She broke up with him, but could she still work for him? That was the question.

Now, she found herself sitting on the dock in the great up-north, trying to decide what to do next with her life and her day.

This was a beautiful spot, it calmed her. She could sit here on… What was the name of the lake? Bear lake? Elk Lake? Not that it mattered, it was peaceful and serene. Shelby threw her arms out wide and inhaled the crisp fall air. "This is perfect," she sighed, Kelly was right. "Almost magical." The morning chill was burning off with the rising sun, she laid back and let the heat from it lull her into a sense of calm as she dozed off to sleep.

* * *

Shelby woke as a shadow eclipsed the sun. Blinking a few times, she looked up to find Tanner looming over her.

"Good, you're not dead. Thought I'd need to perform CPR."

She blinked again at either his joking comment or his dazzling smile, she wasn't sure which. "What time is it?" she asked. She must have slept longer than she thought. The sun was high, the white clouds and blue sky a perfect backdrop.

"One o'clock. I came in to make a sandwich. You hungry?" He held out his hand to help her rise.

She clasped his warm and callused hand, and it enveloped hers, registering its strength as he pulled her up with ease. "I can't believe I slept all morning."

"Easy to do at Moose Lake. Relax, I mean." He added at her confused expression.

Moose Lake. That was the name. I had remembered it was named after an animal at least.

"But I never nap. Not since college," she said as they headed toward the cabin. Her sleep-filled brain was still trying to process their conversation while her body reacted to his touch.

"Not even on the weekends?"

"Nope, I guess I don't need much sleep."

Tanner slowed his stride and looked over at her like he wanted to say something else but kept quiet.

Inside the cabin, Tanner started pulling sandwich fixings out of the fridge. She didn't remember buying all that, and realized he had.

As they made lunch she asked, "Are you done hunting for the day?"

"Nope, just refueling. I'll go out again until dark."

They had pleasant small talk over lunch. After, Tanner grabbed his pack and bow and headed for the door. "I'm off to stalk the ferocious whitetail." He said, almost keeping a straight face, except the corner of his mouth hitched up a notch.

Shelby gave a grave nod, "I hear they are elusive creatures, second only to Bigfoot." Her response was delivered with a dead serious expression.

His stoic features cracked and a full smile bloomed on his face as he opened the door. Upon its closing, a snort of laughter burst from Shelby as she turned to clear the table of their lunch dishes.

She couldn't remember Tanner having such a fun sense of humor. They never talked much growing up, he was four years her senior. She was his annoying little sister's friend. After college, he moved to another state. The last time she saw him was at Kelly's wedding two years ago, and he was engaged. Her friend never mentioned his wedding. They must have kept it small. But then she and Kelly didn't talk about their siblings very often. He and his wife must not have children, she mused, because Kelly would be gushing over a new niece or nephew.

Shelby found herself picturing little Tanners running around the yard, jumping off the dock. She smiled at the scene in her head, until she pictured herself in the scene with them.

"What the hell?" she questioned herself. She had just dumped one married man less than twenty-four hours ago, and here she was fantasizing about another. What was wrong with her? Tanner was good-looking in the rugged all-man sort of way, but she had never thought of him in a romantic way.

Okay, so she had a crush on him in junior high, when he was a senior, but that was years ago, a stupid childish infatuation. It must be her low resistance at the moment, drawing her to every good-looking man in a ten-mile radius, married or not. The last thing she would ever willingly do is date a married man.

Shelby spied an old rowboat on shore and decided that was a perfect way to spend the afternoon. She could work her muscles and clear her mind.

The aluminum boat was heavy. It took her several tries to flip it over. After a short victory dance, she realized she had to push or pull it ten feet to the water. She pushed up her sleeves and started to shove the back of the boat. It didn't budge. Blowing the stray strands of hair from her eyes, she walked around to the front more determined than ever to get the boat into the water. As she pulled, grunting and moaning, the boat moved a couple feet.

"Halfway there," she wheezed, bent over. Resting her hands on her knees, she caught her breath. A couple minutes later, she straightened, wiped her manicured hands on her jeans, and pulled with all her might. The log jammed under the boat gave way. The sudden movement caused Shelby to fly backward and land butt-first into the water.

"Aaah!" she yelped. The water was cold and her jeans were soaked. Standing she flung the water from her arms and stomped over to the log and kicked it. "Stupid log."

She could do one of two things, give up and go sit in the cabin, or change clothes and take the boat out. She was too stubborn to go through all that work, not to take the boat on the water. So while she was wet, she grabbed the rope, and walked the boat into the water, and tied it off so she could go change.

Twenty minutes later, she was in the middle of the lake. It was beautiful. The water was calm, only the occasional ripple to lull her into a peaceful calm. Watching the Canadian geese made her think of all the blessings she had. Family, friends, a good job. She wasn't about to let a two-timing jerk upset her life. She could transfer to a different department. The company was large enough to spend the rest of her career in and never see Justin again.

Shelby didn't want to leave her current position, but she knew it would be easier to make an inter-company move than to get her boss transferred. On that thought, she would look at the job postings when she returned to work.

Spending the rest of the afternoon paddling around, Shelby let the grief of her failed relationship melt away. The hurt and shame of being deceived would take a while longer to shed. The lake worked its magic, by the time she headed for the dock, she was feeling ten times better.

* * *

"Great dinner. I'll help you with the dishes, then I want a rematch." Tanner picked up both their plates and carried them to the sink.

"What? You can't handle losing to a girl?" Shelby flipped her hair over her shoulder and batted her eyelashes at him as she carried their glasses to the sink.

Over the last few days, they had fallen into a comfortable routine. Going their separate ways during the day meeting only at lunch. In the evenings, she would make dinner and then they would hang out by the fire playing games, talking or read for a while before one or both of them were too tired to keep their eyes open.

"I can handle losing, but you cheat."

"I do not!"

"I saw you taking extra points last night. This time I'm pegging and we will see who wins." Tanner leaned in for a menacing effect, but knowing he was playing all Shelby could concentrate on was his woodsy scent which made it hard to think for a moment.

"That… was only once or twice to see if you were paying attention. I was ahead by at least ten points."

He started the water and squirted the dish soap into the sink as he shook his head side to side, tsking. "I see you haven't changed a bit. Still the same little Shelby."

"What do you mean?" The playful light in his eyes had her weary.

"You used to sneak ice cubes into my shoes to see if I would notice. Remember?"

She remembered, she was in eighth grade and sleeping over at Kelly's. Her friend dared her to do it.

"That was all Kelly, I had nothing to do with that." She lied as she picked up a dish towel.

"I think your lying. I may have to teach you a lesson, like last time."

"You wouldn't." *Crap!* She thought as he grabbed the sprayer. The last time he grabbed the ice from his shoe and before she could do more than squeal he had her pinned to the couch and was shoving ice down her shirt.

That was when she looked up into his laughing brown eyes and fell hard, crushing on her friend's older brother.

His devilish smile was enough to make her flinch. *Was he flirting with her? No!* But she realized she was flirting with him. The thought made her take a step back. That and his hand on the sprayer. To break the sexual tension that strummed in her body she said, "Ok, you can keep score this time." And she left the kitchen to set up the cribbage board.

As they played they talked of favorite movies and books, their work, his transfer back to the Twin Cities, anything and everything. The one subject that didn't come up was their personal relationships. He never mentioned a wife, nor she Justin.

After she beat him two games to one she asked, "Don't guys go hunting just for Deer Camp? I thought it was the cigars and poker in the cabin they went for?"

"That's part of it. It's tradition for all the men in my family to come up here for rifle opener, but I also like the quiet of the woods." He shrugged.

She could understand that. She loved the peace of being on the lake with no one else around.

Then he added, "Besides, if you ever shared a cabin with five guys all week, you'd want out, too. Some of them don't shower all week and Uncle Steve snores."

She laughed, "Wouldn't that scare the deer away? Body odor, I mean."

"You would think. We had a guy along one time who sat in the stand eating an apple, smoking a cigar, and listening to the Gopher game, and he still got a deer." He shook his head in disbelief, "It must have been a deaf deer that couldn't smell."

After a week with Tanner, her cheeks hurt from smiling so much.

* * *

Shelby had a long day out on the lake then a walk through the woods. Knowing this, she should have called it a night and headed for the bed. Instead, she sat down on the couch next to Tanner with a cup of tea and a book. Grabbing the quilt off the back, she curled up making a warm cocoon for herself.

Soft snores woke her. She must have fallen asleep instantly because she didn't remember anything after opening her book. Now the fire had died to glowing ambers, and her head was pillowed on Tanner's lap.

Lying still for a moment, Shelby attempted to clear the sleep from her mind without waking Tanner. She wasn't sure how she ended up cuddling with her best friend's brother, but the last thing she wanted to do was wake him and have to face the awkward conversation that would surely follow.

She was sure it was an innocent mistake. Yeah, that was it, she told herself. Even though she couldn't fully convince herself that her feelings for him were strictly platonic. Over the last couple of days, thoughts of Tanner's broad shoulders and make-her-melt brown eyes had been slipping under her defenses.

The snoring stopped, she froze. The hand resting on her shoulder stroked down her side to rest on her hip before she heard the soft snoring continue. Tanner hadn't made even the tiniest flirtation all week. Even if she caught herself flirting with him. He was a complete gentleman. He warned her about walking in the woods at this time of year and gave her an orange sweatshirt to wear. He offered to do all the carrying in of firewood, and told her he would put the rowboat away when she was done using it. She couldn't believe this was anything but an accidental caress.

Slowly, she rose, trying not to wake him, but failing. As she sat up Tanner rubbed her back with the hand from her hip, and he smiled sleepily at her as she turned to face him.

"Umm, I must have fallen asleep, too. You were out in minutes of sitting down."

The look of contentment in his eyes surprised her. It said he could have sat like that all night. She thought his eyes lingered on her lips for a moment longer than casual.

"Well, we should go to bed." His eyes still gazing into hers.

"What?" Feeling like a deer caught in headlights, her heartbeat picked up, and she couldn't look away.

Was he asking her to go to bed with him? Have hot monkey sex all night long? She hoped not, the logical side of her brain said, but she could picture their night together as plain as if she was watching it on an eighty-inch HDTV. Her mouth went dry.

No, surely not. Getting a grip, she quickly blinked to clear lavish lusty thoughts from her mind.

"I don't want to kick you off the couch, but I need to go to sleep if I am getting up at four." He retracted his hand from her back and gestured to the couch.

"Oh, right." He was sleeping on the couch. "Goodnight."

"Goodnight."

Telling herself she imagined the pull between them, she shook her head as she shut the bedroom door behind her.

* * *

Sitting on the dock, Shelby was lost in her thoughts, thoughts of Tanner, thoughts of Justin and thoughts of her future. How could she lust for another married man? Justin had persuaded her and she had to admit she was easily swayed. But Tanner. Tanner hadn't done one thing to lead her on, not intentionally, yet here she was fighting off dream after dream about him. It didn't matter if she was awake or asleep, he filled her thoughts. She was hopeless, she thought shaking her head. She should just join a convent and save all the married men from her roving eyes.

She was still beating herself up when the dock started to bounce with the repetitive movement of footsteps. Turning, she made out Tanner's shape against the sun and smiled involuntarily.

I am in so much trouble, she thought. "Hi," she craned her neck to look up at him as he came to a stop in front of her, "You're in early."

"I got a nice buck." He sat down on the dock beside her, leaned back on his hands and told her how he shot a nice ten-pointer right after sun-up. "It's all ready for the processor so I decided to come out here and enjoy the lake with you."

She watched as he closed his eyes and tipped his face up to the late morning sun. His face was tan and relaxed. He looked at peace with the world. Shelby knew the feeling; the lake did that to a person. Still looking at him, she wondered if maybe Tanner did that for her and not the lake. She would miss their evening talks and games, and there were so many other things she would love to do with him.

"How about I take you into town for lunch today?" His sudden question startled her out of her musing.

His brown eyes suddenly opened and turned to find her staring speechless. "Lunch?"

"Yeah, there's a great café about twenty minutes from here."

After a week in the woods with Tanner, Shelby had forgotten all about civilization. She wasn't sure if she wanted to leave their haven, but the pull of a lunch she didn't have to make was too strong. "All right."

He stood and offered his hand to assist her up. He didn't let go as they walked up the yard. She knew she should release his hand, but she couldn't make herself pull free of his warm, secure clasp until they were at his truck.

The café was a small restaurant with an outdoorsy feel to the interior. The food was delicious.

"This is the best fish I've ever eaten." Shelby wiped her mouth with her napkin as she relaxed back into her chair. She never would have guessed she could find such tasty food this far out of the cities.

"The couple that owns the place brings it in fresh all year round." Tanner reached for the check "Are you up for a little sight-seeing? Or we could head over to the reservation and check out the casino."

"I'd love either. I must confess though, I have only been gambling once and I've never played blackjack."

"Well I'm just the man to teach you. My roommate and I used to go to the casino at least once a month back in college."

He rose from the table and offered her his hand. She took it as they headed off to the local Native American reservation.

The drive was beautiful with the fall colors in full bloom. Tanner pointed out local points of interest along the way while Shelby sat back and enjoyed the timbre of his voice as they drove.

The towns were all small and older around the area, but as they pulled up at the casino, Shelby would have thought they had been dropped into a Las Vegas hotel. The building was newer, a very modern design with flowing curves, an artistic use of steel and wood.

It was busier than Shelby would have guessed at this time of day. Many people sat tapping the slot machine buttons over and over, while others chose the game tables.

Taking her hand again, Tanner leaned down to her ear so not to shout. "The blackjack tables are this way." He led her to a five-dollar table and found two open seats.

The gentleman on Shelby's right reminded her of an old sailor. She had him in height by a couple inches and the hair that ringed his head was pure white. He threw down his cards with flare and cussed at his bad luck.

Turning to find her seated beside him he smiled and leaned in to ask, "Girlie, are you going to bring me some luck?"

"I don't know how lucky I'll be, I've never played before."

The man smiled, showing uneven teeth. "I can teach you. You stick with me," he said with a wink.

"That's what I'm for." Tanner leaned around Shelby and smiled at the older man.

Tanner placed a couple chips on the table in front of Shelby and himself and proceeded to explain the rules of the game. She picked it up fairly quickly with his guidance. And as luck would have it, she started to accumulate a nice size pile of chips, while her neighbor's pile was dwindling.

Just then, an older woman came to stand beside him.

"Honey, I was up one-fifty before she sat down and took all my luck," he fibbed.

"I'm sure." His wife smiled as if she didn't believe a word of it. "Are you ready to go?" she asked her husband.

"Yeah, might as well."

"It was nice to meet you." Shelby smiled as they toddled off in the direction of the doors. She found herself picturing her and Tanner in their eighties as she watched the couple walk off.

Tanner and Shelby played for another half-hour before calling it a day.

They went to the buffet for dinner before heading back to the cabin. Shelby had a wonderful time with Tanner and hated to see the day end.

"That was fun."

"I'll have to take you again, soon."

He didn't mean it. It was just the kind of thing someone said to be polite. But she wanted to believe it. She hoped he wanted to see her again after the week was over. Even if she shouldn't.

She enjoyed Tanner's company and hoped she could get over these little fantasies she was having about him, and remain friends with him back home. Maybe she could invite Kelly and her husband and Tanner and his wife over for dinner one evening. Hopefully she would be dating someone by then. She really didn't want to feel like the fifth wheel.

Back at the cabin, Shelby made them a pot of tea, and they sat on the couch to relax for a few minutes before bedtime.

"Now that you got your deer, will you be heading back to the Twin Cities?" She hoped the sadness at the thought of him leaving didn't show in her question.

"I'll be leaving tomorrow morning. I only took a week off."

"I'm sure your family misses you." Her head never rising from her cup as she asked. She missed his puzzled look then the soft smile that followed.

"Maybe a little."

Not finishing her tea, she put down her cup and turned to smile at him with an overly bright smile, "Well it was nice having company this week. I better let you get some sleep, you have a long drive in the morning."

Before she could stand, Tanner placed a hand on her arm, "Shelby." She froze.

His other hand set down the tea and with gentle fingers lifted her chin. Rich, chocolate-brown eyes gazed into hers. She couldn't look away if her life depended on it, and they searched hers for a long moment before he lowered his head.

Shelby felt her eyes close of their own accord. When his warm lips touched hers she almost sighed. It was a gentle kiss. Feeling her respond, Tanner claimed her mouth with more intensity. Shelby felt herself being swept away in his kiss and open to him. He was thorough in his exploration of her mouth, coaxing her to explore as well.

Coming to her senses, Shelby broke the kiss to find she had not only been swept up in his kiss, but in his arms as well. She was in his lap with her arms around his neck and her fingers entwined in his soft, thick hair. Appalled by the ease which she forgot her morals, she quickly untangled herself from his embrace. She would have been naked with this man in minutes if she hadn't had the mind to stop.

"I, um, I'm sorry. I need to go." She just about ran to the bedroom door.

"Shelby?" He started to stand.

At the door, she paused and turned back to him, staying him with a shake of her head. "No. If I don't see you tomorrow, have a safe trip back." Then she fled before he could change her mind.

Oh, he could change her mind she was afraid, with a soulful look and a gesture to her, she would be falling back into his arms and into his bed in no time. *No!* She would never let herself do that, no matter how much she was drawn to him.

* * *

Shelby woke early after a long night of tossing and turning. She could hear Tanner moving around the cabin, but no way was she going out there to face him this morning. The way she lit up when he touched her was bad enough, but explaining her prior relationship with a married man would be worse than doing the walk of shame from the men's dorm in a short mini and heels her freshmen year at State.

She wished she could call Kelly but she couldn't, not having cell service was only part of the reason. What would she say? "Hey, I kissed your brother last night. I know he's married, but I wanted to ride him like a stallion."

"Yeah, that would go over well." What would her friend say?

She shook off the morose thoughts when she heard the cabin door open and close. Tiptoeing to the door with the stealth of a ninja, she peered out, no sign of Tanner. Closing the door, she slumped against it. She wasn't a coward, not usually, but the thought of facing him had her heart beating wild and her stomach churning.

"He's gone." She took a calming breath and opened the bedroom door, only to find him sitting at the little table, hands folded waiting for her.

Now who was the ninja?

"I see you finally got up." He sat in a relaxed pose as if it was any other day.

"Yes, I thought you left." She said stating the obvious.

"I loaded my truck." He stood and started towards her, "I was hoping to catch you before you ran into the bedroom avoiding me again."

"I wasn't avoiding you." She tried for indignant but couldn't quite pull it off. "I slept late, that's all." She stiffened her resolve as he stood in front of her all strong and male.

"Let me give you a tip. Don't play poker for money. You're a lousy liar." He moved closer, but stopped when she shifted away. "What's going on here? I thought you and I had something good starting. I know you were into me on the couch last night." Her cheeks pinked. "Then it's like I have lice or something. Was I moving too fast?"

Shelby let out the breath she was holding, turning she walked to the couch. Having second thoughts, she sat on the chair instead.

"Tanner, I can't get involved with you."

"Why? You didn't mention a guy. Is it because of my sister? I don't think she'd mind," he asked when she didn't elaborate.

She shook her head, not sure how to continue, then asked, "Do you love your wife?"

"My what?" His brows furrowed as he stared at her.

"Your wife. I met her once you know. And knowing you, I can't imagine you cheating on her if you loved her."

He walked over to her then, kneeled before her and looked her straight in the eyes before saying, "Shelby, what are you talking about? I take things like wedding vows very seriously. I will always love and honor the woman I marry. *When* I marry."

Her heart fell, the thud in her chest seemed audible at the thought of Tanner loving his wife until the day he died. His words replayed in her head, and her own brow furrowed as his last words sunk in. *When I marry.*

He doesn't have a wife? Confused she said, "I met her at Kelly and Al's wedding."

Tanner shook his head. "You met my fiancé. My fiancé of all of a month. We found out pretty quickly we wanted different things for the future. I wanted kids and a house in the suburbs, and she wanted a fast-paced career. I think I got caught up in all the wedding mojo in the air. Jill was never the girl for me."

"So you never married?" He shook his head, "And you like me?" he chuckled at the sophomoric way she phrased the question.

"Very much." He took her hands in his.

Shelby was quiet for a moment, but didn't pull her hands away. "I thought you were married and only wanted an affair."

"I gather that." He looked downcast, dejected even, that she could ever think he was capable of such a thing.

Seeing his expression she swallowed hard, knowing she had to explain. "Tanner, I just broke up with my boyfriend. I found out he lied to me about being married." Her gaze was glued to their hands, she couldn't look at him and see the blame she knew would be in his eyes. "He was my boss. I came up here to figure out what to do next."

"And have you? Figured it out, I mean."

She nodded, "I think so."

"Does it include me?" When she didn't answer right away he lifted her face to his, "I sure hope it does."

She saw no blame or disgust. She only saw caring and kindness.

"Oh, Shelby." He watched as tears shimmered in her beautiful eyes.

Blinking the moisture from her eyes, she smiled softly, "I want it to."

He pulled her into his arms and kissed her. "We can move as slow as you want."

Winding her arms around his neck, she pulled his face down so she could taste his enticing lips. "Not too slow, I hope."

"Good, because I'm a patient man, but I don't think I could wait very long to have you in my life." His lips claimed hers, and then softly added, "Or in my bed."

"Then we should start right now." She walked backward, leading him to the bedroom, never taking her lips from his, thinking the whole time how this little cabin on the lake was magical.

ABOUT THE AUTHOR

Diane Wiggert is the youngest of a large family and lives in her hometown with her husband, son and her two crazy canines. When she's not writing or reading she's hanging out with her family and friends. Diane is currently working on a contemporary romance trilogy set in a small southern Minnesota town with strong friendships and loud opinionated families.

RAILROAD TIES

Rose Marie Meuwissen

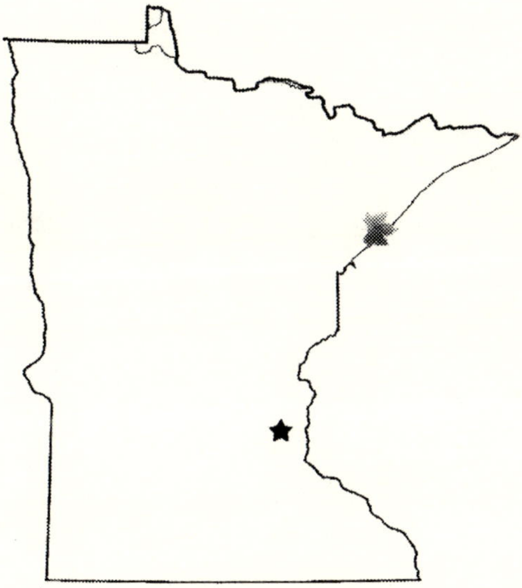

Lake Superior, Two Harbors

Kayla Langley couldn't believe she was doing this. In fact, she was absolutely positive she didn't want to do it and it was most likely the worst idea her best friend, Sara, ever had. Every mile she drove further up north, towards Duluth, the vibrant gold and fiery reds of fall deepened and intensified. The landscape was undeniably a beautiful and amazing scene to behold since Minnesota was having one of its best years for fall colors in a long time. Unfortunately, her mind was inundated with memories of past drives up north with Kevin. He loved their yearly drive up to Duluth every September. Most years luck had been on their side and they managed to catch a sunny weekend. Today, it looked like luck was on her side again as the forecast was for sunny days with temps in the high seventies.

She saw the exit sign for Toby's restaurant in Hinkley and took the exit ramp off the freeway. One just couldn't go up to Duluth without stopping at Toby's for a cinnamon or caramel roll. Breakfast probably would be a good thing since she'd only had a bottle of water so far this morning.

Eating alone in a restaurant wasn't something she liked to do, but since Kevin lost his battle with pancreatic cancer two years ago, she'd learned to be okay with it. Her eyes watered for a moment as she remembered the many times they'd walked into Toby's restaurant together. *Why was she doing this?* She knew this trip would stir up memories of Kevin and she was completely unsure how this was going to help her get over him. Losing Kevin still hurt and she wasn't sure it would ever stop hurting.

"Here's your caramel roll all heated up, nice and warm," the waitress said as she set the plate down.

"Thanks," Kayla answered and mustered up a smile. The caramel had melted and the butter, she placed on the top of the roll, quickly melted and ran down the sides. She took a bite and was swept away in the moment as her taste buds enjoyed the scrumptious flavor of mingling caramel and cinnamon. Of course, there was no way she could eat the whole thing as Toby's was known for their generous portions. No, Kevin was not there to eat his half so she would take it with her and save it for breakfast tomorrow or a snack later on.

Back on the road again, she listened to her new American Idol CD and tried to figure out just what she was going to do once she got to Duluth. In her bag, she had a couple of books to read—the actual paper kind. Her Kindle was also in the bag loaded with more E-books to read. It was the new tech age so she'd purchased the E-reader, but she still preferred to hold a print book in her hands while she read. Old habits just seemed to die hard. Her plan was to relax, read and get started writing her next book. But, what she was going to write about, she had no idea. Hopefully, she would come up with something this weekend.

She had a reservation at the Northern Rail Traincar Inn, just off Lake Superior on Lake Shore Scenic Drive near Two Harbors. It was a hotel Kevin had mentioned and they'd planned to make a reservation to stay there the next year. But, he got sick and they hadn't made it back up to the North Shore again. Kevin loved trains, both small model trains and the large actual locomotives, and the Northern Rail Traincar Inn consisted of authentic train boxcars, complete with graffiti, connected by a walkway and converted into hotel rooms. *Why had she let Sara talk her into this?* Staying there was only going to make her feel more sad and alone. What she really needed to do was cancel the reservation and stay in a hotel back in Duluth. But then, she would lose her deposit, so she just needed to work through it.

It was lunchtime when she pulled into Duluth, so she stopped down at the Duluth Boardwalk area, parked close to the shops and restaurants so she could do a little shopping after lunch before driving the rest of the way to Two Harbors.

It was a beautiful sunny day and actually warm even with the cool wind blowing in off Lake Superior. Ivar's food truck stood parked along the Boardwalk selling fish and chips so she placed an order. She found an empty bench with a view of the lakefront where she could watch the boats coming and going and sat down to eat. Her heart broke as she watched the couples walking by holding hands, smiling at each other. She needed to move on. Her friends told her to, along with her grief counselor, but her heart kept saying no, not yet. But, deep down she knew it was time. She wanted to feel happy again. She wanted to feel all the pleasures and joys of being in love again. But, she couldn't even begin to imagine where in the world she was going to find another man who made her feel happy again, love again. She had absolutely no idea where to begin. Maybe once she decided she was ready to move on, she would find that special man, since it always helped to be looking. At least it couldn't hurt. Right?

After eating lunch, she purchased a few things in the quaint boutique shops along the boardwalk. With her new found treasures in hand, she walked back to her car. She left the parking lot and merged onto the Lake Shore drive to Two Harbors. The houses lining this scenic drive were a combination of old and new world. Some were mansions from a bygone era and some were new ones built according to today's standards with six car garages, swimming pools, and guesthouses. They were all magnificent and pristine.

A little bit further out of town, the road split into the bypass highway or the scenic lakeshore drive. She opted for the latter. Heck, she wasn't in any hurry, so she decided on the road with awesome views of Lake Superior and the incredible fall colors. The two roads joined again right before entering Two Harbors. Highway 61 went right through town and was lined with shops—boutiques, antique stores, touristy stores, bars and restaurants. Kayla debated on stopping to shop, but decided to keep going and get checked into the hotel first. She could always come back later when she became bored, which wasn't going to take much.

She only had a few more miles to go since she had just passed Betty's Pies. Their parking lot was full which confirmed their popularity among the tourists to the area. It was still early, but she was definitely going to have dinner there later. Finally, she saw the sign for the entrance into the Northern Rail Traincar Inn. She drove down the long driveway and pulled up by the front door. The hotel was made out of two rows of actual train boxcars resting on real railroad tracks and hooked together with a hallway down the center. Kevin would've loved this place. No sense sitting out in the car feeling sorry for herself and Kevin, so she got out of the car and went inside to check in.

"Welcome," said the man at the front desk.

Kayla handed him her reservation print out and he proceeded to check her in. "Thanks," she said taking her key card and receipt.

There was a bookshelf in the lobby filled with books and she was drawn to it by her love of books and writing, so she walked over to take a look. It was filled with children's books and adult novels, mostly ones portraying

Lake Superior and Northern Minnesota. She flipped through a couple, but it only made her feel guilty knowing she hadn't done any writing since Kevin was diagnosed with cancer, three years ago. When they found out he wouldn't make it, she felt compelled to spend all her time with him, consequently she hadn't written.

She couldn't write, not when she was surrounded by pain and anger. Anger about the cards dealt her. But, now it was time to start writing again. In fact, that was one of the main reasons she'd decided to come to Two Harbors on the North Shore of Lake Superior, she badly needed some inspiration to jump-start her writing. She knew one day she wanted to write a story about Kevin and his heroic fight against cancer, but now wasn't the time. No, she needed to write about something happy and what she really needed to do was feel like love was still a possibility, because how else was she ever going to be able to write another romance novel? Especially one with a happy ending?

Deep in thought, she made her way towards the door so she could park her car and get her bags. Just then, she walked right smack into a rock hard manly chest that smelled so good she wanted to lay her head right down on it. She felt strong hands on her arms gently pushing her back away from the little bit of heaven she'd just landed on.

"Sorry, ma'am," he said staring down into her bright blue eyes.

"No, my fault, I wasn't paying attention," Kayla said looking up into his warm brown eyes and a beautiful smile revealing perfect and straight white teeth. He was about six feet tall, at least five inches taller than her, muscular with short-cropped dark brown hair. Her body had reacted boldly on its own to this man and she could still feel the fire in the pit of her stomach. *What was wrong with her?* It had been way too long since she'd been with a man, that's what was wrong. Apparently her body knew what it needed even if her head didn't. She backed away a little more, totally at a loss for words.

"Dad, wait for me." The wood door opened and a young boy about ten years old came running through the open door and stopped right behind the man.

"Hi," the boy said. "I'm Tanner. What's your name?" He walked around to stand in front of his dad.

At a loss of how to get out of introductions, she answered, "I'm Kayla.

Happy to meet you." She held out her hand and the boy extended his hand to shake hers. She looked back up to the man who was staring at her.

"I'm Josh. Tanner's dad. Nice to meet you. The two of us are spending a few days up here to check out some special trains in the area. Are you checking in or out?"

"In," she answered. Kayla noticed him looking at her ring finger where she still wore her wedding rings. *Damn!* She should've never been wearing them. They should be at home or at the very least on the other hand. She'd already noticed he didn't have a ring on. Probably divorced. *What the Hell was she doing?*

"Well, we'll probably see you around here then." He took Tanner's hand and they walked past her to the front desk to check in.

"Probably." Kayla smiled and walked out the door of the hotel.

She got into her car and moved it to the parking lot. *What an idiot she was!* She was so intent on not moving on, she was still wearing her wedding rings. If you weren't looking, it just didn't matter, that was why, and she hadn't been looking up until a few minutes ago. This was her weekend to get her act back together and move on. She should've left the rings at home. The diamond sparkled in the sunlight. She loved the ring, it was a part of her. No, it was a symbol of *their* marriage, *their* life together. It was over though. He was gone. She slipped the rings off her finger and put them carefully and lovingly inside the zippered compartment in her purse. There. She'd done it. She was going to move on. Hopefully, it wasn't too late. She got out, opened the trunk and took out her suitcases. As she closed the trunk, she heard a truck drive up beside her. It was Josh and Tanner.

Josh got out and walked towards her. "Just wanted to apologize for walking into you earlier. You are a really beautiful woman… Any guy would find you attractive… You caught me off guard. I noticed the wedding ring afterwards."

"I'm not."

"Not?" Josh asked looking at her ring finger now bare.

"I'm a widow. Just hadn't had a reason to take them off before."

"We're good then?" he asked.

"Josh's mother?" Kayla asked.

"I'm divorced," he stated.

"We're good then," she smiled.

The truck door closed and Tanner stood next to his dad. "I'm getting hungry. When are we going to go eat?"

"A little later."

"I'm going to get settled in. See you later." Kayla nodded and walked back into the lobby.

"Later," Josh said as she walked away.

Kayla got everything put away in her room, the whole time wondering how he was going to see her later if he didn't know her room number.

She took out her laptop and powered it up. A writer always had a file folder full of one page story ideas which was probably the best place to find an idea to get started writing again. She picked one titled, *Heating up the Glacier*, about falling in love on a train ride to Glacier Park in Montana. One about trains. Yes, that would work. After reading the first page of ideas for the story, she started writing. A couple of hours later, she could no longer put up with her rumbling stomach. Betty's Pies was calling her name.

The parking lot was still full, when she pulled into a parking spot around five. Josh's car was still parked in the spot next to her when she left, leaving no chance of running into him again. She put her name on the list and sat down on a bench in the lobby to wait. The twenty minutes passed slowly while she sat on the bench alone observing the other people waiting. Mostly couples, in fact, she was the only one who was alone. She hated this the most. The eating alone at restaurants. It made her want to get in her car and just go home. Her number, 59, was next though, so she would just wait, mainly because she was famished. She got up to look at the pies in the glass case. The pies looked absolutely enticing, she could hardly wait to taste the triple berry pie.

"Kayla."

She heard her name and turned around to see Tanner walking quickly towards her. "Hi," she said and saw Josh walking towards her also.

"Doesn't surprise me to see you here, since it is the only restaurant near the hotel," Josh said and walked over to the counter to get a number. Number 80.

"59," the hostess at the counter shouted to be heard.

Kayla heard her number called and walked over to the counter. "Can I change that to three?"

"Of course, the table seats four anyway," the hostess said.

"Just a moment," Kayla said and walked over to Josh and Tanner. "Would you guys like to join me for dinner? My table is ready now and then you wouldn't have to wait. I'd love the company."

Josh smiled, "Sure, thanks."

The three of them followed the waitress to a table. They ordered quickly. Kayla wasn't sure what she'd just gotten herself into but Josh was definitely a hunk. "What do you do, Josh, besides like trains?"

"I'm the Mesaba Division Supervisor for the Canadian National Railroad. I oversee all the train operations on the Mesaba Iron Range in northern Minnesota. How about you?" Josh asked.

"I'm a writer."

"Wow, didn't think people could really make a living doing that."

"Some people do. I haven't put anything new out in the last couple of years though," she answered.

"I like to draw," Tanner said. "I'll show you some of my stuff later at the hotel."

"I'd love to see it," Kayla said. "I've thought about writing a children's book, but I would never attempt the illustrations. I'm awful at drawing."

"So what do you write?" Josh asked.

"Promise you won't laugh?" she asked.

Josh nodded.

"Romance novels."

"Really? Wow." Josh searched her face for what she wasn't sure. He was silent for a few moments, and then said, "I'd like to read one of your books sometime. You'll have to tell me your last name though. Or do you write under a different name? I heard some people do that."

"My last name is Langley, but I use my maiden name. Kayla Winters."

"Dad, can I read her book, too?" Tanner asked.

"My books are just for adults, Tanner."

"Oh," Tanner said.

Dinner tasted absolutely delicious and the pie was so scrumptious it satisfied every taste bud's anticipation. Tanner talked non-stop with Josh offering more info about his job.

They got up to leave and Josh picked up the tab, "I got this."

"You don't have to do that."

"Of course, I do. You let us butt in line and saved us at least a half hour of waiting for a table."

"Okay, if you insist," she said as they walked out to their cars.

Walking back into the hotel, Tanner ran in ahead of them.

Josh stopped walking, so Kayla did also.

"I'd like to spend more time talking to you. After Tanner goes to bed, would you meet me at the hot tub?" Josh asked.

"Sure, what time?" Kayla asked.

"Does ten work?" Josh asked.

"Yes, I'll see you then."

Back in her room, Kayla was as excited as a high school girl. *What was she thinking to agree to meet a new man in her swimming suit?* Swimsuits just laid it all out there. She wasn't apprehensive about her figure, no, that was definitely not a concern, but still a swimsuit was a little bit too little. Her dark red hair fell just past her shoulders and she needed to decide whether to leave it down or put it up for the hot tub. She decided on up in a brown clip.

She'd never been overweight, in fact, she'd lost weight through Kevin's whole cancer ordeal. After Kevin died, eating had lost its appeal. Today had been different though, she actually was hungry and enjoyed the meal. Especially the pie. Josh would like what he saw and for some reason she really wanted him to. It came back to that old thing called chemistry and she certainly felt it with Josh.

At ten she slid the cover-up over her bikini, walked down to the lobby and outside to the hot tub. The temp had dropped to sixty, but the sky was clear and filled with stars. It always amazed her how much brighter the stars were in northern Minnesota, especially once you got out of the cities. Even though she couldn't see Lake Superior, she knew it lay just behind the trees and road. She could faintly hear the waves lapping the shore. She saw Josh in the hot tub waiting for her. Slowly the cover-up dropped to the ground, she reached down, picked it up and laid it on a chair. For now, they had the hot tub to themselves. The water was hot, but comfortable considering the air temp. She could feel his eyes watching her as she entered the water; she smiled at him.

"Glad you came," Josh said.

"I said I would," Kayla answered sitting down across from him, mainly because she was extremely nervous and way too scared to sit next to him. Besides, it would be easier to talk to him this way.

"Tanner wanted to come along, but I told him it was adult time now."

"Was he okay with that?" she asked.

"Not really, but he knew he wasn't going to get to come, so he went to bed."

"This is really awkward," Kayla said watching his eyes looking at her and a huge smile spread across his face.

"That's because we don't know each other yet, so tell me about yourself. How long have you been writing?" Josh asked.

"Oh, probably my whole life. I was first published about ten years ago. I have an English degree from the University of Minnesota. What else can you do with an English degree besides write or teach? I'm not cut out to teach and I have so many stories in my head needing to be written."

"I Googled you and found you have an impressive list of published books. I think I may have to read my first romance novel," Josh laughed.

"As a guy, you probably would like one of my contemporary novels best."

"I'll keep that in mind, while choosing one."

"What exactly do you do for the railroad as a division supervisor?" Kayla asked.

"I oversee all the train movements on the Mesaba Range, mainly involving transporting ore from the mines to the ore docks on Lake Superior in Two Harbors and Duluth. I grew up around trains and have always liked anything to do with them. That's one of the main reasons we are staying at this hotel. In case you hadn't noticed, it's made out of train cars." Josh pointed back to the hotel train cars.

"I had noticed," she laughed.

"And tomorrow an old World War II steam engine, The 261, will be pulling into Two Harbors. Tanner likes trains, too. Like father, like son, as they say. He hasn't seen a real steam engine fired up and pulling a train before. It is a sight to see, just like out of the old movies."

"I'd like to see it. I've always been a fan of the old movies and the ones with trains usually have romances in them," she said smiling coyly.

"I see. Maybe you'd like to join us tomorrow?" Josh asked.

"Maybe," she answered.

The jets on the hot tub stopped. Josh got out to reset the timer. Seconds later, he was sitting on her side of the tub. She was getting too hot so she got up and sat on the edge of the tub.

"This may be a little forward, but what happened to Tanner's mother?" Kayla asked.

"She became pregnant when we were dating, so we got married, but she was a wild one and after Tanner was born she tried to be a wife and mother for a couple of years. It just wasn't her thing to be married, much less be a mother. She divorced me and gave me full custody of Tanner. She never liked the cold winters here, so she said she was going to California. Haven't heard from her since. "

"Oh, I'm sorry. It must've been hard to be a single dad all these years. And it must be hard on Tanner to have no contact with his mother," Kayla said and slipped back into the water, as she was chilled now.

"All I can do is be the best Dad I can. We do pretty good. My mother helps me a lot with Tanner. She lives in Duluth, too." Josh turned to face her. "Can I ask about your husband?"

"Kevin. We met in college and married after graduation. He liked trains, too. We had, actually still have, a model railroad in the basement of our house in Forest Lake. My house now. He got pancreatic cancer about three years ago. There really isn't much you can do to fight it, but we tried the chemo, which gave him another six months. He's been gone now for two years." Tears filled her eyes as she talked. "I'm sorry, it still hurts to lose someone you were planning on spending the rest of your life with."

"I'm sorry. You didn't say anything about children?" Josh asked reaching over to place his hand over her hand resting on the edge of the tub.

"We hadn't got to it yet. We wanted to. We talked about it, but then he got sick."

Josh brought his other hand up under her chin and their lips met in a kiss. His lips moved slowly over hers and then he deepened the kiss. She responded with every fiber of her being, as her arm went around his neck. It felt good and it had been a long time since she'd felt this kind of pleasure. At least two years. Josh ended the kiss.

She stared into his eyes and became lost to the fire burning in them and inside her. She stood up, stepped out of the hot tub and wrapped a towel around her now chilled body.

Josh got out, grabbed his towel, and wiped off the dripping water from his body. He stood in front of her. "I didn't mean to scare you off."

"No, you didn't. Never was a fan of sex in the hot tub." She smiled and watched Josh's face for signs of approval. He smiled back at her. "I'm in room 220. See you in 15 minutes?"

"You got it!" Josh said and they walked back inside. He left her at her door.

Kayla stripped, dried off and threw on the cover up. This was daring. Josh was a good man, she could tell by the way he'd raised Tanner. He was unbelievably good looking, and the attraction was so strong she wasn't going to bother fighting it. Hell, she'd been with a couple of other guys before she met Kevin, it would be fine. She heard a knock at the door, walked over and opened the door. Josh stood there dressed in jean shorts and a button down short-sleeved shirt, he hadn't bothered to button, wearing a huge grin on his face. He stepped inside and shut the door behind him.

As soon as the door shut, he pulled her into his arms, where she went willingly. His lips descended on hers in a soul-searching kiss devouring both of them. Minutes later, they were lying on the bed wrapped in each other's arms, he was kissing her neck and his hands reached up to cup her breast. She felt the recognition in his hand when he realized she didn't have anything on underneath the cover up dress, which heightened her response. His hand moved to the hem of the cover up dress sliding it upwards, and she felt his finger slide smoothly inside her as her body arched into his touch. Her orgasm came quickly.

The cover up dress slid further up and over her head. She watched him stand to remove his shorts revealing he too hadn't bothered to put anything on underneath them. His hand slid into his pocket removing a condom which he slid on quickly. He was ready, that was apparent. She waited anticipating his entry into her body. His chest was hovering over hers as his lips suckled her breasts one at a time, then moved to her lips as she felt him seeking entrance. He moved slowly in and out, gradually building speed until she cried out and minutes later so did he. He pulled out slowly and moved beside her on the bed. She surveyed every inch of his naked body as he came to lie next to her. *Oh, how she liked what she saw!* Sex with him had met her every expectation. It was a bit quick, but she was in a hurry this time too, since it had been way too long.

"Sorry, that was so quick," he said gently brushing a stray hair from her face. "It's been a while since I've slept with a woman. Next time we'll take our time."

"It's been at least two years for me. I don't think I would've been able to take my time either. Not this time, but next time would be good."

Josh got up and put his shorts back on and Kayla slipped her cover up dress over her head.

"I have to go back to the room. Tanner. Sometimes being a dad has its drawbacks." He put his shirt on and walked to the door.

Kayla followed him to the door. "What time are we leaving to go see The 261?"

Josh smiled, pulled her against his chest and kissed her. "Ten. See you in the lobby tomorrow morning."

Kayla watched him walk down the hall to his room and shut the door. She lay down on the bed and smiled. She'd done it. She'd taken the first step, actually, it was a big step, to moving on. It had felt great, everything she remembered it could be between a man and a woman. It would be a package deal, though, and was she ready to be a mom? She really hadn't thought about it before. She'd always wanted to have children, but a ten-year-old boy. *Could she do it?* Tanner seemed to like her. That was a plus. But the biggest plus was it appeared Josh liked her.

At ten in the morning, she watched Josh and Tanner walk down the hall to meet her. She'd debated the whole morning whether she should drive her own car or ride with them. Heck, she'd just had sex with the guy. She should be able to trust him enough to get in his car. *Right?*

"Ready?" Josh asked.

"Ready. Can't wait to see this steam engine," Kayla said as she watched Tanner's face filled with excitement to go and see the train.

"Me, too," Tanner said and walked up to her taking her hand. "I'm glad you're going with us. I like you, Kayla."

Fifteen minutes later they pulled into Two Harbors' train station's parking lot. The lot was full of families with small children and other train enthusiasts milling about everywhere.

"I brought my paper notebook along. I'm going to draw the train when it gets here," Tanner said to Kayla as they walked towards the platform to wait with the crowd.

"I'm glad you came. I hope you won't be bored," Josh said.

"Not a chance. I'm going to use a train in the story I'm working on, so this will be good writing research," she answered. "Besides, I like your company."

"See the steam down that way, it's coming," Josh said to Tanner while pointing toward the train just rounding the curve in the tracks.

The jet-black, massive, old world, steam engine proudly thundered along the tracks leaving a trail of billowing steam and smoke in its wake. It exuded power as if it was a living and breathing black stallion galloping into town. Lake Superior's sky blue water glistened in the bright sun a few yards away. A totally impressive scene and one she would definitely have to use in a story some time. She was glad to be here with this man and boy who'd literally just walked into her life.

The 261 engine shuddered to a stop at the station and Tanner pulled out his paper and began drawing the proud 261 engine. His concentration was impressive as his pencil flew across the paper.

It was very good. He was talented, that was apparent. Maybe the children's book, she'd always wanted to write, was going to happen. How perfect it would be for her to write a children's story about trains to honor Kevin's love of model trains along with Josh and Tanner's love of real trains. She could even have Tanner draw the train pictures for it.

Josh had been talking to the train engineer and now came over to stand beside her. He effortlessly put his arm around her and casually pulled her to him.

"I never gave much thought to all the stuff about love at first sight, but I know I could definitely fall in love with you. Where do you want to go from here?" Josh asked. His face revealed the sincerity of his confession.

"I think that may be a good starting point. You, falling in love with me, that is. And, I think I could easily fall in love with you, too," Kayla said wearing her heart on her sleeve.

"We may live a few miles apart, but I think it's totally doable," Josh said.

"I can do my writing from anywhere, so I don't see location as a problem," Kayla said and leaned into him as his lips met hers. It was her time to move on and she was finally ready.

Thank God for trains! They'd brought Kevin years of pleasure and now they would hopefully be a part of her new life, too. Along with these two special men, Josh and Tanner.

ABOUT THE AUTHOR

Rose Marie Meuwissen, a first-generation Norwegian American born and raised in Minnesota, always tries to incorporate her Norwegian heritage into her writing. *Real Norwegians Eat Lutefisk*, a bilingual children's book about the tradition of Lutefisk in both English and Norwegian, is her first published book. *Real Norwegians Eat Rømmegrøt*, a bilingual children's book about the tradition of Rømmegrøt in both English and Norwegian, is the second book in the *Real Norwegians* series and is now available. *Dancing in the Moonlight*, a short romance story set on a Mille Lacs Lake, is available in the anthology, *Love in the Land of Lakes*. *Hot Summer Nights*, a short romance story set on Prior Lake, is available in the anthology, *Romancing the Lakes of Minnesota—Summer*.

After receiving a BA in Marketing from Concordia University, a Masters in Creative Writing from Hamline University soon followed. Minnesota is still where she calls home.

She has been a member of Romance Writers of America (RWA) since 1995 and has attended multiple RWA National Conferences and Romantic Times Conventions in Houston, New Orleans, New York, Denver, Orlando, Daytona, Kansas City, Chicago and Atlanta. In 2012, she became co-founder of Romancing the Lakes of Minnesota, a local RWA Chapter in Minnesota.

She has traveled around the world, including Scandinavia, but still has many places to see, enjoys attending Scandinavian events, writing conferences and is usually busy writing Contemporary and Viking Time Travel Romances, Motorcycle Rally Screenplays, Nordic Cozy Murder Mysteries, WWII Nazi Occupation of Norway Historical fiction and Norwegian Traditions Children's Books.

Visit her at www.rosemariemeuwissen.com or www.realnorwegianseatlutefisk.com .

Enjoy!
Kathleen Nordstrom

THE INHERITANCE

Kathleen Nordstrom

Big Stone Lake, Ortonville

"I, Matilda (Matty) Blackstone, leave the Blackstone Ranch and Lodge to my friend Russell Elliott. All my personal belongings Katherine Whitfield can dispose of as she sees fit. My lawyer, Charles Harris, shall handle any financial transactions that occur while settling my estate and any debts occurring from transfer of ownership of the Blackstone Ranch estate.

This is my last will and testament, which releases Katherine Whitfield of all obligations and responsibilities to the Blackstone Ranch estate, thus giving her, her freedom to pursue her life as she pleases.

Signed: Matilda (Matty) Blackstone"

Mr. Harris folded up Matilda Blackstone's will after reading it to Katherine. He took out an old shoebox from his desk drawer, tied up with dirty string and placed it on his desk in front of her.

"This is my inheritance? A beat up, old shoe box?" Kate said sarcastically as tears rolled down her cheeks. She stood up and leaned over the desk towards him with her hands cupped around the edge of the desktop. "This is a joke, right?" She asked in an irritated whisper, holding back tears.

Charles Harris cleared his throat and straightened his tie. "Well, Miss Whitfield. Before you get upset, why don't –"

"Upset!" Kate cut him off. "Why don't I what?" She shoved the shoebox toward Mr. Harris. "Why shouldn't I be upset? You've known my grandmother for years, but you don't know anything about me." Kate snapped the question at him as she slapped down her right palm on the desk leaving a foggy handprint on the glossy finish.

"Now Miss Whitfield," Mr. Harris said dryly. He straightened in his chair. "As I tried to say, why don't you –"

"Why don't I what?" Kate swatted at the shoebox with the back of her hand knocking it closer to him.

His baldhead took on a rosy color while he started to perspire. "Why don't you see what's inside the box before jumping to any rash conclusions." He took out a crisp white hanky from the inside pocket of his tweed jacket and wiped his large brow and pushed the box back towards her.

Kate pulled one side of the string and the box was quickly freed of it. She stared inside the box. "I don't believe it." Kate looked back up at Mr. Harris. "It's full of letters, tied up with more dirty string."

"It's my understanding they are cards and letters from Matty's husband when he was in the Dakotas," he said wiping his upper lip this time.

"This has to be a joke. Why would I want her old love letters?"

"No, your grandmother was quite serious about you having this box of letters."

Kate cautiously sat down again in the brown leather chair in front of Mr. Harris' desk. She whispered, "This is my inheritance. Old letters. You owe me an explanation."

"I don't know what you mean, Miss Whitfield." He poured himself a glass of water from the sterling silver water pitcher sitting on the corner of his desk.

Kate's dark brown eyes turned black as she struggled to control her anger. She fixed her stare on Mr. Harris. "I want an explanation for this nonsense."

"Maybe if you'd read the letters, you'd understand reasons why she did things. Miss Whitfield, I am not the enemy here. I'm just the messenger."

"The messenger? You must have known about this. Didn't you draw up her will?"

"Yes I did. Her will was drawn up about a year ago when Matilda found out she had terminal cancer. I wrote the will exactly as the lady wanted it written," he said nervously.

"She was no lady. She was an old witch. She wasn't happy unless she was making someone miserable."

"I, uh, wouldn't know," he picked up the glass and took a sip of water.

Kate slumped in her chair. "So what do I do now?"

"Katherine?"

"Call me Kate, Mr. Harris. Katherine is too formal."

"Kate," he hesitated. "I think you ought to go home and read all the letters and documents in the shoe box before you make any decisions. I'm sure after reading them you'll have a clear understanding of your grandmother's intentions." He handed her a large envelope, "In this envelope are her burial instructions."

"I'm sure you know what they are. Probably something unusual," Kate said sounding exhausted.

"Well, yes they are," he said.

"Just tell me what they are."

"She wants to be cremated and her ashes mixed with Russell Elliot's when he dies and spread all of them over the ranch."

Kate stared to laugh. "I might have known she'd want something weird."

After a long silence, Kate stood up and took the box of letters off his desk. She shook hands with him. "Thank you for your help. I'll call you after I've read through all the letters."

Kate left the Ortonville, MN, Big Stone County Courthouse and drove back to the ranch. It was a beautiful fall day and the road was lined with majestic trees, their leaves of red, yellow and gold showing off in the breeze. The warm fall air circulated the pungent smell of drying leaves with the foreshadowing of bone fires to come with high school homecoming festivities and football games. All this natural beauty of the season did nothing for her mood as her head was swimming with questions. Why, why had Matty done this to her?

* * *

She drove straight home to the Blackstone Ranch. When she got there, she ran to the horse stables, into the stall of her favorite horse, Deacon, a tall, stately black stallion. She threw the shoebox down in the hay, before she buried her face in Deacon's neck and cried. "Deacon, she gave it all away to Russell. I have no home. What am I going to do?" Deacon snorted and nudged Katherine's head. She cried to exhaustion and fell asleep in the hay.

Several hours later, she awoke to Deacon's snorting. He was nudging the shoebox in the hay with his nose, as if to tell her the answers were in the box. She opened the shoebox. On top of a stack of letters tied with a ragged, faded blue ribbon, were two envelopes. The top letter was marked open first. Deacon nudged her shoulder. "Ok, ok, I'll read it to you," Kate said.

"Dear Kate,

If, you are reading this, I must be dead.

I'm writing this to you because I found out I have cancer. Doc says there's nothing they can do. It's too far along. Since your parents died, leaving you here twenty years ago, in my care, I know you haven't been happy living with me. I know you've been even more unhappy having to take care of things while I was sick and waiting to die.

I've been mad at someone or something ever since I got stuck out here at this blasted ranch on the Big Stone River, so close to the South Dakota State border. My husband Henry brought me here after winning this ranch in a poker game in Deadwood, South Dakota. He was always going off to find his fortune and that's how he got caught up in gambling. A few years after we moved here, I heard he was shot cheating at cards in Deadwood. That's how I came to running things on my own.

Now that I'm gone, I'm going to give you your freedom. You can leave the Blackstone Ranch and go off to the four corners of the earth, or live in the city, to find what you've been longing for all these years. I know you blame your parents for going off to chaperone that church mission trip and leaving you here. It's not my fault they were killed in a bus accident in the mountains of Mexico.

Take what you want for souvenirs, my lawyer Charles Harris will help you get to where you want to go. Just stop being so unhappy and mad at me.

Sincerely,

Matty"

Kate wiped the tears from her cheeks feeling ashamed for adding to Matty's burdens and broken heart. All the years she spent at the Blackstone she thought Matty was mad at her. She cried more while holding the letter to her chest, feeling guilty and ashamed for assuming all these years she was the cause of Matty's nasty temperament. After a long cry, Kate decided she'd better read the other letter addressed to her. She wiped her tears and opened the letter with care, almost afraid to read it.

"*Dear Kate,*

You're probably mad as hell at me by now and in a way, I can't blame you because I left the Blackstone Ranch and Lodge to my loyal friend Russell Elliott. He's stuck by me all these years since I've been living at this ranch alone. Russell helped me raise horses, kept the stables running and helped me keep the lodge from falling apart. He is a good man. He's been a good listener and drinking buddy and a good card player. He's stuck by my side all these years. He took care of me through some hard times.

Since Russell took sick and had to go live in that old folk's home in town, I promised I'd take care of him. I've been paying his bills at that place and promised to do so until he dies. The only way I can keep my promise to him is to leave the Blackstone to him.

Don't go getting any ideas about fighting this. My minds made up and my lawyer, Charles Harris knows I mean business.

So go off to the city and get on with your life Kate. This is no place for a woman to be without a man. The Hills will kill you."

Sincerely,
Matty"

Red Stevens, the stable manager, strolled into Deacon's stall. "Miss Kate," Red said, looking surprised. Her faced was streaked with hay dust and tears. "Are you alright?"

"No. I'm not," Kate, sobbed. "Did you know that Matty left the entire Ranch and Lodge to Russell Elliott?"

"Yes, I found out just a few hours ago myself. Matty's lawyer, Charles Harris called me. I was at his office shortly after you left. He read me the will. Your grandmother left me the pick of any horses I wanted. I don't know what to say. I don't really understand why Miss Matty would do that with you being her granddaughter and all."

"I don't understand, Miss Kate. I've worked here with you and her for the last 20 years. I know Russell was around and helped out a lot, but I never suspected there was anything going on between them.

"So did I. Read these letters and you'll understand." Kate handed the two letters to Red and waited in silence until he read both of them.

"Wow! I had no idea Matty felt that way about old man Elliot. I knew he had been a widower for a long time, but I figured he just needed something to do after his wife died. All these years, I never gave their relationship a second thought. You were about ten years old, when I came to work here. I've watched you grow up."

"I know, Red. You've been like a big brother to me. Teaching me how to ride a hand how to work a ranch. The business end of running the place just came natural and after Matty got sick, I've been running the place by myself. It wasn't until today that I realized how much I loved this place. Now, it's all been taken away. I don't know what I'm going to do. I don't have any relatives left and no place to go. I've never been off this ranch." She started to cry again.

"Don't cry Miss Kate. We can work something out. You don't have to leave. You can stay here as long as you want to. This is really your place. Your grandmother, ah, Matty, was a hard woman to know. All work and no fun. However, after reading her letters you can understand why. She'd been abandoned by the man she truly loved and stuck with a fate she never wanted. She was a stubborn woman and hard to work for, but you've got to see her side of it. Why don't we work this place together?"

"Don't you understand? It's not mine, Red. It's Russell Elliot's," she sobbed.

Red put his arms around Kate. She buried her face in his chest and the tears kept rolling down her cheeks. Red stroked her silky, auburn hair. He leaned back from her and took her chin in his hand and kissed the tip of her nose. "Don't cry any more, Kate. I know I'm several years older than you but I've loved you in silence. I've watched you grow from a skinny kid in pigtails to a beautiful woman."

Kate pushed away from him. "What the hell is the matter with you? What don't you understand? Russell Elliot now owns this place. The whole place," she said as she spun around in a circle with her arms out to indicate what the whole place meant. Red started to laugh making his thick mustache stretch across his mouth as he grinned.

"I don't see what's to laugh about, Red. There goes all my plans for hay rides, bon fires, fall parties, late season fishing crowds, square dances, Halloween party and the corn maze."

"I just told you I've loved you for years and you start howling about Russell owning this place and all your fall plans are going to hell. Woman, I should spank you like a spoiled child."

"What?" She flew her arms up over her head. "I'm a spoiled child now? How dare you suggest I need to be spanked." She kicked the hay in his direction and started pacing in the stall.

"Well, if you think of me as your big brother, then I'd better clue you in on men. They don't like pig headed women and I don't want my woman to act like a brat."

"Pig headed." She knocked his cowboy hat off his head. "A brat am I," she said and shoved her hands on her hips.

"Woman, you try my patience." He pushed her backwards, where she landed in the hay.

"Who do you think…?"

Red knelt down beside her in the hay and took her in his arms. "Will you shut up and listen to me," he said and kissed her tenderly.

When he pulled his lips off hers, for only just a second, Kate felt all her pent up anger melt away and for the first time she noticed his eyes were tender pools, the color of maple syrup. "I never noticed you had only one dimple behind your mustache," she said before she returned his kiss.

He adjusted his body so they were now lying like spoons in the hay, with his arms engulfing her slender body and kissed her again on the lips and on her neck. She was responding to his warmth by pushing against his body wanting more. Her head was spinning, her body ached for him, not wanting him to stop, but he stiffened as his cell phone rang in his shirt pocket.

"Don't move." He rolled away from Kate as he checked to see who was calling him. "It's Matty's lawyer", he said. "Hello, Mr. Harris. Yes, I'll tell her. Yes, I understand. Thank you. Goodbye."

"Kate sat up. " What was that all about?"

"Russell died this morning. In fact, it happened while you were at Mr. Harris' office. He just found out himself."

* * *

"Thank you both for coming to my office right away," Mr. Harris said to Kate and Red. "When I called you a while ago I was at the nursing home where Mr. Elliott lived. It seems he doesn't have many living relatives; in fact, he only had a great-nephew, named as is emergency contact. I have notified him, or at least I left a message with his secretary at his office, that his great-uncle had died. I will contact you as soon as I hear from him."

"Mr. Harris, I need to apologize for acting like a spoiled brat when I was here earlier," Kate said. Red leaned closer to her and squeezed her shoulder. Kate caught his wink at her from the corner of her eye.

Mr. Harris coughed and poured himself a glass of water. "I knew you were upset with Matty's will," he said quickly before he drained the glass.

"Yes I was *very* upset, but that was no excuse for behaving so badly," Kate said and stood up and extended her hand to him. He shook her hand and smiled.

He relaxed and lowered his shoulders. "Please sit down Kath... I mean Kate," he corrected himself as Kate raised her eyebrows at him. "About Matty's request to have her cremated ashes mixed with Mr. Elliot's."

"Oh, that's right. I have to have her cremated, Kate sighed.

"We'll take care of that together," Red said.

"Thank you Red," Mr. Harris said. "I was hoping you would help Kate out with the tasks ahead of her with Matty's affairs, with you working there so long."

"You can count on me to help Kate out," Red said grinning, looking at Kate. Kate saw Mr. Harris caught the grin and looked at Kate with a confused look on his face. She gave Red a look with ruffled brows, silently saying: *behave yourself.*

"As I was about to say, go ahead and tend to your grandmother's funeral and have her cremated. You will have to wait until I hear from Mr. Elliot's kin as to his funeral arrangements. He left no instruction for that. Let me know when the services will be," he said and extended his hand to

Kate to signal the meeting was over.

"I'll keep in touch," Kate said, shook his hand. Red followed her out of the office and escorted her to the Blackstone van with the ranch log on the doors.

Red helped Kate into the passenger side of the van and kissed her lightly on the lips before he closed the door. Walking around the front of the van to the driver's door, he winked at Kate.

"Red, what has gotten into you? First the touching and looks in the office and now the kisses and …" Red kissed her before she had a chance to say more.

"Woman, like I said before. I've longed to do all that for quite a long time. There have been many times I've wanted to pat your back side when you passed by me or kiss your frustrations away."

"My backside? Red!"

"Don't think I haven't noticed how well you fit in jeans."

Kate blushed. "Okay cowboy, slow down. I have to admit you've hidden your admiration well all these, but just because Matty isn't around anymore, doesn't give you the right to start acting affectionate in public. This is all new to me."

"What's new to you?" Red looked sideways at her almost driving through a red light.

"Keep your eyes on the road. I don't want this romance to be over before it really gets started." Her stomach was doing flip-flops and she didn't know if it was from the near miss running a red light or her new romance. Red would be her first. Matty never discussed girl stuff with her and she never had a serious boyfriend before.

"I have to admit it's quiet without Matty shuffling around the kitchen," Kate said to Red while she finished the dinner dishes.

"Yeah, she was always good for an argument over politics or ranching," Red agreed. He got up from the table and put his arms around Kate's waist; nibbling at her neck and pressing close into her back.

"Hey cowboy, I'm washing a heavy pot I need to use elbow grease on." She could hardly move as tingles ran down her spine from Red's kisses and his manhood pressing into her backside.

"I can't believe I can finally kiss you," he breathed throatily in her ear.

I may have never had a serious boyfriend before but I know what his physical advances mean. I'm not ready for the next step, she thought. Shaking the water from her hands in the sink, she spun around, pushed past him, and broke the intimacy between them. She heard him sigh deeply. After grabbing two large coffee mugs the size of soup bowls, she filled them with fresh brewed coffee. She handed Red one of them. "Let's go out on the porch and have our coffee," she said, leaving him staring at her going out the kitchen screen door.

"Man, woman," he said sitting down next to her in the swing suspended from the screened-in-porch ceiling. "You are killing me."

"Like I said earlier," Kate took a big, long sip of her bitter coffee, wishing she hadn't forgotten to add cream before fleeing to the porch. "This is all new to me and you're going too fast."

He stopped the swing from moving and stood up. "Look, Kate, we're both adults and I've waited a long time to let you know how I feel about you." Red's face turned a color like his name. He gulped a mouthful of coffee. "Geez, Kate, all I do is think about you and me together."

"Be patient. I need time to get used to all this."

Red faced her, closed his eyes and took a deep breath. "Okay, I understand." He turned away from her with cup in hand and stared out towards the pastures in silence.

"When did you start noticing me as an adult?"

Without turning around, "I was about the time you graduated from Junior College."

"Junior College! That was a long time ago, about ten years."

"Yeah, ten long painful years," Red sipped his coffee again still not turning around.

"Why did you wait so long to tell me?" After several silent seconds and no response from Red, Kate put her coffee cup down on the floor, left the swing, and stood behind him. "I asked you a question, Red," she said patting him on the back.

"Out of …"

"Red, I don't like talking to your back. Turn around and talk to me face-to-face." When he turned around, Kate saw his eyes were brimmed with tears waiting to spill out down his cheeks. She caught one with her finger to his face that had escaped from the corner of his eye. "Why."

"Out of respect for Matty and you of course."

"Matty?"

"Yes. She was so protective of you. If she knew how I felt about you and my testosterone was in a rage for you, she would have skinned me alive. Matty had been good to me and I didn't want her to fire me or blackball me from working at another ranch. I needed to be close to you." Red passionately kissed her.

Kate quickly broke away from Red's embrace, feeling flushed. "I think I better call it a day, Red. I have a lot to do tomorrow," was all she said has she hurried into the house and fled to her bedroom. Butterflies danced in her stomach and her heart beat fast as she sat at her bedroom window. She watched the sky twinkle with stars and the full moon glowing brightly, smiling back at her. Finally, when her heart slowed to a normal heart rate, she flopped down on her bed. Sleep wouldn't come and the butterflies were still active in her stomach.

* * *

The following morning Kate got up after a restless night, changed her clothes, and got ready for the day. Longing for a fresh cup of coffee, Kate knew five a.m. was not early for the employees at the ranch to be working. She knew there would be fresh coffee at the Chow Hall where the guests ate their meals. "Hi, Berta," Kate shouted at the head cook as she entered the back door of the kitchen of the Chow Hall.

Berta came into the kitchen through the swinging door that led to the dining room, her arms full of dried leaves and flowers. "Hey Kate, how are you," she said wiping her hands on her white, bib apron, After she put the dried goods on the counter next to colorful vases. Without another word, she gave Kate a big hug. "I'm so sorry to hear about Miss Matty," she whispered. Not quite disengaging her hug from Kate, still holding her shoulders at an arm's length, Berta added, "I'm so sorry about what Matty did to you in her will. We all are."

"Thanks Berta. I was shocked, Matty left the place to Russell Elliot," Kate swiped at a stray tear. "I need some fresh coffee."

"Sure, sure." Berta scooted over to the stove where real cowboy coffee was warming on a burner. "Cream?"

"No, I had a rough night. Just black," Kate said and drank deeply of the soothing, dark liquid.

"What's wrong? Why did you have a rough night? Matty?" Berta asked pouring herself a cup of coffee.

"Can we talk, Berta? I need some advice. As a friend, not as co-workers."

"Sure." Berta sipped her coffee waiting for Kate to start talking. "First, about the ranch. Until I hear from Russell's relative, we will all keep running the place as usual. I have no idea what will happen when he finally contacts Matty's lawyer. We have the big family reunion planned this weekend and I want everything to stay on schedule as if the ranch's fate was not hanging in the wind."

"Sure, I understand."

"I will be announcing at a meeting later today for all employees to carrying on as usual. I guess I don't need to tell them about Matty's will. It hasn't been 24 hours yet and I'm sure everyone knows what her wishes are." Berta blushed and nodded in agreement.

"Don't worry Berta. I know how fast news travels in this place. We're like a family. I'll try to keep you all updated on the situation. Um… I … found out yesterday, from Red, um… how he really feels about me."

"Oh," Berta said cautiously.

"And… he says he's in love with me and has been for a long time."

Berta jumped in the air, grabbed Kate in her plump arms, and almost hugged the life out of her.

"Berta, you're hurting me."

"Sorry." Berta placed her hands over her heart. "It's about time."

Kate backed away from Berta. "About time? What?"

"I've known for years how he feels about you. We all do. We've been after him for years to ask you for a date."

"Oh my God! I'm so embarrassed." She put her hands over her mouth and stared at Berta, feeling the heat rise up her neck to her forehead. "Where have I been?"

"Look, he's been right under your nose. You've been too busy trying to please Matty, do the right thing, and work yourself to the bone. You've been focused on everyone else's happiness and making sure the guests got their money's worth, you neglected your own happiness.

"Now wait a minute, Berta. I've had dates. I've had a few guys I liked or lusted after."

"Big deal. They were all guests. Those were only flings for the short time they stayed here. Once they went home after their vacation, you never heard from them again. Right?

"Sort of. There was that one guy I dated when I went to the Junior College."

"Oh, please. He was a nerd. You two got partnered up on a science project for a semester."

Kate started to laugh. Berta joined her. "He *was* kind of a nerd wasn't he?"

"Kind of? Duh! He wore a plastic, pocket protector in his shirt pocket."

"Boy, you sure don't miss a thing do you? I think I need a donut or a piece of cake with this coffee," Kate gave her best pleading look.

Once Berta sliced a piece of German chocolate cake for Kate, she sat down again at the counter. "Something else is bothering you isn't it Kate?"

"Yes," she said sheepishly and pulled her shoulders up. "Red is a really nice, tender guy and has controlled his sexual advances. Um… so far."

"Well, that's good. Isn't it?"

"Oh, yes. That's good because this relationship is so new to me and all, the romance that is just bursting from both of us, caused me to lose sleep last night."

"Kate, don't let him make you do anything you don't want to do," Berta said with a stern voice.

"I know. I understand. That's not the problem?"

"What is?"

Kate forked a big piece of cake, shoved it into her mouth, and said, "I'm a virgin."

Berta shoved Kate's coffee cup at her. "Take a sip and swallow that cake," she commanded. Kate complied choking as she gulped the coffee too fast

"Say that again."

Kate swallowed hard this time. "I'm a virgin."

"Now that's something to lose sleep about," Berta said and hid her face in her apron.

The kitchen phone rang breaking the tension in the air. Berta got up to answer it. "It's the lodge operator. She has a message for you Kate."

Kate took the phone. "Kate, Mr. Harris, Matty's lawyer, called to say, Russell's great-nephew would be coming out to the ranch tomorrow morning." After hanging up the phone, Kate gathered all the employees together in the Chow Hall and explained the status of Matty's wills that was in limbo until Russell's great-nephew showed up the following morning. Once she knew what his plans were, she would plan a memorial service for Matty and take care of her cremated ashes. She asked them all too just go about their business for the weekend and treat the guest as if nothing had happened and continue the preparations for the fall season. They all gave her their condolences but looked very sad and troubled not knowing what their fate would be. They left in silence and went back to work.

Kate encountered Red out back of the Chow Hall after her announcement. He hugged her and gave her a kiss. She returned his passion with lukewarm affection. Feeling a little guilty, when he searched her eyes, looking hurt and confused, she backed away from his embrace. He tipped his hat to her and walked off in silence, never looking back.

Kate spent the remainder of the day avoiding Red and going through Matty's personal things. After finding boxes of Matty's journals in her closet, Kate spent hours reading them, absorbing countless pages of notes about how Matty's husband had left her and how Russell had helped her out with the ranch. She also found ledgers of all the transactions for changes and upkeep of the lodge, guest rooms and the cottages. It all was put together like a timeline of history. "Well, Russell's family will need all these books and documents," she said aloud.

* * *

Kate was in Matty's room sitting in her rocker where had fallen asleep the night before. She stood up and stared at the journal that fell on the floor from her lap. Stacking the journals and ledgers in neat piles, she felt sad knowing Matty would never sit in her rocker again. Sadly, she took a last look at Matty's bedroom before closing the door and strode back to her own room. Once she showered and dressed for the day Kate dragged herself to the kitchen.

"Oh, my God, you scared me," Kate gasped holding her chest as she found Red drinking coffee at the kitchen table.

"Sorry. That wasn't my intention," Red said stiffly, before standing up quickly walking over to the coffee pot. "Coffee?" He held up one of the soup-bowl sized coffee cups in her direction.

"Yes, please," she said and sat down staring at the checkered, plastic tablecloth.

"Cream and sugar are on the table," Red added. He sat down at the table across from her and sipped his coffee without looking at her.

"I think I'll drink it black today." Man this was awkward, she thought.

"Looks like it's going to be a nice day."

Kate saw the sun out the kitchen window, coming up like a big orange ball, which promised a lot of sunshine. "Why are you here Red?'

"Oh, I've been here for hours waiting for you to get your lazy ass out of bed."

"Excuse me?" Kate stiffened and put her coffee cup down on the table a little too hard.

"Well, it's after nine a.m."

"So? How late I sleep is none of your business, Red."

"I guess not," he shrugged and took another sip.

"God, you're annoying. What the hell are you really here for?"

"Not much for small talk in the mornings, are you?

"Red. Stop all this dancing around. What gives you the right to act this way?"

"I might ask you the same thing. What was that attitude yesterday behind the Chow Hall?

"What attitude?" Kate knew perfectly well what he was talking about. She couldn't tell him why she gave him the cold shoulder yesterday and all about her confusion about love and romance. And there was that other *virgin* thing.

"Don't play coy with me. I profess my love for you, and how I've felt for years about you and what do you do? Rip my heart out and blow me off."

"I didn't blow you off." Now she was truly embarrassed, sad and on the verge of tears.

"Don't give me that. Don't pull that girly crap and start crying either."

She wiped her eyes before the tears would spill out. "Why are you being so mean to me?" she asked, going over to the sink with her back to him.

Red was behind her now trying to turn her around to face him, but she wouldn't budge. "Oh honey, don't cry. I'm sorry." He kissed her hair on the top of her head. "It's just that I love you so much. I thought you were in love with me too. Come on don't cry." He leaned next to her, pulled a sheet of paper towels off a roll on the counter, and handed it to her.

"I do love you, Red."

He turned her around successfully this time to face him. "Then what's the problem, honey?"

With the paper towel still to her eyes, she said into his chest, "I'm still a virgin."

He hugged her tenderly before pushing her away from him, pulled the paper towel from her face, tipped her chin up to him and kissed her nose. He smiled, "Is that all it is? He said before he pulled her into him again. They stayed that way until her tears dried up and she could face him again.

"I guess I'm so worried about this place, all the employees, you, new romance I thought you wouldn't want me being so inexperienced."

"I love you just the way you are."

A knock at the kitchen door broke their embrace. It was Mr. Harris with a good-looking, tall man, about in his thirties, standing at the door.

"This is Jason Carlisle, Russell's great-nephew," Mr. Harris introduced him to Kate and Red.

"Come in, welcome Mr. Harris and Mr. Carlisle," Kate said lightheaded, from Red's passion.

Red exchanged handshakes with the two men. "Coffee?" Red asked them.

"Please sit down," Kate offered them a seat at the table. Red served coffee to all four of them.

After exchanging pleasantries, Mr. Carlisle got down to business. "I know we all want to get the situation of Matty's will executed. Can we do that right now?"

Kate's nerves were racing as she wished she was more prepared for this meeting. "Absolutely, let's get started. Would you like to have a tour of your property?"

He cleared his throat. "Let's not get ahead of ourselves. It's not my property yet," Mr. Carlisle said.

Kate and Red looked at each other questioningly. "What does that mean?" Red asked.

"Please call me Jason. May I call you Kate and Red?"

"Sure," Kate and Red said in unison.

"Before I see the property, I want you to look over this report I put together about Matty's estate. With Mr. Harris' help and Matty's tax records I compiled a pretty accurate account of its worth and future earnings, if it continues to operate as it has been."

"What exactly does that mean, *as it has been?*" Kate asked.

"I compared it to other businesses like this one and it won't take long for it to start falling apart, costing more money to run and lose its appeal to vacationers," Jason opened his report and pointed to a profit and loss sheet. "It's all explained here on this page."

"Plain English, Jason. What exactly do you mean? Forget the numbers, tell us what you're getting at," Red said sounding annoyed.

"Well, without seeing the buildings, horses and sporting equipment, you need to upgrade this place. Advertise your services, put together vacation packages to attract vacationers instead of relying on old repeat business. You've got to give people something unique, something different but fun and comfortable."

"I tried over the years to encourage Matty to try a few new things. To draw in customers, but she would never listen," Kate said looking sad.

"That's exactly what this place needs," Jason replied. "Tell me some of your ideas."

"Well, when I went to college, in one of my business classes, I had to present a project where I created a business plan. I put mine together for the ranch, where I created brochures about the ranch and made a list of events we could add that wouldn't take much money."

"Give me more details," Jason continued looking interested in what she had to say.

"First I want to plan trail rides in all seasons. Winter ones to attract December holiday guests. I wanted to try doing this to attract families who wanted to experience Christmas in a log cabin and a ranch. The lodge rooms need upgrading with new rugs and window shutters. I'd like to add activities for kids, business retreats, fishing contests, campfire cookouts, exercise classes and …"

"You get the idea," Jason interrupted Kate. "How about another cup of coffee before I inspect the property.

Kate's enthusiasm died as soon as he said that. She turned to Red. "Would you refill our cups?" She felt edgy again.

Once Red filled their cups and sat down at the table, Jason casually drank his coffee and paged through his report. Kate wanted to scream. The silence was deafening.

Jason put his cup down and leaned across the table, towards Kate. "I have a proposition for you. I know you were disappointed to find out your grandmother left this place to my uncle Russell." Kate nodded. Red started to say something, but Jason put his hand up in a stop motion. "I'm a business man. I think I can come up with a deal that will satisfy Matty's will and give you an opportunity to own this place outright, Kate."

"But how?"

"Hear me out. I never met Russell, and I have no idea what I would do with this place anyway. Besides, I'm a city slicker from the east coast and I've never been up close to a horse much less ridden one. I'll lease this place to you and fund improvements within reason and after five years, if your can prove to me it can be a profitable vacation place, I'll deed it back to you."

Kate almost fainted. "Are you sure you want to do that?" She gripped Red's hand and they both grinned from ear-to-ear.

"Well, if you don't take my offer I'll just have to sell the place."

"No, no don't do that," Kate pleaded. "We'll take your offer."

Jason reached across the table and shook Kate's hand. "Deal."

"Deal," Kate said beaming. She jumped up knocking her chair over. Red quickly stood up. She jumped up and wrapped her legs around his waist.

"Whoa, woman, you're going to break me," Red said and put her down on her own two feet. Mr. Harris and Jason laughed along with Red.

"When can we start?"

"As soon as Mr. Harris here can draw up a contract for you to sign."

"Great, my first project is to plan a beautiful, fall wedding complete with hay rides, a bon fire, and country music for square dancing." She hugged Red around the waist and looked up at him lovingly. "Our wedding."

ABOUT THE AUTHOR

Kathleen Nordstrom is a native of Minnesota. She writes Romantic Mysteries of the Cozy type with no blood and guts or gory murders, or explicit sex, but always has a dead person and an amateur sleuth. She has written short stories that appear in *Romancing the Lakes of Minnesota ~ Summer* anthology. In her other life she was a computer programmer.

She has been a member of Romance Writers of America ® since 1997 and is a co-founder of Romancing the Lakes Writers Chapter established in 2012 in Minnesota.

Kathleen received a two-year AA-Liberal Arts degree from Normandale College, Minnesota, where she graduated with a Phi Theta Kappa designation. Continuing with her undergraduate education, she received her Bachelor of Arts degree from Metropolitan State University, Minnesota with a major in Business and a minor in Creative Writing.

Visit her at: http://www.kathleennordstrombooks.com/ or http://www.romancingthelakeswriters.com/.

THE LEAP

Angeline Fortin

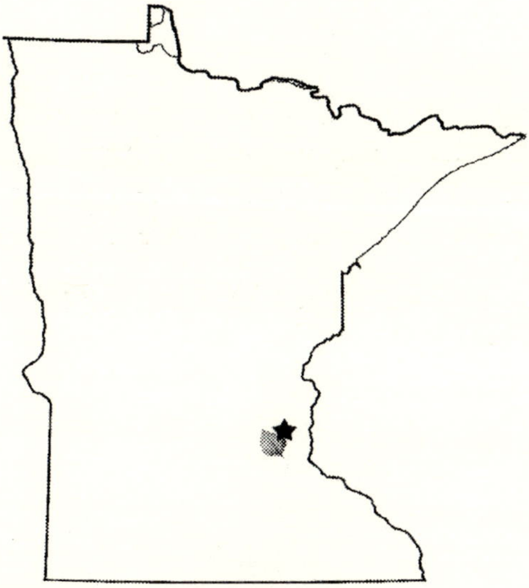

Lake Minnetonka, Wayzata

"What is he doing here?" Kayla Mikkelsen muttered under her breath as her ex-husband walked out of *her* house and on to *her* deck with his young, hot new girlfriend hanging on his arm.

"I invited him," her daughter, Mackenzie, said from beside her.

Kayla stood frozen in disbelief with her wine glass suspended inches from her lips.

"It's my going away party and I wanted all my family here. I hope you don't mind."

Kayla turned to her daughter, trying to keep a grimace from flattening her lips. Mackenzie was eighteen, her only child. Unfortunately she was Tom Mikkelsen's only child as well and she was leaving for college at Northwestern University outside Chicago the next morning. "This is my last day to spend with you alone."

Mackenzie smiled brightly, looping her arm across Kayla's shoulders and giving her a tight hug. "We're hardly alone," she said as they looked out over the crowd milling about the deck around them and spilling over on to the narrow strip of lawn between the house and the lake. Grandparents, aunts, uncles, cousins, neighbors and friends all gathered to give Mackenzie her big send off. "Besides, we had all weekend together and I loved every minute of it. I'd much rather to go off to school with that memory than the one where you bawl like a baby in the middle of my dorm room.

"I wouldn't bawl like a… okay, maybe a little," Kayla shrugged with a sigh. "I'm a mom. It's my job. Dad will probably just drop you at the curb and wave goodbye."

"I doubt it but if he does I'll still be fine," Mackenzie teased. "I'm a big girl now, you know. Now I'm going to go say hello to Dad and Chloe."

"It's such an awful name," Kayla muttered under her breath.

Mackenzie shook her head with a grin. "Don't be mean. She's not *that* bad. Have another glass of wine and try to have fun."

Kayla scrunched her nose in silent disagreement and sipped her wine as she watched her daughter bounce across the deck to greet her father and his girlfriend. His girlfriend! Ugh, Chloe was probably closer in age to

Mackenzie than Tom's forty-two years.

She was young, blonde and beautiful while Kayla would never see the softer side of forty again. Kayla's hair which had once been the same bright auburn as Mackenzie's had faded to a far more vulpine shade. Though she was still in good shape, Kayla had never been as voluptuous as Chloe. Her forty-year-old breasts could never manage to look so pert that she would dare to go braless in a backless halter like that.

A bright orange leaf drifted down from one of the many maples that canopied the deck and managed to land right in Kayla's wine glass. With yet another sigh, Kayla turned toward the refreshment table she had laid out under the large windowed wall of her house. Fishing out the leaf, she dumped out the remainder of her Pinot Gris and reached for a bottle of Malbec.

This definitely called for something red.

* * *

"No, don't jump," a deep, gravelly voice rasped close to her ear as a firm, decidedly male hand slid familiarly down her spine to rest just on the rise of her bottom leaving a startling shiver of awareness rippling in its wake. A darkly tanned hand rescued Kayla's wine glass from her suddenly trembling hand. Setting it safely on the table, he took her hand, sliding his fingers between hers. The unexpectedly sensual brush of skin against skin was even more astonishing than the hand on her back. Kayla turned wide, startled eyes to the reflection caught by the window behind the table and the dark, broadly built man standing so close behind her.

Not a stranger but a very familiar face.

"Bas?" she asked, tugging her hand away from his. A hand she had touched a hundred times before without such an arousing and inappropriate reaction.

"No, don't move."

"What are you doing?" she whispered, subduing the urge to jump again when the warm pressure of his fingers on her back intensified.

"I saw you watching Tom and his little girlfriend. He's expecting you to make a scene over his bringing her along, Kay. He wants it. Don't give him the satisfaction." His lips brushed against her earlobe as he spoke huskily and Kayla shuddered with unexpected and shockingly misplaced desire. "He's dealt you so many regrets, Kay. How about giving him a few of his own?"

It was hard to concentrate with him so close. Why? "What? How?"

A strong arm slid around her waist and pulled her back against a firm male body. Kayla could feel the heat radiating off him. Heat that had nothing to do with warm rays of the autumn sun and everything to do with the fact that she hadn't been so close to a man since Tom had left her a year before.

But this wasn't just any man. Kayla had known Sebastian Cabot as long as she had known Tom. The two men had been best friends, roommates in college when Kayla had started at the University of Minnesota in the Twin Cities. Tom, tall, blond and lankily muscular with All-American good looks, had been an easy target for female eyes and sighs.

Bas, on the other hand, was just under six feet tall but broader, more thickly muscled, with black hair, dark brown eyes under thick brows and a far more piratical edge to his handsomeness. Even in college, probably just twenty years old, he'd possessed a perpetual five o'clock shadow and an aura of danger that fascinated most of the freshman girls.

Including Kayla. He had enthralled and terrified her just the same.

He was doing the same thing now. Sebastian's lips grazed her neck, stunning and arousing her in a way that shouldn't happen after so many years acquaintance. Kayla knew her first instinct should have been to pull away. Instead she was fighting the impulse to arch her neck and invite his lips to meet her flesh. "Bas?" Even the barest whisper trembled as Kayla watched the insanely erotic image play out in the window. "What are you doing?"

"Tom was a fool to leave you," Bas said in his deep raspy voice. The light caress of his breath against her ear left the spot tingling. "He might think that you've lost something along the way but I think you've only gotten more beautiful. Would it hurt to make sure he knew it?"

"You're his best friend." *My friend*, Kayla reminded herself. For the twenty years of her marriage, Bas had been around almost as often as Tom. But the hands on her waist weren't those of a friend. The firm lips nuzzling a surprisingly sensitive spot behind her ear were definitely not expressing anything as mundane as friendship.

It was so odd, so wicked.

So right.

"Yes, and that puts me in the position to be the one to teach him a lesson."

"A lesson?" Kayla asked, putting her cold hands over his warm ones. The dark hair on the back of his hands prickled pleasantly beneath her palms. She'd touched his hand thousands of times over the past two decades without noticing. What was happening? "What lesson?"

Bas spread his fingers beneath her hands, welcoming her to entwine her fingers with his. Kayla gave into the impulse and slid her fingers between his, savoring the carnal glide of his flesh against hers. "What lesson?" she repeated.

"Finders keepers," he whispered in her ear and their eyes met in the reflective glass.

Kayla stared at him in surprise, her blood pounding in her ears. Her heart beating so hard that she was sure he could feel it. *Finders keepers*? What could he mean by that?

"Bas…"

"Kay." Tom's voice boomed with forced jocularity nearby and Kayla jumped in surprise. She stepped away from Sebastian with a flush of embarrassment but he wouldn't let her go far. He caught her hand in his and tugged her to his side as they turned to greet her ex-husband.

"Hello, Tom," Kayla choked out, unable to fight back the flush she knew was blossoming on her cheeks as he looked down at her inquisitively.

"Bas." Tom's gaze shifted to his friend with a questioning lift of one brow but Sebastian merely held out his hand, leaving Tom no choice but to shake it.

"Hey, Uncle Bas," Mackenzie said, eyeing him just as curiously.

"Hey, Kenzie," Bas said with a wink and a grin. Kayla envied his casual ease. "Ready for the big move?"

"Very." Mackenzie nodded and shifted her gaze back to Kayla. Her eyes were full of questions and something else Kayla couldn't quite identify. Pleasure?

Kayla shook her head and turned her attention to Tom's girlfriend with a short nod. "Chloe."

"Kayla. What a… charming house you have," Chloe offered half-heartedly, looking up at the weathered cedar façade of Kayla's 1930s home.

Kayla bristled under the oblique insult. Her tiny two-bedroom home on Halstead's Bay on the far western end of Lake Minnetonka really was charming to her. The cozy, cottage feel, vaulted ceilings and hardwood floors suited Kayla perfectly. Plus, it sat on over an acre of heavily wooded land, facing west and sitting close to the water. A long dock extended into the bay giving Kayla a front row seat to some of the most impressive sunsets God had ever fashioned. Currently a colorful mosaic created by the changing autumn leaves framed the view.

It was heavenly solitude.

And it was all hers.

Certainly, it was nothing like the more impressive home she and Tom had shared for ten years on Gleason Lake in Wayzata. Nor could it compare to the ostentatious, multi-million dollar affair Tom had recently purchased with Chloe on the far more affluent Carson's Bay of Lake Minnetonka. Still, it was nothing to sneeze at and certainly unworthy of that wrinkled nose.

"Such an effusive compliment and you haven't even seen the inside yet," she bit out caustically. "Perhaps I can give you a tour of the bottom of the la…"

* * *

Sebastian's hand squeezed tightly around hers cutting off Kayla's words though there was little he could do to keep her eyes from narrowing on Chloe. How Tom could have decided that the spiteful woman was somehow preferable to the incredible woman he had been gifted with was a mystery to Sebastian. Tom Mikkelsen was a fool to give her up, but he had. Bas wasn't going to let an opportunity like that pass.

"I'm surprised to see you here, Tom," he said amicably as if nothing were out of the ordinary.

"I could say the same." Tom's gaze slid down to where Bas and Kay's hands were still entwined and back up again.

"Why would you be surprised to see Bas here?" Kayla asked. "He has been a major part of Mackenzie's life and has been at every gathering we've had over the years. Why would this one be any different?"

The answer was unspoken but obvious to them all. Bas had started out as Tom's friend solely and he expected it to end that way.

Kayla shook her head and looked up at Bas, meeting his eye directly for the first time. Her light brown eyes softened and crinkled at the corners reflecting more of a smile than the slight lift of her lips. "And he's been my friend for all that time as well. Friends like that don't get divvied up in the divorce."

"Your friend?" Tom asked pointedly, his gaze shifting back and forth between Bas and Kayla. "Can I have a word with you, Kay?"

"Oh, Dad!" Mackenzie laughed lightly, latching on to his free arm. "You can talk to Mom anytime. Come, say hi to everyone." With that, she tugged her father away casting a questioning look of her own over her shoulder as they went.

Kayla's shoulders lifted and dropped with a deep breath as she released his hand. Turning, she descended the steps leading down from the deck and looked back at Bas with a smile he couldn't resist.

It was invitation enough.

Bas followed her past the rest of the guests he had mingled with earlier. Having abandoned the tables of food, they were now gathering around the paved fire pit midway between the house and the lake. Kayla's brother, Steve, and her father were building up a fire against the evening chill that would be settling in soon. Both men looked up as he passed but Bas never took his eyes from Kayla. He followed her all the way to the end of the long dock reaching out into Lake Minnetonka.

The sun was low in the sky, reflecting brightly off the calm waters and highlighting Kayla's warm red hair, her smooth ivory cheek and pointed chin. Her long, tanned legs were bare beneath her denim shorts though she hugged a cable-knit cardigan tightly around her against the brisk breeze blowing over the lake. In his eyes, she hadn't changed a bit since the day they met. She still had the sweetness, that girl-next-door beauty that had ensnared him so long ago. Under arching brows, those beguiling light brown eyes stared up at him – just as a dozen other pairs were likely watching from shore.

Let them watch, Bas thought. There was only one person's feelings he was interested in.

"Thank you, Bas," Kayla said quietly, turning to watch him as he took up position about as far from her as the T-shaped end of the dock would allow. The curiosity wasn't exclusive to the onlookers of that exchange. She wondered what had possessed him to act as he had, perhaps more than she wondered at her own reaction. "You saved me from making a scene over him being here. It was nice of you."

Bas shook his head with a dark frown. That look did nothing to diminish his masculine beauty but roused the untethered fierceness that had intimidated her years before. It didn't frighten her now. Well, not entirely.

On the contrary, it now seemed rather intriguing.

And Bas, in his worn out jeans that clung to his thickly muscled thighs and a grey T-shirt that molded to the sculpted ridges of his broad chest, was suddenly even more fascinating. He shoved his hands into his pockets, the muscles bunching at his shoulders and triceps.

"Nice had nothing to do with it, Kay."

"Then why did you do it?"

"God, Kay," Bas laughed huskily, running a hand through his thick dark hair. "Have you never figured it out? Never seen it?"

Despite his laughter, there was an intensity in his dark eyes Kayla had never seen before. Her heart raced once more as her tongue darted out to wet her suddenly dry lips. His eyes dropped to her lips and if it were possible, darkened even more.

"You're Tom's closest friend," she repeated as a reminder to them both.

Gripping the iron post marking the corner of the dock as if it might somehow anchor her sanity, Kayla watched Bas as he slowly approached. Not in all the time she had known him had Bas ever affected her as he did now. Perhaps it was because she hadn't known immediately who it was behind her at the refreshment table… that she had registered that simmering desire before his identity. She was aware of him now – the heat of his body, his proximity – and it was very disconcerting.

"Yes, I have been for a long time," he said, still watching her closely. "Long enough to know that I should never have gone to such an extreme in the name of friendship."

"What do you mean?"

"I let him pull the 'I saw her first' card all those years ago, Kay. I let him have you without a fight, and I never stopped regretting it in all the years since."

"Let him…?" Kayla licked her lips again, trying to process what Bas was saying.

"Ahh, Kay!" he whispered, his fingers grazed her jaw tentatively waiting for either consent or rejection. Kayla provided neither but lack of action seemed encouragement enough. Sebastian's hands dove into her hair, cradling the back of her head and forcing her to look up at him. "Are you going to make me say it?"

Yes, she was.

Bas lowered his head, brushing his lips across hers without a word.

Kayla gasped at the electrifying contact but it was Bas who groaned aloud. His hand was trembling against the back of her neck as he exhaled shakily. Just a hairsbreadth from hers, his parted lips hovered. Their breath mingled but still he didn't move. His turbulent eyes were nearly black with emotion as he stared down at her.

"Bas?" she whispered, lifting a hand to his hip. Even through his T-shirt, she could feel the heat and tension radiating from him. His chest jumped repeatedly with the heavy beat of his heart. His hand fisted in her hair while his other hand glided up her arm and over her shoulder.

"So long, Kay," he rasped out, stroking her long hair and twisting it around his fingers. "Maybe too damn long. I've dreamed of kissing you but now that I have you here, I don't know where to begin."

He seemed to be doing a damn fine job of it. Some part of her wanted to urge him not to wait any longer but another part was seized by his intensity. Alarmed by it. Just as she had been when they first met. Now she understood what it was that had scared her so long ago. There was something rather intimidating about being the object of such tightly leashed desire.

That she had never detected it before when it was so obvious now was confounding.

Kayla lifted a hand to his forearm. Whether she was thinking of pulling his hand away or urging him on, Kayla wasn't certain but the feel of his taut muscles flexing under her touch drew her full attention and she skimmed her palm up his arm and over his bicep, the full span of her hand didn't even make it half way around the powerful bulge.

"I wish I knew what you were thinking," he said, brushing his lips across her temple.

"I'm thinking that I don't understand this at all," she admitted. "You're *Bas*. I shouldn't even be standing here with you like this."

"I don't want to make you uncomfortable, Kay. If you want me to leave, I'll go."

If there had been anything humorous about this situation, Kayla would have laughed because she had absolutely no idea what she wanted at that moment. Her mind and body were at war. One telling her how ludicrous this all was. The other demanding she just kiss him herself and solve the problem. She, who had never known a moment of indecisiveness in more than a decade, wavered uncertainly.

Long enough for Bas to step back with a sigh of unmistakable regret. "I'm sorry, Kay," he said, looking away. "I don't know what came over me. What made me think…"

"You son of a bitch!"

That shout combined with the shaking dock beneath their feet, parted them further and they both turned in surprise to see Tom stomping down the dock toward them.

In a move reminiscent of his college football days, Tom sped up and lowered his shoulder, tackling Bas around the waist. Though Bas was heavier, Tom had enough momentum behind him to carry them both off the end of the dock. A wave of water lapped over Kayla and she gasped in surprise, but her astonishment was directed at her ex-husband. Tom and Bas surfaced, finding their footing in the waist deep water. "Tom, what the hell are you doing?"

Tom wasn't paying any attention to her, however. It looked like he was trying to strangle Bas and hit him at the same time. "You bastard!" he spat out, while Bas deftly eluded his grasp. "How long has this been going on? How long have you been fucking my wife?"

"Your *wife*!" Chloe screeched in Kayla's ear as she arrived on the end of the dock. Kayla flinched, aware that the rest of her family and friends were gathered on shore, watching the spectacle.

"She's not your wife anymore, Tom," Bas barked out more calmly, fighting off Tom's enraged swings. "You gave her up. Kay's a beautiful, intelligent woman. If you can't see that, I can."

"You bastard!" Tom repeated, slapping the water. "I knew it! I knew it!"

"No, you didn't," Bas said, wrapping an arm around Tom's shoulders and pinning Tom against his chest. "I never said a word to her, never laid a finger on her before the divorce. She was yours and I respected that," he growled, lowering his voice so that their entire audience wouldn't overhear but Kayla still could. "But she isn't yours any more."

"So now she's yours?" Tom laughed, jerking away. "We're not in college anymore, Bas, that we share everything."

"No, we're not," Bas said, his gravelly voice low with emotion. "And I share nothing. But Kayla isn't mine, Tom. Not yet. Maybe never." His eyes lifted to hers and Kayla stared down at him uncertainly. "But I love her, Tom. I always did. You know that."

Tom looked up at Kayla and then at Chloe, who was now quietly fuming by her side. "That was twenty years ago, Bas. Things change."

"Some don't."

Tears stung Kayla's eyes at those softly spoken words, a poignant ache seizing her heart and she drew in a shaky breath.

Tom laughed incredulously again and began to wade out of the water. The crowd at the foot of the dock parted for him and for Chloe who ran back down the dock to give him a firm scolding. Kayla didn't worry for him much. She doubted that Chloe would give up her meal ticket over such a minor altercation. No, Kayla's focus was entirely on Bas as he heaved himself out of the water in one smooth motion and stood dripping on the dock.

His t-shirt was plastered to every dip and hollow of his rippling abdomen. Kayla inhaled with a thankful, yet sorrowful sigh as he pulled it away from his skin and began to wring it out. "We need to get you dried off," Kayla said quietly, taking his arm to lead him down the dock. "Come inside and let me get you a towel."

"I need a towel, too," Tom said, overhearing her as they reached the end of the dock.

"Go home, Tom."

"I need to dry off," he bit out.

"No, you need to leave," Kayla said firmly, giving him a stern look that he would easily recognize after years of marriage. "Now."

Grabbing Chloe's hand, Tom turned and stormed off while Kayla passed on apologies to her guests as she tugged Bas through the crowd. Her family, neighbors and Mackenzie's friends were fairly bursting with curiosity. No doubt it would erupt into an uproar of salacious gossip the moment they went into the house. Her brother even had the audacity to wink as she walked by.

Mackenzie just watched her go without a word and Kayla was glad because she didn't know what she would say to her daughter right then. She was still pretty unclear about what was happening herself.

* * *

"Here are some towels and an old pair of Tom's sweatpants and a t-shirt I adopted from him years ago," Kayla said as she gathered the items and laid them on the foot of her bed. "They might fit well enough until we get your clothes dry."

"Kayla."

"Shower is right through there." She pointed to the door connecting to her bedroom.

"Kay." His voice was noticeably stiff and Kayla looked up to find him lingering at her bedroom door, his hair and shirt still plastered to his body. His sodden jeans dripping on her wood floors. She hardly noticed either one, spellbound by the intensity of his expression. So familiar yet so new. "We need to talk."

"And we will," Kayla sent him a patient smile. "*After* you get a shower and stop dripping on my floors. Like I said before Tom's untimely interruption, I am really confused by what just happened out there."

"Isn't it obvious, Kay?" he ground out, running his hand through his wet hair leaving it stand on end.

Kayla knew from experience that Bas only did that when he was truly frustrated. In fact, she thought she knew almost everything about him. It was clear that she had been wrong about that. "No, Bas, not exactly. I'd prefer to have you tell me."

"What? Tell you that I hate that Tom got to you first?" he ground out. "That I've been holding out for you since you were eighteen?"

Holding out for her? No, Bas had gotten married in his early thirties. "Shelly…" Kayla stammered out, forgetting entirely about his clothes or her floor.

"A last ditch attempt to move on," Bas told her. "That didn't last long, did it?"

No, it hadn't. Only two years. "Bas, I'm sorry. I didn't know."

"You weren't supposed to," he pointed out. "Oh, don't feel sorry for me, please."

Kayla pressed her fingers to her lips as she stared at him. How could she not? He had missed out on a chance at love, a chance to be a father because of her? She had seen enough of him with Mackenzie over the years to know that he would have made an excellent father. "Oh, Bas!"

"Aw, shit," he grumbled, snatching up a towel before turning away. "Forget I said anything at all!"

* * *

Going back outside once she heard the water start in her shower, Kayla was surprised to find Mackenzie sitting alone by the fire pit, poking the fire with a stick. "Where did everyone go?"

"I sent them home," her daughter said simply, looking up as Kayla reached the flagstone pavers circling the pit. "Actually it wasn't too hard. I think it was pretty clear that the party was over. I expect Grandma will call you in the morning though. If she can wait that long."

Kayla dropped into an Adirondack chair and buried her face in her hands with a moan. "Oh, that's just great."

"What will you tell her?" Mackenzie asked, finally expressing her own curiosity. "I mean, you and Uncle Bas? How long has that been going on?"

"It hasn't!" Kayla protested, peeking at her daughter through her fingers. "He said he was just trying to make your dad have his share of regret, too."

"There was more going on there than a little payback," Mackenzie pointed out. "He likes you, Mom. I mean, he always has. I could tell. I mean he really seems to like you."

He loves me, Kayla thought to herself recalling the sincerity in Bas's eyes as he had made that confession to Tom. To her. "It's crazy."

"No, it's awesome! I just couldn't imagine you dating anyone."

"Because I'm too old, right?" Kayla asked. "Because just like your dad, most men prefer someone young, gorgeous and thin?"

"Mom! No!" Mackenzie protested. "*You* are gorgeous! And thin. You take spinning classes like they're crack. Nobody in their right mind would guess you're forty. What I meant was that I couldn't imagine seeing you in a bar or a nightclub to meet guys. Or hooking up with somebody on a dating website. When I saw you and Bas holding hands before, it was just perfect. Like it all just clicked into place. I can see you two together."

"Can you? I'm not sure I can."

Couldn't she, Kayla wondered? She hadn't exactly been appalled by Sebastian's confession.

"Can't you?" Mackenzie asked, echoing Kayla's thoughts. "Whose shoulder did you cry on during my graduation? Where did you turn to get those concert tickets for my birthday? Who held your hand when you were so nervous about passing your ASID certification? Who sat with you in the waiting room when Dad had his surgery? Think about it, Mom. Bas has been there for you, for me as long as I can remember." Her eyes widened as she made the realization. "Oh my God! He's in love with you, Mom!"

Kayla blushed but Mackenzie was grinning from ear to ear.

"This is even better than you just getting your groove on with him."

"Kenzie!"

"What more could you ask for?" her daughter persisted. "It's perfect! He owns his own business. He's stable, reliable and everyone in the family all ready likes him. No breaking-in period at all! Plus, he's hot."

"Kenzie!" Kayla protested hotly again, shocked by her daughter's words and her easy acceptance. Kids were resilient like that but Kayla was still reeling.

"Hey, I don't know but all my friends say so," Mackenzie said defensively then looked up at the house speculatively. "He does work out a lot. I mean, did you see the way his shirt…"

"Kenzie! Enough all ready!"

Mackenzie blessed her with a broad, mischievous grin. "Okay, I'll stop. Listen, I'm going over to Jessica's house for a while and I'll be back later. Much later. So, just have fun."

Kayla buried her face in her hands once more, embarrassed to the core to be having such a conversation with her daughter.

"Well, what are you sitting here for?" Mackenzie asked as she scooped up her purse and dug for her car keys. "There's a big, handsome man up in your bedroom. In your shower. Most likely naked," she called out sweetly before she got in her car.

"I want to die," Kayla said to herself as Mackenzie backed out of the driveway and left her alone. Alone with the fire, the whisper of leaves falling in the cool breeze, the lapping of water against the shore… and, yes, a big, handsome man likely naked in her shower right now.

Between her fingers, Kayla looked up at her bedroom window, brightly lit against the falling darkness. Was it really so wrong after all this time to be fascinated at the thought?

* * *

Wrapping the towel tightly around his waist, Bas left the bathroom to retrieve the clothes Kayla had left for him on the bed. Even ten minutes lost in thought under the hot spray hadn't given him a clue about where to go from here.

If there was anywhere left to go.

"I did have a little crush on you when we first met."

Sebastian looked up in surprise to see Kayla lingering at her bedroom door much as he had not long before. "I thought you were so gorgeous, but you scared me to death," she continued. "So, I went out with Tom because he was safer. And because he asked. You never did." Kayla waited but Bas kept his silence.

He had already humiliated himself beyond recovery; there was no need to add fuel to the fire.

"Why? Because he saw me first?"

Bas's shoulder lifted slightly and he tucked the towel more securely around his hips.

"We were practically forced to marry when I got pregnant with Mackenzie. Times were like that then," Kayla went on, though her eyes had dropped to his chest and she took a few steps into the room. "I'm not going to say that I didn't love him. I did and I did everything I could to make our marriage into one that would last forever."

"I know," he said. Kayla's belief in the sanctity of marriage was strong. Even though it had cost him, it was one of the many things he admired about her. She had been fully devoted to her family.

"And you would have never said anything."

It wasn't really a question and Bas didn't bother to answer. He had said enough already.

"Why now, Bas? Why today?"

"I don't know," he said admitted. More than likely, he had scared Kayla off for good with his impulsive confession. Or even before that. He certainly hadn't thought any of this through. Now, he'd most likely blown his one shot. "I certainly didn't plan that. Honestly, I was still working up to asking you to dinner."

"That would have still come as a surprise. I was never more shocked in my life than I was when you came up behind me like that today. When you…" Kayla swallowed hard when her voice cracked and Bas finally looked down at her, "When you touched me like that. I never expected it. I suppose I should thank you though."

"You already thanked me," he said gruffly.

"Not for that," she said softly.

Bas lifted a brow. "For what then?"

"For not asking me out. I would have said no because we're friends and it would have been…"

"Uncomfortable," he finished with regret. "I know I made you uncomfortable anyway. I'm sorry, Kay."

Kayla blushed becomingly under his gaze and shook her head. "I wasn't exactly comfortable, but I wasn't *uncomfortable* either."

"What's that supposed to mean?"

To his surprise, she stepped closer and laid her hand on his bare chest. His flesh leapt beneath her tender touch just as it had each time she had casually touched him over the past two decades. It was humiliating in retrospect just how thoroughly he had tortured himself over the years, unable to walk away from her even though she wasn't his.

"What you did out there today shocked me."

"Yes, you said that."

Kayla's cheeks reddened even more and she shook her head, skimming her palms up his chest. "You didn't let me finish," she said. Her fingers danced over the tendons of his neck and over his tightly clenched jaw. When her thumb brushed across his lower lip, Kayla caught her own between her teeth. "This is many things, Bas. Terrifying. Surprising. Incredibly exciting, but not uncomfortable. Thank you for shocking me, Bas. For forcing me to see something I might never have otherwise."

Sebastian's heart leapt at her words but he didn't have time to recover his surprise. Kayla tangled her fingers in his short hair and drew his head down even as she lifted herself on to her toes.

Bas groaned in misery but settled his hands on her hips. "God, Kay, please don't lead me on now!"

"Lead you on?" Kayla whispered. "I'm pretty much freaking out here, Bas, but for some reason I can't let you just walk away without knowing."

"Knowing what?"

Bas had told her earlier not to jump but Kayla felt ready to take a leapt of faith. "Just how *comfortable* this might be."

Heart pounding, she looked up at Sebastian reading the surprise in his eyes. Fire leapt and burned it away, leaving nothing but desire burning there. His hands slid up her back, pulling her close to him. Close to the hard angles and sculpted muscles of his broad chest that had beckoned her from the door. His fingertips lightly grazed along her cheek before smoothing her hair back from her temple with aching tenderness. Kayla moistened her lips and waited but Bas still did nothing more than stare down at her much as he had out on the dock. His lips hovered just a whisper away from hers.

Kayla skimmed her palms over his shoulders and down his chest, feeling the erratic beat of his heart beneath her hand. Hers was pounding just as hard with anticipation and something more. "I don't know how you waited all these years for a kiss, Bas. I don't think I can wait a minute more."

The breath he had been holding released in a whoosh and with a low, jubilant chuckle, Bas lowered his head to take the kiss he had always longed for.

ABOUT THE AUTHOR

Angeline Fortin is the author of historical and time-travel romance offering her readers fun, sexy and often touching tales of romance.

With a degree in US History from UNLV and having previously worked as a historical interpreter at Colonial Williamsburg, Angeline brings her love of history and Great Britain to the forefront in settings such as Victorian London and Edinburgh.

As a former military wife, Angeline has lived from the west coast to the east, from the north and to the south and uses those experiences along with her favorite places to tie into her time travel novels as well.

Angeline is a native Minnesotan who recently relocated back to the land of her birth and braved the worst winter recorded since before she initially moved away. She lives in Apple Valley outside the Twin Cities with her husband, two children and three dogs.

She is a wine enthusiast, DIY addict (much to her husband's chagrin) and sports fanatic who roots for the Twins and Vikings faithfully through their highs and lows.

Most of all she loves what she does everyday - writing. She does it for you the reader, to bring a smile or a tear and loves to hear from her fans.

You can visit Angeline's website at www.angelinefortin.com or follow her on Facebook, Twitter @angelinefortin, Tumblr and Pinterest or you can just send her an email at fortin.angeline@gmail.com.

"A story about a witch, a forbidden old flame, and the power of Samhain."

THIRD TIME'S A CHARM

KT Alexander

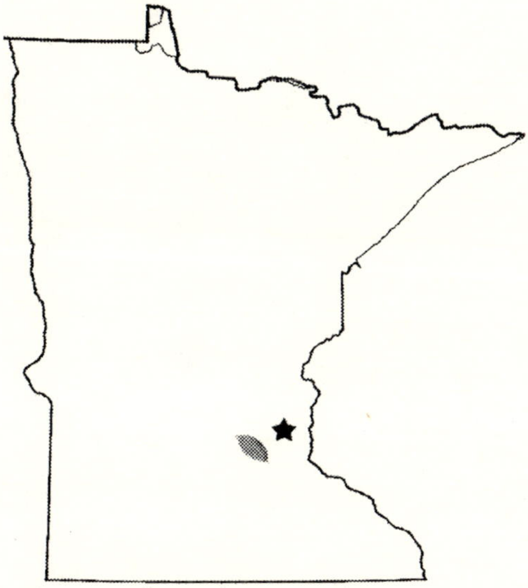

Lake Minnetonka, Excelsior

Mia traipsed down the worn airport stairs toward the throng of grinning Minnesotans. She scanned the crowd. *No one for me.*

Frowning, Mia stomped to the whining conveyor belt in the baggage claim area. It rotated slowly and off kilter as if the luggage it schlepped weighed tons. One forgotten bag spun.

Mia shoved a hand to her hip and arched her back. A throbbing ache had shoved itself under her right shoulder blade.

The circus of vacationers and foreigners amassed around her, crowding Mia closer to the angry hiss of the faded belt as it stopped. The chorus of voices quickened.

The plastic light atop the tunnel from where luggage was supposed to pour lit up on a horrific screech. People gasped, some tripped backward into waiting arms, most flinched. Mia shook her head and grinned weakly.

The throbbing in her back traveled upward, pinching her neck. Mia rubbed the spot.

Her worn leather bag was the first off the plane. It clanked as it slammed into the metal edge of the belt. Mia elbowed her way through the group and yanked her bag over her shoulder.

She emerged from the chaos and searched once more for a friendly face. *Did Val forget?* Resigning herself to an expensive cab ride, Mia resituated her heavy bag.

A warm hand slid down her waist, resting just above her bottom. "Need a hand?"

Mia inhaled and spun.

Dark green eyes, murky and shadowed like the depths of a summer forest, smirked down at her from a great height. Mia straightened and jerked from the man's hold.

"Sean Finch."

"Mia Birch." Those green eyes sparkled from a handsome face she'd crushed on for a decade.

"Why're you here?" Mia dropped the bag and tucked her travel worn braid over her shoulder, quickly re-plaiting the straggled strands. "Val was supposed to pick me up."

Sean crossed his arms and leaned against one of the room's many pillars, the paragon of male contentment.

"I'm here for the same reason you went to Salem and then Europe." His smile froze and did not reach the rest of his face. "I'm looking for a witch."

Mia closed her eyes, and schooled her features. Hiding her pain. The old wounds. The scars *he* inflicted. "Still don't believe I am what I say I am?"

"Witches don't exist, Mia. I wish you'd quit lying to me. Quit pretending." His deep voice whispered across the crowded baggage claim.

"Where are you parked?" She opened her eyes. His calloused hand wrenched her bag from her when she picked it up.

"This way."

Jogging to keep up, Mia took in the sight of the ex she'd fled from twice. The last five years apart had been *good* to Sean. His boyish grin had sharpened into a knowing smile, his green eyes flashed with intelligence, and his jaw had hardened. The shoulders she'd gripped in lust and loathing had filled out, broadened, tightening the material of his black leather coat.

The tense pair dipped out the automatic doors. Rain pounded from the heavens and splashed along the glittering blacktop. A black Ford Fusion was parked illegally in the arrivals' section. The trunk popped open. Sean strode over and chucked her bag inside. Mia grimaced as her possessions clanged together.

"Have a little care with my things," she scolded.

Sean rounded the car and gripped her elbow, leaning over until they were a breath away. "Like you had care with my heart?"

"Where is Val?" Mia tugged herself free and glared right back at the only man she'd ever loved. *The only man I've ever hated.*

"Get in." Sean slid into the driver's side and started the car, leaving Mia no choice again but to follow. She slipped into the soft leather seat. Sean soared down the exit, toward home.

"Where's Val, Sean?" Mia worried her bottom lip. Her older sister would never have forced the pair together unless something serious was at stake.

"She has the stomach flu." Sean blandly answered, swerving in between traffic. "I'm just supposed to pick you up and host you until she's better."

Mia gripped the 'oh-shit' handle and toyed with her pentacle necklace as Sean continued to drive like a madman.

"What brings you home? It's been what, five years?" His knuckles whitened on the steering wheel.

Mia thought about appeasing him by feeding him some fake story. But she never lied to Sean. *Despite his thoughts to the contrary.*

"Samhain, AKA Halloween."

"Some witchy cult sacrifice?" Sean sneered.

Mia chose her words carefully, not wanting to start a fight in the small confines of the vehicle.

"Samhain, is a pagan holiday." She bit her lip. "It's an eve when ancestral spirits from the other side are welcome to visit their living loved ones."

"You mean ghosts?"

Mia could tell by Sean's light tone that he was humoring her. She continued, trying to impress upon him the importance of tomorrow night. "For this one eve, the veil between worlds thins, allowing spirits to cross the great divide."

"Why do you need to be home for that?" Sean merged.

"There are portals—those of us who practice magic call them fairy mounds, or *sidhe*—sacred sites through which fairies and spirits can travel." Mia stole a glance at the rigid man to her left. "The ghost of sweet dead gran isn't the only being who can cross the veil."

"What else can cross?"

Mia stared out the rain-fogged window. "Darker creatures can crawl from the deep. Hungry things, lusting for vengeance, blood, and death."

Sean snorted, not believing her.

"We call them *Aos Si.* And they are not welcome. Ever."

All too soon Sean pulled off the exit for Excelsior, their tiny hometown.

The rain washed over the windows and warped the picturesque place she'd called home until eighteen, and for one brief summer after college. *Ten years since high school and the town looks the same.* Tourist shops, small restaurants, and brightly painted homes, all morphed into a runny painting of old memories.

Sean turned up the wrong driveway.

"Uh Sean, I know it's been five years since you've been to my house, but …"

"I'm not taking you home." Sean overrode whatever insult she was trying to think up.

"But Val, she's sick." Mia grimaced. Illness, especially throwing up, never sat well with her, but Val was her sister.

"Exactly." Sean roared up a smooth driveway, and turned off the purring engine at the end of the circle drive. "I was told that on no uncertain terms was I allowed to let you go home. Val seems to think you need to stay healthy. So I brought you to my home instead."

Mia took in the house before her. The rain lessened and offered her a view through the dappled window.

A Victorian front porch, complete with hanging flower pots and climbing honeysuckle vines feathering the white expanse, wrapped around a cozy old home. A burgeoning Rapunzel tower bloomed above the second story, and a sturdy weather vane spun atop in the fall storm.

Colored stenciling collected in the corners of the porch like painted cobwebs.

The gingerbread house.

"You bought the house next door?" Mia shoved out of the car and yanked her bag from the trunk. Fat drops of water smacked onto her bag. "Why?"

Sean bolted from the driver's seat. "I'm a contractor now, Mia. I fix broken things."

Then fix us.

"Of all the dilapidated mansions on Lake Minnetonka, why this one, Sean? Why?" Mia edged backward toward the forest lining the drive.

Rain continued to splatter down, dampening Sean's dark hair, and shadowing his face. *His remorseful face.*

Moisture beaded her skin. Shivering, Mia backed up until damp grass and dead leaves crunched under her boots.

"Because." Was Sean's only response. He stormed toward the front door and called over his shoulder. "Either you come inside for dry clothes, food, and shelter or you stand in the rain and wonder why you ever came home."

"Already doing that," Mia mumbled.

She hugged her leather bag and jogged indoors. Mia kicked off her black rain boots, and deposited her things on the inlay runner guarding the cherry wood steps.

Decorated in natural materials and pleasing, dark hues, Sean had transformed the molding house into a home.

"The guest bedroom's up the stairs and to the right." Sean poked his head from around the kitchen door at the end of the hallway.

"I'm going to call Val." Mia tossed out and raced up the stairs. In their youth, she and Sean had broken into this house more times than she could count. Mia easily located the guest room, painted a warm auburn.

A wrought iron framed bed took up the center of the small room, a simple dresser and nightstand the only other pieces of furniture. One solitary door led out to a refurbished balcony where the rain continued to fall.

Unzipping her bag, Mia dumped the contents onto the full sized bed. She grinned as her things were revealed: a pair of twelve inch iron knitting needles, a wooden case holding a polished birch branch, a pack of thick and worn tarot cards, five globular candles, and a solid silver German beer stein.

The lid of the beer stein clicked open with the press of her thumb. She had purchased it in Germany during a wild Oktoberfest. Mia had found it on display in an antique store, dark and opalescent, unpolished for decades. It reminded her of the summer she'd turned eighteen, the summer she and Sean had snuck beer into the clearing in the woods.

The summer Sean chose me over Val, seconds after their breakup.

In addition to the pentacle she wore around her neck, each item on the bed was a central part of her practice, representing the five elements required for magic: air, water, earth, fire, and spirit.

Mia picked up a knitting needle and pressed a button at the carved base, unsheathing a slender lance. She brandished it with practiced ease.

***

Sean stared out the large kitchen windows at the forest's border. He could easily walk to the Birch sisters' home. One small acre separated their identical houses.

But he wouldn't walk over. In the middle of their homes, at the center of a perfect copse of maple trees rested a simple earthen mound. In his memory, Sean could see the colored toadstools dotting the ground.

In her fantasy about being a witch, Mia claimed the rise was a fairy mound. A *sidhe.* Imbued with magical properties. Sean ran his tongue along his teeth in frustration.

One night, five years ago, right before she'd hopped on a plane to Scotland, realistic Sean had experienced it. That magical essence which seemed to cloak Mia in a cloud of mystery. A perfect storm of moonlight, fireflies, sweet wine, and potent Mia. The memory of that night still reduced him to a sweating mass of anxiety and desire. No way in hell was Sean going back to that fairy mound. Not for all the sexual allure Mia had to give. Not now. Not ever.

Twice I've fallen for her spell.

And twice she'd fled. Once for college, and again after the death of her mother.

And now she's back.

Sean grabbed the tray of food he'd tossed together. He strode into the guest room to find Mia brandishing a lethal looking lance.

"What do you want?" Mia crossed her arms.

Sean made a show of dropping his gaze to the cleavage she revealed. Mia scoffed.

Sean's mouth lost its grin. A glower spread. *Five seconds in and we're already at odds. Must be a record.*

"I came to bring you food and make you feel at home." He set the tray on the narrow dresser. Mia tossed her black hair and narrowed her blue eyes.

"This town isn't my home anymore, Sean." Bitter anger sharpened her tone.

"That wasn't my fault. I gave you a goddamn choice." Sean bit out, jaw flexed. Mia buffed her black nails on her shirt, looking annoyed. Sean cracked his neck.

"Still haven't shed that nasty habit, boy?" Mia trilled.

"I'm no longer a boy you can order around, Mia." His nostrils flared.

She rolled her eyes. "Nothing's changed."

Without breaking eye contact, Sean nodded. "You're the one who left." He said, softly.

"I think it's time *you* left." Her face morphed into bitter rage as she spoke. "I'm here to help my sister keep an ancient portal filtered, closed off to the evil which lurks in the deep, salivating for your very soul."

I was mistaken. Sean had thought he could take it this time. Could watch Mia lie to his face, again. *I can't do it.*

"When you decide to tell me the goddamn truth, you know where to find me." Sean strode away to deal with his anger over an expensive bottle of Scotch.

***

As the moon to the tide, you always had a knack for taking my control.

Mia flushed, not with embarrassment, but anger. *He still doesn't get it. Still won't accept me for who I am and what I believe in.* Shaking her black hair, Mia stormed out the balcony door her cell phone gripped tightly against her palm.

The rain had stopped. Clouds shifted and unearthed the rotund belly of the waxing moon. A full harvest moon on Samhain meant the veil between worlds would thin at an alarming rate.

A shiver of unease skated down Mia's spine as the wind changed, bringing cool air from the nearby lakes. A rouged leaf, dead and fragile, scraped along the drive. She tapped her cold cell phone against her chin. Fall in Minnesota unearthed colors in every direction and the pale light of the moon highlighted the contrasts, elongated the shadows, and sent a dewy haze along the grass.

She dialed.

Mia closed her eyes and breathed in the sharp scent of earth and the cleansing scent of the passing rain.

"Mia?" Val's quiet voice broke the reverie.

"Hey Sis, how're you doing?" Mia soaked in the sound of her sister's words.

"Horribly, I definitely have the flu." Val coughed. "I won't be able to cast tomorrow night, I won't be strong enough for the harvest moon."

"I'll cast." Mia assured her sick sister.

"Stay safe, stay strong." Val's words scratched through the speaker.

Only one witch was actually needed to secure the fairy mound. Well, one witch and a helper.

"Anyone available to help?" Mia gripped the railing.

"Since mom passed I've been reaching out to the neighboring covens. But that blasted Samhain Bash in Minneapolis means no one wants to help a small town witch protect a stupid fairy portal."

"That leaves me with only one option."

"Good luck, Sis." Val ended the call.

Mia shuddered to think what would happen if she failed. *Nasty little fairies heaving their destruction on an ignorant town. All the little ones trick-or-treating...*

Moonlight danced along the balcony. She squeezed the golden pentacle at her neck. "Damn it all to Hell."

* * *

Someone pounded down the steps. Sean looked up from the thriller he was reading and set down his glass of Scotch as he stood. The pounding intensified until Sean was sure the stairs would crack. He turned and found a pale and panting Mia in the doorway.

Concern eclipsed anger. "Mia, what's wrong?"

Color leeched from her usually flushing face as Mia stepped over the threshold. "Val's super sick."

"We knew that already." Placing a hand at the slender span of her waist, he ushered Mia into his sitting room.

"Yea, well, I thought she'd be better by tomorrow and she won't. Unfortunately I need her help tomorrow night."

She plopped in his chair, lithe legs spread. Her hand automatically went to his Scotch glass. Before he could voice protest, she swallowed the contents in one gulp.

Several sputtering coughs crashed from her ribs. Sean rolled his eyes and patted her back until she caught her breath.

"Damn, that's good."

"*I know.*" He bit out.

"She must have caught the flu from the kids at school." Mia sighed and motioned for more Scotch.

Setting the refilled glass in her shaking palm Sean shrugged. "One of the perils of being an elementary school teacher."

"I need Val's help tomorrow night but I can't afford to get sick, too." Mia handed him the Scotch back and slouched in his favorite chair. Sean didn't like how easily she invaded his space.

"I forgot your aversion to illness." Sean itched to tuck a strand of her dark hair behind her ear wanting to see if it was as silky as he remembered. "Your mom's cancer was a fluke, Mia."

Her blue eyes flashed. "I wasn't talking about that, Sean."

Sean raised his hands in quick surrender. "I didn't mean to bring it up." Five years ago, her mom's cancer had done more than kill the slender Birch woman; it had emotionally ravaged her two daughters. One never left home. The other never wanted to come back.

"I know you don't believe me Sean. I'm not asking you to," Mia's shoulders scrunched in defeat. "But I need your help."

"Help with what?" Sean padded to the sofa and leaned back on the squeaky leather. The vacant exhaustion in Mia's eyes gave him cause for concern.

Air blew out from Mia's lips in a loud sigh. Her blue eyes slowly rose to his, serious and calm.

"I need you to help me cast a spell."

Sean closed his eyes. *How long will she continue this illusion?*

"Before you shut me down, I have a second favor. After tomorrow night, you never have to do another thing for me. Ever."

Sean waved her on. So sure she'd ask for something crazier.

"Can I sleep over?"

***

Sean never ceased to surprise her. He'd nodded. In response to *both* her questions. The borrowed plastic phone in Mia's hand stopped ringing.

"Hello?" Val's soft voice drifted over the landline.

"Sis, it's me." Mia twisted the cord of Sean's old house phone, having left her cell upstairs, and swung her legs from her perch on the granite kitchen counter top. She filled her sister in on the new plan.

"Sean's letting you stay? Good." Val coughed thickly and groaned.

Mia shuddered. "Sean's gonna help me."

"How in Hecate's name did you manage to convince him?"

"Not sure." Mia peered over the half wall in the kitchen. Sean sat in his chair, sipping excellent Scotch. The light cast shadows along his stubbled jaw.

"Perhaps he still likes you more than he lets on." Val supplied and munched on a dry cracker. The noise sent static across the line.

"Don't worry Val, he doesn't like me."

A choking noise blasted from the phone. Mia yanked it from her ear. "Are you laughing?"

Val snorted. "Night sis, check in tomorrow to get the rest of your spell casting tools."

Mia stared at the dead phone, now droning on one long beep. Sean cleared his throat in the background. Mia set the phone in its cradle and found Sean's eyes unabashedly staring.

He raised his glass as if to toast her. "See you tomorrow."

Mia slid off the counter and traipsed upstairs. All those old feelings of young love and lust burst from the dam she'd so carefully built.

We were doomed from the start.

Memories of their past two relationship attempts, forbidden and passionate, occupied her mind as she donned an old shirt and brushed her teeth with a fresh brush. Mia slipped into soft sheets that smelled of man; the dark scent of earth and the spicy scent of rain.

***

The next morning, Sean hoisted the leather bag over his shoulder. The contents clanked and crashed. Val slammed the door behind him, her warning words vibrating in his brain. Guilt turned to acid in his veins.

Sean. We were young and clearly not meant to be. It's been ten years, I forgave Mia's betrayal long ago. Perhaps it's time you two forgive yourselves.

The sack dug into his shoulder and Sean welcomed the pain. Soaked it up like a balm for his soul.

"Sean?" A voice crashed through the woods. Sean perked up, recognizing Mia. She burst from the thicket, red leaves crunching under her black boots.

"Val called my cell—you weren't answering yours." Sean shrugged. "She gave me her stuff."

Mia stalked over and held out a hand for the bag. He ignored her. Water dripped from her dark hair. She noticed his gaze. "I haven't showered in three days and rode on two separate planes. I borrowed your shampoo."

"Good call." Sean smiled down at a fresh faced Mia, so unabashed to be makeup-less and in a baggy men's long-sleeve. "So, what do you need from me?"

Mia glanced heavenward as if calculating the time from the position of the sun. "I slept too long. The sun sets at six tonight."

Sean checked his watch. "It's only one."

"As soon as the sun sets, we must begin the cleansing ritual." Mia glared at the blue sky. "Did Val say anything to you?"

Sean hiked the bag higher. "No."

"Liar." Mia grinned.

***

"C'mon let's get back to my place." Sean stormed past her into the woods. Mia narrowed her eyes. *What is he holding back?*

She gripped her golden pentacle and mentally whispered a spell for peace amidst chaos, knowing tonight's proceedings depended on positive thoughts.

Sean quickened his pace to a jog. The trees thinned and towering red maples dripped leaves through the forest's canopy.

The clearing.

She'd passed it, just now, as she'd gone looking for Sean, and she'd ignored the pull of the *sidhe.* Sean halted. Mia bumped into his firm backside, her own bag clattering behind her.

"Oofta." Breath whooshed from her lungs. "Why'd you stop?"

Sean angled his feet, gifting Mia with his strong profile. He faced the fairy mound with a frown as if preparing for battle. The pull to wander into the clearing was strong. Her boots shifted.

"I can't help you Mia, I'm sorry." Sean dropped the bag with a hammered clang and stormed home. Mia watched him walk away.

"Too much history here, my love." Mia patted the spot over her heart. "Too much between us."

Her whisper dissipated into the sound of water lapping at the shore, just beyond the clearing. She meandered toward the sound, seeking solace. Lake Minnetonka stretched before her like a looking glass, flat and serene.

The storm from yesterday cleared the heavens and nothing but blue sky and sunshine fell. Soon, all too soon the sun would set, the moon taking over.

"The veil will shudder and fade, letting in all the little beasties." Mia tapped her boot against the innocent looking fairy mound.

Mia lugged thick broken branches, dry leaves, and clumps of fire starters into two neat piles on either side of the *sidhe.* She tugged a small barrel of salt from her sister's bag and drew a wide pentacle around the fairy mound, enclosing it. Her arms ached, mud caked her jeans, and twigs tangled in her long hair. The sun dipped below the horizon in a plume of purple fire. The last light cast spooky shadows into the clearing.

Alone on the most dangerous night of spell casting.

Mia sighed and slipped a white robe from her leather bag. She padded to the dark shoreline, appreciating the cover of night for the first part of the ritual. Garment by garment, she stripped.

Naked, Mia strode into the water.

***

Sean marched through the narrow thicket of woods toward the clearing.

"Can't leave chivalry in the feudal system, can you?" Frustrated, he pushed his body into a jog. It would have been so easy to stay at home and sip Scotch.

But Sean wasn't able to push Mia from his thoughts.

"We've got to figure out what's between us, woman. My heart can't take the strain." Sean stopped short at the *sidhe*. Moonlight poured from the starry sky to highlight a nude woman wading into a bay on Lake Minnetonka.

Mia. Even from a distance, without sunlight, Sean *knew* it was her. No other woman walked with the sure and lethal grace of Mia Birch. The evening air chilled his exposed skin and no doubt raised goose bumps on hers. Sean swallowed. Audibly.

An owl hooted nearby, Sean didn't care. A dog barked, the biting sound echoing off the wide lake. Sean didn't care. A leaf drifted from one of the maples and feathered down his arm.

Sean didn't care.

He'd witnessed a nude Mia on countless occasions, knew her every curve, every freckle, but this, this was different.

The moon shone brighter on her skin, water beaded like opalescent pearls as it dripped down her torso. A windless rush of leaves tumbled from the maples and whipped toward Mia, who swayed in the cold water.

Shocked, Sean stood transfixed as red and gold leaves shimmered in the moonlight—*glowed*. They spun around Mia's slender body, at once hiding her curves and exposing damp skin.

He clenched his fists. *Look away.*

He didn't.

A stray firefly joined the dance upon the water. Sean shifted closer. Leaning against a scratchy tree, he realized the firefly, now hundreds of fireflies, weren't insects. *Fireflies don't glow a vibrant orange and glitter like stars. This is magic. This is real.*

The heavens seemed to shine upon a pale and vibrant Mia. Her head was thrown back, water droplets, glittering leaves, and sparks of color tornadoed around her body. Moonlight exploded outward from Mia. The thundering force traveled through Sean, drenching him in dissipating glitter, water, and shards of leaves.

As chaotic as the light show had been, silence deafened him.

Mia jogged from the water with a grin and donned a clean white robe.

Sean moved from behind the tree, heart pounding in his chest. *All I've done is blame her for lies she never told. Belittled her* and *what she believes in.*

Mia gasped when she saw him, her blue eyes flashed.

"I am so goddamn sorry."

* * *

Muddy grass squelched under Mia's toes as Sean meandered from the clearing.

Spying on me naked, Sean?

She wasn't upset in the slightest; he'd seen everything she had to offer. But the apology, that was new.

"I take it you saw my cleansing spell?"

"You're a witch." A shaky Sean reached out and touched a damp lock of Mia's hair. Vulnerability and sorrow etched lines on his twenty-eight year old face. "Oh god. You never once lied. Ever."

"Never ever, Sean." She'd looked forward to the moment when he realized she was actually a witch, when he saw her magic for the first time. Had wanted so bad to wipe the smug expression from his face.

I never expected him to feel guilty, to be sorry.

Suddenly the vengeful joy ceased. Leaving a soft forgiveness in its wake.

"I-I understand if you never want to see my face again. But I'd love to help you with your spell stuff." Shoulders raised once more, Sean looked every bit the conquering hero she'd fallen in love with at eighteen and again at twenty-three.

You wanted to marry me then.

He'd asked her, in the very clearing they were about to enter, if she'd spend the rest of her life with him.

I ran.

"Let's begin." Mia dug into the pocket of her robe, removed a lighter and lit the two fires on either side of the fairy mound.

Sean stood like a sentinel at the edge of her pentacle, waiting.

"Please take a branch from the eastern fire and light the five candles I've placed at the points of the pentacle."

Sean nodded.

"Careful not to bump my salt lines." Mia pointed to the trap she'd set.

"What's the salt for?" Sean lit the candles, giving the lines a wide berth.

"Salt traps spirits and fairies. I also have a slender iron sword to vanquish any evil should it pass through my web."

"You, vanquish?" Sean raised a brow and lit the evergreen candle. She smirked. "Oh just give me the sword."

Mia handed it over and knelt at the edge of the *sidhe*, just outside of the pentacle and closed her eyes. "I need to spell cast right now, this involves extreme concentration."

Footsteps quieted, signaling Sean had moved away.

She called forth the energy building inside of her, energy from the very earth she dug her knees and toes into. Mia began to chant in an ancient dialect.

In her mind she envisioned a wide fishing net, stretching over the fairy mound in crisscrossing strings of light.

The spaces tightened the more she chanted until the whole of the *sidhe* glowed purple, soaked in the rays of moonlight, danced in the flames from the fires.

She opened her eyes.

Sean knelt across from her, his gaze seared her skin with its intensity. An hour passed in silence before the first fluttering of movement began under the visible net atop the *sidhe.*

Sean reared back. "What in the world—"

A cloven leg bowed the net high.

"Stab it, Sean." Pain clenched her abdomen. Sean's green eyes widened, he hesitated. "Please."

Fierce determinate settled over his features. Sean stood, slender lance in hand, and rammed the blade into the flailing creature. A terrified hiss of agony burst from the cloven *thing.* Mia doubled over and pulled more energy from the moonlight tickling her skin. Her spell held in place.

Sean dropped to his knees, azure blood dripping from the sword.

The net shifted again, this time a spectral shape emerged with ease. It hovered over the meshed fairy mound for a moment, as if gathering its bearings, then it raced forward on an invisible breeze, soaring across the lake.

"That one was good?" Sean asked. Mia nodded, focus still on the *sidhe.* "How can you tell?"

"The magic web reads the spirits' intentions and either allows them through, or sends them back. The spell does all the brainwork; I just do the heavy lifting." Mia ground her teeth, a muscle twitching in her jaw. A tender pulsing headache began at the base of her skull.

"You okay love?" Sean stood and rushed to her side.

Mia managed a nod just as the onslaught began.

Hours drifted by with only the shifting of moonlight betraying the time. Sweat dripped from Mia's temples as a veritable army of *Aos Si* fought to break through her net.

Shadows oozed beneath the surface. Prowlers scraped their scales against the reinforced net. Screams of anguish and rage bubbled up from the earth. And every time she ordered, Sean slaughtered the evil, which threatened to break free.

They want out.

Only years of practice and the gentle touch of Sean's fingertips kept Mia centered. Sean sat next to her, iron sword in hand.

"Is it just me or is it getting brighter?" Sean whispered. Mia squinted at the sky. Pale pink light spread through the leafed canopy.

The silver shadows of ancestral spirits drifted across the lake, masking their forms in morning fog. One by one, they slithered back into the earth. Sean shivered as one shifted through him. A form kissed Mia's cheek, hovering at her elbow. A tear trickled down Mia's cheek. *"Mom?"*

A tendril of opalescence drifted down Mia's arm in confirmation. *"May you have many years to come my young one."*

The last spirit drifted into the *sidhe* like steam into the air. Mia released her mental grip on the net. It shimmered like the cresting of a wave before soaking into the fairy mound as rain.

"Finished." Mia deflated, dropping back onto the dewy grass with a well-deserved sigh.

"That-that was ..." Sean trailed off, his deep voice bouncing off the copse of maples.

"Eye opening, frightening, exhausting?" Mia supplied, eyes closed.

"Awesome." Sean whispered. Warm breath tickled her cheek. She shot to awareness. Sean leaned over her, cocky smile in place. "And really freaking dangerous."

Mia rolled her eyes. "Not worried I'll turn you into a toad?"

Sean shrugged. "I'd just make Val turn me back."

Her sister's name acted like a bucket of cold water. Mia shoved Sean away and stood, brushing grass stains off her rear.

"Want help?" Sean winked.

Wanting slithered through Mia. Wanting and sadness. "Sean, we can't be together."

Sean arched a brow and rose to his feet. "That escalated quickly."

"Every time we see each other we fall back into the same pattern. I can't betray my sister like that. Not again." Mia clenched her fists. "She hated me after you two broke up."

"But she forgave you, Mia. She forgave me, too." Sean gripped her shoulders. Mia sniffled and shook her head.

"You don't know that. Sean, I basically *stole* you from her."

"Is that why you run every time? Because you think you should feel guilty, because you believe you've betrayed your sister?" Sean tucked her body into his.

Mia nodded under his chin. "Yeah."

"She told me, yesterday, that she knows how guilty we've felt for a decade." Sean leaned back and looked into her eyes. "She really did forgive us, Mia."

Mia raised a dark brow.

"She and I could never be. Ever." Sean said.

The sureness in Sean's gaze frightened Mia. The urge to run bubbled up. Sean must have sensed her tensing.

"Mia Birch, I swear to goodness, if you run again, I *will* follow you. You will never be able to escape me." Fierce and demanding, Sean pressed his lips to hers.

Mia fell into the kiss. Wanting it. Wanting to believe him. Wanting *him.*

She clung to his shoulders, pressed against his muscled frame, wanting closer and farther in the same instant.

Sean pulled back. They both panted.

"What's stopping you from staying, Mia?" He tugged her dark hair over her shoulder, playing with the strands, seemingly content to wait forever for her answer.

Mia swallowed. "I don't know."

"Liar." Sean beamed.

Mia frowned. "Fine, you want to know why I run? Why I *always* run?"

Sean nodded, still smiling.

"Because what if we fail? What if you decide my brand of crazy is too much. What if you leave?" Mia choked on a sudden sob. Sean trailed the back of his hand along her cheek.

"We won't. I won't."

"You don't know that Sean. You *can't* know that." Mia blinked against emotion. "I can't handle another person I love leaving me."

There. She'd said it. The ugly, undeniable, selfish truth. Mom died of cancer, dad walked out decades ago, and even Val stayed emotionally closed off. Being alone was better than being hurt. Again.

Sean sighed. "Oh Mia, you have no idea how I feel, do you?"

Mia shrugged.

"Come." Sean dragged her, barefoot, over rocks, leaves, broken twigs, and gnarled roots, to his back door. Up his polished steps to the tower room at the end of the hall. Mia followed his lead up the ladder and emerged into a haven of candles, books, and over-large feather pillows dotting the oak floor.

"You know why I bought this house?" Sean asked.

"Because you like to fix broken things?" Mia cocked a hip.

"Partly, but mostly for the view." Sean smiled.

Mia moved to the windows overlooking the misty lake. "It's beautiful."

"Wrong window." Sean steered her to the other side of the circular viewing room.

Mia gasped.

"The fairy mound?" Down below, starting at the base of Sean's door, stretched a slender stone path leading through the thicket to the mapled clearing in which the *sidhe*, so innocent in the daylight, rested.

"The happiest moment of my life took place in that mystical place, despite you turning me down. If I couldn't have you, then I wanted that moment, forever, for always."

Mia faced Sean. "I rejected you."

"Of course you did." Sean sighed. "We were kids. I was an ignorant and judgmental ass. I didn't get it. Didn't love you for the whole package."

Joy beat happy wings in Mia's chest. After all these years of trying, of both of them heaping emotional pain on one another. *He's sorry.*

"If you can forgive me for running when things got too serious ... I'm more than happy to forgive you for not believing I was a witch." Mia smirked.

Sean rolled his eyes. *"Of course."*

She kissed *him* this time, tasting the rain on his lips, the earthiness of his soul, and the love in his heart.

It ended on a bursting grin. "Are we doing this again?"

"Doing what?" Sean tucked a strand of her hair behind her ear.

"Starting over, building a relationship...?"

"Yes, please." Sean kissed her swiftly. He pulled back, their lips a breath apart. "After all, third time's a charm."

Mia laughed and dove right back into his warm embrace.

ABOUT THE AUTHOR

KT Alexander resides in a fantastical realm where gnomes, fairies, elves and ogres come out to play in the evening dusk, the sun is always shining, and roses bloom year-round … She wishes.

In reality, she lives in the Midwest with a loving family and an over-abundance of plants. All of which die a painful and tragic death under mysterious circumstances--the plants, not the family. Her lack of green thumb may be the culprit.

Summer of 2013, she won the Romancing the Lakes Award for her Mystery/Suspense contest entry. Currently she is hard at work on her upcoming releases.

KT also has a short story published in the *Romancing the Lakes of Minnesota ~ Summer* anthology. Available in print and digital format wherever books are sold.

Find out more on her http://www/ktalexanderofficial.blogspot.com or, tweet her @KT_Alexander_ (she loves following new people!), and of course, she's on Facebook at KTAlexanderOfficial. Stop over and say hello!

.

ABOUT THE MINNESOTA LAKES WRITERS

Living in Minnesota, surrounded by lakes, ***Minnesota Lakes Writers*** can't help creating stories of being up North at the cabin, in town at one of the city lakes or Minnesota's own massive Lake Superior. No matter what time of year it is, there is always something going on at the lake. Hey, it's Minnesota! Whether you are sitting on a dock listening to loons calling, taking a leisurely walk around a lake, cruising the lake on a boat or just sitting on a beach, for writers, ideas form and stories begin.

These writers enjoy getting together to set in motion scary stories to be told under the evening stars at a beach campfire or on the frozen ice of Minnesota's winter lakes. And, of course, romances set on sandy lakeshores or on boats skimming over gentle waves.

Minnesota Lakes Writers write stories about Minnesota and its lakes encompassing romance, mystery, and fantasy. Our goal is to enjoy each others love of writing and tell stories about Minnesota and its 10,000 lakes. And since there are so many, it may take us a while!

For more information, find us on our website at http://we-write-books.blogspot.com/p/friting-groups.html.